Parts
of a
Song

***

A Novel

Alexandra del Rosario Romualdez

For Jay

Intro

Set up.

...

1
Manila, 2007

What am I even doing here? Lara Maria Rodriguez Halford thought, sighing to herself.

Clad in her vintage A-line blue dress and a silk scarf, she looked up at the broad building in front of her, the word 'REVOLUUT' carved in gigantic letters across its white stone face. In front of its large, dark doors–like the entrance to a cave, two bouncers in black stood before a line of young people snaking around the club, slurring tsismis in each other's ears and giggling, already half-drunk.

Lara was still very much sober. She had only had time to rush home, shower, get dressed, and munch on a tuna sandwich after work before hurrying to the club. But even if she had been equally inebriated as these other patrons, she wasn't sure she'd feel any more at ease. Her thrifty fashion made her feel like the odd one out in a crowd of glittery, glamorous little black dresses. She wouldn't normally have chosen this scene. On any other Friday evening she might have preferred catching a film, stopping by a jazz bar, curling up with a book, or staying up late painting. But Monique Lopez, a good friend she hadn't seen in a long time, had invited her along and she just couldn't say no.

Her text had read, *revoluut superclub @ the fort. VIP coz ur on my list. will be there at 10pm. can't wait to c u! don't u dare flake out on me. ü*

And so Lara obliged.

Clutching her purse while casting apologetic glances at the other patrons, Lara bypassed the line and headed straight for the men at the door.

"Excuse me," she said in a pitch higher than usual.

They both regarded her quietly—one furrowing his eyebrows,

the other raising his.

"I'm here at the invitation of Monique Lopez," Lara flashed her phone at them. After the bouncers read the text and gave her another once-over, one of them let her through.

"Thank you," Lara said, and she walked through those seemingly cavernous doors and found herself in a large room with high ceilings, exposed ventilation shafts, fuzzy black walls, and stage lights illuminating the DJ booth so that all she could see were the glowing, bouncing silhouettes of the clubbers on the floor.

Fresh out of university in Boston, after a quick visit to Singapore where she'd grown up, it was only Lara's first full week living in the Philippines. Despite being half-Filipino, she did not exude the same comfortable familiarity with the scene and the space as the rest of her peers that night did.

As Lara walked further in, she struggled to see through the crowd and the lasers criss-crossing her vision. *It's these damn pulsing lights,* she thought, gritting her teeth as she made her way to the VIP section, which was a split level above the rest of the club in the far corner of the room. It had the best view of the DJ and the nicest seats in the house. Even from afar, Lara could see shiny black tables and plush purple couches.

"LARA!" A shrill voice rang out amid the blaring music.

She looked up to find Monique—a wide smile on her face, long wavy hair billowing around her shoulders, and a short red dress hugging her figure, showing off her tanned legs. She was waving for Lara to come up to a specific table near the stairs.

In the sea of sweaty club-goers, Lara was relieved to see a familiar face. She threw a thumbs-up in the air and pushed her way through the mob.

It had been two years since Lara and Monique had last met up—in Boston on a school break for lunch. Monique was an old friend from the Southeast Asian international school varsity network, where they met as student athletes, with Lara in tennis and the former in track. Lara had hosted Monique for meets in her home turf—Singapore, and Monique had done the same for Lara in Manila.

Nearly two weeks before, when Lara arrived in the Philippines, ready for her new adventure, she reached out, and Monique was eager to reconnect.

"Would you look at this lady!" Monique exclaimed as soon

as Lara reached her.

Her friend was exuberant and extroverted in all the ways she was not. Big movements, booming voice, smile that spanned the width of her face, round eyes that invited contact.

Lara responded in her own way with a tight, warm hug.

When they let go, Monique steered her towards the rest of the group at their VIP table.

"Everyone, this is Lara," she announced, and then turned to her. "Lara, this is Niko Huang. He's Filipino-Chinese, and he's in plastic manufacturing with his dad."

A guy in khakis and a dress shirt smiled. Lara guessed he was around her age—twenty-one or a little older. She was about to say hello, but Monique whisked her away to the next person: a girl, in skinny jeans and a shiny oversized top.

"Maybe you remember Bianca Torres?" Monique prompted. "She played tennis, too."

"Of course!" Lara said and accepted Bianca's side hug and beso. Bianca was one of her high school tennis rivals; it would be hard to forget her.

"How have you been?" Bianca asked her. Again, Lara was about to respond but Monique was ready for the next set of people.

There was David de Luzuriaga, Bianca's boyfriend who was a Filipino-Mestizo working for his family's conglomerate; Mike Moh, a tall, fashionable twenty-seven-year-old Malaysian-Chinese management consultant based on a project in the Philippines wearing a sport coat and a flashy watch; and Owen Weber, a twenty-two-year-old Filipino-American engineer.

After, Lara scanned all the possible conversations, dances, and drinks that could be had, and she balked. She found it difficult to interact in large groups, especially in loud and crowded spaces. She preferred relaxed conversations—not screaming over a track.

I should've proposed lunch instead.

A server came with a tray of shots and everyone else downed them at record speed.

Well, if you can't beat 'em…

Lara squeezed through the spaces between her dancing companions. *We're here now, Lara,* she admonished herself. *Just make the best of it. A toast to old friends.*

She picked up what looked to be an untouched cocktail on a tray in the middle of their table and sniffed it cautiously.

"That's clean."

It was Owen, the engineer.

In spite of herself, Lara laughed and shrugged. "Cheers!" she said, lifting her glass.

Owen held his bottle of beer up and tipped it in her direction. "Cheers."

They drank in silence together as "Low" by Flo Rida came on, with Lara tapping her foot to the beat of the song.

"Lara, right?" he said, after a while. "I'm Owen."

"I remember," Lara replied. "Hello again."

Owen plopped down on the nearby couch and gestured for Lara to sit as well. Although reluctant, she did, making sure there was enough space between them.

"So," Owen started, "how did you get mixed in with this lot?"

"Monique's an old friend from high school," Lara explained. "She invited me. You?"

"Through Monique, too. She was one of my first friends when I moved here." Owen then flagged down a waiter and ordered shots of tequila.

"And when was that?" Lara asked, moving closer to him. Everything was so loud that it was the only way she could hear him better.

"Bit over a year ago."

"From where?"

"Is this an interview?"

Lara laughed, but was still waiting for an answer.

"Virginia," Owen replied. "I'm from outside DC. But I'm half-Filipino."

"I'm half-Filipino, too! Virginia is awesome. Especially DC." Lara said, enthused. "I love the monuments, and the Smithsonian."

"Ah, I should've known. Where are you from?" Owen asked.

All Lara's life the way she looked—"mixed," "hard to place"—had been a talking point. When she was a teenager, her Singaporean friends and family said she resembled a young Nancy Kwan. Meanwhile, her British and Filipino family insisted she looked like a young Catherine Zeta-Jones. Later on, in Boston, during her university years, her friends called her "The Mixed Bag," because it was a running joke that they could never figure out where she was from just by looking. Everyone had their own guesses–Central

Asian, Middle Eastern, Hispanic, white, and on and on and *on*.

So it went that Lara never really fit in any place.

She considered the question carefully before she answered. "I was born in the UK, but grew up in Singapore. My dad is half-British and half Chinese-Singaporean, and my mother is Filipino, like mestizo. Spanish-Filipino."

Owen nodded knowingly. "My dad's white, and my mom's brown. So they made me. This marble cake of a thing."

She looked at Owen then, a stranger sitting so close to her—something she would usually find uncomfortable, but somehow, in this context, was grateful for. Something about Owen intrigued her. And this was a compromise, the price to pay for one on one conversation in a noisy club.

Lara studied Owen's face—clean-shaven with a strong jaw and rosy cheeks.

From the alcohol? she wondered.

He was not bad-looking. In fact, he was kind of cute. He had almond-shaped eyes and a Grecian nose, and his skin was a warm olive color. Had Lara known at that moment that his instinct had been to move to the Philippines to make it big in music due to his being half-Filipino, she would have understood. Many opportunities in the Philippines often gave mixed-race kids a platform almost as a default, as the standard of beauty was still "that European-look or something like it." Just one of the many effects of over three centuries of colonialism.

Just then, the waiter returned with the tequilas. Owen waved Mike over and the three toasted one another and downed the shots.

"Marble cake can be good," Lara said. "Anyway, these days, isn't everyone from everywhere?"

"Maybe especially in this group," Mike chimed in. He gestured toward the eclectic mix of people around them.

Lara noticed as Mike spoke that he had earplugs in, and she smiled inwardly. "Earplugs?" she asked.

Owen looked and then laughed. "He does that to save his ears. His ears are precious."

"Smart," Lara said.

"The decibel level here is insane," Mike defended himself. "With the plugs, I can actually hear better. They filter out some of the volume and a lot of the ambient noise. Highly recommend it."

Owen turned to Lara again. "So what do you do?"

"Just started in a leadership program for marketers."

"Why did you choose the Philippines?"

"The conglomerate I work for has its largest footprint in Asia, and I thought it would be good to be where the growth is." Lara paused and then added, "And for Asian offices it was either here or Singapore, and I was not going to move back in with my parents again after four years of freedom at uni."

She laughed then, thinking of her loving, overbearing mother, and sweet, protective father. "And what kind of engineer are you?" she asked Owen.

"Environmental," Owen answered. "That's my day job. But I'm also a musician."

This piqued Lara's interest. Her true love in life was the arts, and there had been a time she had hoped to be an artist. Deep down, she knew she still held onto that dream. Though her truest love was the visual arts, she did have a soft spot for music. Ten years of musical training would do that, of course. Piano lessons had been non-negotiables for her mother during those early formative years, and there had also been choir.

"Oh?" Lara said, letting her interest spill over. "What kind of music?"

"Acoustic, and kind of funky stuff mostly."

"We should play together some time," Lara suggested.

"Oh, don't get him started on music," Mike interjected, rolling his eyes. "If you do, he won't stop."

Smiling and scrunching her nose at Mike, Lara proceeded to ignore his advice and handed Owen her phone. "Leave me your number. We can jam next week maybe. I dabble."

"Don't say I didn't warn you! When he found out I had turntables, it opened up Pandora's box. We've been friends ever since. I just can't shake him." Mike wagged his finger at Lara with a playful wink, which only made her laugh again. She appreciated his dry humor, his sing-songy diction.

Then Mike said, "I'm going to dance. You guys coming?" Tiësto was playing on the speakers.

Lara and Owen looked at each other and stood up together and she noticed that he lurched a little. It was such a subtle change in his posture, but she held her arm out so he could steady himself.

He looked at her again just then. "You're not like the other girls here," he said as they headed to the dance floor. "That's why I approached you."

Lara regarded him curiously. She was wary of men who described women in generalist terms like the collective 'other girls,' and it upset her that she was flattered at the same time.

Damn patriarchal programming.

"What does that mean?" Lara asked pointedly.

"Oh, it's not meant to mean anything," Owen said airily.

The two found Mike on the dance floor.

"I mean, most of the girls here are…predictable. In their skimpy little dresses, with all that makeup on. And you," Owen paused. His eyes looked her over again, and she could almost feel him tracing her bone structure, noting her calloused fingers, her large eyes. He gave a thoughtful sigh before saying: "You look like an artist."

2
Manila, 2007

The area of Makati that Lara and Owen lived in teemed with life. Narrow streets lined by tall trees and office buildings co-existed alongside bars, live music venues, and apartments. Nearby, there were malls, restaurants, cafes, convenience stores, and gyms.

During the work week, food trucks on the roadside sold turo-turo style lunches where large dishes were displayed and people simply had to point (turo) at what they wanted. Hot meals of saucy meats and steaming rice were sold alongside deep-fried desserts like turon (sweet, fried banana-filled spring rolls drizzled with caramel and sesame seeds). On weekends, the park turned into a market where one could procure all manner of homemade food and handmade goods.

Filipino cities always ignited Owen's senses—especially that of smell. He noticed that if he breathed deep, he could often identify a hint of fried garlic, sampaguita flowers (jasmine), dried fish, or sweet mangoes in the air, depending on the season and the place.

As he checked his phone once more, reading the address Lara had sent him, he realized he lived only two streets away from her. He looked at his watch as he arrived—a five minute-long walk. Gazing up at the concrete building, he noted its tall, white pillars and wide tinted windows. A tad snazzier than his own brutalist, chunky low-rise apartment building.

The elevator led him up to a mid-level floor and when Lara opened the door, he peered inside—Lara in her home environment, in a tie-dyed tank top and cut-off denim shorts.

Lara's place was a studio. Small but functional. *How long had she said she'd been living here?* Owen thought, as he noticed the art across her walls, and the kitchen counters in various stages of use. In one corner was a desk, and taped to it was a piece of watercolor paper on which stood the beginnings of a painting. From where Owen stood, it looked like a still life of dried flowers. Next to the desk was a guitar case, and leaning against that, a ukulele.

The space was well-loved and well-lived-in.

"Nice place," Owen said, smiling and setting his things down.

Lara nodded. "Thank you. But it's temporary. My company gave me a sort of relocation support package. I get to live here rent free for four months. After that, I need to be in my own place."

"Sweet. At least it's a bit of a soft landing," Owen hadn't received the same treatment from his engineering firm. "I can hook you up with the guy who helped me find my place, if that might help. It's nowhere near as nice as this, though."

"Thanks. I might take you up on that." Lara filled two glasses of water and handed Owen one.

Near the entryway, Owen was distracted by the sight of chalk calligraphy doodled across a large mirror. It was a poem about owning and knowing one's own life, claiming it and beating death by living it. Letting the light in. It was rather inspiring, even to Owen, who was not much of a reader and usually only appreciated poetry when it was in song.

"Wow, did you write this?" he asked.

"Oh god, no." Lara laughed. "Those are excerpts from Charles Bukowski's poem called 'The Laughing Heart.'"

Owen glanced at Lara's loaded bookshelf.

So, an artist, a musician, a reader.

Lara turned away to pull her guitar out of its bag, which brought Owen back to the reason he was there in the first place. He popped his case open and did the same. "I got the list of songs that you said you enjoy covering."

Earlier that week the two had exchanged a series of emails and Lara had outlined some of the music she liked. She had mentioned Jason Mraz ("Ugh," as far as Owen was concerned), but also Smokey Robinson (*interesting*, he thought), and Nick Cave and the Bad Seeds ("Cool," he decided). Owen preferred to cover pop and hip hop, turning the songs into alternative or folk pieces. But he also enjoyed making his own moody, guitar-heavy ballads.

"Anything stick?" Lara asked. "I've been imagining a folksy

cover of 'Love Song' by Sarah Bareilles. That's another one."

Owen cringed on the inside and tried to choose his words carefully so as to not put Lara off without compromising his opinion. *Art is a bold, brave thing*, Owen thought. He wanted to bring those two traits into his music at all times.

"It's just that…*everyone* is playing Jason Mraz and Sarah Barry-worries or whatever her name is. If we decide to play music together, I'd love for us to stand out in the crowd. There were other good ideas in your list. Like…Smokey Robinson. That's got potential. And Nick Cave. I can't imagine a girl covering his music. That could be really cool. Personally, I like doing unexpected covers. Like Shakira. I try to make them my own. If I make originals though, it's more like The National."

"Interesting," Lara said, and Owen wondered briefly if he had been too rude or forward. He was aware he had a tendency.

"I have an idea," he then proposed. "Maybe you could play me a song, and I could play you one, and we can see where we land?"

"You first," she said right when he said, "Ladies first." They laughed and for the first time Owen noticed what that sounded like on Lara's lips. It was a bright, round sound—almost melodic. It made him smile all the more.

Lara shook her head. "Lady's *choice*. You first."

"Fine, then," he agreed.

Lara watched him with her large brown eyes and he suddenly felt self-conscious. He was not sure what to expect from her. He was used to performing, but any performance, big or small, always caused a flutter in his gut.

He stood to shake off the jitters, and walked to the window, tuning his guitar along the way. As he gazed at the newly risen moon and what little of the stars he could see through the light and smog of the city, he thought of a song, recently released, that he liked. He strummed an Am7 and began.

"Electric Feel" by MGMT.

Based on the smile on Lara's face, Owen figured she recognized it. His rendition was slow and smooth. If the original played like a horse trotting through a river, he hoped his cover evoked a stream flowing over rapids on a still afternoon.

It was Lara's turn then. She picked up her guitar, sat at the edge of her bed, and began to play.

"You Really Got A Hold On Me" by Smokey Robinson.

Owen was surprised. Lara, when speaking, had a lower, silky tone. However, she sang in a folksy soprano with a husky catch when she held her vowels, giving her voice a distinct texture.

He watched her intently. With the extra clarity granted by normal overhead lighting and sobriety, Owen noted little things about Lara that he hadn't been able to see in the club. For one, Lara indeed could not be placed. She had high cheekbones over soft round cheeks, nearly black hair, and brown eyes that turned just slightly up at the edges. Her face was framed and accented by distinct lines—long lashes, an aquiline nose, and thick eyebrows. She wore little makeup, if at all, and she was at once incredibly pretty, and yet looked like no one and everyone at the same time.

Owen knew he was the same. The combination of his father—an all-American man who looked as though he had been lifted out of an ad in the 50s and his Filipina mother with a toasty tan and voluminous dark hair created in him a not-anything sort of mix. *Not-short, not-tall, not-brown, not-white, not-Filipino,* and certainly *not-American.*

When Owen looked at Lara, he recognized the sort of ambiguity he felt people saw in himself. There was something strangely comforting about it. Like gazing into a mirror. Even though they looked nothing alike.

When she finished, Owen was smiling.

Lara stared back. "Well?"

She is beautiful, Owen decided, almost like an admission. His usual type was tall, gangly, and glamorous. But Lara was something else. She was earthy–with bare feet that moved lightly across the floor; and artsy–her calloused fingertips testifying to hours of creative and musical work; and athletic–as evidenced by the muscles defined along her calves and thighs. Her eyes were so big Owen thought he might be able to swim in them. Suddenly, he felt caught out, and was confused by the pull she elicited.

To avoid it, he turned away. "This could work."

Owen could hear the smile in her voice when she said, "That's what I thought, too."

Looking around her room, he then took stock of the paintings on the wall. There were Singaporean shop houses, canals in Amsterdam, a European beach scene, the Eiffel Tower, a row of terraced houses in London, and a pagoda in Bangkok. Each had such fine details: a child sitting on the steps of a temple blowing bubbles, a person writing a postcard on a beach towel by the ocean, a testament to the observational powers of their maker.

"So these are yours?" he asked, gesturing to the art.

"Yes," Lara nodded, following his gaze. "I love to paint."

"They're good. You're talented." As he scanned them again, he realized there were none set in the Philippines. "Have you seen much of the Philippines before?"

Lara shook her head. "I've come to visit only a handful of times. I haven't explored the capital, let alone the country. I'm keen to, though. Why?"

"I have an idea."

3
Manila, 2007

Owen's second hand sedan smelled of ginger tea and hot metal—a scent Lara associated with guitar strings and amps. She brushed a couple of dust bunnies off the passenger seat as she buckled in. He was taking her to Old Manila, where he had been on a walking tour when he first moved and thought it might be fun to recreate some of that.

On the way, Owen put on the new The National CD and began to sing along to "Fake Empire." Against the moody riffs of Aaron Dessner, his voice was like a warm blanket—smooth and sure against the wintry minor chord progressions. As she listened, Lara felt a sort of tingling attraction moving up her body and it made her wonder.

***

Old Manila was grander than Lara had imagined. She was aware the Philippines had endured over three hundred and fifty years of colonization—from the Spaniards, to the Americans, and a brief Japanese occupation during the Second World War. But before she had moved there, she had never seen the grand American-esque boulevards in Manila near her office, and that day in Old Manila, not far from where she worked, she saw the vestiges of the Spanish era. There were cobblestone streets, fortresses, cathedrals, and ancestral homes with stone walls on the bottom and wooden ones on top.

Besides a few cousins, most of Lara's relatives lived outside the Philippines, so she hadn't had many reasons to visit growing up. It was usually just a day or two, mainly to attend family reunions in her mother's hometown. As such, she was more familiar with Bacolod than Manila, and even then her cultural knowledge was limited. Lara regretted that now, and was glad for a chance to connect with a part of herself that had been left largely unexplored.

But, she reasoned, if she had explored earlier, she wouldn't have been out just then touring it with this particularly cute guy.

Not a bad consolation, she thought.

But was this a date? It was hard to tell. Probably not. Was she even his type? Lara herself didn't have a type; she just gravitated to the boys in her life by feel. And there were a few feelings she could already associate with Owen. His intensity intrigued her. His smiling mouth and the voice that came out of it made her want to smile and sing along too.

In his presence, she felt seen somehow. Like he was noticing her, really looking.

That day, they headed in step with one another from monument to monument. She was glad she had worn sneakers because there was plenty of walking.

To his credit, Owen was a fine tour guide. He tried to tell stories with a flourish. "Here is where Jose Rizal, the National Hero of the Philippines, was kept. He wrote his final goodbye—'Mi Ultimo Adios,' and was killed by a firing squad. Supposedly, he asked them to spare his face. The ladies thought he was a looker, so I guess he had a high opinion of himself. Boy was a player. Wrote long-ass love letters. You know, I think he was a Reformer, not a Revolutionary."

"Oh, I know about that a little. I mean, I did read his books," Lara interjected. "In English, of course. Not the original Spanish. In the first, he does sound more moderate. The second is more jaded."

Owen's eyes widened. "Have I been preaching to the choir?"

Lara laughed. "No, I don't know much else. Just read the books and know he died a hero."

Standing at the gates of Fort Santiago carved of wood and stone. They both gazed up silently for a moment, Lara marveling at all the historical wonder around her.

"You know, my office is near here and I can't believe I hadn't thought to visit sooner," she mused. "Thanks for today."

"Wait, what?" Owen exclaimed in surprise. "My office is

also really nearby. Maybe we should carpool."

"First, you live near me, then you work near me… Are you stalking me?" Lara narrowed her eyes at him but she was smiling.

Owen laughed and poked a finger at her. "Hey, I was here first. Obviously, you're stalking me." Then he added, "But let me know. I'm serious. For the environment. And the gas money."

Lara pondered this for a split second. It was an easy answer, really. "Yes, I'd like that. I'm all for saving the whales. Closing the ozone. Reduce, reuse, recycle." She pointed at her red sneakers. "These are the only things I'm wearing that I bought new. Everything else," she gestured down her outfit– distressed jeans and flowy white top, "ukay-ukay."

"Thrifted? All of that?"

"For the good of the Earth, my friend."

***

To end the tour, Owen took Lara to a coffee shop nearby with a view of the sunset over Manila Bay—a splash of vibrant colors behind clouds of every odd shape and size. Everything was bathed in a sort of hazy golden light.

It felt almost romantic.

"So what got you into music?" Owen asked.

"Like every good Tiger Mom, mine insisted I learn the piano. I was in lessons until I was fifteen," Lara said. "But unlike my sister, I fell in love with it. Taught myself the guitar and ukulele in high school as well. Sang in the choir. What I wanted was to start a band, but I never got around to it. At one point I wanted to learn the drums, but that was a definite no—from my parents, I mean. You?"

Lara was not the type to divulge too much information about herself, but Owen was rather disarming.

"My parents were musicians. They left me with my grandmother to advance their music career." At this Owen shrugged and scoffed at the same time, almost as though he was shaking off his cares. *A touchy topic, maybe?* Lara wondered. She hoped *not too touchy,* because the more Owen told her about himself, the more she wanted to know.

"What kind of music did they play? Do they still play?"

"Kind of jazzy stuff. I'll play you an album in the car later. You might even know some of it. They retired in 2001." Owen took a sip of his coffee then changed the subject. "Anyway, tell me something else about you, something I don't know yet."

"Like what?"

"Anything. A quirky fact, a joke, a story." When she didn't answer, Owen added, "Like, when and how did you get those?" He pointed at Lara's face where two little pock marks adorned her nose.

Lara scrunched her nose up and touched a finger to the scars. "Chicken pox. Circa 1993. Or thereabouts."

Something about the way he looked at her made her heart flutter. It felt so purposeful—his penetrating gaze, squared shoulders, always a small smile at the edge of his lips.

"Ah, of course. I have a couple on my butt. For the same reasons." Owen smiled, wiggling his eyebrows. "And other scars, too."

Through the window, the golden light of the setting sun cast dramatic shadows across Owen's profile. For the first time, Lara noticed features she hadn't seen before—a mole on his cheek; a white birthmark on his collarbone; a round scar on his elbow—rough-edged, dramatic looking.

"Like that?" She pointed at his elbow. "Where's that from?"

Owen looked at his elbow and shrugged. "Old wounds."

4
New York, 1993

Owen's mother's favorite song was "Smile." She liked the Nat King Cole version best, and sang it all the time. Some of Owen's only fond memories from his early childhood were set against the backdrop of that song.

Owen could still clearly remember one morning in the little apartment he lived in with his parents in New York. He must have been six. His mother had been singing as she fried bacon. She was more focused on the song than the food, and before either of them knew it, the bacon was burning and the alarm had gone off.

The sprinkler above activated automatically, drenching mother, son, and the entire tiny kitchen. In her shock, Owen's mother dropped the pan and it clattered onto the floor, splattering boiling oil right onto Owen's elbow. He screamed and the neighbors came banging on the door.

By the time first responders from the fire department arrived, Owen was calm. His mother and neighbor had run his elbow under lukewarm water, and the sprinkler had ceased its deluge.

One of the first responders, a fireman who introduced himself as Kurt, gazed from mother to son as he examined Owen's burn. "How did this happen?" he asked.

Owen's mother, wide-eyed and ashen in the face, just shook her head. "I must have been distracted as I was cooking."

Kurt seemed concerned. Brow furrowed and eyes on Owen, he gave him another once-over. "Are you okay here, son?"

Owen remained silent.

"Does this kind of thing happen often?" This was said

in his mother's direction, and then he turned toward Owen and looked him dead in the eyes.

What was he trying to say? Even at that young age, Owen did not like the tone he was hearing in the man's voice. It was stern and low, like the old priest who said mass on Easter Sundays and always put extra emphasis on the word *"died"* as he said Christ was crucified and rose again.

"I'm okay," Owen replied finally, leaning closer to his mother.

Kurt looked between the two once more, stood up, and turned deliberately to Owen's mother. "You should have that looked at. And more importantly, try to be more careful."

Owen watched the helpers leave then turned back to his mother, but she had already gone back to her song and cooking. He decided to retreat to the living room and flip on the TV.

His mother never took him to have it looked at. She had completely forgotten. She was deep in her music once more and Owen wondered if she'd noticed it still smarted. Or if she even cared. At school, the other parents were always involved. Someone would fall and get a little scratch and they'd have fun Teenage Mutant Ninja Turtles Band-Aids to show for it.

What did Owen have?

5
Manila, 2007

Coming into the end of 2007, Lara and Owen had spent every single day together since they jammed that one evening.

They carpooled, taking turns driving one another to and from work every day. Occasionally, Mike joined them midday. Driving his long-term Mercedes Benz rental, he'd pick them up and they would go to Mall of Asia to eat or catch a sneaky matinee showing if work was light.

Mike wore his earplugs at movies, too.

***

One evening, Mike had the pair over for dinner. Kicking off the night with beers, he showed Lara his spare bedroom, which had a little stationary bike for exercising and turntables for sound mixing.

Owen had been there before and was a big fan of Mike's set up. As a Management Consultant a few years their senior, he had more disposable income, and could afford top-line equipment for his interests. Owen was almost envious. All he had were his amps, his instruments, and his looping pedal. He could imagine doing a lot more if he could mix his own tracks more professionally.

That evening, Mike showed off by mixing them a boppy sample combining a track off a Eurythmics record with a Chicane one. Owen, Lara, and Mike bobbed their heads to the beat and Lara sang a couple of lines.

"I can't lie, no, I can't lie to you... So please don't ask me for the truth, cause I can't lie..."

Her sweet, raspy voice made Owen smile and tugged at the

edges of his imagination. He jumped in.

"But it's a secret, and I must try to keep it… It'll kill me unless I kill you, but I can't lie…"

Mike clapped and hooted, and the trio laughed.

"Hey, that was cool! Did you improvise that?" Mike asked.

Owen and Lara nodded, grinning.

After, Mike cooked and they ate at his dining table with a city view. They toasted to the lights blinking at them along the skyline, and both Lara and Owen were dazzled by the papillote of sea bass, dauphinoise potatoes, and mint dark chocolate lava cake.

"Where did you learn to cook like that?" Lara demanded.

Mike gave them a cheeky grin. "I have my ways."

***

One Saturday night, Owen left Lara's house at nearly three in the morning after a night of playing his new set list for gigs for her, and working on a few covers for fun. He returned before lunch on Sunday and when she let him in, he saw she had her guitar on her bed with papers stacked next to it, notes and lyrics scribbled all over even in the margins.

Against one wall was a large canvas with an expressionist portrait of a woman sitting with a dog at her feet. On her desk, her work laptop was open and one mug with tea, another with coffee, and a glass of water flanked the keyboard.

"You're nuts. Did you sleep?" Owen asked incredulously.

"Yeah." Lara stopped to think, then said, "For four hours."

"But…what is all this?" He gestured around.

Lara pointed at her laptop. "Work emails." Then at the painting. "Just a feeling I had to paint." Then at the bed. "Oh, and a poem I read inspired me so I tried to write a song."

Owen looked across the work before him. So much of it was good, but it could be *great*. He could see that. He *believed* that.

Lara reminded Owen of two of his favorite quotes from the only novel he ever enjoyed—*The Catcher in the Rye* by J. D. Salinger. The first was about how nice it was to see someone excited about something; the second was about the importance of finding out where one should go and going there right away.

"But what's the point of all this?" he found himself asking.

Lara looked at him with those deer-in-the-headlights eyes and said, "I don't know. You know that...itchy hands feeling? Figuratively? Art is 'release' for me. I want to go everywhere with it."

"I don't know," Owen mimicked uncharitably. "Everything should have a point. Even art." He paused. "No, especially art."

"Well, what's the brilliant creation *you're* working on exactly?" Lara's voice was clipped, biting, defensive.

"Nothing, but I'm not actually brilliant like you. I don't have your natural talent, or your Filofax brain full of inane information."

"Not true. You're good at what you do."

Owen shook his head. He was not a natural talent. He worked to warm up his voice. He bled his fingertips to stubs learning songs. But Lara had the tools—naturally. She could be great.

"I'm middling at best," he insisted. "And I'm fine with that. I'm used to doing the extra shit, sweating, getting shot down. But you have the potential to skip all that. What you do—whatever that ends up being, needs to be worthy...needs to *transcend*."

6
Virginia and New York, 1960s-1990s

Virginia, 1960s-1980s

Owen's mother, Maria Victoria Jalbuena Pineda, otherwise known as Vicky, had been born in Richmond, Virginia to Bethel "Beth" Natividad Narcisso Jalbuena and Paolo Virgil Marquez Pineda. Her parents were immigrants from the Philippines who had left their country, like many others, in search of more—more money, more opportunity, more for their children.

When she was six, though, her father disappeared.

It would be years before Beth would manage to make sense of what had happened. She would eventually explain that, from what she could tell, her husband had lost his job and abandoned them in a fit of shame.

Beth had done her best with everything left behind. She worked hard at a store until she was promoted to manager. She did so well that she was later taken into corporate to manage a network of stores.

Later on, as a performer, Vicky would think of her parents whenever she had to call up a strong emotion. When she thought of her father, she could call up longing, bitterness, and anger. When she thought of her mother, she could call up triumph, hope, and redemption.

Vicky was a musician. She had dedicated her life to her craft. After her father had left them, she became obsessed with the musicians she saw on TV—all the glitz and glamor. They wore beautiful clothes, sang catchy songs, and rode flashy cars.

So Vicky trained herself to sing. She sang in the shower and the kitchen, and under her breath while waiting tables at a local restaurant. When Beth moved them to Arlington after she got another promotion, Vicky sang on the bus to work after classes at a local community college. It was on one such day that she met Oskar Weber.

Oskar was a student at Georgetown University. He was tall, broad-shouldered, and beautiful, and had a look that suggested good breeding. He wore preppy sweaters, Ralph Lauren jeans, and suede boots. His wavy blond hair was parted on the side and combed just so. He looked like Ryan O'Neal.

And Vicky loved Ryan O'Neal.

She was Oskar's opposite. She wore floral dresses and cowgirl boots. She had round sunglasses like she was one of the Beatles, and her hair was always in some variation of messy bun. She crocheted her own sweaters, and wore nail polish the color of sunflowers.

Oskar was drawn to her. *Who was this vibrant creature?*

Vicky was singing "Smile" as she read the paper on her usual commute. Oskar slid into the empty seat next to her and said hi.

***

Vicky and Oskar were quick with everything—from liking to loving, from inspiring to creating, from fighting to making up. They were like a wildfire in a forest. Oskar left his family's promises of comfort, inheritance, prestige, and he joined Vicky on what Beth characterized as a fool's errand. She told them often what she thought of their naive desire to become "rockstars." But she gave them a roof and a home, and when their baby was born, she took him in her arms and vowed to protect him.

That baby was Owen Victorio Pineda Weber.

Owen's earliest memories of his parents were just fragments. More feelings than events. More songs than occurrences.

The touch of his mother's soft hands on his cheeks.

Her beautiful voice over his head.

Vicky singing a jazzy tune. Oskar singing the blues.

His mother when she shouted—a painful, sharp sound.

Mean. Discordant.

His father when he whispered—a scary echo in your bones. Shrewd. Unforgiving.

The kisses they gave each other—sloppy, urgent.

The kisses they gave Owen—tentative, a caress.

Their hugs were soft and warm, but his bed was hard and cold. Owen lay in it often, believing he was alone and listening to the sound of their music wafting through the house. Hearing things smashing, followed by a gentle melody—a fragile reconciliation. When he was older he'd imagine that even as a baby he would have thought, *"How long have I been crying?"*

Then Lola Beth's hands would find him.

***

New York, 1993

By the time 1993 rolled around, Vicky had been living in New York for exactly eighteen months, pursuing her career in music. They had left Beth's house once they had felt Owen was old enough to need less oversight and could be brought along to gigs if need be. Lola Beth disagreed, but there was no use arguing.

Vicky and Oskar went by the band name Vic & Oz, and had recently graduated from playing seedy pubs and three-star hotel lobbies to signing with a small record label called Orion Sounds.

At eight, Owen was acquainted with the bars in the area and the music scene. His parents played a sort of intersection between jazz, easy listening, and folk. They made folksy melodies and harmonies, but played against blues notes and complex jazz chords.

By this time, Elvis Presley was getting stamps made in his honor; Patti La Belle got a star on the Hollywood Walk of Fame; Aretha Franklin received a Grammy Lifetime Achievement Award; and Whitney Houston was the primary hitmaker. New rock bands were also emerging, from grunge to metal. Owen loved all of it.

It would seem a little odd for an eight-year-old to be so into music, and because of his long hours following his parents around, helping them carry equipment, and attending their gigs, Owen found it difficult to make friends. He was not allowed on play dates (who would pick him up after?), and he found those boring anyway, because other kids didn't like the same things he did.

He would never forget coming into school one morning that year, late as usual. He was excited for the day because he knew they would have music class.

But when the teacher pulled out a guitar and started singing a popular campfire song, Owen made a noise of disgust. He hadn't meant to, but he was used to the crowds at his parents' gigs. Sometimes the opening set would be disappointing and hecklers would call out names or boos. The kids all giggled when he had groaned audibly. Emboldened by their response and the behavior he was exposed to at live music venues, he said, "Boo! This is shit! Play some real music!"

Some kids laughed, but the teacher was livid. Owen received five days of detention and a note for his parents.

That day, when he returned home with the disciplinary slip, his mother was livid. Vicky may have been an artist, may have seemed a free spirit, but she was raised a certain way and she believed it was the only way to grow a backbone. So she disciplined her son the way she had been disciplined as a child.

"OWEN!" Her voice was so loud Owen winced. "You should know better! Kitchen. *Now.*"

He did as he was told, his heart racing.

On the kitchen floor, Vicky poured dry, raw white rice onto a small patch of tile. She pointed. "Kneel."

Owen bit his lip and closed his eyes, willing himself not to cry as he got down on his knees on top of the grains. They were hard and sharp and the longer he kneeled there, the more he could feel them digging into his skin. He resisted the urge to adjust himself, knowing it would only make it worse. He felt each grain pressing against him, sketchy and coarse, like kneeling on pins.

Vicky watched quietly. Owen refused to make a sound. What seemed like an endless five minutes later, she grabbed him by the arm and pulled him up. Rice sat embedded on his little knees. He tried to pick them out or brush them off. Vicky looked away as she said, "Now go to your room."

In his room, Owen put John Coltrane's "A Love Supreme" cassette into his Walkman. He lay on his bed and stared at the ceiling, feeling frustrated and alone, but comforted by jazz music.

Jazz. There was something so visceral about it—the way the meter and time and percussion could be felt in one place in the body, while the brass played in another.

That day, Owen felt the drums in his chest, beating with his racing heart. He felt the piano in his mind, minor chords of thoughts in overlap. And he felt the saxophone in his soul—an almost playful sound over everything else saying, *"It will make sense one day."*

After that day, Owen no longer attended his parents' gigs. They left him at home alone with the TV and a sandwich, and sometimes a glass of milk. He had strict instructions to call the club they were performing at before calling 911 if anything happened.

Owen missed the live music, and had begun resorting to staying up late with his ear against the wall between his and his parents' room—listening to them practice.

Some nights, this would backfire, and he would hear things he knew he shouldn't.

Vicky and Oskar were practicing a specific song once. They had gone over it at least a dozen times already. Through the wall, Owen wanted to scream, "It would be way better if you brought the harmony in earlier!" But he was a kid, what did he know, and they wouldn't have listened anyway. So he sat there and endured.

On the fifteenth replay, though, there was the hard sound of a smack. A sick, flat noise like something hard hitting something soft. A whimper. Then Oskar's voice, "You're killing me, Vicky!"

Then a similar sound again, and a growl—low and menacing.

"Touch me like that again and I really will, Oskar!"

"Don't you dare talk to me like this. Blessed with a voice like yours and you can't even get this right!"

Owen pulled his face away from the wall and nestled into his blankets, closing his eyes and wishing he hadn't heard any of it.

A few weeks later, his parents finished their new album. They had a meeting with their record label and were told they would begin touring as the opening act to a famous jazz trio. Lola Beth was called in and just like that Owen was sent to a new home.

7
Virginia, 1995

When Owen was ten, he could be found in any one of three places: in Mrs. Stone's homeroom at Abingdon Elementary; on a stoop somewhere between Arlington Apartments and Abingdon, dribbling a basketball; or on the floor too close to the TV in his grandmother's little flat.

Arlington Apartments was a squat two-storey building in Arlington, Virginia, just outside Washington DC. It had red brick walls, and was built in the late '50s. It was infested with mice, and the heating left something to be desired, but as far as Owen was concerned it was the safest, kindest place in the world.

His grandmother, Lola Beth (though she always called herself "Bet" as she was not good at making the "th" sound), was constantly on her feet, cooking, cleaning, decorating.

If it was Christmas, she would construct elaborate miniature Christmas villages in every window sill, and put out an heirloom nativity (*"It's a belen, Owen,"* she'd say). The house was filled with the mixed culture scents of turkey and gravy, but also of kare-kare, a Filipino peanut curry.

If it was Easter, there were reusable Easter egg stickers on the corners of every mirror, and papier mache bunny statues from the '80s that she continued to dust off and prop on shelves and counter tops. Then the kitchen was filled with the sweet aroma of pastillas de leche or leche flan.

If it was Halloween, she would carve miniature pumpkins with happy faces and angels. She'd tell anyone who would listen that Halloween was about honoring the dead, not cursing the living. Those days, there would be pumpkin pie, mango floats, and chocolates galore.

The home was small but cozy and filled with mementos. Black and white framed pictures adorned the walls with Owen's sad attempts at artwork squeezed between them. There was Beth at fifteen with her mother on a farm in a province in the Philippines. There was Beth twenty years later with her husband and four children in front of a house in Richmond, Virginia. There was a picture of a small but beautiful ancestral home with stone walls on the ground floor and wooden ones on top.

She also had images of all manner of Saints whom she claimed blessed every type of affliction. When Owen had first moved in two years before, she explained them to him. There was Saint Anthony of Padua, whom she had a little stampita of that she stuck next to the front door.

"He's the Patron Saint of Lost Things, Owen. In this house we ask for the blessing of never losing anything. But especially not our minds." She'd widen her eyes and give a silly cackle. Owen thought she was hilarious.

There was also Saint Nicholas, whose stampita she stuck next to Owen's bed.

"He's the Patron Saint of Children, Owen. He will protect you."

Owen's favorite, however, was Saint Jude.

"He's the Patron Saint of Lost Causes, Owen," Lola Beth explained. *"That's why I put him next to that."*

Owen looked, and there right next to a framed image of Saint Jude on Lola Beth's mantle over the fireplace was a picture of a petite, pretty Filipina woman, smiling brightly, and a large blond man with the build of a quarterback. They were sitting on the hood of a sports car and holding hands.

Owen's parents.

He enjoyed almost everything about Lola Beth's eccentric decor. He loved that each piece had meaning. However, he did struggle to get over the large (*"Gruesome,"* he would say) crucifix with a bloody Jesus Christ nailed upon it. It hung over the front door frame facing into the flat all year round.

"To keep us honest," Lola Beth would tell him.

She did not say "I love you" much but instead, she talked about food, and she called him "hijo" or "anak," and she spoke his name. She always asked, "Have you eaten already?" and ended every other sentence with "Owen."

"Come here, Owen. Yes, get the chair, too. That's right, Owen. It is almost time to eat. You are so skinny, Owen. You have to eat. Come, oh, eat already, Owen."

When Lola Beth said "Owen," she pronounced every syllable. It rolled out of her mouth through the sides like the "e" stretched wide—arms open, a welcome. The "n" slipped out with her tongue against her front teeth accenting the name, distinguishing it from the rest of the words in the sentence.

"Oh-when," it almost sounded like. Like a question. Oh, when?

The American way, in contrast, was short and curt. *"Own,"* they'd say, the "e" swallowed by the "w", and the "n" held inside the mouth, just touching the roof. Almost a groan. Like the sound his classmates made whenever Mr. Delgado announced a pop quiz. Or like a whisper. Like the way his mother said goodbye the day she'd dropped him off.

Owen preferred Lola Beth's way.

8
Manila, 2007

"Owen, can you pass me the coffee grounds?"

Lara and Owen stood in Lara's kitchen—a small sojourn from their usual state. Evenings had quickly become reserved for music and art. Lara would come to Owen's, or Owen to Lara's, and they would practice duets, watch art films, and debate the merits of different forms of expression until the wee hours in the morning, regardless of whether the next day was a work day.

That night, though, they were not making music, they were making tiramisu.

This had been Lara's idea, and Owen decided to indulge her. Lara had many different creative urges, he was learning. It made sense—all the art, and the books, so why not in the kitchen, too?

He looked in the cabinet for the grounds.

"Owen?" she called again.

Whenever Lara said his name, it was like a song. Her accent sat somewhere between generic American, thanks to international school, and Transatlantic, owing to her father and her hometown. The 'O' was round, an opera note; the '-wen' somewhere close to 'win.' A happy sound.

He liked it.

Owen pulled the sack from a shelf and passed it to Lara. "So where did you learn this?"

"Old roommate in college. She was Italian-American."

He watched as she poured out the grounds and mixed them with boiling water.

"You're supposed to whip the mascarpone," she pointed

out.

"Right. By the way, I was thinking of adding funk to my set," he said as he whisked the light cheese in the bowl in front of him.

"What kind of funk?"

"Stevie Wonder? Or the Isley Brothers."

"Ooh, could be fun. Throw one into your gig tomorrow and let's see how it goes." Lara touched Owen's arm to stop him mixing as she noticed the mascarpone had turned thick like tasty clouds.

Owen was getting paid for gigs on Fridays and Saturdays, and Lara had begun attending and observing, taking videos, and notes.

"Which would be better?" Owen asked. "I really like 'Superstition,' and that's pretty crowd-pleasing…"

"Yeah, that's fun."

"Let's finish this and I'll play it for you." Owen rubbed his hands on his jeans as Lara began to lay the ladyfingers in a dish.

"Okay, okay. You're hilarious, you know," Lara pointed out.

Owen turned to her, surprised, "What do you mean?"

"Even when we're trying to do something different for a change, it still goes back to music."

She was smiling, which made Owen think that she kind of liked it. This made him smile a little, too.

***

The next day, at Owen's gig, the two showed up separately, both wearing a white T-shirt and khakis. Lara had made hers more her own with little sunflowers she had embroidered onto the seat pockets.

"Seriously?" they said at the same time, and then laughed together.

As Owen watched Lara, on her own accord, reach over and help him haul an amp, he pictured what they looked like as he walked alongside in virtually the same outfit, with the rest of his equipment in tow. He realized then that they had somehow grown so attuned with one another. It was foreign to him—this familiarity. He liked it, yet there was discomfort, too.

Do I like her like that? She's not even my type, he wondered. *If I fall, is there a safety net, or does it just lead further into an abyss?*

These kinds of thoughts made his chest constrict. Owen had never been in love before. His previous girlfriends had been likable—he'd been drawn to them physically, and they'd been fun. But Lara was different. He struggled to even consider it, and the one thing he could do was sing it out.

In the middle of his set, Owen looked at Lara and said, "This one's for my friend, Lara." And then he played "Electric Feel" by MGMT.

As he sang about connection and urges, he identified an electricity in his own soul. Filipinos had a special word to describe the giddy, heady exhilaration of a romantic moment. That word was "kilig." Perhaps this was that. When Owen played music, he felt mixed up, full of light, overcome. And when he looked at Lara, he felt embers of that, too. And that was a little scary.

At home after each gig, Owen listened to Lara read out her notes.

"The joke about the difference between men and women fell flat;"

"The blue shirt is too similar to the backdrop there. White would be better;"

"The mic in that venue has a tendency to drop down. You'll have to adjust between songs."

After that, they would play a few songs and Owen would give Lara feedback, too.

"When you hit that note, your voice catches a little, it's nice;"

"You have to learn to play to the viewers more—look up, smile, interact—we'll work on it together;"

"Once we liven up your set list, I think you'll be ready for a gig."

9
Manila, 2007

Owen rejoined Lara and Mike at their usual table after yet another Saturday gig. The place was fuller than normal, and the restaurant staff had set up extra lights trained on the stage. Over the buzz of conversation and the clanging of drinks, a young man in steel-toe boots, leather pants, and a ripped Eraserheads T-shirt climbed onto the stage and took hold of the microphone.

"Owen Weber, everyone," he gestured in Owen's direction and everyone clapped, with some enthusiastically and others obediently.

Mike and Lara whooped and threw their hands up in the air for added support.

Owen bowed in their direction with a playful smirk on his face. "Thank you, thank you very much," he said in a mock Elvis Presley voice.

"Owen is here almost every weekend so be sure to come catch his future sets, too. They're always fun. I'm Nilo, as most of you already know." He waved. "And every month I host an open mic here that goes well into the early morning. So. If you are a musician, stand-up comic, karaoke king or queen, this is your sign. This is your turn. It's time."

Owen's head whipped round and he stared directly at Lara. "Do it," he enthused, grinning widely, nudging her with his shoulder.

"Ha-ha, very funny," she rolled her eyes, nudging him back.

"I'm serious! We play music every day, you are so ready for this. Just one song. Just to try," Owen urged, poking Lara in the side.

"What?" Lara stared at him and realized he was serious when his eyes didn't flinch even a second. "No!" she exclaimed. "I'm not ready!"

"Well, what have we been practicing and jamming for then, if we're never going to actually play?" Owen said, his voice flat, one eyebrow raised.

"Ooooh, shots fired," Mike said. He was looking between the two, smiling at them both. "For what it's worth," he said, turning to Lara. "It would be awesome to hear you play."

Lara's stomach churned. She hadn't expected to perform that day and had zero ideas. "I don't even have my guitar," she said and then groaned, knowing this was a flimsy excuse at best.

Owen rolled his eyes and said, "Use my guitar, then."

Lara sat for a moment as the first performer came on stage and introduced herself. She was petite, with dyed blue hair, and a cello in tow. Over the noise of her own thoughts and insecurities ("You're going to suck," said the devil in her ear), she could just make out a Bach piece cutting through the room.

"I believe in you," Owen said, grabbing Lara's hand and squeezing it. This movement—so intimate, so familiar, so encouraging—sent a shock of electricity from Lara's fingertips up to her heart and she almost winced.

She sighed loudly. "Fine," she relented.

"YES!" Owen pumped his fist in the air. "She's next!" He called out to whoever would listen, and then he got up and approached Nilo himself to get Lara on the list.

Two more musical numbers later, Lara found herself on stage, sweating and panicking, and trying not to overthink anything. With Owen's guitar strapped to her, and her heart palpitating in her chest, she took a deep breath and squinted into the bright lights trained her way.

"This is," she said, faltering for a moment, and then saying the first song that came to mind, "'Kiss Me.' By Sixpence Nonethericher. Please, sing along if you know it."

Climbing off the stage minutes later, in a state of shock and awe, Lara was greeted by high-fives, hugs, and smiles, with Owen's largest and warmest of all.

As his arms wrapped around her, he said in her ear, "That

was good." His tone was light, encouraging. He squeezed her one more time. "A worthy first choice."

***

Later that night, still buzzing from the high of her first actual solo public performance, Lara chewed on her lip, pencil in hand, paper before her, ukulele in her lap.

Her mind kept drifting back to a video she had seen on the Niger food crisis the year before. She set pen to paper and began to write. The words flowed like she was a little glass flute and a popped bottle of champagne had just been poured into her, bubbling out and over–effervescent, intoxicating.

With a strum of her ukulele, she began to sing the words she had written, allowing the melody to give them a life of their own.

A song.

No not ever enough
Is the falling grace of feeling failing appetite
No not ever does it
While the sand swallows the sea
And drinks up the rain
Mouths bigger than his lips
Parted under
A selfish sky
Holding back the tears he cries.

Oh, life…Oh, life…

So tight the stomachs of the sunburnt children
Backs against the scorched sky
Dissolving like no one as clouds go by
Into ashes
To the sand
To drink the sea
And swallow the rain again.

Oh, life.

On her second pass through, she recorded it on her computer. She played it back and it felt almost like an out-of-body experience. Her voice in the air, in waves, in music.

Her own music. She *loved* it.

She named the file "Hunger," and attached it to an email to Owen that read: *Trying something new out...Let me know what you think.* Then she clicked 'Send' and closed her laptop. Inside, she had that heady feeling, light and soaring. Had she actually made something good?

Just as she was getting ready for bed, Owen phoned her.

"Lara, this is beautiful. I'm coming over." A pause, and then, "Okay?"

Lara's stomach did little happy flips at the word 'beautiful.' "Sure," she said.

Owen was there in just a matter of minutes and when he came in, he sat at the edge of the bed and looked at Lara. "Play it again," he urged. "Please."

Lara, feeling self-conscious but also excited, picked up her guitar and began to play the song live. It felt raw and naked, but somehow also right. Owen was staring at her fingers, then her mouth, then her guitar. His brow was furrowed, eyes narrowed, totally concentrated. When she finished, he said, "Again."

Lara started from the top. Owen picked up a paper, and began to write notes. When she was done for the second time, he said, "And again."

"Owen, really I was going to go to bed—"

"Please," he said again.

Lara sighed and rolled her eyes but complied. This time, Owen sang along in harmony during the last two lines of each verse, and all throughout the chorus. He pulled out his own guitar and began to pluck a light bass pattern to carry the song.

Their voices seemed to fold into each other like sheets tangling, creating warmth and friction and comfort.

In that moment, it was clear they had heard something special, but Lara's heart still skipped a beat when Owen suddenly exclaimed, "Lara...would you start a band with me?"

Looking at him, he seemed almost surprised himself, eyes wide and mouth just a little agape.

Lara had loved the arts longer than she could remember,

but music had always been a hobby. A casual pursuit. Still, as she sat there, soaking in the wake of her first original composition, she had the sudden inkling that perhaps, at this specific juncture in her life, it was the direction she was *meant* to go. A path not only with music, but with Owen.

"Don't you think what we just did was amazing? You wrote this amazing song, and then we made it more amazing together?" Owen enthused, brows furrowed, eyes wide and asking.

"So eloquent," Lara teased. "Amazing, amazing, amazing."

"Lara, come on…" His eyes were pleading.

She knew she didn't want this to end—this energy in the air between them, this electric connection.

So she said yes. "Fine. What's the plan?"

10

New York and Singapore, 1990s-2000s

New York, 1993

Lara was a precocious child who always carried with her something to read, something to sketch with, and something to listen to. She had everything in a leather backpack, soft, and supple from years of use, handed down by her grandfather. The moment he had gifted it to her was when she first fell in love with vintage.

She was seven when she spent her first summer in New York. Her mother had taken her, Yaya Luz, and Adora along while she completed a certificate course at Columbia University. In the daytime, Aurora would be in classes and Yaya Luz would bring the girls on little excursions.

On this day, they were at the Met.

Lara had been to the Met before. Her mother had taken her there, and they walked its hallowed halls with breaths held, practically tiptoeing as they gazed at the pieces of art and history with love and longing. She imagined she was Claudia in *From the Mixed-Up Files of Mrs. Basil E. Frankweiler.*

Yaya and Adora had never been, though, and Lara felt it was her solemn duty to properly introduce them to the wonder that was the Metropolitan Museum of Art. In her bag, she carried a copy of her current favorite novel—*Little Women* by Louisa May Alcott. Lara fancied herself a Jo and Amy meshed together with a sprinkling of Beth—a wild storyteller, an aspiring painter, who loved the piano and would one day bloom into…well, she hadn't quite figured out that part yet. Tucked behind *Little Women,* she brought with her an old favorite picture book called *Linnea in Monet's Garden*.

"This is the starting point," she said to Yaya Luz and Adora, who trudged along slightly begrudgingly, more interested in the ice cream that had been promised her after the museum visit than the museum itself. Lara pointed to the cover of *Linnea In Monet's Garden*. "We need to find the water lilies."

Adora perked up at the suggestion. "Flowers?"

"Yes." Lara grinned.

Adora nodded enthusiastically. "Like a scavenger hunt?"

"Sure!"

Without a map, the three wove their way through the museum, in and out of wings. Lara read passages of her book to Adora and Yaya Luz as they searched for clues.

Eventually, they figured it out: Claude Monet's work would likely be amongst the European paintings.

When the girls found themselves in the first hall of European masters, Lara felt her heart begin to race with excitement. She had always loved art. The first time she picked up a pen and drew, she was only eleven months old, and she drew a sun with a smiling face.

And that was just the beginning. Thereafter, she blew through notebooks at such a pace that her mother had to purchase a chest to store them all. And it wasn't just visual art, it was all art.

At five, she began taking piano lessons, and sang occasionally in the church children's choir. By the time she was six, she was in her "anatomy" phase. She would open her parents' heavy leather-bound academic books and sketch body parts. At seven, she had just begun dabbling in watercolor and writing poetry that she would illustrate or sing melodies against.

Everywhere she went, she had a story in her heart, pictures in her hands, music in her ears. At restaurants, she would sit with her notebooks and her pens, a tune in her head—the backdrop to her masterpieces.

"They're not yet good but I will be," she often said to herself as she regarded her own work.

Right then, as Lara stood in front of Monet's "Water Lilies," she almost cried. Her heart thudded in her chest and she held her book up next to the painting and noticed the texture of the water, the movement in the strokes, the soft colors. If one stood close, they would have little to no idea what it was, but if they stepped back and saw the whole picture, they would understand the scene in its entirety much better.

Adora counted the flowers with Yaya Luz before moving to a Clara Peeters' painting not far away that was more vibrant, dark, and bold.

But Lara remained anchored to the spot. She slipped out her Walkman and pressed play. In it was John Coltrane's "A Love Supreme," a cassette she had swiped from her father's collection because she loved the rhythm of it. It made her feel like she was in an old film—the kind her grandparents watched on the Classics Network where everyone spoke in a sing-songy drawl and danced their way across sound stages. The one she liked best was called *Young Man With A Horn*, where Doris Day and Kirk Douglas danced through the highs and lows of an art, love, music-filled romance.

While listening, Lara tapped her feet and swayed a little, examining each stroke with a deep focus and appreciation. In that moment, she felt certain: if she could fill her life with music and art, it would be complete.

***

Singapore, 2003

Nearly a decade later, Lara found herself staring at two envelopes in her hands, both of them heavy and promising. One of them read Rhode Island School of Design, and the other, Boston University.

She already knew what her mother would say.

From the front of the house she could hear the noises of people arriving–her mother's voice, Adora's footsteps, and the rustling of paper packages and plastic bags. They had been shopping.

"Si Lara?" She heard her mom ask in Filipino.

"Sa dining, Señora," Yaya Luz replied.

Adora and Aurora materialized in the room moments later. Adora draped herself over one of the chairs feigning exhaustion. "We had *such* a good time shopping. You should've come."

This recommendation made Lara giggle a little. She loved her mother and sister, but she really was not the high street fashion type. She much preferred thrift stores and flea markets–which, of course, Adora knew.

"Yeah, no thanks. But glad you guys had fun. What did you get?" She and Adora were incredibly close, as many sisters only a year apart in age would be, but that didn't mean they were anything alike.

Adora threw her feet into the air and said: "Shoes!" And indeed she had on a beautiful new pair of designer flats.

"Nice."

Adora shrieked. "Wait! Are those what I think they are?"

"Indeed, they are, " Lara answered, waving the envelopes in the air.

Aurora shook her hair out of her clip and her eyes grew wide. "Oh my goodness!" She rushed to sit next to her eldest.

"Shouldn't we wait until Dad is home?"

"We can always show him later. Let's open them now!"

Lara took a deep breath. Prior to opening these envelopes she could still dream that she would be allowed to accept an offer at a design school to pursue art. Once the envelopes were open, she could already tell what her mother would say.

"Open it!" Aurora said again, nudging Lara.

Lara sighed. "Okay." She slipped the RISD envelope open first. The acceptance letter slid out and Adora cheered. "YES!"

"Oh, that's nice." Aurora smiled. "Congratulations, dear. What was the program again?"

"Fine Art or Art History."

"Mm, nice. And the second?" Aurora's eyes betrayed her even though she was squeezing Lara's arm encouragingly.

Typical. There had to be statistics that would show what percentage of Asian or part-Asian homes supported their children in careers in the arts. *0.001%, perhaps.*

Lara smiled and set the RISD envelope aside as she opened the next. The Boston University letter slid out and Aurora clapped loudly. "Such an excellent school, don't you think?"

"It is…" Lara admitted.

"They have such a good Communications program. I've heard." Aurora had of course done her own research. "Communications is so much like art. You can do all your creative stuff and still have all the qualifications to do marketing or creative work in a stable corporate job."

Lara smiled and nodded. She knew her mother was right, and of course, taking up communications would be the more practical way to go. But she still felt a tug in her heart.

"You can be an artist at any age, you know. But you only get this one chance for us to pay for a degree that could take you places and provide you with the security in your life to do all the things you want to do," Aurora went on. "Imagine how fun it will be. You'll live in Boston and it will be such a wonderful time for you. Independence, learning, academics, FUN! All that and there's no reason you can't still keep your little artsy hobbies, of course."

Little artsy hobbies. It stung. Lara was known across her school as the Art Girl. Her work was featured all over the building, she performed acapella with the choir at competitions, and she represented them in arts competitions the region over. Yet, when it came down to it, to her mother, all that passion and work could only ever amount to a hobby.

A little artsy hobby.

Still, Lara struggled to find it in her to argue. She also excelled academically, and was an adaptable person, so while deep down, she wanted to do art for life, she also wanted to do right by her parents. They were bankrolling her education. And they were simply advising her out of personal experience.

Lara looked between the envelopes. "I'll think about it."

"Yes, do." Her mother nodded enthusiastically. But she must have known, the choice had already been made.

***

Later that week, Lara went to the Singapore Art Museum on her own. She sat amongst the paintings, and the sculptures, and the photographs, and then opened her sketchbook and drew. Lines, scribbles, patterns, doodles. On her Discman, she listened to a mix she had made of John Coltrane, Smokey Robinson, the Beatles, and Joni Mitchell. She sang along softly about life, the carousel, agony, ecstasy, and sweet harmonies.

She sat for three hours until a docent approached her and mentioned they would be closing in a few minutes.

Lara was not ready to leave, so by way of response she pointed at one of the works on the wall that had been baffling her. The painting was figurative abstract, by a Filipino artist, and appeared to depict a beautiful young woman who appeared to be working on a weave.

"Why is this called The Champion?" she asked.

The docent looked at the painting thoughtfully, tipping her head one way, then the other. "I believe this artist is from Mindanao—in the South of the Philippines—and if you look closely, I think those are a Spanish flag and an American flag being unwound and rewoven into a Philippine flag. I'm not a Filipino but," the docent shrugged, "Maybe it's a statement about national identity."

Lara looked at the painting again and did notice upon closer inspection the colors of the flags coming apart and blending into something new—the Philippine red, white, blue, with her stars and sun. She felt a sudden wonder bubbling up in her. How beautiful it was to be able to tell such a profound story in a single image.

"Thank you," she said, and as she got up and began packing her things, another thought occurred to her. She turned to the docent once more. "I just have one more thing…"

"Of course."

"Have you been working here a long time?"

"Since it opened in 1996, yes."

"Would you say most of these artists started young? Or do you think anyone can be an artist, no matter how old they are?"

The docent seemed to consider this then said, "I think that anyone can be an artist, regardless of age. All you need is the mind, the heart and the hands for it. And it helps to have experience, too. Claude Monet started really painting in his forties after his wife died. Ed Hopper sold his first painting in his thirties, and before that he had to struggle. And have you ever heard of Grandma Moses?"

Lara shook her head.

"She didn't start til she was in her seventies I think. Look her up. There are artists in every specialization who start at all stages of life, or persist even into old age. In painting, in sculpture, even in music. Just look at Tony Bennett. He's still kicking it."

"Thank you."

"Do you want to be an artist?"

"I thought I did. I mean, I think I do."

"Are you about to go to uni? You look about that age."

"I am…"

"And your parents want you to do something practical?"

Lara laughed sheepishly. "You must get this a lot."

"Not as often as you'd think." The woman's lips turned up at the edges while her eyes and knitted brow betrayed a bittersweet, kindred sadness. "For what it's worth, I think that whether you take the long way or the short way to your dreams, if you stay focused, and if it's for you, you will get there at just the right time."

11
Manila, 2007

On one rare evening when Lara was otherwise engaged ("girls' night" with Monique), Owen and Mike went for sushi at a popular hole in the wall.

"So what's the deal with Lara?" Mike asked over his plate of salmon belly sashimi.

"What do you mean?"

"I mean, you guys are together every day. Is that something or…" Mike trailed off.

Owen knew Mike had reason to bring this up. He and Lara were together all the time; they were so close, so kindred, that any sane person would have assumed they were dating.

But Owen didn't know what he and Lara were. He hadn't spoken to her about it, and although something about her kept pulling him in, he did not want to ask how or wonder why. Besides, since they had begun making music together, a relationship seemed off the table anyway. After all, look how awful that had been for his parents?

When Owen didn't reply, Mike started again. "Seriously, Owen," he insisted. "You probably see each other more often than my parents do. And they're *actually* married."

Owen laughed again but then was silent for a moment. "I don't know," he lied.

Mike's eyebrows shot up and he almost looked upset for a moment–making Owen suddenly aware that perhaps he needed to find a better way to talk about this with their friends. The truth, of course, was that he and Lara were not only busy being friends, they were busy working on something *specific*. Their music. But Owen and Lara had not told anybody about their project. They were three songs into their album and, in Owen's words, they didn't want to "jinx" anything by letting anyone else into their creative cocoon. That day, however, confronted with Mike's line of questioning, Owen thought it a good time to tell just one other person about what they were up to.

Plus, Mike did have some good music equipment. Maybe he could help them. And maybe telling him would put an end to these cross, loaded looks of judgment—like the one Mike had on his face right then.

"Okay, I'll tell you what's really going on," Owen said as he took another bite of sushi. "Lara and I are music partners." He had not said this aloud to anyone and when it came out it felt incredibly right. "We've decided to make an album together."

Mike looked taken aback for a moment. "Wait, are you serious? So it's not just some playful jamming you guys are doing, you're actually making music and booking gigs?"

"Well, we haven't booked gigs, but we're making music, yeah." Owen admitted. "We've done the first few songs for an EP." The sushi on his plate was finished so he picked up the menu again.

Mike sat back in his chair and nodded, his lips drawn into a smirk and his eyebrows raised halfway up his forehead. "Okay, I'll buy it. So. It's not a wife-wife thing, it's a work-wife thing?"

Owen shrugged. "Call it what you want."

Mike laughed. "Okay. Certainly explains why you guys practically live together."

Owen just chuckled in response.

Mike sat back. "Isn't she supposed to move out soon?"

"Yeah, in a couple of weeks."

"Has she found a place yet?"

"No, actually."

"Think maybe she should come live with me? I'm going to be traveling more for work and don't want to pay the full rent anymore. She could stay in the other room. I can leave the music stuff in the living room and you can use it when needed."

Owen's eyebrows shot up and he smiled at the thought. "Really?"

"Just don't break anything or it's on your head."

Owen laughed. "Deal. I'll ask Lara what she thinks later."

"Later?"

"Yeah, I'm going over to hers after this." He checked his phone and saw that Lara had messaged her ETA (*"midnight"*). "I still have time though. Should we order some sake?"

12
Manila, 2007

Four months after meeting Owen and Mike, Lara found herself moving all her things into Mike's apartment after having agreed to rent the second bedroom. Owen had taken Friday off work to help, and he stood in the middle of her new room holding a stack of books he'd taken from one of the boxes.

"You're going to need to buy another bookshelf." He gestured at the built-in shelving. "Your one thousand books aren't going to fit there. Have you ever heard of an e-reader? It's a new thing. Amazon just released one. May want to look into that."

"I like the way they smell," Lara said, rifling through another box of books. Owen glanced across the spines—Mary Oliver, Maya Angelou, John Steinbeck, Kazuo Ishiguro, Toni Morrison, Gabriel Garcia Marquez, Haruki Murakami, Søren Kierkegaard, Jane Austen, William Shakespeare, F. Sionil Jose. And so many more.

"What?" he asked. Had she said something about smell?

"The books," she said. "I like the way they smell."

"That's a thing?"

"You are obviously not much of a reader." She fished a hardbound volume out of her stack and walked up to Owen, opening it up under their noses. She was standing so close all of a sudden that Owen could see that a sprinkle of freckles across her nose bridge formed the shape of the Little Dipper. Endearing.

"Take a deep breath," she said.

He blinked, trying to focus on her eyes instead. Which right then looked like brown portals into another galaxy. Being close to Lara, physically, was confusing. He wondered whether she was aware of the power she could have over some people. Like himself.

"Just do it."

He refocused and obliged. As he did so, she closed her eyes and did the same. A small smile started at the edges of her mouth, and Owen watched her. The little cupid's bow above her lip was damp—just a hint of sweat from the effort of the move.

Focus. Owen tried to pay attention to the book. It smelled like paper And old leather. And ink. A pleasant, benign smell. Lara, though, looked like she was floating off somewhere else.

"It's nice," Owen found himself saying. "And I do like books."

Lara tilted her head at him and gave him a curious smile. "Name one you loved enough to finish and remember."

"*The Catcher In the Rye.*"

Lara seemed surprised at this. She squinted at him. "Name another. One that doesn't have a whiny teenage narrator."

"No."

Lara just laughed, tossed the book onto the bed before following it down with a plop. "Tell me more, what do you like about *The Catcher In the Rye?*"

"I like how relatable it is. I read it at a time when I was feeling such similar things as Holden was."

"I can imagine that."

"And I like it because of who gave it to me."

Lara perked up at this. "Who gave it to you?"

Owen paused, then cleared his throat. He was not ready for this topic of conversation, so he changed the subject. "I don't think you have any other choice than to unpack, Lara." He looked around at the three boxes and suitcase in various states of unpacking.

Lara didn't press. Instead, she groaned and said, "I'd rather just lay here. You can unpack. Or you could lie with me, too." She shrugged and Owen thought of that Snow Patrol song.

"Now isn't the time for Lara Halford to become lazy for the first minute of her life." Owen walked over and poked Lara's side.

Lara veered away. "Hey, wait! I'm ticklish."

This was dangerous information to hand to Owen. He poked her again on the other side playfully. "How did I not know this about you!" Owen said, reaching over and grabbing both her sides, sticking his fingers under her ribs.

Lara began to howl with laughter.

Owen climbed over her and brought his hands up under her arms. "What about here?"

Lara was laughing so hard she was crying, and Owen couldn't help laughing along. He had never seen Lara so loose. Her face lit up, her smile wide and eyes soft. Owen felt he had found a button that released her into the wild.

When Owen let up, it took a moment for them to stop laughing. As they did, they realized they were on the bed, and he was on top of her, hips pressed against hers, and there was something else between them, too. Literally.

Hearing Lara clear her throat, Owen felt a blush creeping up his neck and rushed to get up.

"So, um," he started to say.

Owen hoped she would not bring up what had just happened. It was a natural effect of being in close proximity with the opposite sex, he reasoned with himself. He had, after all, not had sex in a long time. It was just a biological effect. Owen did not want to do it with Lara. He had seen through his parents what it meant to be in love with a partner. One could love a partner as a friend, but to be in love with them was another thing entirely.

Owen also felt privately protective of what he had with Lara. It was impossible to explain to anyone else, but everything felt so delicate, so deep, and so any time he tried to look past the present moment with her, he pictured himself falling with nothing to catch him. He imagined them in love, and making music, and eating each other alive the way his parents had. It was too frightening. What they had could not be cheapened by a label, or jeopardized with a "relationship."

13
Manila, 2007

Lara could not remember the last time she had been tickled that way. Perhaps not since childhood. Or maybe ever. She felt light, happy even. She was pleasantly surprised that her joy and clarity of mind expanded as her laughter had. But now she was distracted again. She rolled onto her side and gazed at Owen searchingly. Were they going to ignore what she was sure she had felt between them?

Owen did not look like he was going to respond to any confrontation on the matter. His face was closed off, eyes glazed over, mind somewhere far away. Lara got off the bed and quietly began unpacking again. Owen just lay watching her, then after some time had passed, he stood and helped in silence.

Later as the two were eating dinner and assessing the work they had done, Lara was still feeling rather out of sorts. This unspoken conversation was maddening. Every time she looked at Owen his body and his eyes told different stories. His eyes said, "let's not," but his body, so close to hers, legs touching, said something else. It didn't make sense. She thought, *If you're creating such deep work with a person, didn't it often follow that you loved them deeply, too?*

Owen poked her with his elbow. "Hey," he said. "You okay?"

"Yeah, thanks for helping."

"Any time. Are you too tired to make music tonight?"

Lara looked at him for a moment. If she said she was tired, Owen would go home and she would not see him until the next day. If she said she wanted to make music, even though she wasn't in the mood to, he would stay longer, but the music they would make would be bad, and they would bicker.

Lara liked when Owen stayed over. She was in her twenties and single, and that combined with work and art could feel like a rather lonely thing sometimes. It was always nice to have someone sharing space, a bed, breakfast. Mike was out of town for five days and Lara would have her first night completely alone in a much larger apartment. But without the excuse of the music, why would Owen stay?

When she hadn't answered for a time, Owen said, "We could just watch another movie, if you prefer?"

Lara looked at him. It felt like an olive branch. Like the conversation inside his words said, *We won't talk about this afternoon, but I'll stay. I'm here if you want me here.*

For the briefest of moments, in those words, she felt little embers of falling. Of love. She shrugged them off in her mind, and focused on the current reality.

"What do you want to watch?" she asked.

"Got any more French art house films to put us to sleep?"

Lara laughed. "Always. And it's French New Wave."

***

The next day, Monique invited a large group over for a house party. Though Owen had stayed the night, the awkwardness of what he and Lara had felt between one another still hung in the air.

They arrived at the party together, but once there, Owen turned to Lara and said, "We should walk around apart. Hang out with other people for a change. I'm sure you get it."

It was so abrupt, Lara's first reaction was confusion. Then she shook it off by saying, "Okay." But he was already walking away.

She ventured into the party, scanning the crowd for someone she knew. She spotted Bianca, David, and Niko, each with a beer in their hands. They waved when they saw her.

"Hey!" she said, walking over and plopping down in an empty armchair near them.

"Hey, where's Owen?" Bianca asked reflexively.

Lara shrugged, trying to act nonchalant. *Like you couldn't care less*, she thought. "Oh, here somewhere."

"Oh, okay. No gig tonight?"

"Yeah, none this week. I just moved into Mike's spare bedroom so he's been helping me with that."

Bianca nodded knowingly as though this were to be expected. *Did that sound weird?* Lara thought, self-conscious. "He's a good friend," she said–her tone stilted and awkward.

Niko laughed and Bianca kicked him in the shin, her eyes wide as she smiled.

"Right, a *super* good *friend*." David grinned and then Bianca kicked him, too.

Just then, Lara spotted Owen and Monique across the room. She was about to greet the host when she remembered what Owen said. She faltered, and her eyes darted between the two. Then she saw the way Monique was looking at him—with one hand on his arm, and the side of her lip half in her mouth, chewing on it just a little flirtatiously, almost sensually.

Monique was a lithe, beautiful woman, and suddenly, Lara could imagine Owen liking that. That evening, Monique, in her own home, wore red lipstick, and a sleek silver dress that went to her knee and had a slit up the side. Glamorous. Adult. Lara, in contrast, was in jeans that she had embroidered with little daisies on the pockets, vintage pumps, an old Foo Fighters T-shirt, and a spot of tinted lip balm. She hadn't even brushed her hair—just thrown it into a half-ponytail and said, "That'll do."

Why would he be attracted to me if he could have a Monique?

Niko and David picked up the heirloom sungka set from under Monique's parents' coffee table and started a game.

Bianca sidled closer to Lara, following her gaze. "Oh," she said. "That."

"What?" Lara turned to her.

"Nothing," Bianca said, shrugging.

"No, what?"

"Nothing, just Monique and Owen. I saw you looking at them. Nothing's happening there, I think."

"Oh. I mean, not that it matters. But. Oh."

Both girls fell silent.

"I mean, that's what Monique told me anyway. And you know Monique, she's just...flirty...effervescent...that's just. Her."

Lara watched them as they talked and Monique twirled a strand of hair around her finger. Lara felt a sudden wave of jealousy. An uncomfortable acidity in her stomach. She wanted to kick herself. And even though she knew Bianca was right about Monique's personality, it didn't really allay her anxiety over the idea that there may be something brewing there between her two friends.

He's not yours, Lara, she scolded herself. *And you like Monique. She's your friend. And a nice one, at that.*

Still, Lara decided to stick with the group she was with. Owen could do what he wanted. But later, when Lara felt she had had her fill of debauchery, she went in search of Owen who had ridden with her. When she found him, he was on a couch with Monique, another girl, and a couple of guys she did not recognize.

"Hey, I'm heading home. Are you coming?" she said, and then nodded to her friend. "Thanks for hosting, Monique."

Monique grinned broadly. "Thanks for coming!"

Owen looked around and took another swig of his drink. "No, I'm good. I'll catch a ride with someone else later. Thanks."

"'K." Lara turned on her heel and walked away. As she was getting settled in her car, her phone chimed. She pulled it out and was surprised to see a message from Owen.

From Owen (Music Dude) Weber
Are you sure you didn't drink? Drive safely. Text me when you get home.

Lara couldn't help it—she smiled. She felt that little sensation of falling once more—of love.

Have you eaten already?
Did you sleep well?
Let's do what you want to do.
I missed you.
I'll stay.
Text me when you get home.
Love—a word four letters long but a thousand lines deep, and equally wide.

<h1 style="text-align:center">14</h1>

Fairfax, Virginia, 2000

Owen wrote his first song when he was fifteen. By then, he had been living with Lola Beth for seven years, and had seen his parents all of ten times: three birthdays, seven Christmases.

Christmas was the worst. On his birthdays, he would often have a party and some friends over as a buffer. But Christmas was just Lola Beth, his parents, and him. For Noche Buena, his mother's brothers would come by with their kids, and then the rest of the week, it was just the four of them grasping at straws for conversation starters.

Owen did not know how to act around his parents. As far as he was concerned, Lola Beth was raising him, and she was doing a fine job. Vicky and Oskar's duo had expanded to a full band, and they were charting in a strong middle range for their genre.

When Owen turned twelve, they began earning enough to relocate him and Lola Beth to a bigger house in a better district. Owen missed the little apartment in Arlington, but Fairfax was nicer, and Vicky wanted Lola Beth to retire and focus on home life, rest, and Owen.

The house on Hollowview Court would allow Owen to attend well-ranked schools, but it also meant that Owen was in a less diverse environment than he had previously been. If he had felt different from his friends and classmates in New York and Arlington, it grew only steadily worse in Fairfax.

Luckily, he managed to find a small niche within the school's Karate Club. But while he progressed through the belts nicely, it created its own problems, with half the school nicknaming him Bruce Lee and the other half Little Jackie Chan. He didn't even look like either of the Asian stars, but just the fact that his ethnicity was adjacent to them seemed to seal his fate. He let the jokes slide off of him, rolled with the punches, joined in the merrymaking. It felt shameful, but it felt like survival.

Eventually, he began swimming, too. Sports, music, and Lola Beth's support—including the delicious lumpia she always served him and his friends—made school just bearable. Owen knew he was getting by okay without his parents.

The truth was, Vicky and Oskar could have picked Owen up any time. They could have taken him to live with them in Los Angeles. But they didn't.

"It's not the life we'd want for our son. LA is soul-crushing."

He had overheard them in conversation with Lola Beth after Noche Buena when he was thirteen and everyone thought he'd gone to bed. Lola Beth was asking if they planned to bring him like they originally thought they would. Curiously, nobody had ever asked him what he wanted. Not that he knew. But it would have been nice to have been asked.

The Christmas before Owen's sixteenth birthday, Vicky and Oskar arrived, as always, three days early. They rolled up in their vintage sports car, both in a terrible mood. It seemed they had argued some time along the long cross-country drive over. They loved to take the car all the way from California to the East Coast. Each year, they considered it a musical pilgrimage, where they could stop at special places and write new songs. And each year, they arrived in such a state—red in the face and barely speaking. Owen had no memory of a Christmas where it wasn't like this.

It made him wonder if one had to be argumentative and sour or sad and angry to make music. It certainly seemed to be the driving mood behind his parents' art. They always seemed more ready to write raging break up punk rock rather than easy listening jazz. It made Owen think, *Why do people work with the people they love? Why, when it can destroy them?*

That day, as they got out of their car, not even glancing at each other, a certain stiffness in their gaits, Vicky looked at sixteen-year-old Owen. "My goodness, Owen, you are so grown."

In the almost year since she had last seen him, he had shot up three inches, and grown his wavy hair out. She gave her son a kiss on the cheek, and then walked past to hug her mother.

"Big man." Oskar grabbed Owen and gave him a bear hug.

Owen smiled, and helped his parents with their things, taking them to the third bedroom and setting them on the floor. This time, they had a new guitar and case, the brand emblazoned on the side. *Taylor.*

He looked at it.

"That's for you," came his father's voice.

Owen turned and saw his father in the doorway watching him.

"Open it," Oskar said.

Owen's heart skipped a beat. He had purchased his own guitar secondhand earlier in the year. It was no good, but it was his, and he loved it. Still, a Taylor in hand was like a gift from the gods.

In the years since his parents had left him, the one thing that could truly lift his heavy heart was a good song. It drove Lola Beth crazy—the worry and trauma of raising a free-wheeling musician like Vicky. But she allowed him space to create, and she was proud.

When he opened up the case, he saw before him a beautiful Taylor acoustic. It was crafted out of a light wood with a cutaway, a dark fretboard, and small diamond inlays. It was the most beautiful guitar he had ever touched. He wasn't surprised at all to find that as he ran his fingers across it, he found that they were trembling. With a deep breath, he began to pluck at the strings.

"Maybe this summer you can come be with us in LA." Oskar's light, hopeful tone surprised Owen.

"What's this now?" Vicky's voice was pinched, annoyed.

Owen looked up to see his mother coming up behind Oskar.

"Dad said maybe I can come stay with you guys in LA for the summer," Owen answered.

"He can even roadie for us. We can pay him a small wage," Oskar suggested, enthusiastically.

Vicky shot her husband a look that seemed to say, *"I can't believe you'd do this without consulting me"* before saying, "That's our busiest season. We tour all summer. It's going to be very unstable for a teenager."

"He's old enough to decide how he feels about that."

Owen looked at his parents. In that moment, he realized he scarcely knew them, and they him. A summer together would likely come with both blessings and curses. Was he ready for that?

He stood up with the guitar. "Thank you for the guitar. I love it." Then he walked out.

That night he wrote his first song. It went:

> *If I walked a thousand miles just to get to you*
> *Would you want me to?*
> *If I swam across a sea to wash off all your sins*
> *Would you let me in?*
> *If we knew each other even just a little bit*
> *I could manage it…but I can't*
> *If we loved each other even just a little more*
> *I could make it work…but you can't*

15
Los Angeles, 2001

In the end, Oskar had won the argument, and Owen had indeed been able to make the choice himself. And so once school had let out, he got on a plane to Los Angeles to spend his first summer with his parents in many years.

Lola Beth had done the very Filipino-grandma thing of sending Owen off with Tupperwares full of food with notes on them describing freezing and reheating directions. That and a blessing, crossing his forehead with Holy Water and hugging him so tightly he could barely breathe.

Upon arrival, Oskar came to pick him up from LAX in his sports car. Oskar looked happy to see him, and Owen was hopeful the trip would be a proper bonding experience. Their first in memory.

"What's in the suitcase?" Oskar asked after he had lifted it into the car. It was very heavy.

"Lola Beth's frozen delights."

Oskar laughed.

"Where's Mom?" Owen climbed into the passenger seat.

"Oh, she had an appointment," Oskar replied vaguely, pulling out and beginning their drive home.

The pair had not been alone together many times in Owen's young life, and he found it rather daunting attempting to have a conversation with his father.

As if thinking the same, Oskar pulled up a carry case full of CDs and handed it to his son. "Pick your poison."

"Thanks," Owen said as he began flipping through it.

There were two hundred CDs in there, so he was spoilt for choice. At the very back, his father had placed all of the Vic & Oz albums together. There were four full-length ones in total, plus two EPs. Owen was familiar with each one—he and Lola Beth kept them on the mantle—but they never listened to them. He knew Lola Beth was angry with his parents and that there seemed to be no room for anybody or even anything else in that dysfunctional little family. Still, he noticed that confrontation did not come easily to Lola's Filipino sensibilities, so he observed that she preferred a more silent sort of disapproval.

Owen did not ask to listen to his parents' music at home. However, he had thought it a good idea to familiarize himself just a little once he had confirmed that he'd be helping them over the summer. He took the CDs into his room the week before he'd left, and listened to each front to back, and over again. The familiar sounds of his parents' voices mingling with one another in silky harmonies, and the colorful jazz in the background, transported Owen back to his early childhood.

He could almost smell the pancakes and bacon, the longganisa, the fried lumpia. He could feel his mother's hand over his as they danced through the living room in their tiny apartment. He could see his father's face, laughing and lit up by the Christmas lights as they put up their first tree. It was a pleasant reminder that it had not always been lonely, or difficult.

"Do you have a favorite from our albums?" Oskar asked.

"I don't really listen to them much, to be honest. But I like this one. It's more bluesy than the others." He pointed at their sophomore release.

Oskar smiled. "That's my favorite, too."

Owen finally settled on a Foo Fighters album.

Oskar nodded his approval. "Great choice."

The two men bobbed their heads to "Learn to Fly" as Owen watched the LA traffic with fascination. There were large highways and boulevards in Virginia and sometimes they did get backed up—especially on a Sunday morning along Leesburg Pike just before all the mega churches in the area held their services. And New York had traffic, too, but on smaller grids, with people yelling and weaving in and out. But LA was its own beast. There, it was lane after lane of all manner of cars, trudging along like a school of fish on a single current.

Oskar seemed to read his son's mind. "It's crazy, isn't it? I miss New York…Do you ever miss it, too?"

"I don't really remember it much."

That wasn't true. Owen remembered it well, but it seemed easier to end the conversation there. If he had spoken more, they might have talked about something he didn't want to touch—like why they left New York in the first place. Or, more importantly to Owen, the manner in which they had left him and New York.

"We're in West Hollywood now," Oskar announced. Owen looked out the window and gazed at the tall palm trees, low rise apartments, and streets lined with shops and bars and clubs.

They pulled up moments later at a Mediterranean style apartment building. Oskar parked the car and unlocked the doors. "Home sweet home!"

Owen looked around, puzzled. He had somehow imagined that his parents were living in some comfortable, if not swanky, pad in Beverly Hills, or Hollywood, or Malibu, or wherever fancy people in LA lived. Wasn't that the life of a musician? Even if they were not world famous, they had a steady following that included big fans as well as casual listeners who knew them by name and enjoyed catching them on the radio. Owen's teachers at school, for example, were always slightly star struck to hear who his parents were. He hadn't expected them to live in a walk-up in the middle of the city.

Oskar caught the surprise on his son's face and gave a forced smile. "Your mother and I are trying something out. She lives in our house in Silver Lake, and I'm renting this place here. It's closer to our record label, and…" he trailed off.

Owen shrugged, trying to seem nonchalant, but inside he was surprised. His first thought was, *Damn. They're separated.* His second was, *Lola Beth is going to kill them. Or at least light another three candles every day after mass.* He made a mental note to tell her all about it on his first phone call.

***

Oskar's apartment was charming—well-lit and smartly furnished with modern, cream, wooden, and white interiors. It had a single bedroom, but there was a pull-out couch in the living room, and Oskar had set it up with pillows and covers.

Owen nodded awkwardly. "Thanks for setting all this up. Is there anything you need me to get to work on today?"

"No problem, son. It's my pleasure. No work today. I was thinking after you've settled in, we can go for a walk and I can show you our label, and we can have dinner somewhere nearby?"

"Will Mom come around?"

"Not today."

"Okay. Sounds good."

"Okay, I'll just leave you to it. Bathroom's through there."

Owen nodded. "Thanks."

Oskar walked off in the direction of the semi-open-concept kitchen. "Can I get you anything to drink in the meantime?"

"No, I'm good, thanks. And thanks, Dad."

"What for?"

"Picking me up, and…arranging for me to be here at all. It's going to be fun." Owen surprised himself saying so, but he did hope he was right.

Oskar smiled. This time a genuine, wide, bright smile. Owen found himself thinking, *Oh. We do look alike.*

"I'm glad you're here too. Thanks for agreeing to come."

***

Owen was in LA for a whole week before he saw his mother. In the time between his arrival and their first get together as a family, Oskar had put Owen to work on small tasks—sitting in on meetings; taking notes; cleaning and organizing instruments; loading and unloading the vehicles; and learning the ins and outs of each piece of equipment. He spent most of his days with Oskar and members of their backup band, listening carefully as they showed him things like how to load the lights, or which cords matched with which amps.

As Owen watched them work, he could hear Lola Beth's judgment in his own mind falling away. She always said musicians were flighty and impulsive and could not be trusted to stick to a schedule.

"There's a reason they call a diva a diva," she would scoff.

However, Owen felt that the musicians Oskar worked with—and Oskar himself—were hardworking and precise individuals. Owen couldn't imagine Oskar doing anything on a whim. With the tour coming up, it seemed every minute was allotted preciously toward preparation so things would be just right.

On day seven, Oskar arranged for Owen, Vicky, and himself to have dinner at a restaurant called Campanile. It had a beautiful interior courtyard where one could dine under lofty ceilings amidst the once-neglected architectural project of Charlie Chaplin—the icon, and original composer of Vicky's favorite song, "Smile."

Oskar and Owen were already seated when Vicky arrived. His mother waltzed in in a sleek black dress, a silky batik shawl draped around her neck and shoulders. She looked every bit a superstar. The two men stood when she approached the table and they exchanged kisses on the cheek.

"Oh, Owen," Vicky said, taking her son's chin in one hand and turning his head left and right to look at him and smiling, as if in approval. "You've got a nice tan from the summer sun."

Regarding Oskar, Vicky nodded and said, "Fine choice."

"It was designed by Charlie Chaplin long ago, and then abandoned," Oskar supplied. "I thought you would enjoy that."

"That's sweet of you," Vicky said. "I've been here actually. It's delicious."

Oskar looked taken aback for a moment, and then recovered and spoke, "Oh, wonderful. Then you must recommend something."

A staff member swooped in with a menu. Everything looked delicious, and very expensive. They placed a few orders, and sat in silence, looking at each other for a minute. Owen could not remember the last time they were just the three of them together, without the buffer of friends or uncles or aunts or Lola Beth.

"So what has your dad gotten you up to all week, dear?"

"Mostly learning the ropes. Roadie work. I'm liking it."

"It's hard work."

"Yeah. I mentioned it to Lola Beth. She sends her regards."

"How is Mama doing?"

"Lola's well. Says she's bored without me to clean up after."

"She's got to be joking. She makes a bigger mess than you do in that house," Vicky teased.

Oskar, who had been quiet, slightly snorted as Vicky and Owen chuckled along. The ice had broken a little.

"Sorry it took us so long to bring you over," Oskar said.

"The idea came up often but we could never come to an agreement..." Vicky elaborated. "And it's not a great environment here for you. Especially before eighteen months ago, it would have been a mistake to have you come. Everything was so unstable."

"Well, if some of us had not—" Oskar's tone had taken an edge to it, and he was clearly addressing Vicky, not Owen now.

"Don't start!" Vicky interrupted, but her face looked sad, and her voice trembled just slightly.

"Do I hear shame? Defensiveness?" Oskar's words left his mouth in forceful breaths.

Owen was suddenly transported to obscure childhood memories. The machine gun-fire sound of his parents bickering, interspersed with the sensations of song, the touch of cold hands, the drip of tears, the sight of white-knuckled frustration.

"Oskar, don't start now. You make it out like I was the bad guy when you know that it was a two-way street. You know what choices you made and how they contributed to this outcome. "

"Fine." Oskar huffed, chastised, but still upset. He took a second seemingly to compose himself then turned to Owen again. "What we're trying to say is, we're sorry it took us so long to do this. It never seemed like the right time."

"It never was the right time," Vicky affirmed.

"But now it is?" Owen asked.

Oskar nodded. "Now, it is."

"You're old enough for a taste of LA life," Vicky explained.

Owen was silent. Somewhere in his stomach he could sense irritation, disappointment, the metallic taste of betrayal. On the one hand, who were these strangers who had chosen to exclude him conveniently from their lives, only showing up when it suited them? Only letting him in when they felt like it? Who were these people taking him to dinner, calling themselves his parents? And yet. There they sat together, all three of them, by some kind of miracle, and amidst them stood the future of this summer. A strand of connection.

Could Owen be allowed to hope?

"So what's the rest of the summer going to be like?" he asked in an attempt to focus on the tangibles.

"Well, you'll come with us on tour. We're going to hit the road in the buses and go from here to Vegas, and we'll start from there. We'll pass back through LA, then through up to Oregon, playing a live venue every few days."

"Cool." Owen had not seen much of the country, and just then he felt quite excited.

"But your father and I wanted to tell you something, so that it doesn't come as too much of a shock."

Ah, the catch.

Owen looked to Oskar, whom he felt more a kinship with after more time together. But Oskar simply kept his eyes on Vicky. Owen glanced back at his mother, who seemed uncomfortable.

She cleared her throat. "We never mentioned this… because we didn't want to worry you and Mama…but…Dad and I have been separated for a while. I've been seeing someone. He is going to come stay for a week at the end of the tour, and I'd like you to meet him."

Owen took in a small breath. He was unsure of how he should react. He supposed his parents expected him to have some emotions or an opinion but he was unable to call up anything. Not remorse. Not compassion. To a child, it only mattered that their parents were married if the marriage was part of their household. And Owen's household consisted of two people: Lola Beth, and himself. As far as he was concerned, his parents could have been just another musical duo announcing they were separating. Sad but…c'est la vie.

"Okay," he said.

Oskar coughed. Vicky tilted her head to one side and looked at him. Owen thought he caught a hint of sadness in her eyes, perhaps even regret.

He looked away.

Owen had heard the stories before from his grandmother. In a moment of charity, she'd explained once that his parents hadn't wanted to leave.

That the move to LA for Vicky and Oskar had not been easy. Their first label had said, *"Go on tour."* And a tour was no place to raise a child.

Their second label had found them on that tour and said, *"Move to LA, record a new album, and tour again."* So the problem persisted. Vicky had asked Beth if she'd move with them to LA and be Owen's guardian, but Beth had refused. She'd explained to Owen that the notion of disrupting four people's lives versus two seemed inherently selfish.

"Plus," Lola Beth had said, "You were so settled here with me already. Why uproot you again? Let them chase their dreams. You and I can chase your own here."

Owen loved every minute of the tour. He was surprised at how much he enjoyed California in particular, and a part of him pictured himself there one day—in the northern reaches perhaps, enjoying the mountains, writing music in a cabin.

After the tour, Oskar, Owen, and Vicky discussed things briefly and decided Owen would spend the last week of summer with Vicky. He would get more time with her and her new boyfriend, Jack Brown, a banker from Manhattan who visited nearly every weekend. Owen would also help her renovate one of the bedrooms that had originally been designed for him so that he could always feel like he had his own space there.

When Owen had arrived at the house and seen the bedroom, it was shockingly sentimental. They had painted it light blue, and in it sat a wooden bed with rocketship sheets. On the walls, they had hung up frames of his favorite vinyls as a child: an eclectic mix of John Coltrane, the Jackson Five, Miles Davis, A Charlie Brown Christmas, and Sesame Street's "Aren't You Glad You're You." There was a desk in the room, now too small for him, and a large bear stuffed toy in one corner with a ukulele strapped to him.

"So this is yours. I'm sorry that we'd never shown it to you before. I wish we had done all of this sooner," Vicky told him.

***

The next day, Jack arrived. Jack was a tall man with a broad smile, and kind eyes. He regarded Vicky with equal parts awe, respect, affection, and playfulness.

That first morning, Vicky introduced them at the door. "Owen, this is Jack. Jack, this is my son, Owen."

"I have heard so much about you, Owen." Jack offered Owen his hand and they shook respectfully.

Owen had been apprehensive, but something about Jack was disarming. Perhaps it was the way his eyes and the bridge of his nose crinkled when he smiled, which he did often.

Owen and Vicky let him in, and they settled around the coffee table with some ice cold soda to beat the summer heat.

"I got you a small gift. Not sure if you'll like it, but at your age these were some of my favorite things." Jack handed Owen a box.

It was not wrapped. It was simply a wooden box with Owen's name carved into the front on the bottom right corner. Inside it, Jack had placed an assortment of things: a paperback copy of *The Catcher in the Rye* by J. D. Salinger, a voucher for four tickets to a drive-in theater in Virginia that Owen was curious to know how he procured, a gift card to Tower Records, and a harmonica.

It was a thoughtful present, and although Owen was not an avid reader and preferred the study guides of classics rather than the books themselves, he felt motivated to give this one a try.

He took the harmonica out first and blew a few notes into it.

"I learned that when I was in my teens. It's a nice thing to whip out on a date if you can learn some of the pop music of the times." Jack laughed—a jolly sound.

Owen smiled. "Thank you. This is a really thoughtful gift."

Later that afternoon, when the conversation seemed to be going well enough that Jack could tell Owen was comfortable, he offered to drive Owen to Home Depot. The idea was to pick up materials to spruce up his room.

In the car, Jack was very forward. "I like your mother. No, to be clear, I love your mother. So I hope we can get along."

"Sure," Owen said, looking out the window as Jack drove them through town. "I don't see why not."

"I'm not here to replace your father. But I'm glad we're getting some time together, one-on-one."

"Yeah, I'm not sure how much my mother's told you about our relationships, but I don't really think you need to worry about me thinking you're trying to replace anyone."

"Ah, I think your mom's been pretty honest with me thus far. I know you live in Virginia with your grandmother. And that you don't see your folks very much. I know what that's like. My parents were also divorced. They worked really hard, and I grew up mostly with my grandparents. And my mother when she was around."

"Oh."

"Yeah." Jack seemed thoughtful for a moment, "You know, as an adult, I look back and I kind of think…I was lucky."

"Really?"

"Yeah, I was lucky, because my granddad is awesome." Jack laughed. "Cooler than my parents combined." He winked in Owen's direction, which Owen found both annoying in that 'don't treat me like a kid' way, but also endearing in a 'this guy is so nice' way.

"But also because my parents were not really in a place to raise me," Jack continued. "And the most responsible thing they could have done was hand me over. Just glad I didn't end up in foster care." He whistled and shook his head. "Dodged a bullet there."

They pulled up at the depot and stepped out. Owen chewed on this information as they picked a new color for his walls, some shelving, and planks that Jack said he would fashion into a new desk.

The next day, Vicky, Jack, and Owen got their hands dirty in the room. They spent the morning painting. In the evening, with sore backs and burning arms, they sat in the living room and watched the *Home Alone* movies while eating pizza and popcorn.

It was the closest Owen ever felt to having a nuclear family. That night, after Jack and Vicky went to bed, and Owen tucked into the couch for the night to give the paint time to settle, he pulled up *The Catcher in the Rye* and began to read.

***

Over the week, Owen learned to enjoy Jack and Vicky's company. From the earlier half of the trip, he had developed a new bond with Oskar. But Jack was a different sort of man, and he could understand why Vicky liked him better. Owen appreciated his candor and thoughtfulness. Often, he was more forward and open than Owen's own parents were, because there simply hadn't been any baggage there to carry into the conversation.

Before he left, when Jack and Vicky dropped him off at LAX and Oskar came to say goodbye, Owen found a moment to speak to his mother privately.

"Thank you for the summer, Mom. I had fun and I feel like I learned a lot about music, and about you guys, and about myself, too. Oh, and I like Jack a lot. Hope that works out."

Owen, who was not showy in his affection, then gave his mother a quick hug. Vicky nearly cried. Owen could tell she was also grateful for that summer, and he finally felt that the three, or even four, including Jack, made a sort of family.

16
Fairfax, Virginia, 2001

Back in Virginia, Owen found himself already looking forward to the following summer, which Vicky and Oskar had agreed could be done exactly as the previous—with Owen in LA, and on the road with them.

In the meantime, he was content with long distance calls scheduled regularly with both his mother and Jack, and Oskar.

"On Thanksgiving, Vicky and I are going to plan a trip to New York," Jack one day enthused. "You can take the bus over and we can have dinner at my apartment with my daughter. I think you would get along. She's older, and can give you tips for college."

Owen started school again at the end of August. He felt, for the first time, the embers of home in his gut—a feeling of knowing, and being known, and having plans, and having people. His people.

The day had begun normally. Owen was trying to stay focused on the math problem in front of him.

At 8:51 a.m., there was a commotion outside in the hallway. Mr. Smith, his teacher, stepped out to find out what it was, then came back in, taking wide strides to the TV that was always parked in the front right corner on its dolly. He rolled it to the middle of the classroom and turned it on, fiddling with the channels before stopping dead on the news.

Matt Lauer and Katie Couric filled the little screen, and the students all watched in silent confusion.

The journalists were only on for the briefest of moments before an image of the famous World Trade Center in New York City replaced them. Tower 1 was in shambles. A massive plume of black smoke billowed upward. There was a gaping hole on its side.

A witness was giving an interview.

The broadcast seemed to only have been going on for a couple of minutes. 'LIVE EDT' it said at the top left corner. Years earlier, there had been a terrorist attack on the World Trade Center, and the anchors were saying this event was being treated with utmost caution for that reason.

"A bomb?" one of the other students cried, frantic.

"We don't know what this is yet, kids," Mr. Smith said. "Does anybody have family who work in the World Trade Center? If you feel that you need to call somebody, I will grant people permission to head to the phones two by two."

Owen sat glued to his chair, staring at the scene before him. Family at the World Trade Center. He thought about how they had lived in New York for those years, and how he loved the New York skyline, and how those two tall, beautiful buildings seemed a monument to American ingenuity. He wondered if they would just patch it up and things would go back to normal. He wondered what kind of people worked at the World Trade Center. Bankers, probably. Like Jack. Where had Jack said he worked?

They hadn't been watching for long before they saw, right out of the corner of the frame, a fast-moving, white shape slide into view and then, fire. Fire everywhere. Fire billowing out of Tower 2. His teacher immediately cut the feed, the little screen going black.

A couple of kids started crying.

Owen's heart thudded in his chest. His mouth felt dry. He swallowed. No luck. He tried again. Still nothing. He could not swallow, in fact, he almost felt he could barely breathe.

He thought of his mother in LA, and of Lola Beth at home, no doubt watching this unfold and fretting. And he thought of Jack. Jack Brown, the investment banker.

"You okay, man?"

Owen turned to look at the kid next to him—Charles Kehoe, one of the "popular kids"—a wrestler, a candidate for Homecoming King, that kind of guy. He was not Owen's friend, but that day he looked at him with such worry and kinship, Owen felt how arbitrary friendship in high school could be.

"Yeah, I'm fine," Owen managed, trying to sound casual.

"Okay, cause you're... And I just thought..." Charles pointed at his own cheek, and then gave Owen a genial punch in the shoulder, and looked back at the screen.

Owen touched his cheek. *Oh.* He hadn't noticed he'd been crying.

***

On September 14, 2001, a large newspaper published an article with a roll call of the companies in the World Trade Center. After days of sitting on her hands, staring at the TV, calling Jack, Vicky looked at that article, her eyes nearly swollen shut from crying. The very first line read out the name of the firm on Floor 104, and underneath, it said: *"Seventy-eight unaccounted for."*

Another day later, Jack's daughter called Vicky herself to deliver the news.

Then Vicky called Oskar, and then her label, and then her mother. She packed up her life into a suitcase and moved back to Virginia where she would spend the next year in her room, crying through her sheets and refusing to speak, not even to Beth or Owen.

Once, Oskar flew over, and Vicky let him in. He stayed in that room with her for two weeks straight, leaving only to pick up trays of food from the kitchen or drop empty ones back off. He wouldn't speak with Owen or Lola Beth about Vicky except to say she was in a state.

One evening, Owen overheard the two fighting in Vicky's room. He could hear things being thrown, both words and books, and perhaps a hair dryer, too.

The next morning, when Owen woke up, Oskar was already gone.

"You know, Owen, your mother is experiencing a new kind of pain," Lola Beth said. "Pain can be a powerful tool. I built a good life for my children using my hurt as fuel. But pain can also spread. We have a saying in Tagalog that goes *'Ang sakit sa kalingkingan ay ramdan ng buong katawan.' The pain in a pinky finger can be felt in the whole body.* What it means is, when one in a group is hurting, everyone is hurting. Your mother is hurting. She is hurting so much that she can hardly exist outside of her hurt. She is the pinky finger, and she is in pain."

And we are the body.

17
Singapore, 2007

Owen stood at Changi Airport the day after Christmas with his hand carry and guitar in tow. When Lara found out Owen had no plans for the holidays, she was affronted. *"But Christmas is the best!"* She insisted he visit Singapore while she was there for ten days.

Visiting Lara's family at Christmas in Singapore seemed a little intense, even though she was easily Owen's best friend. So he compromised and agreed to come the day after and stay for New Year instead.

"Boring," she had rolled her eyes, but helped him book the trip anyway. That was how he ended up at the arrivals bay, waiting to be picked up.

Moments later, a black BMW pulled up and the passenger window rolled down. "Your chariot has arrived, sir." It was Lara. She gazed up at him over the rim of her sunglasses and Owen felt a sudden rush of joy at the sight of her face.

He laughed and he slid his belongings into the trunk before climbing into the passenger seat. "Sweet ride."

"It's my mom's." She checked the rearview mirror then turned to him and smiled. "Welcome."

Owen was happy to see her. It had only been four days since she'd gone, but he realized it was the longest they had been apart since they'd met. He leaned in and hugged her. "Merry Christmas!"

"Merry Christmas indeed! What did you end up doing?" Lara pulled the car out and began driving.

"I still have a couple of distant titos and titas living in

Quezon City so I did Noche Buena at their house. Then I watered your plants, had a call with my lola, and went to a party at Monique's."

Lara glanced sideways at him at the mention of Monique. and he caught it but didn't acknowledge it. He took it to mean she had suspicions about his relationship with Monique. But he was not sleeping with Monique, and he didn't owe Lara any explanations. Nor did he feel like talking about sex with Lara anyway.

"How's your lola?" Lara asked, signaling to turn.

"Ah, she's been better. It's freezing now. Not good for her arthritis. But she and Mom made leche flan, and my titos visited for a bit. That's enough to keep Lola happy for the next few months."

"That's nice. Did you get to chat with your mom, too?"

"Mom and I don't talk much. Anyway," Owen said, changing the subject, "what are we doing today?"

"We'll drop your stuff at mine, have coffee with my parents, and then we're going to meet my sister Adora and her boyfriend for dinner. They work near where we're eating so they'll walk over and meet us there, then we can commute home together."

"Cool." Owen gazed out the window. He had never been to Singapore before. He hadn't known what to expect and was delighted by the large trees, wide boulevards, and skyscrapers. For a few minutes, they drove in silence passing a commercial area full of malls. Then they turned and drove up a grassy, hilly, and tree-lined residential area, and pulled up at a free-standing property.

The house was black and white, and charming. Owen imagined that this type of landed property cost a pretty penny in a place like Singapore. They parked in the driveway, unloaded his things, and walked up to the house.

A small Filipina woman opened the door for them. "Hello, 'day," she greeted Lara.

"Hello, 'Ya!" Lara said and then turned to Owen. "This is Yaya Luz. Yaya, this is Owen."

Owen smiled and offered his hand to shake.

"Yaya Luz has been with our family for twenty years," Lara added, giving Yaya Luz a side hug.

"Guapo, 'no, 'day," Yaya Luz gushed, telling Lara that she found Owen handsome.

Lara laughed. "Yaya, he's also Pinoy."

Owen laughed. "My mom is. But my Tagalog is not good. Masama. But thank you. You are also maganda."

Yaya Luz beamed. Lara smiled at that, charmed in spite of herself, and then shook her head. "Yaya Luz doesn't speak much Tagalog either," she told Owen. "She's from where my mom's from. They speak Ilonggo there. It's a bit like Malay-meets-Spanish."

"Sir Owen's room is ready, 'day, but your mom and dad are in the sala."

"Why does she keep saying 'die?'" Owen asked Lara softly, making sure Yaya Luz was out of earshot.

"It's not d-i-e. It's spelled d-a-y. It's short for 'inday.' It's used to refer to a young girl, and sometimes like a term of endearment," Lara explained. "She often called my mother that. And now, me too."

Lara showed Owen where to set his things aside, and walked him to the living room, where she found her parents, both reading.

When she and Owen walked in, her father smiled from his seat, and her mother stood.

"You must be Owen," she said, approaching and giving Owen a hug. "Call me Tita Aura. That's Lewis."

Lara's father, Lewis, stood and offered his hand with a nod.

Owen smiled back, slightly intimidated by his silence. "Thanks so much for having me."

"Well, if Lara's going to be living with boys, we should at least know who they are," Lewis said with a laugh afterwards that suggested he did not find this very funny.

Lara rolled her eyes and cast a side-eye at Owen. He read that as, *"We're going to keep this as short as possible."*

"Owen and I don't live together, Dad, and you would love Mike,my actual housemate. He'll come on New Year's Eve to say hi."

Lewis shot her a small, suspicious look, but then smiled and turned back to Owen. "Coffee?"

As if on cue, Yaya Luz appeared in the living room with a tray of coffee cups, two pots, and a little wooden tea box.

"Come, sit. " Aurora gestured to the vacant seats.

Lara and Owen sat side by side on the love seat.

Everyone picked up a cup and Yaya Luz went around with the two pots in her hands saying, "Coffee? Or tea?"

Owen sipped his coffee politely. "Singapore is beautiful," he enthused. "This is my first time."

Lewis nodded. "Ah, there's plenty to see."

Aurora was looking with a curious smile at Owen as though assessing him. "Lara tells me you are working on some music together?"

Ah, there it is, Owen thought. Based on Aurora's tone, there was a judgment there. He knew Lara was close to her family, so it was no surprise they had heard about their little project, but he wondered if Lara had certain insecurities or reservations about what they thought of the whole thing. His eyes flitted toward Lara and he noted her squirm just slightly. He guessed his inklings were correct.

Lara cleared her throat. "It's just a small project, Mom."

"I hope it isn't distracting her from work. Lara can get so caught up in things. She was already doing well," Aurora said, and then looked at Lara pointedly. "The program you're in is prestigious, you know."

"Yes, Lara is doing great at work. They love her," Owen said encouragingly. He shared a glance with Lara and offered her a small smile. "And she's also doing amazing things with music. She is responsible and productive in both areas. It's impressive."

Owen saw Lara squirm again from the corner of his eye. To steer the conversation, he searched the room for something to comment on. His gaze landed on the fine blue and white china they were using. "This china is beautiful. Is it an heirloom set? It looks hand-painted."

This pleased Aurora. "Yes! It's from my grandmother…"

After another cup of coffee and a few more compliments from Owen on Aurora's interior design and Lewis' taste in coffee beans, the two managed to break away to shower and unpack. By the time Lara and Owen were ready to go, Aurora was beaming. She turned to Lara, and right in front of Owen, she said, "I'm glad you have such nice friends in Manila, sweetheart."

Owen caught Lara's eye and he saw that she was smiling—a whole-face, whole-being smile. He smiled, too.

Once out of the house, Lara walked Owen to the nearest bus stop and they headed toward Lau Pa Sat, a famous hawker center in the middle of the Central Business District.

"In my opinion, there are other places to grab a bite, and we'll try those too across your stay," Lara said. "But Lau Pa Sat is an institution. It's in a refurbished Victorian structure, with beautiful cornice trims, and a delightful asymmetry. I think you'll like it, Owen."

When they alighted and were walking through the well-lit, buzzing streets of the city center, Owen found himself watching Lara. He felt that he was seeing a different side of her. From her stories, and her own sometimes incessant optimism, he almost imagined her parents to be warm, fuzzy pushovers. But seeing the way they had interacted, how they loved but didn't always understand her, made him feel a sense of kinship that he hadn't realized was there. It certainly explained a little about her frenetic energy and drive to succeed. Before he could bring it up, though, they arrived, and Lara was waving to a small group nearby.

Owen saw them eyeing him and felt a rising panic. He noted their teasing eyes and realized they probably thought he and Lara were seeing each other.

When they reached the group, Lara made the introductions. Adora was the first to strike up a conversation. As Lara went to pick out food with Adora's boyfriend, Adora recommended she and Owen stay back to chope the table.

"Chope?" Owen asked.

"Yeah, reserve. Normally, you throw a packet of tissues on the table and people know it's taken, but I figured we could just sit and chope with our butts. It's nice to finally meet Lara's creative partner."

The way she said it, with emphasis on the word 'partner' grated on Owen, but he smiled. "Yeah, do you like music too?" he said.

"I do like to sing. Covers and stuff."

"Oh, what kind?"

"I like lots of stuff. Everything from Jay-Z to Sufjan."

Owen was impressed. "Nice," he said. "Lara doesn't seem to listen to a lot of rap. I'm always recommending we try more off-beat covers. To surprise people. But she likes what she likes."

Adora cocked her head to one side "Well, music doesn't have to always be surprising. If it's performed well, with style, and earnestness, then that's enough isn't it? I think Lara likes what she likes and chooses songs specifically because she knows she'll do them well."

Owen nodded slowly. "Maybe."

Just then, the others returned with their first course: two platters piled with forty mixed satay sticks smothered in peanut sauce.

"Let's dig in!" Lara said excitedly.

18
Singapore, 2007-2008

The next afternoon, Adora, Lara, and Owen were out shopping on Orchard Road, a strip of boulevard lined with tall trees and massive modern shopping malls with large glass faces and big brand names shining across their facades.

"How are you liking Singapore, Owen?" Adora asked.

"Too humid for my taste." He tugged at the front of his shirt for a little ventilation. "Need to find a solution for how sticky it's making my pits. But it's beautifully engineered. And very clean."

"Owen is an engineer," Lara clarified.

"An environmental engineer," he added.

"By day," Lara shot back.

And they smiled at each other.

As they walked on, they spotted a tall model-looking girl up ahead—legs for days, flowing dark hair, toasty skin like cafe au lait.

Owen nudged Lara with his shoulder, "That's the kind of girl I should date."

Lara felt an annoying pang inside at Owen's comment, but she recovered quickly and raised her eyebrows at him. "By all means. The question is if she'd date you."

Just then, Owen spotted a shop selling men's suits and jeans. He excused himself and headed in while the girls ate outside.

"What is his deal?" Adora asked, once he was gone.

"What do you mean?" Lara explained.

"Pointing out other girls when I thought you guys were a thing?" Adora said pointedly.

"We're not a thing. And that's just him being himself—funny, forward. You know."

Adora sighed. "Mm-hmm, what's your deal *together*, then? Since he's just a Funny Guy you don't have A Thing with."

"Ah," Lara waved her hand dismissively just like their mother might, ignoring Adora's sarcasm and laughing in a way that she hoped sounded light and airy. "I've already told you. We're like…business partners. We're work spouses."

"We, we, we," Adora teased, though Lara didn't think she looked particularly approving, eyebrows raised and lips pursed.

"What do you mean?"

"Tell me, what do you like to do on a Friday night?"

"Well usually we stay in to play music but sometimes we go out too. Live music. We—" Lara stopped in her tracks. "Oh." She smiled sheepishly and cringed.

"We. There's no going back from the big *WE*." Adora could have probably gone on but just then Owen walked out.

"Did you buy anything?" Lara asked.

Owen shook his head. "Not really." He eyed her ice cream. "But while I was there, I was thinking we need to work on our image if we're going to market our music. I tried on some pants and I think the rich food we've been eating is getting to my stomach. Literally." He patted his belly. "I think I have a new New Year's resolution. Drop five kilos and get *ripped!*" He turned to Lara. "Do you want to join me?"

Lara thought about that for a moment, even as Adora rolled her eyes at her, and not even discreetly. "Maybe…"

"Suit yourself. I just feel like…style, aesthetics…all that matters when performing. Anyway, fitness is a good thing," Owen pointed out.

He had a point. And she had also been working out less. When did she have time to exercise if every free minute was spent with Owen? But now he was proposing they work out together.

"That's true," Lara said finally. "I do miss a good sweat."

"Awesome! We can come up with a program and get smoking hot together," Owen said. He squeezed Lara's shoulders and gave her a wide, infuriatingly handsome grin.

Lara, in spite of herself, began to imagine what it might look like—*the two of them, sweaty, scantily clad, exercising together.* She stopped herself. *Dangerous territory,* she thought and pushed the thought away.

***

Later, Owen, Lara, her parents, and Adora, with her newest beau, started a game of Pictionary in the living room.

Everyone paired off, and Lara was with Owen by default.

"Okay, lay it on me!" Owen braced himself at their first turn.

Lara laid out her first clue and as Owen puzzled over it she growled. "Focus!"

"Draw better!" He shot back, "I thought this was supposed to be one of your *talents,* little miss *artiste.*"

"Well, I can't do anything if you're *dense!*"

Everyone laughed, entertained by the pair's spirit.

"You guys are leading, you know," Aurora pointed out.

"Lara's always been so competitive," Lewis commented.

"Well, looks like she's found her match." Adora said sardonically just loud enough for everyone to hear.

Lara stuck her tongue out at her sister. "Pff. We are not even in the same league."

"Indeed, I am way ahead of her," Owen piped up.

Lara rolled her eyes at him. "You're fighting a losing battle."

"Oh my *lord,* you guys are on the *same team,*" Aurora reminded the pair with an exasperated sigh.

***

That night, when everyone had gone to bed, Owen knocked on Lara's door.

"Hey," she heard him whisper through the crack, "you up?"

Lara stood up and walked over quietly, opening the door just a smidge. She was wearing an oversized football jersey with only her knickers underneath, and she wasn't sure she wanted to broadcast her body for Owen that way.

"Yes?" she said through the crack in the door.

"I've been meaning to do this since I arrived, but I didn't have any opportunities to do so. So I gave up waiting for the right moment," Owen said, his voice soft and urgent.

Lara's heart skipped a beat. What was this about?

"What are you talking about, Owen?"

"Can I come in?"

Lara sighed but she stepped back and let him in, her arms crossed over her chest. She climbed back into her bed and drew the covers around herself protectively. She reached over to her bedside and flipped on a lamp.

As her eyes adjusted to the warm, soft light, she realized Owen was holding a box in his hands. It was wrapped in red and green paper with a big bow around it.

"It's your Christmas present," he said, handing it to her.

Lara realized she hadn't gotten him anything. "You didn't have to."

"I know, but I wanted to. Open it." Owen smiled.

Lara peeled the paper open carefully to reveal a pretty navy blue box. It felt heavy in her hands. She pulled it out and lifted the lid off to reveal a whole mix of things. Tucked right in there was a tabletop microphone she could plug in to her laptop, a little plastic holder of new picks with her initials engraved on them, and a brand new external hard drive.

"I couldn't choose just one, so I figured why not all." Owen shrugged. He did so in such a casual way that it almost infuriated Lara. Not because she was angry at such a lovely gesture, but because she was frustrated at what it might all mean. Did people who were just friends do such thoughtful things?

She resisted the urge to reach over and kiss him.

She tried not to imagine pulling him into her bed.

She wondered what he was thinking at that moment.

"Thank you," she said finally. "It's a lovely gift. I feel bad I didn't get you anything."

"I don't need anything. You're already so generous with me. And this trip has been more than a present."

"But you paid for it yourself."

"But you're hosting me and doing all the legwork. Anyway, we're not arguing about this. I wanted to give you something nice."

"Well, thank you. Again." Lara got up and gave him a long, tight hug.

When she let go, he was smiling, and she thought she caught a hint of color in his cheeks.

"Anyway, good night," he said as he made his way back to the door. "Looking forward to recording more music together and using some of your new tools."

Verses

Shape and Form

It was a dark night in a noisy place
I looked sideways and I saw your face
You were watching me with piercing eyes
Telling me all your secrets, all your lies.

You were standing in the light of moon
I was the one soft feature in your room
I was writing songs into your heart
You were falling right into my arms.

19
Manila, 2008

"So, I was thinking," Lara said one morning as she and Owen lounged in her room strumming listlessly on their guitars.

Owen looked up at her from where he sat on the floor and raised his eyebrows in response, awaiting the rest.

"I was thinking that most artists draw inspiration from other sources, too," Lara continued. "Other forms of art. Maybe we can do some art afternoons every few weeks?"

Owen ran a hand through his hair and gave it some thought. "I don't know much about any other forms of art." He wasn't overwhelmingly interested in other manners of creative expression, but Lara had a point. Didn't Don McLean write that song "Vincent" about the Van Gogh painting?

"But I do," Lara sat up suddenly, eyes wide.

Owen looked at her and smiled, appreciating once more her open enthusiasm.

"Let's go to the Ayala Museum," she gushed. "We can walk there. And I can show you my favorite set of paintings."

Owen thought about this. He wanted to keep working, but the music wasn't coming to him anyway, so a break was a good idea and would give him decompression time before his gig that evening.

"Sure," he said. "Fine."

The pair packed up their instruments, set them aside, and walked the short way to their destination.

The Ayala Museum was a beautiful, gray modern building with a strong stone face and long, tall glass windows stretching across the side of it. It stood nestled next to the lush gardens of the

Greenbelt Mall nearby and provided a sort of cultural centerpiece for the central business district.

Once there, Lara walked Owen straight into a wing filled with work by a man named Fernando Zobel. The walls and displays were adorned with abstract pieces depicting moths in flight, or other dynamic creatures in stark high-contrast acrylic.

"This place was one of my first stops when I arrived last year. I went on one of their free tours," Lara said as the two gazed up at one painting. "They explained that some of the work in this collection was done not only with brushes, but also syringes."

"Oh." Owen looked up, admiring the lines, the sort of organized chaos on the canvas, "I can see that."

"I love that idea. Using alternative tools. The effect is that they look as though they're perennially moving."

"Is that what you like about it?" Owen looked from Lara to the painting then back again.

"What?"

"The movement," he said.

She nodded, still staring.

Owen followed her gaze. "It does look like it's flying."

"It's based on a genus of moths," Lara said. "It looks… free."

Owen looked from the painting to Lara, and then back again. He admired her ability to love so many things, and to cultivate such knowledge of each of these. It seemed that often there were no limits to her passions. He wondered if he would ever find the edge with her, or if she just kept going, and going, and going.

***

The next morning was their first official workout session for the year. Owen had researched and put together a list of things to do: box jumps, burpees, 3-km run, and stairs. Lots and lots of stairs. They would begin their workout in the park and then head back to the apartment, where they would climb twenty flights up to Lara's flat.

"That's the cool down." Owen pointed at the paper where it said *STAIRS*. "I call this workout the 'Booty Blaster.'"

Lara made a face that indicated she was not thrilled, but she clenched her jaw and nodded anyway. "Let's do it then."

They went through the first series of movements with ease. Owen watched Lara's body and could see her muscle memory was doing her favors. Her hair, in a high ponytail, bounced against her back as a thin sheen of sweat developed on her shoulders.

"Done," she said breathlessly, plopping on the grass. "Your turn."

Owen blinked, realizing he'd been staring. *Oops. Get it together, man.* He cleared his throat and turned his eyes to the ground as he got down and started his set of burpees. *Just focus.*

20
Manila, 2008

By the third set on their first day of Booty Blaster, Lara was on her knees.

"You did so well in the beginning, and now that we're almost done you're acting so weak!" Owen groaned and Lara nearly threw a handful of grass and dirt at him but when she turned she saw he was smiling—a cheeky, joking grin.

She huffed and collapsed onto the ground, her back to the grass. "I haven't worked out in ages. Give me a break!"

"NO! Recording, performing, all of that takes a lot out of you. We're going to PUSH," Owen said, but he lay down next to her.

Lara rolled over onto her side and looked at him. "Oh my God, Owen, this isn't the army. We don't have a record deal. We aren't touring. We're just making songs together."

"It's not the army, but it's still boot camp…booty boot camp. And it's not *just* songs. If you want to succeed, you have to act like a winner and think like a winner!"

"Where'd you read that? A poster in your therapist's office?"

"Ha ha. Just stop whining and let's go finish this with the stairs, Lara. Maybe you'll even get a guy from all this work. Then you'll thank me after."

"When on earth would I have time to have a boyfriend if I'm constantly around *you*?"

"Good point. Maybe we should change that?"

Lara's heart skipped a beat. She didn't want to drive Owen

away, actually. Was that even possible? She doubted it. He was attached to her too, after all. "I doubt you'll be able to stay away. Who's to say you're not the one who's going to be after this booty when we're done with it?"

"Ooh, that's nasty." Owen scrunched his nose up and stuck his tongue out in her direction, but after he smiled and threw his arm around her shoulder. "Just kidding."

Lara tried not to think too hard about decoding his mixed signals.

One impossible, painful task at a time. First, the stairs.

21
Manila, 2008

The two scheduled their first gig at a little open air venue near Manila Bay. By then, they had four original songs, and Owen felt they were ready to test the waters.

Before their set, Lara was ridiculously nervous. Owen could tell because she was sweating through her top—a vintage oversized golf shirt tucked into a pleated tennis skirt. She wore just a hint of mascara and tinted lip balm.

She looked very cute. He tried not to stare. Instead he said, "Dude, relax." A little to himself, but mostly to Lara.

"I can't! I've never performed original music for a crowd."

"You'll be fine. You perform in front of me all the time."

"We're together so often. That might as well be the same as performing for a mirror."

Owen laughed but instead of taking Lara's bait to bicker, he reached over and pulled her into a hug. "You are brilliant. Every single day, when you play these songs, you blow my socks off. You're going to do just fine," he whispered into her ear.

He then felt Lara's muscles relaxing as she took a deep breath. He let go. "Better?"

"Thanks…" Lara let out a long exhale and paused. "Did you mean that, though?"

Owen rolled his eyes and poked her gently on her side, smiling. "Don't make me take it back."

Lara smiled back. "Fine. Let's do this."

"Yes!" Owen cheered. He was glad he had made Lara feel good. And he was excited to see their efforts in the wild at last.

As they walked to the stage, he tried to drown out the noise in the crowd, but he picked up the snippets anyway.

"Ugh, is this going to be some indie duo?"

"Oooh, I love her outfit!"

"Uy, what a cute couple!"

Suddenly, Owen felt a kernel of panic in his gut. *Couple.* To be part of sometimes indistinct halves of a whole. To be at risk of being broken in two. It was one thing to catch himself staring, to catch himself wanting. It was another thing for this to be the definition of them. He shuddered. From the inside, Owen did not feel like a part of a couple. In fact, sometimes, it felt like more than that. And both those things were scary.

Owen did not have many people that he liked to be around. Besides Lola Beth, constancy and attachment were not familiar constructs for him. But now, he had Lara, who showed up every day, despite his stupid jokes and his chaotic energy. Despite his pushing her and poking her and teasing her. Despite the weight of the work they were inflicting upon themselves.

In the Philippines, Lara was the closest Owen could get to a feeling of home. The thought was so intimidating that he tried not to think of it at all.

On stage, Lara and Owen found their stride. Owen played to the crowd, but he noted as he watched Lara that she sang from a deep place that reached out into the hearts of the audience. He could see it in the way that they reacted to each little hum and crack in her voice.

It mirrored, somewhat, how he was feeling inside whenever he heard those sounds himself.

Their first song was a cover to get the crowd going—a Filipino classic from the turn of the millennium called "Torete" by Moonstar88. It worked. There was something endearing about Lara singing in Filipino.

Before the gig, Owen had looked up the lyrics and learned the song was about uncertain, unrequited love. In the first verse, the song was about making a plea for something to be granted, and a request to hold hands. The words seemed on the nose. Owen tried not to think too hard about them every time Lara glanced his way.

For the middle songs, they played originals. "Hunger" elicited swaying in the crowd, and Owen gazed at the hundred or so people enjoying their music, feeling triumphant.

It's happening.

The penultimate song was a cover—"Delicate" by Damien Rice. This time, Owen was looking to Lara as his muse. The song was just about delicate things people didn't want to break, and the ways in which they hid what they felt or what they wanted to do. And though he was singing he wasn't scared, he knew he was a little bit.

They ended their set with another crowd-pleaser—"No Diggity" by Blackstreet. Some of the crowd got on their feet and cheered at the end. Mike yelled for an encore.

The venue booked the pair immediately for every Saturday in the coming months. The fruits of their labor were becoming clear.

***

After their set, Lara and Owen retired to his place. It was late, and they had only taken one car, and under the guise of laziness, mixed with the high after a good performance, they both agreed Lara should just sleep over. Technically, they preferred Lara's place—more bed space, more comfort, more privacy. But Owen kept a lot of their gig equipment–amps and such things, at his flat as he performed more often. So they settled in there.

On his cramped super single bed, the two lay face-to-face on their sides, recounting the highlights of the day.

"I think it went really well," Lara gushed.

"It did," Owen responded. He squinted at her face in the dark and smiled.

Lara just sighed–a soft, contented sound.

"So, tell me," he said, meeting her gaze. "How did you find your first official performance?"

She pursed her lips and turned to look up at the ceiling thoughtfully. "It was...exhilarating."

"Right?"

"I can see why you love it. I performed a lot in high

school but always with choir. This was totally different. There was something so unfiltered about having to lay all that music bare."

"Like a piece of your soul just"—Owen made a sound effect like wings batting in the air—"flying off into the world."

"To meet and greet other souls."

"Namaste."

Lara giggled and turned back to Owen. "What made you want to be a musician?"

It was his turn to look up at the ceiling then. Some people had a moment, a day, or an instance where they could say, *That was it. That's when I knew.* But for Owen it had been a life. A life that had steered him into music.

It had been his mother's voice when he was little, his father's crooning in the morning.

It had been Lola Beth's sweet attempts at lullabies; all those nights tagging along to bars in New York.

It was the moment he had moved to Fairfax County and realized Dave Grohl was from there, too.

It was the guitar his parents had given him, and the first song he'd written with it.

And it was the night that the asshole at the frat party had heckled—*"Looks like a case of yellow fever in here!"*—when he'd walked in and seen Owen and his fellow bandmates on stage—a group which included himself, a half-Korean med student, and a Japanese international student. "Yo," Owen had said into the mic, *"Rein that shit in."* But the guy just threw his beer bottle in the boys' direction and yelled, "Go back to your own countries!" Owen had then rushed off the stage and slammed his fist into the guy's face, then before anyone could even respond, he had jumped back to the safety of the platform and launched immediately into a cover of the Foo Fighters' "Monkey Wrench," giving the few stunned drunks who noticed something flashy, new, and fun to focus on instead. To say he had felt triumphant then would have been an understatement.

Music had saved Owen many times. And it was still doing so. Whether as a salve, a distraction, or a sense of purpose, music was his lifeline. His means of making sense of and responding to a world that he often felt lost in.

"Owen?"

He realized he had been spacing out. "Right, sorry. You asked why music?"

"No, why musician?"

Owen nodded and took a deep breath. "I'm only telling you this because we've just shared perhaps one of the most intimate things two people can share—original music, written together, performed for a crowd."

Lara nodded.

He went on. "I love engineering, you know, the structure of it. And for me, it's the closest career I can find to music that isn't music. I mean barring pure math, engineering has that same sense of structure—making sense of chaos, building something, following precision, meter, form, function. Throw in the environmental aspect and you've got something that responds to the world around it. But music…" He paused and whistled softly, "Music is the one thing helping me make sense of the world. It's the only avenue in which I'm entirely honest and…entirely me."

Lara nodded again, taking it all in.

"Music may have been the reason my parents left me, but it's also the reason I'm still here today. I kind of want to share that with other people. You know what I mean?"

"Yeah," Lara said with a smile, even though her eyes betrayed a sort of empathetic sadness as well. "I understand. Thank you for sharing that with me."

Owen smiled back. "Don't get any ideas. We aren't going to have sappy moments like this every day. That was just your performance bonus."

She laughed. "Literally."

"Literally." He scrunched his nose at her.

"Wonder what I get if we sign a record deal," she joked.

Was she flirting with him? He swallowed hard and looked away. Why was it that every time they opened up to one another, there was a trigger that would make him want to recoil?

"They'll want the full package for that, so," Owen said, and then poked Lara's stomach, "Better work on those abs first."

She swatted his hand away. "Ah, there he is. The usual Owen. Welcome back. You weren't missed." But she smiled and he knew she must have known that, even just for the briefest of moments, she had closed a gap. He had never shared those thoughts with anybody else.

The truth was, nobody had ever asked.

It was so like Lara to be the first. It felt odd to answer her, but he found himself thinking, *It would have been stranger not to.* It felt like they were on this journey together now. This musical adventure.

22
Manila, 2008

"I'm tired. Going to rest. I'll watch you." Owen stretched out on Lara's bed after a tiring evening of rehearsals and songwriting.

"You mean critique me?"

"Your words, not mine. Need critique?"

"I have a new song."

"Let's hear it."

This new song, like many of her good ones, just flew out of her one evening. It felt like a confession, and she began to fret that she was digging a hole for herself.

Maybe I should back track. Play something else. Something more neutral, she thought for a moment.

But then she had an almost irrational inkling Owen would know if she wasn't playing the one she had originally intended.

She paced the room and pretended to tune her guitar.

"Oh my god, just get on with it already, I'm falling asleep. Do it or don't. If it's shit, don't share it. I'm too tired for that."

Lara rolled her eyes–why was he so crass sometimes? But she sped it up anyway. One more deep breath, then she began to sing—a sweet melody filled with symbolism of houses and birds, and a chorus that begged a question:

So tell me then, darling
Do you, do you love?
Do you, do you love
As I love, as I love

As I love you

The song was light, lyrical—almost playful. When Lara finished she was facing the wall so she didn't have to look at Owen.

He was silent.

She turned to see if he was still awake and when she did, he was sitting, staring at her with a curious look in his eyes.

"It's no good. It needs work," she said awkwardly.

Owen rolled his eyes. "Are you kidding? Don't fish for compliments, Lara. It's beneath you. It's brilliant. I mean, the chords are a little standard, but you applied them well. It's a good song," he said. "I can imagine a harmony over the chorus, and maybe shorten the last bit so it doesn't go on and on but…it's great. You're so productive."

If he had any inkling that he knew the song was about him, he didn't let on. Lara blushed. "Your turn. Show me something."

Owen opened his mouth once and then closed it again, drawing his lips into a thin line. A small sign of hesitation. Lara knew he had been working on something because often when they'd work side by side one another without really talking or collaborating, she'd heard the same chords and whispered lyrics. She was curious. She wanted to know.

"Please?" Lara gave him the most earnest look she could muster.

"Fine," he sighed, picked up his guitar, and began to sing:

Oh, I feel something
It's coming up from underground
Your eyes pull me deeper—
I reach for you, I'm going down.

Nothing can be promised,
But your lips, they part as I draw near
Something deeper calling, and I'm paralyzed by my fears.

I don't know if I can be
A better man—A better man, they say that a better man
Only a better man could be worthy—A better man.

Owen cleared his throat. "So, there." Then before Lara

could even say anything, he launched himself in her direction and poked her in the side, tickling her.

"Hey!" she said, laughing, swatting him away but it was no use. He was strong, and they were there, and they were a tangle of bodies, and between them in the air hung their music, and her desires, and she tried not to think too hard about what that all meant. She tried not to think at all.

***

One Saturday morning a few weeks later, Owen and Lara lay in bed reading and ignoring their self-imposed deadline to complete the last two songs for their album.

"We need to mix it up," Owen said, putting his book down. It was something random off Lara's shelf that he could hardly focus on.

"How so?"

"Maybe listen to new music or ask Mike to mix a sample for us to sing over. I don't know. We've got enough of your melancholic love songs." His tone was teasing but it still stung.

Lara's brows furrowed. "I thought you liked my music?"

"I do. It has enough character to make up for the generic pop chord progressions."

"Look, that's the second time you've brought up the chords. Maybe we need to revisit some of the arrangements and compositions. If something is bad, we should fix it."

"Oh, but all pop music has overused chords, Lara. It's fine. It's not an insult." Owen waved his hand dismissively, which only confused Lara. Wasn't he the one who'd called her brilliant? So she was brilliant, but also overused?

But also, why did she want to impress him so much anyway?

Owen went on. "Look, I like the music we make together. And anyway it doesn't matter if I like it, it matters if the people who buy albums like it. And I'm sure they will."

"If we ever sell albums," Lara said pointedly. She had not reflected much on whether she wanted to become a full-time, professional musician. Her entire goal was to follow through with the plan, and do her best. And the mention of albums made her

102

anxious. It seemed like a lot. In fact, lately all of the work—and even Owen—seemed like a lot. Mike had been traveling often and without their usual buffer, Owen and Lara were marooned in their own little world most of the time. It was getting a bit stuffy.

"Maybe I just need to get laid," Owen huffed.

Lara laughed, then realized he was serious when he didn't flinch.

"I thought you were getting laid?" She thought about the times Owen attended parties at Monique's and stayed after Lara had gone home.

"Nah. I think you stop me from getting laid."

"So I'm some kind of cock block?" Lara was taken aback and unsure if she should believe him. Not that it mattered. Since they were just friends. Work spouses. Whatever he wanted to call it.

"Yeah. Not in a bad way. I don't mind. You keep me honest."

"Who exactly do you need to be honest for, Owen?"

"Myself."

Lara had so many questions. Owen practically lived at her place. They slept next to each other often enough. The first night he had asked if he could join her on the bed, she thought, *Oh my god, something's going to happen tonight.* But they had lain there instead next to one another, and indeed simply gone to sleep. Like a slumber party. Her body burned; she had urges, too. So if it was a lay he needed, why weren't they having sex? It wasn't as though she had given him any indication that she was not interested.

He must not be interested in me then, she told herself.

Owen was still groaning and complaining. "Honesty is great and all, but it's been a while, and…a man's got needs."

Lara rolled her eyes. "You need a burst of inspiration."

Owen caught on. "I need to *grind out* a good song," he added, wiggling his eyebrows.

"You need to *release* your inhibitions."

"I need to *stroke* the keys a little harder."

"You need to get *real deep.*"

The two laughed.

"Doubt it'll make it that deep. You forget—I know some

things." Lara teased, referring to the one time, months earlier, when his erection had made a guest appearance on her bed.

Owen's eyes widened, taken aback. "Are you questioning my manhood?" He rolled over, straddled her, and began to tickle her.

Lara gasped and laughed, wiggling around, but not really trying to get away.

This time, Owen did not hide his arousal. Lara knew she was flirting and teasing them into a corner. She didn't know if it was right but the song she had written played in her head. *Do you love as I love you?* She thought of what he'd said, *A man's got needs.*

Well, a woman does too.

So, as his hands traveled along her body, as he asked if they could strip down, as they lay skin to skin, body to body, she allowed it to happen. Because deep down she wanted it to. A burning question in her gut, perhaps closer to an answer. She surrendered to the moment, closed her eyes, and breathed.

***

Lara may have thought, or hoped, that having sex with Owen would make things clearer for her emotionally, but she had been wrong. Owen deflected discussion on the topic whenever possible. It seemed his main intention was to just keep moving forward.

The evening after it happened, Lara tried to bring it up. "So… About this morning…" she said as they drove up to the bar and restaurant where they played every week.

"Yeah, let's not talk about that," Owen said immediately.

Lara, taken aback, raised an eyebrow. "What do you mean?"

"I mean, we don't have to talk about that. It was just about getting a thing out of the way, you know?"

"Is that what it was?" Lara said flatly.

"We had to clear the air. Aren't you glad it's over with?"

Lara was, in fact, not glad it was over with. It seemed only to have called up more feelings and more questions. "So, it was just like an itch you wanted to scratch?"

"Yeah, sure, something like that." He picked up his amp and a stack of other things so that his arms were full and his face was half covered, making it hard for Lara to make eye contact with him. "Besides, I think it feels good. Didn't you wonder what would happen if we'd do it? Well, now we know. No biggie." The pair walked backstage and put down their things. As Owen straightened up, he looked at Lara, smiling. "Right?"

Lara did not dignify this with a response.

That evening, she attempted to perform as professionally as she could, sticking to her script and looking at Owen as little as possible. When they were finished and sat with Bianca and David to the side of the stage at a table reserved for them, a girl in a cute denim jumper with plaits in her hair approached. "That was an *amazing* set," she gushed, then she turned to Owen, "I *loved* your solo—"Hips Don't Lie." Sexy." She winked. "I'm Theresa."

Lara looked at Owen, Owen looked at Theresa, Theresa smiled, and Lara felt her blood boiling just slightly.

Owen scooted over to make room. "Would you like to join us for beers?" he said.

"Oh, really? Hope I'm not interrupting anything?" Theresa glanced at Lara when she said so.

Lara kept her gaze on Owen, who looked in her direction but avoided her eyes.

"No," she said finally, smiling at Theresa. "It's totally cool."

***

It was a mistake, Lara decided a few days later. It seemed the only real positive development from their little tryst was that Owen indeed had a burst of inspiration, and the two were able to finish their fifth song, co-write the sixth, and wrap their first EP.

Their first listener was Mike. The three sat in Lara's room on the floor listening intently to each song, sometimes playing one twice, three times in a row. They listened in complete silence. Lara took notes, as she always did. The work could never be done.

When they finished listening, Mike smiled. "It's good, guys. Look at that! My two closest friends, making something awesome."

Lara chewed on her lip. "Do you think it's missing anything?"

"Honestly? No."

"I think this is the best we can do, Lar. And I know I never say this kind of thing but I think it's good enough," Owen chimed in.

"What's next?"

"Now we just need to shop it to labels."

"What labels? Local labels?"

"That was my idea, but I'll ask my dad. He'll have advice."

Owen burnt the files onto a couple of disks and decided to send it the next day with a small package of Filipino snacks. He sent one version of the package to Lola Beth and another to his dad.

"What do we do in the meantime?"

"We wait."

***

Waiting proved to be a harsh game. Even for Lara, whose feelings were mixed on the whole matter, anticipating the coming feedback Owen's father might have on the little baby she and Owen had made together was nerve-racking.

"I know what we can do," Owen said one Saturday as they prepared for the evening's gig, going over the set list and packing up the instruments.

"What?" Lara asked, testing the strings on her ukulele.

"We can design an album cover." Owen was grinning as though this had been a real lightbulb moment for him.

Lara thought about this. "We don't even have a name," she shot back.

"We'll think of one. A name and album art. Something we can use over and over again. Our first album cover can be like a logo for who we are." Owen was on a roll now it seemed, his eyes wide and his smile not faltering for a moment.

Lara had to admit it was smart. From a marketing perspective, if they made their first album cover like their logo, there would be great brand recognition if they were ever to get big. She almost laughed at her own inner monologue—fusing her passion for the arts with her corporate profession a little. "That's not a bad idea, actually," she said, sitting back. What medium might lend well to that sort of work?

"It could even be a stamp, maybe?" Owen suggested.

"Yes!" Lara said, a bit of excitement bubbling up in her chest then. "Linocut! I can hand carve a stamp out of rubber and it can act as both our logo, and the actual album cover. And our name. All at once. And the beauty of that is we can use the original linocut carving to stamp on shirts, posters, and more in the future."

Owen laughed and punched an arm skyward triumphantly. "Now you're talking!"

"Okay, now for a name?"

"What about Lawen," Owen wiggled his eyebrows and stuck his tongue out indicating to Lara that this was clearly a joke.

She made a face at him in response. "How about we write some ideas down and ask our friends what they think?"

***

"I like The Wanderers," Bianca said.

Monique, Bianca, David, Niko, and Mike all sat together at a booth near the stage, looking over the piece of paper Lara had laid in front of them.

"Yeah you guys give that folksy, indie, emo, wandering traveler vibe," David agreed.

"I like The Bandits," Niko said. "It has a nice ring to it."

"I still think you should go with Beauty and the Beast," Mike suggested, chuckling.

"That's not even on the list." Monique rolled her eyes at him, but she turned to Owen and Lara and nodded. "But he has a point."

"And I'd be the Beauty in that scenario, right?" Owen squinted at Lara.

She smacked him on the arm then pointed back at the list, "Focus, guys."

"I like Two People best," Monique said, obliging Lara.

Lara smiled at her. "Thank you. I like that one, too."

"It's so obvious," Mike pointed out.

"But that's what makes it perfect. Isn't that what we are?" Lara asserted.

She liked the name. It had no pretenses. It said what it was. They were Two People. Two People Making Music. Two People Writing Songs. Two People Telling Stories.

"The album could be Making Music. So it would be Two People, Making Music. Then the concept for all the titles would be to finish that sentence. Two People Singing Folk. Two People Running Wild. Two People Eating Pizza," Owen enthused, seeming to get on the same train suddenly. He was nodding slowly as though his mind were working on this concept, kneading it into a puffy, delicious, workable dough to bake into a toasty masterpiece. Lara could see the cogs turning in his head, and it made her smile.

"That's not half bad, actually," Mike conceded.

"It's settled then. We're Two People." Lara grinned at Owen and they high-fived one another.

Later that night she carved the first draft of their album cover: the two people, a ukulele, and a guitar. Around them, flowers and patterns and textures. She spread ink across the rubber pad and stamped it onto a square sheet of paper. On the top left corner she wrote "TWO PEOPLE."

23
Manila, 2008

For Lara's twenty-second birthday, Owen decided to organize a party.

He invited Mike, Monique, Bianca, David, Niko, and Monique's brand new boyfriend, Mateo. It felt like a big deal to plan a thing for Lara, But then again, he'd reasoned, who else would? He and Lara were best friends and creative partners, and he was at every liberty to do something nice for her occasionally.

On the Friday before her birthday, Owen picked her up from work as usual. But instead of driving her home, they stopped at a large condominium complex with two imposing skyscrapers.

"What's going on?" she asked.

"I have to pick up something."

"Oh. Should I just wait in the car?"

"No, come. It might take a while."

They parked and walked up into the lobby of one tower, where Owen led her to the lift.

"So how was your day?" he asked.

"Tiring…uninspiring…"

"Quit for the music," Owen teased.

She shrugged. "Maybe."

Ever since they had had sex, Lara had seemed a little off. She'd tried to bring it up a few times, but Owen genuinely had nothing he wanted to say on the topic. He could tell Lara was frustrated, and he was himself confused. If he could have verbalized one thing, he would have said, "I don't know what to do with how I feel about you." Perhaps that might have helped. But he didn't do it.

When the elevator doors opened, there was a popping sound followed by a shower of silly string coming from every direction. Owen laughed as Lara turned to him looking dazed.

He wrapped an arm around her shoulders and pulled her in for a hug. "HAPPY BIRTHDAY TO YOU!" he began to sing.

Mike, Monique, Bianca, David, Niko, and Mateo were all standing in the hallway leading up to a spacious apartment. They were each holding canons of silly string, now empty. The group sang a rousing chorus of "Happy Birthday" and then yelled "SURPRISE!" together after for good measure.

"What!" Lara exclaimed, eyes wide.

"You had no idea, did you!" Mike grabbed her and hugged her tightly. "Gifts and drinks and music inside!"

Monique and Mateo approached too and kissed Lara on the cheek. "Happy birthday! I want you to meet Mateo, my boyfriend."

Mateo was a dark-and-handsome type in jeans and a light pink polo. Next to Monique, with her long, flowy hair and form-fitting black dress, the two looked like a smart couple.

Lara smiled, throwing a glance at Owen. He could imagine her thinking, *So you really aren't sleeping with Monique.* He just smiled with his eyes in return as though to say, *Didn't I tell you?*

"So nice to meet you! Thank you, guys. I had no clue at all."

Monique laughed airly. "Ah, it was all Owen." She winked, grabbing Lara by the hand and pulling her into the room.

"Monique's parents own the flat and are between tenants so they let us use it," Owen explained, following close behind.

In the apartment, the dining table had been set with all manner of food and drinks. They had leaned into a Filipino party theme and there was a tray of Filipino spaghetti (a little sweet, a little spicy, with sliced hotdogs and melted cheese), alongside barbecue sticks skewered through mini hotdogs and marshmallows.

On another plate there were fried chicken wings, and cheese pimiento sandwiches on rainbow white bread. On the coffee table was a stack of board games. Mike had brought in his turntables and stood behind them, mixing a bopping set that featured his own playlist of EDM tracks, Top 40s hits, and some of Lara's favorite alternative tunes. In particular, there was an eclectic rendition of Joni Mitchell's "Circle Game" mixed with a sample from Usher's "Love In this Club." When it came on, Lara scrunched her nose in Mike's direction and smiled knowingly. Mike saluted her and nodded to the beat.

When everyone had a sufficient amount of alcohol, the group pulled out a game of Monopoly and declared a team challenge. They broke into pairs. Bianca and David, Monique and Mateo, and Mike and Niko paired off. The latter two declared themselves the extra wheels, leaving the birthday girl to her Work Husband. Lara and Owen were too drunk to protest. They sat close to one another, knees touching, and played as the Scottish Terrier.

"Let's name him," Lara told Owen as she gazed at the little dog figure on the Go square.

"Scottie," Owen declared.

"Isn't that his real name? Like, in the game?"

"Oh, I don't know."

"That's lame. Scotchy, maybe?" Lara suggested.

"Scotch."

"Scotchy Scotch."

Owen shook his head. "Sounds like Scratchy Crotch."

"It does not."

"Fine, Scratchy Scrotch it is. I mean, Scotchy Crotch."

"I think you need to get your head out of your crotch."

Lara rolled her eyes, exasperated. "That's not an expression."

"Oh my god, guys! Can we just start playing?" Monique interjected, throwing the die.

Owen leaned on Lara's shoulder. "You're going to have to lead this one a little, I think. I am…drunk." He felt the warmth of her body right next to him and it was comfortable. He smiled.

Lara leaned her head against his in return. "We'll make do."

***

The game went on for hours and the group lost track of who the real winner was and where the money was going. Mike, who was always quickest to sober up, declared Monique and Mateo winners and ordered everyone to bed. He and Niko took the couches, whilst Monique and Mateo went into one of the bedrooms, Bianca and David into another, leaving a third vacant.

"A very big bed for the birthday girl," Owen said, standing in the doorway as Lara slid under the covers and switched the AC on.

She groaned and waved her hand. "Come here, Owen. I'm so wasted I need someone who can hold my hair back while I try to avoid throwing up all over Monique's parents' furniture."

She was drunk. He knew that. How drunk? He wasn't sure. But far enough gone that maybe she wasn't fully aware of what she was saying. Should he oblige? The shape of her body under the covers suddenly seemed soft and inviting. With his heart thudding in his chest, Owen closed the door behind him and climbed in next to her.

"You're so needy," he whispered. A tease. Something to lighten the mood.

"Mm," Lara seemed not to care about his silly comments just then. "You like it."

"Maybe." Owen looked at Lara. With the temporary courage and clarity granted him by the liquor, he could see her with more honesty. She was a little insecure, and way too nice. Compassionate. There. All the time. Present. Such a gift. One he was not used to.

His mind was full of questions he directed at himself. *What do you do with someone who is there for you? How do you not take them for granted? If her presence was scarcer would you love her better? If she made it harder for you, would you recognize it as a love that you deserve? Does she scare you?*

Owen took deep breaths, trying to avoid his inner voice. They were so close that he could see every movement of her chest, every flutter of her lashes. She was flushed from the alcohol, her lips deep red, her cheeks as though she had been standing too long in the sun. He gazed at her. This kind, talented woman, silly sometimes in her need for validation. He felt, just then, such deep affection.

Owen's lips were against her ear. "Are you awake?"

She nodded.

"Can we…"

She turned around and faced him. Opening her eyes, she gazed quickly into his and nodded again.

And so they did.

May 30, 2008
Email from Oskar to Owen

Subject: Two People EP

Hi son, I trust you are well. I received your EP. This is good!
Congratulations. Don't send it to anyone there yet because
I know just the label for you over here. Have you heard of
Brave Brothers? If you haven't, they distribute a lot of this
kind of singer-songwriter kind of stuff. I know that's not
what you initially wanted, and that you kind of wanted to
make a go of it in the Philippines, but just think of it: LA
could make this BIG for you! I've already forwarded it to a
contact at Brave. I will update you when I hear from him.
Hope to see you soon.

Dad

24
Manila, 2008

"Guess what!" Oskar said through Owen's phone, on loudspeaker, which he held between Lara and himself. "The guys at Brave loved your music! They want to fly you over to meet. They'll pay for the flight, and you can stay with me so you don't have to shell out for a hotel. Lara, too. Just for a week. Can you swing that?"

The pair sat in Owen's bedroom five days after Oskar's email had come in. They were surrounded by copies of their album and all their instruments and equipment as they prepared for the evening's gig. As Oskar delivered this news, Owen's eyes grew wide, his cheeks flushed, his smile lit up his entire face.

But Lara was apprehensive. She felt an acidic sort of panic developing in her gut. When she had first committed to making music with Owen, she had enjoyed the idea of a project. And of course she had wanted to do it well. But traveling cross-continent to meet with record label executives was a different ball game. What would her parents think? Her boss? What would she have to give up? Going into music meant exposure, and the possibility of failing publicly. She shuddered at the thought, her feet going cold.

"It's going to be fine. It's just a meeting."

"I don't know, Owen. I really enjoyed the process, but I wasn't fully aware of the commitment it was going to take."

"You were totally aware. You're just chicken now."

When Lara didn't respond, Owen threw his hands up. "Lara, you knew just as well as I did what we were spending all those sleepless nights on. Or did you think this was some game?"

It stung because, sometimes it did feel like a game—

specifically, Owen's game. One that she was just there to play. Or worse, to gamble. To wait.

"Sorry, I'm just excited," Owen said after a moment of silence. "Please. Let's just meet them and see what they say. If you hate the deal, then you don't have to take it."

"What am I going to say at work, though?"

"I don't know, tell them your boyfriend wants you to meet his family and you haven't taken more than a day off since you started, and your results show that you deserve a break."

Lara raised an eyebrow at him. Mostly for his use of the word 'boyfriend.' "I see."

"Whatever. Tell the truth, or lie. Just don't be chicken shit."

"God, Owen, if you think that's going to convince me—"

"Lara, I mean it. Don't be afraid to seize the chances you deserve. Your work on this is so good. Now, come to LA and bask in it for a minute, damn it. Your parents should—no, WILL be proud."

How did he even know that was something she was considering?

The two blinked at each other for a moment, all the possible futures this path led to running through Lara's mind.

Finally: "Fine."

25
Los Angeles, 2008

Eight weeks after they had first sent Oskar their EP, Lara and Owen were on a plane bound for LAX with a stack of their own CDs, the artwork she had made emblazoned on the front of little inserts with their music, lyrics, and acknowledgements written out. Owen had insisted on bringing a few to give out to Oskar, his friends, contacts, and anybody else who might be interested.

"Just in case."

When the plane landed, Owen was well-rested and chipper but Lara had barely slept, her back uncomfortable, her brain racing, and her heart thudding in her chest. The massive step of going from a garage band style project to going to Los Angeles to get signed was exciting, but also confusing. And of course, she had a plethora of mixed feelings about Owen, too.

This trip was not just a work trip—it was an introduction to Owen's father and a part of his world she had only received snippets of in conversations. It felt like they were so invested in each other that their assets were getting more and more tied up. Signing a record deal felt like signing a marriage contract, almost. Suddenly, they would not just be sharing space and emotional baggage, they would also be sharing a job and finances. Adora had been the one to plant this idea in her head when Lara called with the news.

"That's awesome, Lar! But do you really want to be work-wedded to Owen? You do know you guys are like secret boyfriend-girlfriend, and that is already super weird because everyone knows it but never says it. So if you ever want to date anyone else, you can probably say goodbye to that if he's hanging around you like a little…"

"Little what?"

"Nothing. I can't find the right word."

***

Oskar picked up the two at the airport. He drove a vintage sports car, and looked remarkably like Owen, just taller and lighter.

He was also incredibly warm and friendly. He helped the pair with their bags, exchanged pleasantries over the weather, and let them choose the music for the ride.

"How was your flight?" Oskar asked.

"Long," Owen said.

"You slept the whole time!" Lara countered.

Owen met her gaze in the rearview mirror and smirked. "Or did I just pretend so as to avoid you talking my ear off, whining about how long the flight was or whatever?"

"Ugh, you're such a jerk. For the record, Mr. Weber, I wouldn't do that. I don't do that. That's more your son's style."

Oskar laughed and also met Lara's gaze momentarily in the rearview. "I think I'm inclined to believe you."

Lara gave Owen a smug look of triumph and he laughed.

Oskar drove the pair to his home in Silver Lake. The house was a charming three-bedroom. It had been built in the late 1930s, and had white trimmings, a powder blue exterior, and a red front door. It had a large open concept kitchen-living-dining area, and a sizable backyard.

One of the bedrooms was being used to store music equipment with no room for a bed, and so there was only Owen's room left.

Oskar pointed, "Not sure if that's going to be a problem," he said, referring to the new queen-sized bed in the middle of the room.

"That's okay, Dad," Owen answered. "We'll be fine."

"Sure," Lara said, trying not to sound too uncomfortable. Barring an official diagnosis for their particular affliction, she was not overly thrilled to be "Owen's not-so-secret-girlfriend."

Oskar seemed to hesitate and turned to Lara. "Are you sure? Because Owen can sleep in my room with me."

Owen shook his head again. "It's fine, Dad. Thank you. This is great. We're used to each other."

Lara sighed inwardly but smiled. "Yeah, this is perfect."

***

Oskar had arranged for a meeting with Stuart Kline and Harold Bishop from Brave that coming Friday. It gave the two a couple of days to sightsee and attempt to get over their jetlag. It also gave Lara the opportunity to bombard Owen with questions.

"Who are these guys?"

"Stuart is the co-founder, and Harold is the head of A&R."

"What does A&R mean?"

"Artists and Repertoire."

"Is our EP really considered an EP or is it more a demo?"

"They will think it's a demo, but we know it's an EP."

"What is the difference?"

"An EP is technically already produced and ready to go out into the world. A demo is just a rough cut of something."

"Why didn't I take any of the music electives attached to my Communications degree? Don't answer that. It's rhetorical."

"I'm going to, anyway. Because you didn't know what you had until you met me!"

***

On Friday morning, Owen and Lara went on a quick shop to choose appropriate outfits. He wanted something that said creative and professional, cool but open, polished yet adaptable.

There were many non-starters according to Owen—the white dress that "made her look like a baby," the green suit that "made her look like Hilary Clinton."

Finally, Lara settled on a flowy A-line summer dress with quirky silver buttons. She wore it with her oxfords, and pulled her hair into a wavy half-pony. When she walked out of the bathroom, with exactly a dash of makeup on, Owen grinned at the sight of her. In spite of herself, she blushed.

He had chosen blue jeans and a gray buttoned-down shirt

119

that was tucked under a light linen sport coat, which complimented Lara's outfit.

They stood together in front of Oskar's mirror and Owen put one arm around her. "What a pair we are, huh?"

Lara's heart fluttered and she nodded. *Indeed.*

***

The meeting was scheduled at the Polo Lounge of the Beverly Hills Hotel. The intention was to go for cocktails before dinner. Oskar said that if the execs were inviting them there it was a good sign that they were taking their work seriously. Apparently, many deals had been made in the Polo Lounge.

For good measure, Owen had pre-booked a room for the weekend. "I have a good feeling about the meeting," he'd said. "We'll toast to the close of the night in a room at a Los Angeles institution."

Lara never expected to spend her first fancy staycation with her work husband-best friend-not boyfriend, instead of a romantic interest. So, although she found this sweet, it was also a bit disturbing and uncharacteristically optimistic of Owen. It revealed how invested he was. It made her nervous that his hopes were so high, there was a chance he would be disappointed.

She teased him. "You went from someone who didn't want to tell anyone about the project for fear of jinxing it, to someone booking a five-star hotel because of a good feeling."

"And you went from being my yes-woman music partner, albeit a little insecure, to this like, really critical naysayer."

"You exaggerate."

"Blah, blah. You're just anxious. It'll be fine. They'll love it. If it was shit, I wouldn't have loved it, and we wouldn't even be here."

"You're not a record exec, Owen."

"No, but I grew up around this. Trust me. Let your light shine this time, Lara. Just give it a try."

Lara sighed. He was right. She probably was just nervous. And maybe a little bit afraid if things did go well. Was she ready to change course? What would her parents say? Did it matter? She thought of that Yeats poem that went, *"The greater grows*

120

my light, the further that I fly."

She took a deep breath and closed her eyes for just a moment. When she opened them she decided.

I'm ready.

***

Stuart Kline was tall and broad-shouldered, with curly brown hair graying around the temples, a wide smile, and piercing blue eyes behind black-framed glasses. Lara guessed that he couldn't have been older than forty.

Harold Bishop, on the other hand, was even taller than Stuart, with beautiful skin like the night and soft, kind eyes. He was built like a basketball player and dressed like a jazz musician, a houndstooth flat cap on his head.

When Owen and Lara walked into the restaurant, they recognized the two right away from an image search they had done earlier. He nudged Lara in the side and pointed with his chin at Stuart. "Maybe you should get with that one."

Lara rolled her eyes. "Sure, in our hotel room. Let's just have a foursome while we're at it. You get first dibs."

"Someone's feisty. I like it," Owen teased.

"Let's just get this over with. We're almost late."

***

Stuart and Harold were interested.

"I love the quality of the lyrics," Stuart enthused.

"The harmonies are spot on," Harold added.

"I'm curious who the artist is behind most of the songs. I know you work as a pair, but there's often one who writes more."

"That would be Lara." Owen beamed at his partner. He was lapping up the praise, and he felt that she should be encouraged along as well. She smiled and patted his leg under the table.

"Yeah, I thought that. I could really feel it in your voice, especially on the third track. 'Hunger?' Oh, and 'Do You Love…'" Stuart made the chef's kiss hand gesture and flashed his pearly whites again, his eyes boring right into Lara.

She cleared her throat softly. "Thank you, but Owen did most of the producing, with a little help and feedback from another friend, Mike Moh, who is very talented at sound mixing."

"Ah, you're being modest. Is she always like this?" Stuart flashed another wide smile in Owen's direction. Then he turned back to Lara, which made her wonder if he was flirting with her.

Owen nudged her knee under the table, and Lara shot him a look. Could Owen tell he was flirting? Was he egging her on?

She nudged him back and stopped herself furrowing her brow. "Thank you," she said graciously.

"We are keen to sign you guys," Harold interjected. "We will of course have to re-record the music. In their current state, they're great, but they could be better. They could be actual hits, you know."

"Of course," Owen agreed. "We'd love to hear your feedback, and what you think is best for us as artists, and you as our label."

Harold nudged Stuart and Stuart grinned. "I like these guys."

"Well, if the co-founder is on board," Harlod said, "then that makes my job easier. I've brought a draft agreement over to precede an actual contract—"

But Stuart interrupted him. "Ah, Harold is always right down to business." He waved his hand dismissively. "All of that will come in due time. Why don't we order drinks and get to know each other first? I like to know my artists intimately."

When he said this, Lara wasn't sure if she was imagining things, but she felt like he had glanced her way. She swallowed hard, her instinct kicking in.

As Stuart ordered drink after drink and downed them faster than they could be made, Owen joined him as though it was all hearty merrymaking. Harold, to his credit, tried twice to slow his boss down, but after his gentle suggestions fell flat, he excused himself saying he should be getting home to his wife and children.

Lara, feeling vulnerable and uncomfortable as Stuart began to sidle his chair closer to her, began to do the opposite, sliding hers closer and closer to Owen. She had long stopped ordering drinks, and was subtly trying to get Owen to stop as well.

"Oh, it's all good fun, dear!" Stuart grinned again, an expression Lara was beginning to hate.

She placed her hand on Owen's knee and squeezed it. He brushed it away—eyes narrowed, confused. "Hey, that tickles. What's up?" he whispered to her when Stuart turned to order more whisky.

"I want to go to the room now," she pleaded quietly.

"Oh, sure. Tired?" Owen checked his watch and Lara felt a surge of relief. "Wow, it's pretty late!" When Stuart returned, he said, "We've had a great time, Stuart. Thanks for your consideration. And for this evening."

Stuart shook his head. "It's nothing. Consider everything done. We are going to make you stars."

Lara was no longer impressed or excited. If she hadn't been sure she wanted this before the meeting, she was increasingly less interested with every minute they spent with Stuart.

"Thank you. We are very excited," Owen said graciously. "But you'll have to excuse us; alcohol and jet lag don't seem to go well together. Can we reconnect this week on the next steps?"

"Oh, feel free to go if you're tired," Stuart replied. "Lara and I will just stay and chat more." He then looked at Lara. "We can talk and she can report back." His tone was pointed, his eyes piercing through her.

Lara saw Owen's body language change in an instant. "Actually, I can stay," he said, a hint of uncertainty in his voice.

Fright, flight, fight was in Lara's mind but she did not want to throw the deal away. She knew how hard they had worked on their songs and didn't want to let Owen or herself down.

I just need to get out of here in one piece. Everything will be okay.

"It's better you go," Stuart said. "Lara is the creative one, right? You and Harold can talk. You're the smart, commercial kid. I want to talk about artistry. And lean into some feedback."

Lara cleared her throat, feeling defensive for Owen and afraid for herself. "Owen co-produced my music, and wrote several songs, too."

But Stuart was adamant. "Ah, my favorites are yours.

Your talent is so…raw."

Lara could tell that stung. She knew Owen, and when she looked at him and saw that pale, crestfallen look on his face, she could tell he'd gone somewhere into himself. She reached for his hand, but he pulled away, and her heart tumbled further into her stomach.

"I'll just go to the bathroom," Owen announced. "You guys can chat, and when I'm back, Lara and I will head up."

Owen waved for the check as though this was a final decision, and then patted Lara's shoulder. His face had regained some color, and he looked as though he had some resolve—a solution he had come up with in his mind perhaps. But Lara was reeling. *No*, she thought, *don't go.*

Owen seemed to almost read her mind. "It'll be fine. You're a superstar. Don't let him intimidate you." He said—loud enough for Stuart to hear. Then he walked off.

Lara felt a rising panic as she watched him go.

"I think I need the bathroom, too," she declared, standing up.

But as she did so, Stuart's hand went right up the back of her skirt, squeezing her inner thigh hard. He then snaked his hand around her hip. Holding on to the edge of her panties, with his nails digging into her pelvic bone, he pulled her back down into the chair.

Lara couldn't breathe, she couldn't move.

Then Stuart slipped his hand out and she almost gasped in relief, as though coming up for air. It only lasted a moment, though, because next thing she knew, his hand was on hers, directing it right to his crotch.

"Lara, I know talent when I see it. And I see a lot of it here."

"You're drunk," Lara managed.

"A little alcohol won't hurt anybody."

You're hurting me right now, she thought, but what came out of her mouth was: "I think I should go."

Stuart had his hand around her wrist. He was much bigger and stronger than her, and his fingers pressed against her pulse as he kept her hand on his crotch. With his free hand, he undid his zipper and slipped her hand inside his pants. She tried to resist, but to no avail, pulling her hand away only seemed to make his grip tighter, more unforgiving. Underneath, he wore no underwear. She tried to hold her fingers as still as possible and willed Owen to return, but it was no use. Slowly and methodically, Stuart began to move his hips against her hand, and she felt his fleshy appendage responding.

Their table was in what Lara realized now was quite a quiet, private section of the restaurant, and they were seated facing the crowd so that it would be easy for Stuart to spot anyone before they were spotted themselves.

She felt trapped.

Stuart pushed her hand against him. "Come on, don't be afraid."

Lara could not bring herself to do anything. But it seemed it didn't matter what she did or did not do.

"I think I should go," she repeated, more firmly this time, even as her voice trembled. "You are drunk."

"If you want this deal, you're going to have to stay," Stuart slurred, spittle following his words.

Lara's skin crawled. "I thought we were talented?" she sputtered. "That you guys were excited about what we brought to the table?"

"Oh, you are. But there are a thousand other demos on my desk as we speak. I need to know you excel in other areas, too. Areas that would…" He paused. "Set you apart. Starting with making a deal under this table. I think your partner is aware of the trade-offs in this business. Or didn't he tell you?"

Then he leaned his face in very close to her, and licked her on the neck. There was nothing sexy or sensual about it, it only made Lara feel sick.

Boiling over at last, with her free hand, Lara slapped him. Hard. She fought to hold back tears.

Right then, Owen returned.

Stuart let her go with a sharp exhale and a grunt. He rearranged himself then stood abruptly.

"It seems, after further discussion with your partner," he said, turning to Owen "we aren't seeing eye-to-eye after all, Mr. Weber."

The check came and Stuart signed it without looking.

"We won't be in touch." He looked at Lara when he said this.

Owen glanced at Lara then turned to watch Stuart go. When he looked at Lara once more, his face was red and his voice was tight as he said, "What the fuck just happened?"

***

The room was beautiful and spacious. A mix of pinks, taupes, creams, and greens adorned the walls and floors. The textiles were luxurious and soft. And there was only one king-size bed.

Lara had not spoken since Owen reappeared in the restaurant. She took a head pillow, placed it on the chaise at the foot of the bed, and lay face down. She wanted to be alone, but Owen kept talking and talking. She was taking deep breaths, trying to slow her heart, but Owen kept asking and asking.

"Lara, what am I going to tell my dad?"

"Lara, what can possibly go down in five minutes?"

Lara, Lara, Lara.

Lara had not been assaulted before, though she knew girls who had. She felt both totally alone, and totally together. She had read before that one in five or six women were assaulted in their lifetime.

Lara counted in her head the girls she had known who had experienced some kind of sexual abuse. Then she counted in her head the microaggressions she had endured leading up to that moment.

Seemingly innocuous cat-calling on the street, an eerily similar vernacular of misogyny across every country.

A cheeky hello, wiggling eyebrows, whistles, the words "smile" and "beautiful" and "make my day" and "look at me" in every language, an "ooh," an "ahh," smooching noises.

Being stared at or followed.

Being honked at by passing cars.

Lara realized it was not quantifiable, so she stopped. She thought, *It's not so bad. It was close, but barely anything happened. Maybe we can still smooth things over.*

But even as these thoughts formed, she could identify the

bitter taste of failure and disappointment in her mouth preventing her from verbalizing them.

The wrist Stuart had gripped was still smarting. She looked at it and noticed, for the first time in ages, the little scar on the base of her palm where she had cut herself one evening, stretching her own canvas in high school.

"Scars," she whispered to herself.

She had a few others. The pockmarks Owen had noticed on her face. Another on her collarbone. They had once itched and burned so much, she'd scratched them raw, enough that they'd be reminders on her skin forever.

Lara wondered if it was the same with other things that hurt, even ones that went further than skin-deep. Like wounds from past relationships. Or breaks in your heart. Or the pain she was feeling in her wrist. The injury, the indignity of everything that had just transpired. Would these also just become part of her skin? Help her build a thicker hide? Battle scars?

"What? What did you say?" Owen huffed, leaning slightly in her direction as though straining to hear her whispers, her breath, her very thoughts.

"Nothing."

"Lara, what the fuck happened?" Owen sat on the chaise—at her feet. He had talked himself nearly hoarse.

Lara heaved a big sigh and curled up further into herself before finally answering, "He propositioned me and I said no."

Owen stared at her. "That's it?" he said flatly, his face falling.

"I mean he propositioned me and I slapped him."

Owen threw his arms up. "WHAT THE FUCK, LARA!"

"Stop saying 'fuck,' Owen."

"What the FUCK. Grow up, Lara! You've blown it now."

"I think I recall specifically asking you if we could go. He was making me uncomfortable."

"I tried. I tried but he backed me into a corner. You could've thanked him and walked off. You should have been like, 'Thank you, hot record label executive.' In fact, it was a compliment! A hot guy like that…I'm surprised he went for you at all!"

Lara could not believe what she was hearing. "You are such a fucking asshole." She said it so softly that even to her own ears it sounded menacing. She didn't know whether to wince or to cry. The things she liked about Owen—his passion, his assertion, his seemingly confident posturing, his love of music, all of these suddenly paled in comparison to the anger she felt at everything he had just said. The salt he had rubbed into her wound.

"Oh, please, Lara. Don't pretend you weren't flattered!" The words coming out of Owen's mouth were bitter and sharp, jagged edges cutting right into her heart.

In her head, she was explaining: *Owen, he violated me. He put his hand where it shouldn't have been. He grabbed my wrist. He touched me in ways and places I didn't want him to.* The train running next to these thoughts said, *You're an adult. You could've walked away. Maybe you gave him signals—didn't you think he was hot when you first saw him?* These trains, both at the same velocity, would soon reach a crossing and crash into one another, and Lara would not be able to make sense of them anymore.

"I can't believe you made such a big deal of this. This shit happens in this industry, Lara. You have to grow a thick skin."

"Just because something happens doesn't make it right. If that's your main defense, then I don't want to be in this industry."

Owen took a deep breath and backtracked. "You don't mean that, Lara. I mean, you're right, it's not right. But we worked hard on this. Don't say that." He seemed to be coming down from his tantrum. He swallowed hard. "Maybe we can still salvage this?"

"Good night, Owen. I'm tired. Why don't you call them tomorrow and tell them you'll do the deal without me." Lara didn't want to fight. She was too tired. Too mixed up.

Owen quieted himself for a moment. Finally, he said, "I don't want to do this without you. Let's regroup when you're ready."

Lara sighed. She wanted Owen's dreams to come true. She saw how he lit up when he made music. She saw how proud it made him and his father. She saw this was a life he hoped to live even just for a moment. But she also struggled to see past the hurt he had inflicted on her just then. And she couldn't deny that, with her first foray into the world of record labels culminating in absolute disaster, she didn't feel particularly motivated to make it in the industry. She needed time. So she said: "Okay. But I want to take a few months off. Until the end of the year."

Owen breathed. "Okay. Now why don't you come to bed?"

Lara did not want to be touched. She worried that if she slid into the bed, Owen would touch her, and she would start shaking. Or worse, crying. She did not answer and pretended to sleep.

Wordlessly, Owen picked up his pillow. He placed it on the floor at the foot of the chaise, and he lay there next to her.

In the middle of the night, Lara woke. She sensed that Owen was awake on the floor next to her and she turned and looked down at him. He gazed back at her. Lara squeezed her eyes shut and began to cry. She rolled away, ashamed, exhausted, sad, confused. *Stop it,* she commanded herself. *Enough.* She didn't want him to see.

Owen reached over and rubbed her back. "Do you want to move to the bed now? It's really nice up there…You'll sleep better."

She nodded, and together they walked to the bed and lay down. Owen wrapped an arm around Lara's waist from behind and buried his face in her hair.

The next morning, Lara opened her eyes and realized she was still in her clothes from the night before. She and Owen were on the bed but were now as far from one another as they could possibly be. As she gazed at the curve of his back, she felt like he was oceans away. She got up and ran herself a bath. In the water, she let herself cry until there was nothing left.

26
Manila, 2008

That night in the Beverly Hills Hotel had been excruciating. If Owen had ever felt he and Lara were delicate before then, it trumped every other time. As he held her on that bed, in that ridiculously fancy room, he felt as though his hands were made of jagged rock, and he was holding a crystal champagne flute that could shatter with one small, wrong move. Or had it already?

This feeling was only made more intense when Owen and Lara arrived back in Manila, and Lara had still not returned to her normal self. Quiet, reserved, even distant sometimes, she seemed distracted and moody, and she wouldn't pick up her guitar.

When Owen would ask if she'd like to jam, she'd shake her head and say, "Remember you agreed we could take a break? Give me until the new year. "

Owen thought she was being a little dramatic. If some hot, older woman working in the industry had come onto him, he might have had less principles about it. He might have even enjoyed it. Though he couldn't say that for sure. He felt guilty for having uncharitable thoughts. But he was also annoyed. He knew Lara wasn't telling him the whole story, and he thought, *If she wanted me to empathize, she should have told me everything.* But he didn't say it aloud. There were too many feelings, not just around this subject, but around Lara in general.

In the past, Owen felt his feelings in one of two places. Either the bottom of his stomach, buried under something to dull the knowledge of them. A shadow of acidity, a hint of queasiness, but there was Lola's lumpia to make it better. Or sometimes in his head, at the back of his ears, but there was Coltrane to dampen the frequencies of his reverberating heartaches. This, though, this entire situation had lodged his feelings in his throat. Confusion, anger, frustration, worry.

He imagined himself choking on them all. He thought about Stuart, in the five minutes he was away, propositioning Lara. What had he said? What had he done? Owen said stupid things all the time and Lara never slapped him. It had to have been more. He thought of how he had left because he wanted to preserve the deal. How he had chosen the music over Lara. Without whom the music would not have existed in the first place. Right at the top of the feelings, sitting in his mouth like a bitter pill, was shame. Shame that he hadn't been there for Lara, but shame also at the failure of a dream.

He had had to explain to the bar they were playing at that it would just be him for the time being. They were not thrilled, but they let him stay on, and every Saturday, he came with his guitar and played his set.

His first night back, Lara came too, surprising even him.

"Are you sure?" he asked her.

"I'm not suddenly allergic to music, Owen." She rolled her eyes as she helped him load his equipment into his car.

That night, Owen played "Delicate" by Damien Rice again, but it seemed to have taken on even more meaning. Was something broken between them? Would they ever get it back?

***

"Hey, what are you doing this weekend?" Owen asked one Thursday after work as he and Lara shared a platter of sisig—finely diced pig face and ears, crunchy and sizzling on a platter with soy sauce and garlic and calamansi juice.

"I have plans with Monique," Lara answered, taking a bite.

"Oh." Owen was almost surprised. He usually knew Lara's plans beforehand. Especially for the weekend.

"Why?"

"I don't know, I thought we could do something different. Like climbing a mountain or something." He didn't really know why he'd said that. It felt a little like he was grasping at straws. If they weren't making music, what would they do together?

"That could be fun, actually."

Lara's answer surprised Owen so he ran with it. "I heard a colleague talking about Mt. Pinatubo. Maybe that's an option?"

"The volcano? Isn't it flat?"

"Yeah, so like, not a mountain, really. But a fun physical challenge. Something different for a change?"

"Sure." Lara shrugged. "But maybe in a couple of weekends. This weekend doesn't work. I'm playing tennis with Monique and some other friends on Saturday. Then on Sunday, my tito is in town and we're going to have lunch."

Owen felt a small pang. Shock at not being invited? Discomfort over being excluded? Had that been intentional? "I didn't realize you guys were doing that now," he said, knowing he sounded jealous.

"I didn't realize you were interested in my every movement?"

Oh, and she was catty now?

Owen held his tongue and turned to take another bite of sisig. "I think I'm going home to practice some guitar after this."

"Cool, I'll head home, too. Carpool still on?"

"Yeah. See you tomorrow, then?"

"See you tomorrow."

***

That weekend, with Lara spoken for, Owen attempted to go on a date with a girl he had met at one of their gigs.

Tall, slim, dark-haired with long lashes, Owen remembered thinking she looked like Olive Oyl from the *Popeye* series.

When he picked her up, she was wearing a red top and black skinny jeans. He had to resist the urge to call Lara right then to tell her so they could laugh together.

The girl's name was Ella. They went to dinner at a pretty Filipino bistro near Owen's home. Owen liked the crispy adobo flakes and rice there. Ella said she was watching her weight ("Where is it?" Owen had thought. She was so skinny he couldn't imagine there was anything to watch). She ordered bangus and proceeded to push the rice off her plate into a bowl on the side.

She was nice, but in true Owen fashion, he just could not

get invested. He was a little bored, watching her across from him talking about her Catholic school upbringing, and the local college basketball league. And her favorite song was "Bubbly" by Cobie Caillat, which almost gave Owen hives just thinking about it.

After the date, he went home and texted Lara:

From Owen Weber
Went on a date with Olive Oyl tonight. Red and black outfit and everything.

She didn't reply until the next morning:

From Lara Halford
Haha! Pics or it didn't happen.

***

The one thing Owen observed that Lara did seem to enjoy doing with him was working out. So they did that almost every day. Lara would wake early and message him that she was going on a run, and he learned to set an alarm and come along.

They jogged alongside one another mostly in silence. Then they would stop somewhere, usually in Salcedo Park or on a quiet street, and Lara would say, "Want to sprint?" And they would take turns sprinting.

One such morning, Lara went an extra four sprints more than Owen. He watched her go. Her legs, her back, her arms, her. He couldn't help it. When she sat on the curb next to him to catch her breath, he smiled.

"What?"

"Nothing," he said, scrunching his face up and laughing.

"No really. What?" Lara looked at him expectantly with an eyebrow raised and Owen wondered if she expected him to start teasing her.

But that was not what he wanted to do. So when he finally replied, he said, "You're looking good. Strong."

Lara looked pensive. Then she let out a long exhale and smiled—wide and genuine. "Wow, look at you. That's probably the nicest thing you've said to me in months."

"We haven't been speaking much," Owen countered.

"That's not true. We speak all the time."

"You know what I mean."

She nodded. "I just…was processing something."

"Did I do something wrong in LA?"

Lara looked at him, surprised, eyes wide. Owen wondered if she was surprised because she felt he had done nothing wrong or because she never expected him to notice that she was hurt? It was obvious. He knew it. She must know it, too.

"I think you not taking the Stuart thing seriously was hurtful," she said finally.

Owen chewed on that for a moment. He could not pretend to think or feel a certain way about something if he just didn't. "It's just that…people get propositioned every day and they reject people everyday and life goes on."

"It wasn't just that."

"Then what? Why won't you just tell me the whole story?"

"Fine. I'll tell you," Lara said.

And then out it came. The whole disgusting story.

Owen felt like a ton of bricks had fallen over his head and those feelings of confusion and frustration flashed through him like wildfire. "What the actual…" he started.

"Don't say 'fuck.'"

He punched one closed fist into an open palm then slapped his hands against the pavement. "Lara, you should have told me then, we could have—"

"What, Owen?" Lara interrupted him again and when he looked at her he could see the resignation and hurt in her eyes.

He suddenly was very disappointed in himself. "I shouldn't have left you. I'm sorry. And all the awful things I said, too."

Lara shook her head. "It's all water under the bridge now."

"Gross, dirty water."

"Well, you're an environmental engineer. What would you do to fix it?"

Owen smiled at this. He loved the way her mind worked— with creative, compassionate solutions. How she managed to find and see the good in people. In him. How she was still making him smile even after he had failed their friendship.

"Ah, I don't deserve you, Lara," Owen said in earnest.

"You are too good a friend."

Lara smiled at him. "Well, I'm glad you know that."

It was quiet again for a minute, and Owen sat with his thoughts. The most important thing to him was tying up any loose ends hanging between them. So he said: "Are we okay now? Like, are you still mad? Is there something I can do?"

Lara looked at him, and in that moment, she seemed to really be looking. It made him feel naked, vulnerable. What was she seeing? Work? Friendship? Trust? Companionship? Love? Knowing?

She nudged his shoulder with her own. "No, Owen. I was never mad at you. I just needed time. I do have one request, though."

Owen looked at her as though to say, go on.

"Can we pause the music for the foreseeable future? I mean, I know we're on pause until the New Year but to be honest I just…" she trailed off. Then she took a deep breath and said, "I don't think I have it in me. Even after the New Year." She looked down at her palms, her hands in her lap, as though she was almost embarrassed. She seemed tired. And he had been so hurtful. It was clear she needed the break.

"Yes." Owen's answer almost surprised himself, but he knew it was the right thing to do. He had an impulse to take it back, to push her and say, *No, I believe in us, I believe you can do it.* But he shot himself down quickly. *Now is not the time,* he thought.

Lara looked up at him and smiled. "Thank you."

Owen smiled back and felt as though a weight had lifted off his shoulders. At least they could go back to normal now. With that out of the way, he thought it was as good a time as any to let her in on his plans. "I'm planning to go to Virginia in late November."

"Oh?" Lara said, eyes wide in surprise.

"Yeah, I looked at flights and it's too expensive to go for the holidays, so I thought I could spend ten days there two weeks before Christmas instead. Then I'll be back here mid-December."

This would be the longest they'd be apart across the entire duration of their friendship and saying it aloud felt strange. It almost made him nervous. He wanted to push that sensation away.

"That's a great idea," she said.

Owen shrugged. "I should make an effort to see Lola and Mom, don't you think?"

"Of course. Can you get the days off?"

"I hope so. The deal's good. Do you want to come?" he said in a teasing tone. "Up for the Virginia cold?"

"I can't take more time off right now," Lara said, "Besides, won't your Lola think we're getting married if you fly me all the way there?" She laughed at this, teasing him too.

He grinned. "Nah, she knows you're not my type." He winked at her.

"So you keep reminding me," she said and then cleared her throat. "So what will you be doing at Christmas then?"

Owen shook his head. "No plans yet."

"Not even Noche Buena with your relatives like last year?"

"Nah."

He didn't want to be with distant relatives on Christmas. He would rather be alone in that case, although the person he really wanted to celebrate with was already right there with him.

27
Manila, 2008

Owen's earnestness was so endearing, and Lara could feel all her cold resolve and hurt thawing. And as he said *"I don't deserve you,"* she found herself thinking, *is this romantic? Or? What?*

Then of course, right after all that she had to learn he'd be alone for the holidays. Lara tried to imagine Owen alone on Christmas and her heart went out to him. She couldn't help it. Owen was her best friend, even after everything. He had said and done hurtful things, sure, but nobody was perfect right? Besides, wasn't that what Christmas was all about? Love and forgiveness, yadda yadda?

Christmas was Lara's favorite holiday, as it was for many of the Filipinos she knew. Her family always had an awesome dinner, whether in Singapore or the UK. It just so happened that year they were hosting a massive Christmas reunion for her relatives on her mom's side at the old hacienda in Bacolod, an hour's flight from Manila. Plus ones were welcome.

She weighed the pros and cons. If she invited him, he wouldn't be a pathetic kid stuck at home. But her entire family might think they were dating, if they didn't already. But did that even matter?

"You can't do nothing at Christmas, Owen. Why don't you join me for my family Christmas this year? It's a much cheaper flight than me going all the way to Virginia."

"Singapore again?"

"No, actually this year we have a reunion in Bacolod. From the 22nd to the 27th."

"Oh wow, that sounds special."

"Very! It's a proper Filipino Noche Buena, plus all the fanfare of a Filipino family reunion. We haven't done one in maybe seven years? People will be flying in from all over to celebrate at our ancestral home. There's probably going to be like a hundred people there. Accommodation is free, so you'd just have to swing the ticket."

Owen's eyes grew wide, which indicated to Lara that he was surprised. She knew it was a big leap to go from visiting Singapore for New Year's to attending a family reunion. She could already imagine him overthinking all these things, so as though anticipating the conversation she said, "Don't worry. It's a plus-ones welcome thing and I'm sure my cousins will be bringing friends, too. It'll be fun. And I'm not just asking you to be nice. I cannot stand the thought of you having a depressing Christmas in your flat. It's so pathetic, it's giving me a headache just thinking about it. So it's almost a favor to me if you think about it on those terms. Come on."

"I've never been to that side of the Philippines. I'd love to see more of the country…" Owen thought about the proposition. "Sounds good. But I'm doing it for you. So you don't fret about poor pathetic me."

Lara smiled. "Deal."

***

"Thanks for giving me a ride," Owen said to Lara as the two unloaded the trunk of her car at the airport.

"It's not like there were any better options," she pointed out. *And to be fair, I just wanted that last bit of extra time.*

Since their conversation, things had reverted somewhat back to normal, and Lara felt a lot more at ease with Owen once more. So when the date of his trip to Virginia drew steadily nearer, she began to feel that looming sense of separation anxiety. Taking him to the airport was the least she could do–both to help him skip the hassle of taking a taxi or having to pay for some sort of long term parking solution nearby, and to help herself miss him for just that extra hour less than she might have otherwise.

Owen reached over then and pulled Lara in for a hug.

She returned it in earnest, squeezing him tight.

"Be safe," she said in a tone that she knew sounded too motherly, too caring for her own good, but she just couldn't help it. "Message me when you land."

"I will," Owen replied, arranging his things and waving as he began to walk off. Just before he entered the terminal, he turned back and called to her, "Besides, if anything happens, I've listed you as my In Case of Emergency on my phone and basically every form. So. You'll know if I don't make it." He said this in such a light, playful tone that for a second it barely even registered.

"Wait, what?!" Lara exclaimed incredulously.

"See you soon!" Owen responded, willfully ignoring her reaction and laughing as he disappeared through the sliding doors and past the x-ray machines inside.

I'm his emergency contact? Lara thought to herself, a mixture of warmth and confusion swirling in her stomach. It seemed Owen would just forever have that effect on her.

28
Fairfax, Virginia, 2008

Ten days without Lara were going to be even harder than Owen had initially imagined. Everywhere he went he thought, *Oh I should tell Lara about that.*

He resisted the urge to send her every little thing (a funny sign, graffiti, a joke), and instead coursed the bigger things her way (the title of a book he thought she might like, or a song he thought was special—that year was all about "White Winter Hymnal" by the Fleet Foxes).

Lara, though, did not hold back. In their emails, she left long lists of links, and would attach pictures of both the mundane and exceptional. Owen teased her about it but he secretly liked it. It was nice to be thought of.

One morning, Lola Beth and Owen were eating breakfast while Vicky was on a walk with her little chihuahua, Pebbles. Owen was quiet and pensive. He usually had stories to tell, music to share, or questions to ask, but not then.

Lola Beth took a homemade pandesal and sliced it in half. She buttered one side and put guava jelly on the other and squashed the bread down and took a bite.

"So. How is life in Manila, hijo?" she asked after.

Owen, who had been busy slicing a piece of Spam into little cubes, looked up at his grandmother and smiled. "Good, Lola."

"Anything interesting happening? Your father wrote that you were in LA and met some important people for your music."

"Yes, yeah. We did that."

"And?"

"And it didn't work out."

"Oh, mi hijo, I'm sorry to hear that." Now Lola Beth looked concerned. "Is that why you're so quiet?"

Owen still hadn't figured out the core details of what went wrong in LA. But he knew that that ship had sailed. It was disappointing, sure, but that wasn't what was on his mind.

Things had improved with Lara, and she was no longer cold or distant. He was going to spend Christmas with her family. But inside he still felt ghosts of the lumps in his throat. Confusion. Frustration. Worry. Losing the record deal was one thing, but what he had done—putting the music before Lara, judging her, feeling angry and uncharitable—that was another thing. That was a Vic and Oz thing. It shouldn't have been an Owen thing. And yet.

"Lola. Do you think it's normal to let people down when you're chasing your dreams?"

"I think it depends on who you are letting down."

"I sometimes worry that my ambition is hurting Lara."

"Is that what you're really worried about when you think about her?"

Owen fell quiet.

"It is normal to let yourself and the people around you down sometimes," Lola Beth said. "But you need to strive to be and do better. And one of the best things we can do to help ourselves and each other, is to be true." She patted Owen's hand then placed a pandesal on his plate. "Now eat, anak. You're so skinny."

***

Towards the end of the trip, Owen and Vicky sat together with Pebbles and a game of backgammon as Lola Beth slept.

"How was LA?" Vicky asked.

"Ah, you know. LA was LA."

"Your father wrote to us about it. He even sent pictures."

"I heard." Owen stared at the board in front of him. "That's nice. I'm glad you guys are civil."

"I'll always love your father, you know," Vicky said candidly. "Creating together was our lifeblood and our kryptonite, I guess. We used to fight all the time. Music was the heart of that. We would fight over priorities, over you, but all against the backdrop of music. We would hurt each other. Even hit each other. And say the most awful things, and then we would try to make it all better with a song." She trailed off a moment then sighed. "Things have gotten better over the years. Since I moved here. Without the pressure of our dreams and expectations, we can love each other in a way that's good for us both." She moved a piece. "Plus, it's good I'm with Mom again."

Owen nodded. "I'm glad you're with her, too." It was a rare thing for him to speak to his mother, so this too felt like a gift. Just in time for Christmas. He didn't want to acknowledge the first half of her statement, but it sat with him, leaving an impression. Without the music, there were other ways his parents could love each other.

After another quiet moment, Owen looked at his mom and asked: "Do you ever regret leaving the music business?"

Vicky looked back at him. "It was time. I had run out of my own songs. Plus, I needed time to get over Jack."

Owen nodded, resisting the urge to make a sarcastic or snide remark like, "And how's that going for you?" The phrase "to get over Jack," felt like a rude downplay of everything that transpired in their family after 9/11—the understatement of the year, pretty much.

Vicky didn't just take a year off to get over Jack, she took a year off from living at all. She had not been entirely present for Owen before Jack passed, but after she was basically invisible. Or, he was. He had ceased to matter at all. He would never forget the year she had spent locked in that room. And perhaps he might never forgive her for it either.

All these thoughts were unraveling in Owen's head, but right above them he could somehow see an important truth: this was Vicky, vulnerable. She almost never spoke about Jack, and in that moment, at the simple mention of this shared pain, Owen felt a little knot in his own chest loosen.

"I miss him too, you know," Owen heard himself say.

Vicky looked at Owen again, this time her eyes wide in a bit of surprise. He had never said that to anybody at all ever, but it was true. In the short time that Jack had been in their lives, he had been a sort of glue, a symbol of hope.

"Of course." Tears formed in Vicky's eyes and she reached

a hand toward Owen gently. He let her grab his hand. "I forget sometimes, you know, that you both had grown close. We were a mini family for a few short months. I'm sorry, Owen."

Owen nodded and they sat together like that for a moment.

Vicky let his hand go and regarded him then with dewy eyes, and a small, bittersweet smile. "Love, hey? It really can mess you up."

Owen gave a small chuckle.

"But better to have loved and lost!" Vicky declared.

Owen rolled his eyes and turned back to the game. "Where were we even?" On the outside, he played it cool, but really, for the first time in many, many years, he felt a little lighter in his mother's presence again.

Later on, as they were packing their things away, Vicky posed a question. "What happened in LA, Owen?"

Owen startled and looked at her, "What do you mean?"

"To the music. Your album or demo or EP. I listened to it. It was promising. Did you guys not like the terms of the agreement?"

"Something like that."

"You know there are tons of other labels."

"I think Lara wants to do something else, to be honest."

"Oh. Do you think you'll go off and do your own thing?"

Owen thought about the lumps in his throat. Confusion. Frustration. Worry. "I don't know," he said, thinking about what he'd said to Lara all those months ago in LA: *I don't want to do this without you.*

29
Bacolod, Negros Occidental, 2008

Christmas for Owen had always been an intimate affair. His parents would come and shower him with gifts as though in penance for their sin of abandoning him. He'd smile awkwardly for pictures. Lola Beth would make delicious food. His mother would lead them in carols. Uncles, aunts, and cousins would come for a few hours with presents, tsismis, big voices, and karaoke machines.

He was not prepared for what he faced at Lara's Christmas gathering. A massive family of siblings, spouses, children, cousins, uncles, aunts, and friends descended upon Hacienda Rodriguez.

The grounds were sprawling.

To get to the main house, one had to follow a sloping driveway, which ended in a rotonda around a large fountain. This structure—affectionately nicknamed "The Big House" was made in the classical colonial Spanish-Filipino style—half stone, half wood. It boasted ten bedrooms, a massive living room with high ceilings, and a dining room with a table that could seat twenty people.

Behind the Big House there were three smaller guest houses, built later on land that had once been used for farming and keeping fighting cocks.

"Who are you?" Owen marveled, staring at Lara. He had seen her life in Singapore—a well-kept historical home, fancy cars, well-bred parents. But he had never learned about her mother's background in detail. Who was this person whose family was of the landed gentry, yet who drove a crappy car, shared rent with Mike, and preferred thrifted clothing from ukay-ukays? Who had he been hanging out with for a year and a half?

Lara laughed airily and waved him off. "My great-great grandfather came from Spain and I don't know the rest. This is the family's land. My uncle still manages the properties and the farms, but everyone until my mom's generation has shares and it's all just distributed." She shrugged. "Later on I guess we'll inherit some, too."

Owen rolled his eyes. "You could have funded our album."

"No," she corrected him. "My older family members could have funded it. Then it would have been a total mess."

"Okay, can you run me by everyone who's going to be here?"

"Maybe I need to print you a booklet with names and faces."

"If that'll help!"

Lara just laughed. "You'll be fine."

Owen felt out of his depth. One part of him was saying, *What if they hate you?*; Another, *Does it even matter?* And yet another felt such admiration for Lara that despite her background, she was so gracious, down-to-earth, humble. *Elegant. Beautiful. A wonder.*

***

The Christmas activities were manifold. Owen was grateful that he had already met Lara's immediate family, which made it more straightforward to ease into the festivities and meet people.

There were many colorful characters. A tito who led visual merchandising for a high street brand in San Francisco, and his long-term partner whom Lara affectionately called Tito Sweets. A tita who was a talented concert pianist and had played in all the biggest halls in the world, including Madison Square Garden. Lara's grandparents—sweet, funny people who tore it up on the dance floor whenever the jazz music came on. Cousins who loved karaoke. Owen met and enjoyed them all.

On Christmas Eve, the night of the biggest party, a large tent was pitched in the garden, and a buffet of roast lamb, lechon, cochinillo, steak, turkey, and the Bacolod-classic inasal had been set up alongside an abundance of sides of salads, roasted vegetables, pancit palabok, kare-kare, and garlic rice. There was even a kakanin station, and cakes and fresh fruits.

Owen and Lara sat with her family. Her parents to Lara's right, and her sister, Adora, to Owen's left.

Later, when everyone was stuffed and waiting for the next feast to begin at midnight, Adora, Lara, and Owen swiped glasses and a couple of bottles of Philippine rum from the bar and ran off to hang out behind a large acacia tree in the garden.

They chatted for a few hours until they were discovered by Aurora calling them over for the midnight toast, gifts, and feast. On the tables there lay a spread of hot chocolate, ham, queso de bola, and ensaymada. Owen saw the cornucopia in front of him, and Lara beside him, and smiled, his heart full of sweet, festive gratitude.

That night, even Owen had gifts to open—a handsome pineapple-fiber barong from Lara's parents, a book from Adora, and from Lara a beautiful leather wallet with his initials embossed on it. She had folded a note into it that read: *For you, Owen. Love Sounds the Music of the Spheres (Rumi), The Messenger (Mary Oliver). Merry Christmas.* He supposed they were poems and tucked them into the zipper section for later.

Once everyone had eaten their second fill, music began to play and some family members turned in while others stayed behind, cleared the tables and began to dance. The lively jazz and Christmas music were replaced with Top 40s and '80s hits.

With too much alcohol and an abundance of Christmas spirit, Owen found himself filled with a warm feeling of love and family. He stayed on the dance floor. And he danced. Particularly, with Lara.

As they danced he realized this was the first time he had really held her hand, fingers interlaced. Although they had lain together before, he'd never touched her hands this way. He felt the warmth of her palm on his palm. He felt her smooth fingers between his. He spun her around and watched her hair billow in the breeze, her vintage green tulle dress all cinched and tapered in the right places fanning out around her. He looked at her. He took her in.

Caught up in the moment, he pulled her to him and nuzzled his face in the crook of her neck. Confusion. Attraction. Inebriation. He could not make heads or tails of it. He did not want to ask why.

Lara reached for him in a way that seemed so second nature, even that was so much to bear and he stumbled away.

Still, she followed after him. "Owen! Where are you going?"

"I don't know." He stopped and turned around. They swayed a little in the December breeze, and Lara knocked into him as she approached. They steadied each other, laughing.

"Is something the matter?" she asked, placing her hands on his chest and looking up at him. Her fingers began tracing his collar bone and, instinctively, his hands pressed into her lower back.

"No. No..." Owen shook his head and squeezed his eyes shut.

I love you so much I can barely breathe. I need to get away from you or I'll fall too far and there will be no net to catch me.

"Do you want to head back to the room?" Lara asked.

Owen looked at her, trying to steady his gaze and body. The moon cast a soft white light across her brow, illuminating her large eyes. There was such a deep, physical, emotional rumbling in him. He wanted to ravish her. He wanted...so many things.

"Okay," he said.

The event had been planned by a few of Lara's cousins. Everyone was assigned rooms, and Lara and Owen had one together, with twin beds. As they went, hand in hand, Owen lamented over the irony that this was the first time they didn't have a bigger bed to share.

They stumbled into the room, laughing about their own drunkenness, and when they fell upon one of the beds, tangled up in each other, Owen put his face near Lara's ear and whispered, "I think this is the best Christmas I have ever had."

Lara pushed him back and flipped them over, sitting astride him and looking down, she smiled boldly. "It's about to get better."

30
Manila, 2009

The biggest news of the New Year was Mateo and Monique were engaged. It was everyone's first week back at work in the new year, and decompression days were very much called for after all the hectic holiday celebrations and the floodgates opening in everyone's work inboxes. To celebrate this engagement, and to let off a bit of work-related steam, the boys were out at the driving range while the girls had gone to do yoga and get facials.

Mike took a large swing with his club and watched as the little white ball flew far across the range. "So, I have news too," he said after.

Owen stood up to take his turn. "What?"

"My project here is ending," Mike said as Owen swung.

Owen botched the follow through and his ball did a silly little arch and fell many meters short of Mateo and Mike's. "No. So soon?"

"It's been nearly three years now. Probably not soon enough!" Mike chuckled, but his eyes betrayed the bittersweet feelings that came with this moment.

"Shame, man," Mateo said, standing to make his own swing. "Where are you going now?"

"Singapore. Time for me to dedicate myself to the family business." Mike replied.

Owen looked at Mike and felt a sadness at the inevitability of the passage of time, of the promise of change. *At least Lara's here,* he thought.

"You and Lara can visit." Mike nudged Owen, wiggling his eyebrows, a cheeky grin on his face. "See your in-laws."

Owen scrunched his face up at Mike and nudged him back. "Whatever, man."

"What's happening there, though, really?" Mike pressed.

Mateo laughed. "Ah, the question on everyone's minds that no one dares to say aloud."

Owen laughed, unable to hide that bit of defensiveness in his tone. That little panic. "What's that supposed to mean?"

Mike hit another ball into that seemingly sky high green net before them and laughed a big, hearty laugh. "Oh, please, Owen. People don't just attend their friend's family reunions. Friends don't practically live together. Except maybe you and I. Since you practically live with Lara, and I actually do. So like, I guess you and I live together by proxy. But that doesn't count."

"Look, just tell us already," Mateo chimed in. "What are you two? We're all dying to know? How was Bacolod? Are you in love? TELL US. Please. It's like watching the OC." He referenced the mid-2000s teen soap Owen had hated with a passion as a show, though he had appreciated its soundtrack.

Owen was quiet. Bacolod was amazing. But faced with the question, he could hardly bring himself to say so. The bubble Owen and Lara had lived in in Bacolod could not have been real life. The only times he'd ever been that happy always ended in disaster. And it terrified him.

Since LA, it had felt like he was trying more, like he was missing Lara more, like he was putting himself in places he knew she wanted him more. And, worse, in Bacolod, he had put words to it. Every night there he had thought that dreadful thought, I love you madly. It echoed like the lyrics of his parents' most popular song: *I love you madly, so very madly, you ask me nicely, but you can't have me, 'cause even though I love you madly, I'll treat you badly, and that's our tragedy.* That song was about his parents. He knew in his bones that his fragmented memories—the smarting red on his mother's cheek, a scratch across his father's face, his father's roar, his mother's scorn. Then always a song. Frantic apologies. Beautiful music. The sense that everything was sacred, yet nothing was safe. *I love you madly.* It could not be.

For Owen, almost all love was to be abandoned. Or to burn and scream and fight. He could not put himself through that willingly. Lara was not just a friend. She was not even just a lover.

She was his person. His family. And 'family' was scary.

But Owen in that moment, used this to his advantage as he said, "I just don't have any family here, guys. So Lara's that. A best friend. Family."

Mateo and Mike exchanged a glance. Owen chose not to read into it. Then they continued knocking those little white balls around, avoiding the elephant in the room once more.

31
Manila and La Union, 2009

Lara sat in the corner of the coffee shop with a copy of *Tulips and Chimneys* by e.e. cummings. Ella Fitzgerald played in her ears and she tapped her foot and hummed along.

"Sorry I'm late."

She looked up to see Owen in front of her, smiling, looking just a little sheepish. He wore jeans and a white T-shirt and had his laptop bag slung cross-body.

She smiled back. "It's fine."

Mike had begun packing his side of the house, and Lara found the whole thing rather depressing so had asked Owen if they could spend that Sunday out. He had recommended coffee and a movie and perhaps dinner, and she'd gone with it because on top of Mike's move, the ambiguity of her relationship with Owen, and the pressures of work, she had little mind space to think of much else.

"I brought you something," Owen said, opening the flap of his bag and pulling out a little paper bag that had been folded over. He handed it to her and sat down.

"Oh!" Lara said, surprised. "Okay." She took it and opened it to reveal a beautiful leather bound notebook with thick watercolor pages and a tin case with three watercolor brushes.

"I bought this for you when I was in Virginia and totally forgot to give it as part of your Christmas gift but while I was doing a bit of spring cleaning I found it in my backpack."

Is something happening here? Lara imagined, for a moment, what 2009 could bring if this version of Owen–the openly appreciative and affectionate version, would no longer revert to being emotionally unavailable and perennially avoidant. Would they finally have a chance to say the things they had been talking and living and tiptoeing around?

"Thank you, Owen," she said. "You didn't have to."

"I know." He shrugged. "But the museums always make me think of you."

Lara smiled. "Well, thank you. Hey, your birthday is coming up. Have you thought about what you want to do?"

Owen shrugged. "I kind of just want to do dinner and something outdoors with you and Mike."

"Okay, maybe we'll plan something."

That was how, weeks later, Lara, Owen, and Mike found themselves in La Union for a weekend of surfing.

The resort that Lara had booked was a quaint B&B. The three were to share a room with a single bed and a bunk bed, and to make the atmosphere cozy and celebratory at the same time, Lara had packed slingers and a birthday sign which she proceeded to hang up with much enthusiasm when she sent the boys to sign them up for surf lessons the next morning.

When Owen and Mike walked back in, surf lessons booked and cases of beer in tow, they both smiled. Lara had hung up all the decorations, and upon their return, blew a nostalgic paper and plastic party horn in their faces.

Mike high-fived Lara. "Nicely done."

"Sweet." Owen reached over and pulled Lara in for a hug. Over his shoulder, Lara saw Mike giving her wide eyes and wiggly eyebrows. She narrowed her eyes at him, mouthing "Shut up."

Mike put both hands up in surrender and turned away with a cheeky smirk.

When Owen pulled away, he didn't leave Lara. One arm still around her shoulders, he looked around the room and squeezed her against his side again. "This was really thoughtful."

Lara wiggled away from his grasp and from her suitcase produced her ukulele. "And I figured just for this weekend, we can make some music again. If you want."

At this, Owen seemed to beam with joy—his eyes wide, and a smile spreading across his face. "A thousand times yes."

The next evening, after a full day of surfing, the three sat on the beach and watched the sun setting in the horizon. Orange, blue, pink, purple—a gradient of vibrant colors bathed the entire sky. It was gorgeous.

Lara pulled out her uke and began to pluck a small tune.

Eyes still on the sunset, Owen bobbed his head and began to hum. As the song progressed, he threw in occasional gibberish, and then finally a real verse.

> *Seasons come, the wind it blows,*
> *the summer rain, it ebbs, it flows;*
> *and in the waves, across the sea,*
> *I know you're swimming after me.*

Lara jumped in.

> *The evening wakes, the sun she sleeps,*
> *the moon, she has secrets to keep.*
> *And yes I know, you're free—it's true,*
> *but I'll keep swimming after you.*

Her heart pounded in her chest. Was this the moment? Or was this just another song? Owen's voice grew softer as he responded.

> *Don't get me wrong, I want you to,*
> *Cause there's this thing with me and you.*
> *But if we let the water in,*
> *And we keep diving deeper then,*
> *We may not get back home again.*

Lara was silent. She had no response, her mind a jumble of thoughts and feelings.

Owen looped back into a new verse.

> *I know the risks—the deep abyss.*
> *I can't keep swimming out like this.*

Your options lie upon the shore.
You deserve oh so much more.

Lara could see Mike eyeing her as she stopped playing.

"Bathroom," Mike said, getting up abruptly and leaving.

"Owen..." Lara began when Mike had gone, her heart squeezing in her chest. Was that song for her? Was that their song? Did he mean it? What "more" could she possibly deserve?

"Lara..." Owen said, still not looking away from the sun. "Let's not. Okay?"

She sighed and looked at her feet. It felt like she was stuck in a neverending verse.

32
Mt. Pulag, 2009

On a weekend in March, Owen and Lara scheduled a Mt. Pulag climb with Mike. A send-off. To train, they ran together three days a week and did uphill sprints on weekends. Lara never brought up the spontaneous song she and Owen had sung together the month before. It all felt so raw and real, and much too delicate, and she just couldn't bring herself to expose all the little bits of her if Owen was going to hold his own cards to his chest. It didn't make sense anymore. So she waited.

Mt. Pulag was a popular hiking destination, boasting a maximum elevation of over 2,900 meters. It had spectacular cloud-capped views of the Cordilleras and Lara was beside herself with excitement. She could already see all the photographs she'd take, the paintings it might inspire, and the joy of the climb itself.

The day of the climb, the group took a bus together up to Baguio. It took six hours, and when they arrived, it was foggy and a little chilly. They stopped by a street-side vendor and ordered a few cups of taho. They then took a separate car to the ranger station by the mountain run by the local government. The road zigged and zagged, and Lara and Mike both complained of motion sickness, which Owen teased them about, but helped them with anyway, handing them cold water and bread whenever needed. When they reached their destination, they received an orientation about the climb while tucking into bowls of arroz caldo–Filipino rice porridge with ginger and garlic and chicken.

The best time to climb Pulag was before daybreak so as to catch the sunrise at the summit. Thus, that afternoon, while waiting, and under orders to rest and prepare for a near-midnight rise, Lara, Owen, and Mike stayed at Kino's Homestay, a cozy little inn with dorm rooms, communal bathrooms, and the softest fleece blankets Lara had ever snuggled in.

They lounged around, took pictures, and basked in the scenery, which was already breathtaking from where they were. After an early dinner, the group slept.

The group was in great spirits. They were all excited to be making more memories in the Philippines, and it was a bonus to make them with their closest friends. It was also a little sad for everyone, though. They knew this was a despedida for Mike.

Lara had not figured out what she was going to do about her housing arrangements, and she knew she would miss him, the counterweight to her and Owen's intensity.

At one in the morning, everyone awoke for the climb. It was cold. Lara took deep breaths of the damp air, smiling at the day ahead. The group climbed quietly with purpose, following their guide named Mang Tonio. They reached the summit in four and a half hours and sat on the grass, looking out across the clouds, waiting for sunrise.

As the first rays of light broke through the clouds, over the peaks, the three were greeted with a meeting of earth and sky. They were immersed in hues of blue, yellow, white, and cream. It was a swirling mix of colors as the wind blew around them, treating their senses to the smell of grass and dew.

Mike stood between Owen and Lara and put his arms around their shoulders. "I'm going to miss you guys a lot."

Lara felt emotional, like she might cry. But it was impossible because she was simultaneously so happy. "Singapore is not far," she quipped.

"You should take over my side of the lease, Owen," Mike said softly. "The flat would suit you perfectly."

"Only if it's okay with Lara?" Owen looked across Mike toward Lara. His eyes somehow told her, It'll be good. I promise.

Lara looked at the two young men next to her—the people who had made the Philippines her true second home. She thought about the history behind them, and the future ahead, and she smiled as she gazed at the clearing sky.

"Sure," she said to Owen.

33
Manila, 2009

Mike sealed his last box and helped Owen move his own in.

"Well, I think that's that," he said as Owen rubbed his hands on the seat of his pants and looked around the room. It had been emptied of Mike's things and was replaced with Owen's own sparse belongings—two small boxes and two suitcases, and an abundance of musical equipment.

The two friends shook hands and then pulled each other in for a hug. Owen held on just a second longer, sad to see Mike go.

"Are you and Lara going to be okay without me?" Mike said when they pulled away. He said it with a smile that did not reach his eyes, which made Owen think he was being serious right then.

For a change, Owen fought the urge to say something silly or sarcastic or defensive in return and was quiet for a moment. "Yes," he said finally. "We're fine. We'll be fine."

"'Cause in La Union..." Mike cocked his head at Owen and then trailed off.

Owen knew that Mike was thinking of that evening when they had jammed and improvised that song that Owen sort of regretted every moment of now that he had a bit of space and hindsight. He couldn't understand why he had done that. The moment had been so raw, and he had felt so many things. But it had opened up sides of him he wasn't ready to expose, and he was not in a position or of a frame of mind to make any grand gestures or keep any promises. Perhaps he never would be.

"Lara is a wonderful person, you know," Mike said.

"Of course."

"So…all I'm saying is…" Mike sighed and shrugged. "Handle with care. That's all."

Owen furrowed his brow and frowned. "Obviously."

Mike shrugged again. "Anyway, I'll miss you guys. Keep in touch, okay? And every time you're in Singapore, call me. I mean it."

"We should take one more picture all together," Owen said, then he turned and called out into the hall. "Lara! Get in here!"

He heard Lara's door open and close and her footsteps. She appeared in Mike's doorway wearing cut-off denim shorts and a vintage bowling shirt that she'd cut to reveal her midriff. She was sticking with her workout program and it showed. Owen tried not to get distracted by all the little patches of skin he could see. He gestured for her to come closer.

"Group picture," he explained.

"Oh, I have an idea." Lara perked up, smiling and disappearing once more. When she returned she had her camera mounted to a tripod and a little remote in her hand. She set up the tripod and directed the boys to stand in front of all the packed boxes and then she ran to join them. Standing between them, both boys put their arms around her.

"One, two, three, cheese!"

And the flash went off.

34
Boracay, 2009

In the Philippines, the despedida de soltera was designed as a celebration for the bride involving the entire party, including the groom, his friends, and his family. Monique's was a couple of days before the ceremony right on the powdery white shore. She had specified it was a barefoot party, and everyone came in fresco outfits, leaving their shoes by the floral archway at the entrance.

The bridal entourage, which included both Bianca and Lara, wore Lara's favorite piece of her entire wedding wardrobe—linen mini-dresses, cut very low in the back, and embroidered in honeysuckle-colored traditional patterns and curls as popularized by those from the Batangas province who embroidered on piña textile. The soft, slightly see-through fabric with intricate cubist stitching was both elegant and free.

A bar made of bamboo had been built next to the matching DJ booth, and Wayne Wonder was playing on the speakers.

Lara stood with the other bridesmaids, fawning over Monique's short, white, shimmery number, and the tropical tiara she wore woven out of rattan and bedazzled with seashells.

From a distance, she saw Owen walking with the groomsmen toward the bar. He wore a linen shirt and khakis, and his sun-kissed skin shone in the setting sun. Just then, he turned and caught her gaze, as though he felt her looking. These moments of contact always felt like finding a piece of herself in the middle of a crowded room.

She was thinking these things and spacing out before she realized Owen was right in front of her. The song was "No Letting Go." Wordlessly, he held his hand out and she took it. That night,

159

they danced just like they had in Bacolod, not holding back. Lara could tell that when she and Owen allowed themselves to be quiet and use their bodies, it was as though many things were being said at once. As they moved together, she noted the weight of his palm on her back and it was like "I'm here." She felt his gentle gaze on hers and it felt like "Always."

Why couldn't they say these things out loud?

***

The next day was the wedding. Owen watched Lara march toward him and they met in the middle to walk up the aisle as a pair. She in her flowy gown, him in his barong. Arm in arm, they walked and watched Mateo beaming proudly in anticipation.

Lara had never thought about getting married. She had assumed it would happen but she hadn't considered what she wanted in a husband, in a wedding, in a marriage.

She thought about how Mateo and Monique were a good fit. They fought, but made up well. They communicated. They were from similar backgrounds. They understood each other.

She thought about Owen, on whose arm she was hanging. Of how they fought, but also how they fit together. She tried to imagine marrying him but could not see it. She tried to imagine marrying someone else, but drew a blank. It almost disappointed her.

***

The morning after the wedding, Lara woke with a splitting headache. Owen approached her bed at 9:30 a.m. to rouse her for breakfast to no avail. She mumbled a complaint about a migraine and rolled back over pressing her fingers to her temples.

Owen slipped out and, ten minutes later, came back with water, electrolyte drinks, and a sachet of ibuprofen.

He sat at the edge of her bed, rubbing her neck and head gently. "Do you think you'll make it to the send-off brunch?"

Lara squinted up at him. The light from the window was giving her a headache. He noticed her glancing in its direction, and hurried over to close the curtains. "Is that better?"

160

She nodded and willed herself to smile.

Owen stroked a strand of hair off of her face and tucked it behind her ear. He began to slowly, gently rub her head and neck, his fingers working their way along her nape and cervical spine. A certain tingly lightness came over her, and she felt her breath catch in her throat. She lamented that she felt too sick to properly enjoy the attention, but she would have been lying if she said she wasn't basking in the affection.

"Shall I wake you at 11 to see if you're okay to go?"

She nodded and smiled into her pillow.

***

At 11 a.m., Owen woke her and she felt a little better. With his help, she got out of bed and got dressed.

"Thanks, Owen," Lara said as they walked toward the hotel restaurant to send their friends off on their honeymoon.

35
Manila, 2009

"So, how's it been since your husband moved in?" Monique's voice on the other end was sing-songy and teasing.

She and Mateo were out of town on their two month-long Southeast Asian honeymoon tour. Mateo had gone off to play a round of golf and she had called Lara to show off her hotel room and insisted on the latest tsismis.

Lara nearly choked on her tea. "Excuse me."

"I'm sorry, I had to." Monique laughed, sounding not at all apologetic. "It's just that you guys are so weird, girl."

Lara sighed and sat down at her desk, opening up the watercolor sketchbook Owen had given her and flipping through the first few pages of sketches—each a small representation of her favorite tropical fruits being held by a tanned, weathered hand— an exercise of her skills in still life and figure painting. The most recent piece, though, was a watercolor of Owen's face—his eyes, a small smirk at the edges of his mouth. She cringed and closed the book.

"What do you mean?" She feigned innocence.

"Oh, please." Monique sighed and Lara could imagine her rolling her eyes. After a moment of silence, Monique seemed to change tactics and a more serious tone came into her voice—lower, softer, more considerate. "Lara, are you sure it was a good idea to move in together?"

"We're friends. Why not?" But as the words left her mouth, Lara almost felt stupid.

"You aren't just friends, Lar. And you know it. You know

that's never ever what you guys will be."

Lara sighed.

"Are you honestly telling me you've never had any… moments?"

Then the floodgates opened. Lara had kept these stories to herself so long that once she'd begun, it was hard for her to stop. She told Monique everything. How they had slept together—several times. How he avoided conversations on the topic. How he was sweet and kind, but also unpredictable, and clearly deeply hurt somewhere in a place he wouldn't let anyone see in full.

When she was done, Monique whistled. "That's…a lot, Lar…"

"I know." Lara flopped back onto her bed, near tears. "But I don't know what to do. I don't want to confront him because I don't want to push him away, and I don't want to force anything on him that he doesn't want. He's had a lot of childhood trauma, and I want to respect his space and allow things to happen in their own time. But it is hard to forever be in this limbo."

Monique was quiet for a moment. "Lara…I can tell that you and Owen care a lot about each other. And I can tell you that he and I slept together a couple of times, but he never ever seemed even slightly interested in me the way that he is so clearly in love with you. You guys are sitting on a ship right now. Docked. And either you start captaining that ship into the open ocean to find out what's out there for you both…or you get off. Now. Promise me you're going to give him an ultimatum. This can't go on. You are worth so much more! You could date. You could meet a proper nice guy. You don't have to wait around for Owen to change or get over his traumas. You can have a wonderful life, with someone or even as a single person. Just without the drag of a hanger-on leading you on."

Was that what Owen was? A hanger-on? *No, never.* He was her best friend. But once the words had touched Lara's ears, she knew they were partly true. Owen was hanging on, sure. And she was too. But he was leading her on. And that in particular made her a little angry.

…But she loved him. How sad was that?

"Fine," she said finally. "I will. I will talk to him about all this. If nothing changes by year-end, I'll give him an ultimatum."

"That's the spirit, girl! I love Owen as a friend, but I love you more, and you deserve to be happy."

Lara couldn't help herself, she smiled, even though inside she already felt the edges of anxiety creeping in on her.

36
Manila, 2009

For New Year's Eve, Owen and Lara decided to host a party at their flat. Though it had been a couple of months since Lara's talk with Monique, the chat remained fresh in her mind. It was not just something she'd said to appease Monique. She knew that the promise was more for herself than anyone else, but the thought of bringing it up terrified her. To make matters worse, Monique would be there that night, and would surely not shy away from reminding Lara of this ultimatum.

Guests trickled in from seven in the evening, particularly Bianca, David, Niko, Mateo, and Monique.

"We're all here!" Bianca cheered when the recently-weds finally arrived.

Both Mateo and Monique stood at the door with large platters in their hands. "Balinese delights!" Monique declared. Fresh off their honeymoon across Indonesia and Thailand, the pair had clearly brought home a piece of the trip with them.

"Wow!" Lara said, letting them in.

"We couldn't resist. The food in Bali was so good we just had to bring you some. We secreted home our favorite delights frozen and heated them up at home," Monique gushed, shrugging her shimmery bolero off and draping it onto the back of a chair as she handed Lara a tray of sate lilit.

Lara thanked them and helped set the food down.

Owen came back in from the kitchen where he had been popping a bottle of wine. "Did you guys bring us something?"

"Balinese food," Lara confirmed.

"Sweet. It smells awesome."

Once the food had been set down and everyone was settled

around the couch picking at the charcuterie, Lara turned to Monique and said, "So how was the trip? Tell us all about it!"

"It was amazing, Lar, you have to go. Especially to Bali. We went scuba diving, white water rafting, and had barbecued seafood on the beach while watching the sunset."

"We also rode a glass-bottom boat," Mateo piped in.

"We did water sports, too. And had the most delicious coffee I have ever had!" Monique enthused.

Lara turned reflexively to Owen. "Ooh!"

He nodded with enthusiasm, as though reading her mind. "We should make the trip."

"I haven't been since I was twelve. I bet there's more to do now."

"For sure. It's pretty developed now," Mateo said. "There are a lot of hip places. You can choose your chill."

"Maybe for New Year's?" Owen offered. "We could take a few days extra off of work and rent a villa."

"Maybe!" Lara enthused.

"Where did you guys stay? Was it a villa or a resort? Maybe we should split it and do a bit of both. See different sides of Bali." Owen turned to Lara. "We could do a mixed itinerary."

"Ooh, white water rafting would be fun."

"Surfing."

"And maybe a cooking class. This food is delicious."

"Have you tried one of these? It's a revelation." Owen offered Lara the stick of sate lilit on his plate and held it up to her mouth. She took a bite and her eyes grew wide. Owen's eyes followed hers and they nodded enthusiastically at each other in agreement.

The friends around them exchanged awkward looks. Lara pretended not to see and hoped the moment would pass but then—

"You guys are driving us crazy," Monique declared.

"Wait, what?" Owen asked, a confused look on his face.

"You two!" Monique threw her hands up in the air. "I mean, just get a room already!"

"We already live together," Lara and Owen joked in unison, and then they nudged each other with their shoulders and laughed, even though Lara's heart was palpitating with anxiety.

Nobody laughed along.

"No," Monique said flatly. "It's been weird forever!" Then she turned to Lara. "Have you spoken to him yet? It's year-end. Have you spoken to him?"

Lara sat, mouth half-open, both shocked and convicted.

"I knew it." Monique rolled her eyes. "I guess you guys are satisfied to remain in this nebulous, co-dependent state of affairs." She crossed her arms over her chest and leaned back.

Owen gave Lara a sideways glance as though to say, Yikes. But Lara was looking right at Monique. The rest of the party had gone dead silent.

"What Monique means is," Mateo said slowly, "we love you, guys. But it's weird that you live together, do everything together, and are clearly crazy about each other, but refuse to admit it."

"This is an intervention," Monique declared.

Niko whistled from his seat and Lara caught Bianca reaching over to punch his shoulder, shooting him a "shut up" glance.

Lara saw Owen lay his hands in his lap as she avoided his eyes.

"Oh, so you guys get married and suddenly you're the relationship experts and know better than we do what kind of relationship this is?" He gestured between him and Lara. "The only people who can say what this is are Lara and I, and we're fine."

Monique rolled her eyes. "You're not fine."

"We're fine."

"You're not fine."

"We. Are. Fine."

Monique turned to Lara. "Are you fine with this, Lar? Are you fine with Owen being your plus one to everything? Are you fine with him acting like your boyfriend without ever admitting he is? Do you want to grow old with Owen, and be best friends for life with all the stupid things you aren't saying?"

Owen looked at Lara searchingly, but she looked away.

"That's what I thought." Monique stood up. "I'm leaving. This is dumb. We'll come by for the dishes another day. Let's go,

Mat."

Mateo shrugged apologetically. "Sorry. But. She's right." He turned to the rest of the party and smiled awkwardly. "Happy New Year, guys!" Then he and Monique headed for the door.

At the door, Monique turned back once and addressed Lara directly. "I told you, Lar. Either captain that ship away from the dock and find out what's out there in the ocean, or get the fuck off and find some other fish in the sea. Before you sink." Then she was gone.

"Wow, way to back me up there. What was all that about?" Owen whistled. "Do you think she's on her period? Maybe she's pregnant. That would be fast. But cool."

Lara inhaled deeply then exhaled, counting in her head. *One…two…three…four…five…six…*

Then she turned to the rest of their guests. "I'm really sorry, guys, but maybe you should leave?"

Bianca was already getting up, pulling David along with her. "Don't have to tell us twice."

"Here, take a tray of food." Lara handed one of the charcuterie platters to their friends. Nervous. Awkward. She could feel her cheeks flushed with embarrassment.

"We can head to my place," Niko said cheerfully, trying to lighten the mood.

David nodded quickly. "Yeah, fun," he agreed.

"Wait, no. This is stupid, Lara, come on, just 'cause Monique and Mateo had some weird tantrum doesn't mean we can't—" Owen was talking, but Lara wasn't listening, and neither were their friends.

Lara walked the rest of the group to the door and everyone hugged and kissed goodbye, exchanging New Year's blessings. When the door shut, it was just Owen and Lara again.

"What the hell did you do that for?"

"Owen, I've been meaning to have a conversation with you," Lara started, her heart was going what felt like a thousand beats per minute, and she kept thinking, *This is it. The ultimatum.* "I wasn't going to until everyone was gone, but I guess the party got cut short anyway, and now's as good a time as any."

"Why so serious?" Owen teased, his voice playful.

"Please, can we talk about this finally." Lara felt stupid and tired and confused. Were they ever going to say the things they should?

Then Owen suddenly reached over and began to tickle her.

Lara's heart dropped. She did not want to be touched like this. She wanted to have a mature, respectful conversation. The unexpected, unwanted breach of her personal space—so tone deaf—felt like a white hot iron on her skin. She had not thought consciously about LA in a while, but right then it felt like Owen had set off a trigger. In spite of herself, with his fingers in her rib cage, she began to laugh even though what she really wanted to do was to cry. She stood and pushed Owen's arm away.

"Okay, enough," she said with a warning tone.

Owen poked her again in the underarm. His hands where she didn't want them. Her body, trapped. A feeling she remembered.

"Stop," Lara said, firmly this time.

When he reached over and started again, she reflexively, with an open palm, slapped him gently across his cheek. "I said enough!" She was shocked she had done it, but relieved she had kept it soft, playful. She had never slapped anyone except Stuart, but in that very moment Owen seemed cut from a similar cloth and it made her sick. But he wasn't Stuart. He wasn't. Right?

Unsure what might happen next, she looked at him, frozen for a beat. His face was devoid of expression. She thought perhaps they might both begin laughing. Then, without a word, and with a closed fist, Owen hit Lara on the side of her head.

Lara's left ear throbbed. Her temple pounded. She stared wordlessly. Lara had never been hit by anyone except her mother, who would spank her open palm when she misbehaved as a child.

"Never slap me again," Owen said, his voice cold, his face devoid of emotion.

Lara's words sat in her throat. A tangle of everything she wanted to and didn't want to say. She had gone into this wanting to have a specific conversation, and now she was at the cusp of a totally different one. She swallowed hard. Everything she had felt about Owen seemed to have flown out the window. Right then, all she could see was a pathetic little man. A stranger. Who gave and did only what he wanted, whenever he wanted.

"Get out," Lara seethed.

"Say you'll never do it again."

"Okay. Now get the fuck out."

Owen's face began to change, as though his rage had passed and he realized what was happening. His neck was red, but his face drained of all color. He turned to the door, slowly, as if in shock.

"Owen," Lara said as he went to open the door. He stopped and turned back to face her. "I never want you to touch me again. I never want you in this room again. Get away from me."

So he did.

***

The next morning, Lara awoke to a series of messages.

From Owen (Music Dude) Weber
Hey, can we talk this morning?

From Owen (Music Dude) Weber
Just a few minutes of your time. I promise.

She took her time formulating her response. She didn't even want to imagine what he was thinking or feeling. She didn't want to dignify him with her empathy. Not with her temple still smarting. Still, a conversation surely had to be in order.

Best get it over with, she groaned to herself, unsure whether it was a moment to rage or to cry. Perhaps a bit of both.

From Lara Halford
K. But don't come to my room. I'll come out.

She was irritated with herself. She went over the events multiple times. She thought about the very moment that night when it happened. When she had slapped him. Had it been hard? Had it been in self defense? If he was doing something and she asked him to stop, was he the instigator? Had she been a fool? Could she have anticipated this? Did she know him at all?

Lara settled into the couch in the living room. This man who had hit her, he lived with her, he was half her life. They were together all day, every day. How could she get away now?

In the decorative hall mirror, she caught a glimpse of herself. She had not slept much the night before and it showed—bags under her eyes, a small welt on her temple where he had hit her—hidden under a wisp of her hair.

A moment later, Owen came out of his room and pulled a chair over and sat down some feet away from Lara. He looked awful. His shoulders were slumped, which was so unlike him. His hair, disheveled, a thick mane of bedhead. His eyes were puffy, skin splotchy, brow furrowed.

Lara felt a pang she could not control. Worry? No, pity, she decided.

"Hi," he said slowly.

"Hi," Lara replied. She waited a few beats. One…two…three… "So."

He looked sad and lonely, regretful and pathetic. She didn't know whether to laugh in spite or cry in heartbreak.

"I'm sorry," Owen said finally. He took a deep breath as though there was more so Lara sat, waiting for the rest. "I'm so sorry…I crossed a line. I wasn't thinking. I don't have an excuse. It was shitty. I was shitty. Maybe I'm no good for you? Maybe I'm just a verse in your song, and it's time to move to the next part?"

When Lara did not respond, Owen forged on. "Maybe my purpose in your life was to push you to grow and own your talent, and now all we're doing is pushing each other around. I don't want to hurt you any more. All I wanted was to show you how brilliant you are, and encourage you because I know you're so talented."

He was blabbering, and Lara admittedly liked seeing him vulnerable and honest for a change. But as he spoke, she realized she had a role in this. She had tried to start conversations, but never openly shared her feelings. When he bantered, she bickered, too. Suddenly, she felt convicted and sad.

"Anyway, I think you know what I'm trying to say. I'll move in with Niko for a couple of weeks while we figure out the whole lease and…whatever. Then I can be out of your hair for good."

When Lara looked at Owen, she realized he was crying. It seemed so extreme to go from a hundred to zero overnight and yet where else could they go from here? From this hurt?

Lara tried to imagine how she would fill her days without

Owen. She tried to picture how long it might take for her to no longer think of him in a song, or a painting, or a book, or a movie. How hard it might be not to want to include him in a conversation. Or ask what his thoughts were on a topic.

She felt a hole forming in her heart—the shape and magnitude of missing someone. Of missing a future she was not even sure would have been hers. Of missing an answer she may never find, to a question she could not ask.

"Okay," she said finally, nodding.

Owen took another deep breath. "I'm sorry…"

"I'm sorry, too," Lara replied sincerely. "I didn't mean to slap you. The tickling triggered me. I just…"

"I know," he said. "I crossed the line. I should have listened when you asked me to stop. After what happened in LA, too… I should have known… I should have been more sensitive to your boundaries…"

They were quiet for a while.

"So is this it then?" Lara blinked back a tear, and she was now angry at herself for being so sad. Is this what a broken heart feels like?

"I guess? I mean, we'll need to talk about logistics soon but otherwise, I guess this is it. Have a nice life?"

"You know…it sucks because…you're the only person I've ever let…" Lara trailed off. In, she wanted to say. He was the only person she had ever let into her deepest depths, to the point of creation, in the sense of two souls making a thing of nothing at all.

"I know. And…you're like home to me."

That, said so openly. So honestly. So plainly.

What now? Lara stared at him. Something fluttered in her stomach. Butterflies. Painful ones. Butterflies with razors for wings. The metaphor made her think of that Smashing Pumpkins song—"Bullet With Butterfly Wings." Well, she did feel caged. And lost. And wondered, what can still be saved? Perhaps none of it.

Owen stood. "Good-bye, then?" His posture reverted to how he always carried himself—straight, squared, self-possessed. It almost angered Lara because it felt so dishonest. She realized then that what she had originally identified as a sort of mature confidence in him was yet another layer, another wall built into the fortress that guarded Owen from the joys and perils of connection, love, and life.

Lara stood, too. They looked at each other. Owen reached over then, drew Lara in, and hugged her so tightly that she thought she might break, yet so tenderly that she thought she might disappear.

Then he was back in his room. Lara could hear him shuffling things around behind his door, no doubt packing a bag.

37
Manila, 2010

Owen lasted exactly one week. Living with Niko was fine, but he missed his room, he missed his apartment, and he missed Lara. Everywhere he went there were reminders—a song on the radio, a book on a shelf, a movie trailer, a joke overheard, the fact that he was driving alone to work on the first week of the year.

On one hand, he was terrified. The way he had hit her made him question himself. What had possessed him to do that? Had it always been in him? Was it yet another part of his childhood that he'd never be able to weed out? His love for her scared him. Perhaps he was one of those in whom fear triggered fight responses.

In the middle of all these thoughts was the truth that Lara was his place, and without her, he was homeless. Perhaps she could forgive him? He knew he could be better. Controlled. He would never do it again. It had been hasty to say "goodbye forever" when there were still so many loose ends. Perhaps they could work it out?

On Friday, Owen stared at his phone as his day neared its end. To text, to call, to sleep, perchance to dream? Owen knew he was in dire straits if he was thinking in Shakespearean verse. Especially since he'd never read any of Shakespeare's plays in full.

He shook off his procrastination and drafted a message: *Hey.*

Did he always start messages with 'hey' or had it usually been hi? He scrolled through past conversations and then settled.

38
Manila, 2010

From Owen (Music Dude) Weber
Hey, Lara. How are you doing?

From Owen (Music Dude) Weber
Got plans tonight?

From Owen (Music Dude) Weber
Do you think I could come home? And we could hang out?
Maybe we can paint for a change? Or if you don't want to,
that's fine, too...

Lara's heart skipped a beat when she saw Owen's messages. She had not been coping well. She spent their first two days apart journaling in various states of duress—crying, laughing, raging. Lara missed Owen. The place she lived in was half his, his things were still everywhere. His favorite cereal, the soy milk he loved, his running shoes, the records he'd left in the living room.

She vented to her sister, and friends, particularly Monique. They told her it was a good time for her to meet new people. When Monique asked about the ultimatum and apologized for possibly triggering the fight, Lara brushed it off.

"No, you were right to call us out," she had said.

Because it was true. Monique's intervention had revealed irreparable cracks in their life together.

Lara hadn't told Adora or Monique what had really happened that night. She had described it as "a lovers' quarrel for non-lovers." *If either of them knew...*

But Lara shook her head. They didn't know, and would never know, because nobody had to.

It was a one-time thing. Owen wouldn't do it again. She knew he cared about her. He'd said so himself, *"You're like home to me."* And who would burn their own home to the ground?

She stood and paced. She had already been planning an evening of painting. She had been listening to Joni Mitchell's "A Case of You," crying and feeling pathetic and thought she'd mix it up with something productive for a change. The only thing she'd managed to get herself out of bed for all week besides work had been running or painting. His proposal was almost too on point.

I could reply to Owen, and we could set boundaries. The little devil in her ear added, *Everyone deserves a second chance.*

Lara sat on the edge of the bed with a sort of naive hope in her chest. She picked up her phone, and texted back in the affirmative. Half an hour later, Owen was at their door. Rather than walk right in, he rang the bell.

Lara opened up.

"Hey," Owen said awkwardly, his eyes downcast.

"Hi," she said, but she didn't move. The hope she had had earlier was still there, but at the sight of him it had become tempered somewhat by the reality that Owen was still Owen, and she was still Lara, and that he had hit her, and hurt her in many other ways, and that she was still angry. Lara almost never felt angry for more than a day or two, and the fact that this vice grip on her heart at the sight and sound and even indication of Owen could have outlasted the week felt like a sure sign that the road to reconciliation and recovery was not going to be the easiest one. *Is this what it's like to have a broken heart?* she thought.

One second. Two seconds.

Finally, abandoning her thoughts momentarily, she stepped back in the door frame, and Owen leaned forward and wrapped his arms around her.

Is this *what it feels like to be heartbroken?* Her mind repeated that question. Her chest was constricted, her throat tight and dry, and she felt such a consuming sadness just then that she tried not to cry. She returned the hug stiffly and stepped aside so he could come in and shut the door behind him.

"You want to paint?" she said, sitting on the couch, remembering what he had mentioned on the text and what she had planned herself for the night.

Owen sat down next to her. "Yeah, and I brought provisions to power us through." He handed her a little box of cake like a peace offering.

"Thanks. What do you want to paint?"

"I was thinking of some figure drawing? Maybe a lady in the nude?" He nudged her shoulder with his own.

She scoffed. "Lying on a blanket," he added, his eyes on his feet. "Made of hairy caterpillars with the faces of her ex-lovers."

Lara snorted. A soft giggle. They both relaxed. *Okay, he's not all awful, we can still make this work*, she thought, that small glimmer of hope appearing before her once more—a testament to how mixed up she was inside.

He turned to her. "It's a metaphor."

She smiled back and repeated: "It's a metaphor."

***

Three awful paintings and some laughs later, Owen and Lara lay on their bellies on Lara's bed watching a movie on her laptop and sharing the slice of cake he had brought. They had opted for one of Lara's favorites: *A Bout de Souffle*—a Godard masterpiece. As they got to the end, Lara put the laptop away and Owen turned on his side, drawing closer to her.

"Time for bed," she said, feeling both the strangeness as well as the comfort of being in this position again after all that had happened. She faced away from him, still sitting in the conflict of her feelings.

"Are you awake?" she heard him ask.

"Mm-hmm…what is it, Owen?"

"How are you?"

"I'm fine, Owen. Really." But was she? Her heart was pounding in her chest, and even though they had just had a wonderful time together, being so close again, sharing breathing space, she felt a certain persistent sadness too.

He shifted on the bed. He took one arm and wrapped

it around her waist, settling his chin into the crook of her neck. "Did you miss me?" His voice was so soft she almost wondered if he had meant for her to hear it.

She exhaled. "What? In the week that we were apart?" It came out a bit more biting than she had intended, but she was tired and at war with herself, so how else could it have come out?

"WEEK? No, it…that wasn't…was that it?" he sputtered.

"Yup."

He seemed to pause to do the math. "Oh. Well. Did you?"

She was silent for a moment and then, "A bit." She conceded with a shrug, trying to sound nonchalant. Bold. "I bet you missed me," she teased.

"Yeah, I did," he said with certainty.

Lara closed her eyes and drew in another breath. She tried to silence her own questions, her own frustrations. She resisted the urge to allow her heart to erase the hurt Owen had inflicted on them both, she valued her own forgiving nature but there was a difference between forgiveness and forgetting. And to forget so soon would be wrong. She willed herself to save her mixed feelings for another day and was close to dreamland when he said softly: "I think this is just something nobody else would understand."

"Mm." Lara was too tired to argue.

"Sometimes we don't even understand it." That last bit sounded as though he was speaking mostly to himself.

Lara scoffed inwardly, *ah, there's the rub.*

39
Manila, 2010

The next day, Lara and Owen sat on the couch face-to-face. The two had decided that they would come up with agreed upon boundaries. Owen felt good about it–in fact, it felt almost too good. He was so undeserving, and yet, there in the air between them was not just forgiveness, but also reconciliation in the air. And not just reconciliation even, but also hope.

It was one time, he kept repeating. *I'm not violent. I'll never do it again.*

"You first." Lara poked him in the leg with a finger.

"Okay…from now on, I swear not to cross any more physical lines, and to respect your personal space and boundaries."

"No more sex," Lara declared.

When she did so, Owen felt himself color immediately and there was a small pang in his gut–disappointment? A physical response? He tried to mask it with a smile.

"Darn." He said, nudging her with his foot. "Kidding. You're right, of course. No more sex." *She's right,* he insisted to himself.

"Friends?" He said.

"Friends," Lara nodded in the affirmative.

A part of Owen knew that the elephant in the room remained. He knew it was there. The things that he and Lara had not been able to say–the unresolved conversation Monique had tried to trigger between them on that New Year's Eve.

"I think I know what you wanted to talk about," he found himself saying–almost in spite of himself. *What are you doing,* he scolded himself. *Well no turning back now.*

Lara looked at him with a curious expression on her face–like she was surprised he'd brought it up.

You and me both, Owen thought.

"It's just…we just would kill each other, you know, Lara?" Owen said.

It was true. He knew it. He watched his parents' love destroy them. He knew Lola Beth's love had abandoned her, had broken her, and forced her to rebuild. And he now knew, on top of all that, just how well he could hurt Lara whenever they got too close, whenever it was too intense and the feelings got too big and confusing to hold in.

"Ah, Owen. You're killing me already," Lara chuckled. She said it like it was a joke, but he could see something in the way she was sitting, the way her shoulders had turned away from him and her mouth had drawn into a line–an unsuccessful attempt at a smile. It all made his heart hurt just a little.

"We can focus on other things. Maybe we should travel the country, or something," he proposed. "Or make more art."

"Yes, sure. I like the idea of a travel buddy and the promise of more art." But she didn't offer any more suggestions after, she just got up and stretched, "Well, that's that then," she said, "I'm going to call Monique. We were thinking of going to the Polo Club later to play tennis."

Owen watched her go. He was grateful for the clear grace she had extended him, but he could tell already something had shifted. It made him nervous. But he pushed it out of his mind. *This can work,* he thought. *Things can be okay. We can move forward.*

Pre Chorus

Anticipation

If you cast a line into the ocean,
Drop the anchor through the waves,
A thousand hopes remain uncertain,
What becomes of all this yearning?
What to do with all this hurting?

40
Manila, 2010

In the third quarter of 2010, Lara graduated from her marketing leadership program and was given a new role as a Brand Manager of her own product unit.

After another long work day, Owen picked her up to find her in a terrible mood.

"What's wrong?" he asked as he drove them home through the sluggish Manila traffic.

She sighed. "So many things."

"Try me."

"I just hate the new product they've assigned me. It's one of those sachet things sold in sari-sari stores." Lara huffed, her brows knitted together as though this worried her. "It generates so much plastic waste. It doesn't belong in the future."

"Have you mentioned this to your boss?"

"Yeah, I spent my entire lunch hour formulating a proposal to move to bars that could be stored in paper packaging, but the others insisted it wouldn't sell. I mean, isn't that our job? Marketing? Educating to make it sell?" She groaned and rubbed her forehead with one hand.

Owen kind of loved how passionate she was about everything she did. She always gave a hundred and ten percent.

"Would it help if you and I made a full presentation about it together?" he said. "I've got lots of environmental data up my sleeve."

But Lara wasn't in the mood for solutions, clearly, because this just made her shake her head. "I don't know, Owen. I'm just tired. Let's change the subject."

"Okay." Owen switched on some music to fill the silence. "A Sentimental Mood" by John Coltrane. He remembered how, as a child, this music had always brought him up from his lowest of lows. He hoped it might help her, too.

And as though in answer to this, he felt Lara's mood seem to shift at the first measure. She smiled then and gazed out the window. Owen cast sideward glances at her, admiring the way the street lights flickered across her face as the car moved.

"I love John Coltrane," she said softly. "You know, I used to listen to his music on repeat while painting." She paused. "I actually can't remember the last time I did that."

"Feel like an artsy night in?" Owen proposed. "We can swing by the store to get some supplies."

Lara turned and smiled. "Let's do it."

***

When the pair got home with canvases in tow, they holed up in Lara's room and began to paint with Coltrane in the background.

Owen watched Lara with a sense of wonder. It had to have been one of his favorite things to do with her—working quietly, side-by-side–whether on the same thing or on their own projects. The look she got in her eye of utmost concentration, the little smile on her face like she was sharing a secret with herself.

They painted and created all night, only noticing how long they'd been awake when the first rays of sun streamed into Lara's room. Owen's work was abstract—red forms on a cream backdrop, both the color of blood, and a symbol of love. It was objectively bad. But his pride from that night was a song he had played around with on his guitar—full of bluesy chords and playful progressions, the lyrics of which he had not yet sung aloud.

> *It's hard, too hard to say,*
> *Can we still afford to make a brand new day?*

Lara's work was, to Owen's eye, transcendent. She had painted a woman seated—cerulean blue curved around her silhouette. Was she swimming, was she flying, was she sleeping?

"It's beautiful," Owen said, "I love the use of color. It's so dynamic."

"I like yours, too." Lara tilted her head at his work with a sort of sideway grin, teasing and sweet.

Owen laughed and together they said, "It's a metaphor." And it meant more things than one. *It's a metaphor,* as though this could cover the breadth of the things they weren't saying aloud.

***

After that, most nights when Lara would paint, Owen would join her. Even though he didn't want to be a painter, he enjoyed the atmosphere of creating together.

On one of their weekly calls, Lola Beth asked Owen what he and Lara were up to. When he mentioned painting, she laughed out loud.

"But you never were very good at that!" she exclaimed. "Have you found a hidden talent somewhere?"

Owen laughed. "No, I'm still terrible."

"So why do you do it? Just for fun?"

"Yeah. Besides, it's what Lara wants to do."

"I thought you wanted to make music together."

"I still do, but I don't think she wants that anymore."

"But she wants to paint?"

"Yes. So I don't mind. It's a good way to pass time together."

Lola Beth nodded knowingly, but said nothing. What sat under his words was a peek of the truth: it didn't matter what they were doing, as long as they were together. Owen didn't care what they spent their time on, it's simply that Lara was who he wanted to spend his time with. Even if he couldn't say so out loud.

41
Manila and Singapore, 2010

For Yaya Luz's fiftieth birthday, Lara wanted to go back to Singapore for a long weekend. And Owen thought that it would be a great opportunity for them to travel together and reconnect with Mike too.

"Would it be terrible if I ask if I can come along?" he said one afternoon as he and Lara sat together on the couch with jazz music in the background, and Lara's laptop was open on a flight booking page.

She turned to look at him as though this was a weird question, "You can go to Singapore whenever, I'm not your keeper."

These days, Lara was always one of two things–either her incredibly sweet, generous self, or this slightly sassier, cattier version that Owen felt he may never get fully used to. But he didn't feel he had much to bargain with. After all, he had, quite single-handedly, gotten them into their biggest mess yet, and if she needed days, months, or years to overcome that, well, he wouldn't stop her.

"I mean, would it be nice *if we went together?*" he said, placing careful emphasis on the last half of his question, but trying to sound as light and hopeful as possible so as to be more likely to receive a yes.

Lara seemed to consider this for a moment before finally saying, "Well, actually, Yaya Luz does love you." She smiled and that small chip on her shoulder slipped away a little. She went on, "And we could see Mike."

"Exactly," Owen replied, "You read my mind."

"You can stay at mine, I'm sure, I'll just let Mom know." Lara went on, "But make sure you buy Yaya Luz a gift."

Owen's heart soared just a little bit. It felt good to be planning to travel together again. It was like one more step back to all the things he loved about them together. Just two people… making music, traveling, climbing mountains…

"Of course I'll get her something," he said, "What might she like?"

***

So, a couple of weeks later, Lara and Owen arrived via taxi to Lara's parents house and both yelled, "SURPRISE!" at the door when Yaya Luz opened it wide.

Hugs, kisses, and gifts were exchanged. Owen had, in the end, purchased her a leather handbag, and Lara had gotten a matching wallet and put some Singaporean dollars in it.

For dinner that night, Yaya Luz was relegated to anywhere else in the house that was not the kitchen so that she could rest while Adora and Lara worked to whip up a nostalgic Filipino party meal of pancit palabok and chicken lollipops.

"Do you guys need any help here?" Owen asked, poking his head into the kitchen after the first hour that the girls had been holed up.

"Fry the chicken lollipops, maybe?" Adora gestured toward the tray of battered chicken pieces sitting on the counter.

Lara pointed at a pot with some oil in it over the stove, "Check if that's the right temperature and start dropping them in there," she recommended. "The recipe is on that paper next to the tray, I believe."

Owen got to work, picking up the now greasy piece of paper and reading across the steps.

As he worked, a song came to him and he began to shimmy in place, singing softly to the lyrics of Joni Mitchell's "Big Yellow Taxi." Out of the corner of his eye, he saw the two girls begin to sway along as well and within moments they had joined the chorus. Ladles in hand, singing into their spoons, into the room, into the ceiling.

Owen watched them, the music emanating from

somewhere deep inside of him, gleeful. It felt like family. Then he caught Lara's eye, and thought he saw something flicker, just the slightest change in disposition, a faltering smile, an unspoken word. He looked away, now a mixture of gratitude and grief.

He wanted to reach for her, dance her through the room, but he stayed in place, finishing his task as they finished the song. He knew the time for such affections had passed. He thought, in that brief moment where their eyes had grazed upon one another, he'd seen their new boundaries between them, fresh and strong, a wall, a warning even. Was it the beginning of the end?

***

The next day, Mike, Lara, and Owen decided to take a bumboat ride from the Changi Ferry Terminal—near the airport, to the nearby island of Pulau Ubin. Popular for its cycling paths and walks, it was a small escape from the urban jungle of the big city.

The group rented some bikes and went quietly through the trails, stopping here and there to spot a bird or a boar or a monitor lizard.

At midday, they stopped at an open-air seafood restaurant by the water for lunch.

Lara excused herself to the bathroom and Owen and Mike sat with the menus puzzling over what to order.

"How's it been, man?" Mike asked, pulling his water bottle out of his backpack and knocking back large gulps.

"Oh, good, you know," Owen said, still looking at the menu. Mike, of course, didn't know anything about his and Lara's disastrous New Year or the fight—at least, Owen hadn't mentioned anything. But perhaps the other friends might have told him about the outburst on New Year's Eve…and Owen had also stayed at Niko's…he suddenly became self-conscious over what Mike might know, and what judgments he might have. He pushed the thought away and pointed at a steamed dish that looked particularly appetizing.

Before Owen could say more though, Mike spoke up. "I heard some things."

Oh, here we go, Owen thought desperately wishing for

literally any other conversation but what he suspected might come.

"Heard you were staying at Niko's for a week or so?" Mike said, looking at Owen then sort of meaningfully, searchingly even.

Owen cleared his throat, "I did."

"And that there was a bit of drama at the New Year's Eve party..." Mike went on.

Jeez, does tsismis have to be the default? Owen was irritated but tried not to let it show. After all, Mike was one of his closest friends and it wasn't like he was overstepping by bringing these things up. A good friend would, of course, be concerned.

"Yes, Monique went a bit off her rocker," Owen said. "Wanted to call an intervention on Lara and I."

"I mean, go Monique," Mike replied, a sort of smile playing at the edges of his lips.

Owen narrowed his eyes at his friend. "You guys just all like the drama," he said, trying to keep his tone light. Don't be accusatory.

Mike, who Owen knew was too mature and too cool to bicker along, laughed a little at this. "No, we just want what's best for two of our most awesome friends. So, I'm guessing that the intervention got you and Lara talking and the results were not favorable, so you had to have some kind of cool-off period at Niko's?"

It would be an understatement to say that Owen was filled with relief to hear Mike's version of the events. *Ah, so this is what everyone thinks happened...*

Then Owen felt ashamed. Ashamed, because he knew that the truth was worse, and that he was lucky Lara wasn't telling everyone about it. He wasn't worthy.

"You could say that," Owen responded. "It definitely went south after the intervention and staying at Niko's was necessary. It was nice of him to help me out then."

"But things are okay now?" Mike said. "Like, so okay that you flew here with her again?"

Owen nodded silently.

"So, was it Lara who didn't want anything to do with you then? Sorry, I'm just curious. You guys are so close, seem so well-suited I really thought...I guess we all just assumed..."

"Well," Owen interrupted softly, "You assumed wrong."

Then Lara walked up and the conversation shifted and apart from an occasional look from Mike—a question, a wonderment, a confusion, the boys didn't bring it up anymore.

42
Manila, 2010

Lara, Bianca and Monique had begun to make a habit of weekend tennis afternoons at the country club. They would play doubles with a trainer–alternating the pairs to make for fair games.

On one such afternoon, the girls finished a particularly sweaty session and headed to the open air lounge to order refreshing mango shakes and sit by the pool.

Lara had been thinking, more and more recently, about her next steps. With work being as uninspiring as it was, she had begun to wonder if it was time for a change. *But what sort of change?*

As if reading Lara's mind, Monique propped her feet up on a nearby chair and took a sip of her fruit shake before addressing the table with a question.

"Any fun plans for you guys over the coming months?" she asked.

Monique worked at a local gallery. Her job required odd hours, usually managing particular exhibits, visiting artists, wining and dining with collectors, but it was incredibly flexible, and as a result, she and Mateo–who worked for the family business–often had extravagant travel plans peppered throughout the year.

"Hmm." Bianca took a sip of her own drink, thoughtfully gazing out at the pool, then went on, "Work, work, work. And maybe a week or two at the beaches to go surfing. Zambales. La Union."

"Nice," Lara said, "No plans on my end yet. Just Christmas in Singapore with my family."

"And Owen?" Bianca asked, at which Monique threw her

a dirty look.

Lara caught it but just let it slide. She shook her head. "Actually," she said, "no. Just me this time. He did ask what I was doing, and I think he would have liked to plan something together, but I think I want to just be with my family this year."

Monique and Bianca both nodded as though affirming Lara in her decision. She was glad for that, too, because when Owen had asked, it had almost made her feel guilty not to invite him along. But…it felt important at the same time. Important to her to just be by herself with her family for a change.

"Also," Lara added, "I've been thinking of leaving Manila."

Monique and Bianca shared a quick glance—which was not lost on Lara, before they turned to her.

"So soon?" Monique said.

"No, no. No." Lara laughed then, "No. Not so abrupt as that. Not before year-end. Just…think I'll start planning ahead from now on. Not sure yet, though."

"What would you do?" Bianca asked.

"Maybe go back to school?" Lara had thought about it more than once and it kept occurring to her again and again. She had done the safe thing before—taking the Communications degree. She was years into her corporate career now. She felt she had perhaps earned, at last, the privilege of studying something within her true passions. Art? Art History? Perhaps, finally, the realization of a dream was in the near future?

"An MBA?" Bianca guessed.

"No, actually, maybe something in Fine Arts."

Monique and Bianca whistled together in approval.

"I like it," Monique enthused. "Maybe show us what you've been working on lately. I'd love to see. Imagine, one day, hosting your work in my gallery." Monique said this with a dreamy tone in her voice, and Lara felt grateful just then to have good girl friends.

"And you and Mateo?" Lara said, changing the subject for the moment.

"Well," Monique said, rubbing her hands together, looking mischievous and excited at the same time, a sneaky smile playing on her lips. Her gaze lay steadily on the pool now and when Lara followed it she realized her friend was watching a young family splash about.

"Are you…" she trailed off, looking directly at Monique with a demanding question in her eyes.

"No, not yet. I'm not pregnant yet," Monique replied quickly, "But, we're going to stay put this summer and start trying." The smile on her face was huge and hopeful, and Bianca and Lara both blushed and grinned with an overwhelming happiness for their friend.

"That, my friends, deserves a toast," Lara raised her tall glass—filled with crushed ice and fresh mango, and they all clinked their drinks together, smiling.

***

"You should totally do it," Adora was saying for only the tenth time.

She and Lara were on one of their weekly video calls—a loosely held tradition that had become more and more regular as of late. The last year had been a rough one for Lara, and leaning on her girl friends and sister was one of the highlights of the past several months. She had just told Adora about her thoughts on going back to school, and Adora was, as usual, her encouraging self.

"It's just been such a hard year, you know, with how things went down with Owen, and work being what it is," Lara said. She knew she didn't have to rationalize anything to Adora, in fact, she knew she was doing more work convincing herself than anyone else.

"Girl, don't even, you don't have to explain anything to me," Adora replied, waving her sister off, "I think it's awesome. And if you go to Paris or New York, you can be damn sure I'm visiting you, like, *all the time.*"

Lara chuckled.

Just then, there was a knock at her door.

"One sec," Lara turned away from her computer and called back, "Yes?"

Owen must have just gotten home from work, she guessed. He poked his head in just then and waved. Adora, spotting him through the camera, waved too.

"Hey, look," he said, still standing in the doorway, not daring to encroach on Lara's space uninvited. Things had, indeed, changed quite a bit since the new year. He waved his external hard drive in the air, "I managed to get a download of *In the Mood for Love*. I thought we could watch it. I've never seen it, and I know it's a classic."

Things may have changed, but Owen still knew how to get Lara's attention. *An evening of Wong Kar-wai? Say no more.*

Lara nodded, "Sure, I'll come to the living room and we can order in pizza and watch it over dinner. It's really good. Can you make the order while I finish up this call?"

Owen nodded and waved once more at Adora to say bye.

When he had gone, Lara turned back to her screen and caught Adora rolling her eyes as she said, "It'll never not be weird. But you know, I guess you guys are legit best friends now, so at least that."

Lara laughed and replied, "Well, if I move out, then I guess it'll stop being weird then."

"Hmm. Yeah, I guess that's true." Adora agreed. "Okay, go watch your movie. I'll catch you later."

"No, you still need to give me the full update about your promotion and the new boy in your life," Lara said.

"Okay, okay," Adora said, and the girls spoke for another half hour.

Afterward, Lara joined Owen out on the couch and realized, with a certain sense of triumph, that it felt good not to be eagerly putting things down to be with him. It felt nice not to be putting him first anymore. It felt…right.

43

Singapore and Tokyo, 2010

Lara, Adora, and their parents sat around the living room on Christmas Eve–a Kenny G album playing in the background, and a delicious spread of charcuterie and kakanin prepared by Yaya Luz before them.

"This is nice," Aurora commented, "Just us four for Christmas. Something a little more subdued."

All four of them exchanged smiles of agreement.

Then Adora rubbed her hands together, "Shall we exchange gifts?"

"Ah, as good a time as any!" Lewis declared, patting his hands on his knees and standing up. He reached under the Christmas tree near the corner of his couch and picked up a stack of gifts.

He grinned. "To the women in my life," he said, handing them out.

The Halford women opened their presents simultaneously– discovering in each beautifully wrapped package a long, flat, rectangular case. Jewelry.

The piece Lara got was perfect for her–a vintage golden tennis bracelet filled with aquamarine stones. "Aw, thanks, Dad," she said, getting up to hug her father.

Everyone began handing out what they'd gotten for each other. Lara had decided that that would be the year of making things and had painted a watercolor scene for each family member, then framed them with a signed dedication on the back.

Lewis and Aurora fawned over each of theirs–for her father, the Bodleian at Oxford; for her mother, the facade of the

Rodriguez ancestral home in Bacolod.

Adora's was a painting of the sisters as children–based loosely on a photo of them on the beach.

"You've gotten so good!" Adora enthused, reaching over and pulling her sister in for a hug. "This is priceless. I hope mine can compete," she said with a cheeky wink as she handed Lara an envelope.

When Lara opened it, she found a card and a piece of paper. She folded it out and saw, to her absolute shock, two tickets to Tokyo for the coming New Year.

"What?" She exclaimed.

"You seemed like you needed a break. And you got that big promotion. And, honestly, you need a girls trip."

Lara reached over and hugged her sister–perhaps like she had never done before. It was possibly the most thoughtful gift anyone had ever given her.

"I know the last year's been a lot," Adora whispered as they held one another, "I just wanted some us time."

"Totally," Lara whispered back, and her heart filled with warmth and cheer. The perfect way to end the year.

***

Lara and Adora had actually never traveled just the two of them without the buffer of family, so it was a real thrill to do something totally new together.

"I am so excited," Lara admitted as the girls found their counter and presented their passports.

The woman behind the desk tapped away on her computer and then handed the girls their boarding passes.

Lara checked their boarding passes, and noted, "Wait, is this a middle seat?" she asked, pointing at hers.

The woman nodded. "Yes, it is a middle seat. It's a full flight. These were the only ones next to each other I could give you."

The girls thanked her and walked away. "Boo to middle seats," Lara said.

"Ugh, seriously," Adora empathized, "I'd switch, but you

know how claustrophobic I can get. The window makes a big difference for me."

Lara shrugged. "Don't worry about it." She wouldn't let such a small thing ruin a great start to the trip. She gave her sister another side hug and said, "I'm just glad we get this time together. No questions about who gets the Best Sister Award for this year."

Adora squeezed Lara back and gave a small laugh.

As the girls made their way to their gate, Lara–from a distance, saw a young man in a black suit helping an old lady lift her bag onto a chair. He had tousled dark hair, and she could just make out a strong profile, and soft eyes.

Cute guy, she thought, but then Adora pulled her toward a seat nearby and she lost sight of him

"Aw, snap," she said.

"What?"

She laughed at herself. "I thought I spotted someone cute."

Adora looked up eagerly. "Where?"

"Well, we've lost him now." Lara shrugged, settling into her chair and opening up the book she'd picked up on the way out of Singapore, which was *On Love* by Alain de Botton.

Adora nudged Lara and jutted her chin towards some seats across from them just a few rows away. "Is that Cute Guy?"

Lara looked over the shoulders of those in front of them and indeed spied Cute Guy, sitting near their gate, on the phone.

She smiled and said, "Yes."

From this vantage point she could see him better. He wore a white dress shirt, crisp and tailored, under a black sport jacket, with slacks. His golden olive skin, and the curl in his hair made Lara think, *Greek God but also Superman.*

Adora smiled approvingly. "I can dig it."

The girls giggled privately then turned back to their books and waited to board.

When it was their turn, they walked down the aisle with their things. As they neared their row, they noticed someone already seated in the aisle. Lara looked up at the number and down at the passenger, and realized with a start it was Cute Guy.

What are the odds! she thought as Adora reached over and pinched her in the arm.

Cute Guy turned to them and smiled—a sweet, close-lipped smile. "Sorry, can we get past?" Lara asked.

He stood immediately and stepped into the aisle. "Of course! Can I help with any bags?"

The girls shook their heads and squeezed into their seats.

Cute Guy then sat on his own and buckled in. Once everyone was settled, Lara pulled a notebook out from her bag. It was one of the free Moleskines Mike always had lying around—a green leather bound book with the name of his former consulting firm embossed on the front.

"Hey!" Cute Guy said, fishing in his bag and pulling out an identical notebook. "Fellow consultant?" he asked, flashing his.

Lara startled, then laughed—partly because it was so unlike her to be a consultant, but also because of the incredible coincidence. "God, no. Definitely not. My friend is. He brought home free swag all the time and gave them out to us plebs."

"Oh, small world." Cute Guy put his own back in his bag. "I'm Andres," he said. He had a low, formal voice, and a British accent. When he said his name, he smiled, his eyes crinkling at the sides.

Lara tucked her notebook onto her lap. "I'm Lara."

"And I'm Adora," her sister piped up.

"What brings you guys to Tokyo?" Andres asked.

"Girls' trip," Adora supplied.

Lara nodded, "A sister trip for the holidays. You?"

"How lovely! I'm also on a bit of an Asian vacation. First Bangkok, then Singapore, then Tokyo. I was traveling with one group in Bangkok and Singapore, and now I'm meeting another in Tokyo."

"Oh, and are you based in the region?"

"No, actually, I started off in London a few years back, and have spent the last six months in a new role in Boston. Certified expat life, or some such."

"Oh! How funny, that's where I went to university," Lara exclaimed.

"Small world!" Andres said for the second time.

"It really is. What is your impression of Asia so far? Is it your first time here?"

"No, I have to travel to both Tokyo and Singapore a couple of times a year for work," he answered and then he gave both girls a conspiratorial wink, "I really don't mind. The food here is spectacular. What about you? Are you from around here?"

"Sort of."

"We're from everywhere," Adora piped up.

"Our mom is Filipino, our dad is British-Singaporean."

Andres smiled proudly. "Ah, we're cut from the same cloth, then! Sort of. My Dad is British, and Mum is Argentinian."

"Would you look at that!" Adora beamed. She reached under Lara's arm and pinched her again. Lara pretended not to notice.

"Don't consultants usually fly business?" Lara asked Andres.

"For work, certainly, but seems rather frivolous for a short flight on a vacation. It's probably bad for the environment."

"How virtuous of you."

"We all try, don't we?"

"Sure," Lara said. "So who are you meeting up with for this leg of your trip?"

"Colleagues, actually. Well, colleagues who've become friends."

"So is it work-related still, or is it all fun?"

"Well…I'd be lying if I said that it's all fun, though I certainly hope it is plenty of that too. But," he paused and looked around as though about to tell her a secret, "To be honest, I'm trying to position myself for a promotion and a move to our New York office. I haven't quite started the process, but the colleague-turned-friend I'm meeting here is rather high up and cozy with the Partners, and he promised to give me some mentoring while I'm in town."

His admission made Lara laugh, and it wasn't lost on her that he had mentioned New York—wasn't that on her list too?

"Your ulterior motives are safe with me," she said. "And I don't blame you. Not into Boston?"

"No, I like Boston fine. But New York has the kind of energy I'm looking for at this stage in my life. Plus, in London

I was far more accustomed to working with a lot of financial clients, and I think my skills and experience better suit a role in Manhattan–with the same sort of clientele."

"I get it. I'm angling for a change of scenery too, and New York is on the short list. Maybe our paths will cross once more in the near future." *Hmm, am I flirting?* She felt a sudden thrill accompanied with a small side of panic.

The drinks cart came and the pair each ordered white wine. Adora, who professed she was tired and wanted a snooze, slipped her eye mask on and turned toward the window.

Andres held his drink up. "Cheers to you, and the holidays, and the possibility of our paths crossing once more."

"And to your ulterior motives," Lara teased.

The two met gazes and clinked glasses.

Over the seven and a half hour flight, Lara surprised herself. Not only did the pair stay awake, they talked the entire way, too. Andres was interesting, but also interested——asking thoughtful questions, and listening well.

They traded stories about the adventures they had been on. Lara highlighted her Mt. Pulag climb, and Andres recounted a riveting tale of a trip in the Andes. When he mentioned his love of music, they each let the other listen in on a favorite playlist. Andres liked the Red Hot Chili Peppers and John Mayer. Lara let him hear her mix featuring Bon Iver and Vampire Weekend. Where their tastes truly intercepted, though, was in jazz, and they sat listening to Tony Williams together as Andres pointed out key moments in one explosive, dynamic drum solo on a Miles Davis collaboration.

Lara was intrigued and almost felt sad they were hitting it off so well. After that flight, they would part ways, and there would be an ocean between them.

Ah, well, she thought, *it's still a nice story, isn't it? Met a guy on a plane. Had a nice time. A good story.*

By the time the captain called the landing announcement, Andres found it in himself to ask Lara for her contact details.

"In case you have time while you're in Tokyo and want to hang out," he said, saving them to his phone as he put his coat back on, "And if you don't then let it be of some use in case we're on the same continent again."

As Lara and Adora waved Andres off, Adora pinched Lara's arm again. "Did you give him your number?" she hissed.

"Yeah, but that's a no-go." Lara laughed, pinching Adora back. "He'll be an ocean away."

"But he's in Tokyo right now," Adora said, rolling her eyes. "I think you guys were totally into each other."

Lara turned to look at her sister to see if she was teasing, but her face was totally straight. In fact, her brows were arched in that exact way she did any time she felt she knew she was right. The expression took Lara all the way back to their childhood and the endless arguments that Adora never backed down from. Somehow, it made Lara giggle.

"What?" Adora said, one of her eyebrows shooting up even more dramatically.

Oh, that did it. Lara doubled over with laughter.

"Whatever, Lara, you have totally lost it." Adora waved her hand dismissively. "Mark my words," she went on, "He's going to text you before tomorrow's over."

***

Adora had been right. Andres indeed sent a message by the next morning.

Lara wasn't annoyed that Adora had been right. No, Lara was annoyed that Adora had been right and then decided that it would be hilarious to schedule a massage at the hotel for the exact time Lara had agreed to meet up with Andres.

Lara sat at the small udon place near Roppongi, tapping her foot and watching the customers receiving their orders—large, steaming bowls of springy, thick noodles. She was very early, partly because she was rather nervous, but also because she had underestimated her own ability to navigate the train system.

Just then, the door to the little restaurant opened and in walked Andres in a gray wool coat, a Burberry scarf around his neck.

At the sight of Lara, he waved and quickly grabbed a seat across. "Hi, apologies. Am I late?" he asked, turning to check his watch.

He wasn't.

"No. I'm just early."

"Oh good. This is one of my favorite places to eat here," Andres said, putting his scarf aside and smiling, "It's near my office."

"That makes sense. I did think the area was rather corporate."

"It doesn't negatively impact the food, I promise."

"Oh, I didn't think so," Lara assured him, "In fact, wouldn't it be even better—given the working crowd?"

"I suppose the demand would be high, as would expectations. The Japanese are serious about their food."

Andres helped Lara order, and together they ended up with a bowl of tempura udon, and a cold version with a dipping sauce.

While waiting for the food to arrive, Lara was surprised at how much more the two could find to chat about. Part of her own hesitation to come alone had been the idea that they'd already had that seven hour journey to cover a wide array of topics. Who was this stranger that she was now going to spend yet another few hours with? And what if that lovely connection they'd had on the flight had just been that—a sort of vacuum? A contained occurrence? Like a scene from a movie, and not from real life?

But her anxieties had been for naught. Andres was still just as interesting that day as he had been on the plane.

They exchanged stories about politics, New York, Boston, London, books and art. They spoke about the theater, and they talked about music again, and again. As they ate through their dishes, the conversation flowed.

"I can't say I have any favorites, really," Andres said when Lara asked if there was a specific artist or genre he really identified with. "I think all music has its merit."

"Even serialist music?" Lara said, a teasing tone in her voice—because who on earth likes serialism?

"Even that post-tonal rubbish has its reasons," Andres replied, and for a brief, surprising moment Lara felt an in explicable surge of attraction.

Feeling rather overwhelmed with this totally uninvited sensation coming over her, Lara decided to change the subject.

"So what does the rest of your trip look like?" she asked as she worked her way slowly through her bowl.

"Not too busy. I'll be sightseeing with my friend–"

"The one who'll be mentoring you?"

Andres gave a hearty laugh. "Yes that one. Then we'll probably go out for drinks and meet a larger group for a New Year's Eve party tomorrow. Perhaps you and Adora would like to join for that?" He paused and took another bite, then added, "Where is Adora?"

"She had a massage she couldn't rebook," Lara answered. She thought briefly about cursing Adora in her mind, but she felt so at ease, not at all stressed or self-conscious, and she realized Adora had been right about a lot of things. Lara did need a break. It had been a year. This was nice. This was necessary. This was good.

"Ah, shame."

"Seriously, she's missing all this good stuff," Lara said, slurping up a bite of noodles and grinning with genuine satisfaction.

After their meal, Andres paid, and walked Lara out of the restaurant. "I'd have loved to stay and chat longer, or even invite you along with my friend, but…" he trailed off.

Lara shook her head, "No, don't worry about me at all! Adora and I have our own list of things to get through." She had had zero expectations of spending even more time with Andres, and was frankly just glad for the respite from her life in Manila–from Owen, from work, from…everything. Tokyo, Adora, heck even Andres, they were all part of the remarkable, escapist holiday unfolding before her.

Andres nodded and reached over and gave Lara a friendly hug as he said, "Well, I'll be in touch about the party tomorrow anyway. Hope to catch you again."

And then the two parted ways.

44
Tokyo, 2010-2011

For New Year's Eve, Lara wanted to return Adora's favor somewhat, and reserved a fancy kaiseki experience at a Michelin-starred place called Komuro. By some miracle, she had been able to book a table, and so the girls found themselves that evening in the cream, wooded, minimalist interiors of the storied establishment.

"You didn't have to do this," Adora gushed–though her face said slightly otherwise. She was obviously pleased at the gift of indulging in Japanese haute cuisine.

"I know," Lara said with a playful nudge, "But I wanted to treat my best sister to something special."

The girls sat down at their spot on the bar.

"So, you didn't get too much into it yesterday, but how was the meet up with Andres?" Adora asked.

Lara had indeed skirted the topic a little, choosing to focus more on how Adora's massage had gone, and what they might want to do–even indulging Adora's every window shopping whim.

"It was fine, the udon was delicious," Lara said vaguely. She didn't know why she was withholding about Andres. There was just something so deliciously mysterious and exciting about him–this beautiful creature she had met on a plane. This unbelievably cinematic encounter. It all felt unreal. Like a dream. And perhaps it was that notion of a dream being a wish and a wish being sacred and not something to be spoken of for fear of it never coming true...*Or something like that,* Lara thought.

"You've said that already," Adora replied exasperatedly.

Just then they were served some plum wine in a beautiful, dainty glass. The clear, almost syrupy liquor glistened and smelled of fruit and flowers.

The girls took their drinks in one go, and Lara turned to Adora once more and said, almost cheekily, "Yeah well there really wasn't much else. Do you want me to record all my future conversations with men to play them back for you?"

Adora rolled her eyes and laughed, shaking her head. "Fine, whatever. Rain on a girl's parade, why don't you? He is cute. You should allow yourself this bit of fun, Lar."

Her sister was right of course. Lara knew that. But she had grown so used to the chaotic weather patterns of her relationship with Owen that the prospect of a fun fling seemed remote and maybe even scary.

"Didn't you say he'd send you details for some party tonight?" Adora went on.

"Yeah, he did." Lara pulled out her phone and opened up the last message from Andres, showing it to Adora.

It was an address for a party at some snazzy penthouse. *Open bar*, it stated.

"Ooh," Adora said with a whistle. "We should go."

"Maybe," Lara replied and turned to focus on their food.

By the time their last course had been had, Lara and Adora were both tipsy–and they couldn't tell if it was because of the occasional alcohol they had consumed across the meal, or if that tingly, heady feeling was thanks to the special, foreign, delicate, romantic otherworldliness the entire kaiseki experience had been.

As they stumbled out of the restaurant, leaning on each other and giggling a little, Lara's phone went off.

Answering it without looking, she said loudly, "Hello?"

"Lara? Are you alright?" A formal, British voice sounded from the other side.

"Who's this?"

"It's Andres."

"Oh!" Lara smiled and Adora squeezed her in the arm.

"Are you coming tonight? Just doing the final headcount with my friends–I'm here early and helping with a bit of set up, it won't be very many people, I don't think–" he was saying, then there was a pause and Lara overheard someone speaking in another language in the background, and then more garbled English, "one moment–okay–all right now, I'm back. Anyway, it looks to be around fifteen of my mate's friends, and some of their plus ones. Do come and bring Adora. There will be drinks and dancing and good music."

Adora was pulling Lara's arm now incessantly mouthing, "Let's-go-let's-go."

Lara rolled her eyes then finally conceded, "Okay, we'll be there soon. We just finished dinner."

"Fabulous! See you soon, then."

Then the line went dead.

***

Lara deduced, upon arrival at the party, that it was being hosted by the friend-colleague Andres had referenced who was clearly high-up, and obviously loaded. Because a penthouse like that in Tokyo must have cost a fortune.

The owner of the place, a tall Japanese man in a tailored gray suit, had opened the door to Lara and Adora and seemed immediately to know who they were. "Hello, you must be Lara and Adora, welcome! Come inside, please. I'm Sōta."

He let the girls in and led them to the large living room with its floor to ceiling windows, kitchen island, and a dance floor cleared in the middle. The space was stunning. Everywhere Lara looked there was glass and wood and steel juxtaposed against designer furniture in a mixture of Asian and mid century modern styles.

"Thank you for having us, you have such a beautiful home," Lara said graciously, handing Sōta the Californian merlot they had picked up on the way. It suddenly seemed a very understated gift, especially as she gazed at the exposed bar with what appeared to be a shelf full of Japanese whiskeys.

But Sōta took the bottle with gratitude, bowed very slightly, and smiled wide. "Arigatou gozaimasu–thank you very much. Please, make yourselves at home. Can I get you anything?"

Adora, who really didn't have much shame in anything at all, immediately answered, "Oh thanks very much, if you have a Japanese whisky you would heartily recommend, I'll take that."

"I have just the one. I've been serving it all evening so

far and it is the hit of the night, I think," Sōta said, and then he turned to Lara. "And same for you?"

"Yes, whatever is easiest," Lara said with a smile.

Sōta walked off to the bar and the girls then turned to survey the room and the company. There were around ten other people there already–a few dancing, and some lounging on chairs or by the windows to admire the view. Just then, Andres materialized from one of the clusters. When he saw Lara and Adora, he immediately made a beeline for them. In his brown tweed suit he looked every bit the British aristocrat and in only the best of ways.

Lara felt her fingertips tingle and she blushed.

"Lara, Adora! So lovely to see you both again." Andres gave the girls kisses on their cheeks.

Sōta returned just then with drinks and they bowed to him as they took them.

"Good choice." Andres raised his own glass. "Kampai!"

It was in this convivial atmosphere, with the assistance of booze, and that feeling of being suspended in time–in that bizarre vacation dimension, that Lara found herself dancing with Andres all night. It had been so long since she had last done that with anyone but Owen that it all felt new and odd on her skin. A prickly, uncertain feeling, but also bold and exciting.

Unlike with Owen, whom she always found herself inadvertently entangled with or in, Andres was not dancing too close to her that evening. There was nothing overly intimate about how he moved, but he was open, and she was open, and the music was free, and they were dancing. Just dancing.

Just after midnight, she spied Adora in a corner with one of the other guests, playing a spirited game of chess. The other woman was getting worked up, throwing her arms in the air, and Adora was laughing in a way that Lara guessed was likely inappropriate or out of context. Lara realized perhaps it was time to go.

Regretfully, she pried herself away from the dance floor and further from Andres. "Sorry, but I think it's time for me to go. This was so fun," Lara said, squeezing Andres in the arm.

He smiled at her, and–unprompted, she noted her mind wandering to a rather involved image of how it might be to kiss those lips. Shaking off the thought, she gave him a peck on the cheek instead.

"Thank you for coming. We must keep in touch," Andres said, an insistence and kindness in his voice.

"Will you be in this region again in the coming year?"

"Of course," Andres called out over the music as the bass dropped in what Lara identified as a Skrillex song. "For work, for sure."

"Perfect, message me when you're in Singapore. Maybe we'll see each other there. And, otherwise, there's always stalking each other on social media," Lara said, feeling a little thrill go through her at how flirty she knew she was being.

Andres nodded and gave Lara one last half hug. Then Lara made her way out of the party. She first bade goodbye to Sōta (whom she by now called Sōta-san, like most of the other younger friends in the room), and extricated herself and her sister from the apartment.

***

"I think he likes you," Adora pointed out as the girls settled into bed for the night–back at their hotel, "Andres, I mean."

"Ah, we barely know each other," Lara said, waving her off. "And we don't even live on the same continent. But he was nice."

"And cute. And you don't live close to one another right now, but that could change. You both said it yourselves on the plane. Both in search of a change of scenery. Imagine if one day you both end up in New York?"

This possibility had not been lost on Lara at all, and she tried not to think too much of it. Instead she said, "He is cute. Yes. Cute Guy."

"Totally," Adora said, turning on her side to face Lara and give her a cheeky grin. "You suit each other. Cute, kind of serious, kind of cerebral, and whatnot. You know. Also, I totally noticed that you ignored everything I said about New York."

Lara laughed then and turned out the master switch. The room went dark. "Good night, Adora."

"Good night, sis."

And they fell into a much needed slumber.

45
Manila, 2011

"So how was your Tokyo trip?" Owen asked.

He, Lara, Monique, and Mateo were seated around the young married couple's newly delivered dining table—a live-edge masterpiece from Bali that they had matched with beautiful Kenneth Cobonpue chairs.

Monique wanted guests over to serve tapas and pintxos and inaugurate this work of art—as she called the set of furniture. She wasn't wrong—Owen had to admit that much.

Platters of Iberico cheese, hams, chorizos, grilled pulpo, breads, and aiolis were laid out in the middle of the seated pairs, and a jug of sangria stood already half-empty at one end of the table.

"It was great," Lara answered as she served herself some pulpo.

"Just that?" Monique pressed, poking Lara in the side, "Tell us more about Cute Guy."

"Cute Guy?" Owen turned and looked between both women, his heart beginning to race. *Stop it,* he thought, a little annoyed at himself. But that only seemed to add to the anxiety and he noticed his palms were a little sweaty.

"Yeah, Lara's drunken New Year's Eve text mentioned meeting a cute guy on the plane. You didn't even give me his name, girl," Monique said playfully, taking a large bite of fried manchego.

"Andres," Lara said easily.

Drunken New Year's text? Owen hadn't received one. He had received a sweet, short message on the day itself, but not the night before…

And Andres?

"Yeah, he was really nice," Lara went on casually.

"Ooh, exciting," Mateo piped up.

Something stirred in Owen.

"And you met on a plane. How cute," Monique gushed.

Annoyance, Owen realized. That was what had been stirring in him. No, perhaps jealousy. *No, annoyance, Owen thought firmly to himself. Annoyance at…Monique. For making this sound like big news, or something. It's just a guy, for god's sake.*

Lara seemed to blush at this and that only served to frazzle Owen more.

Discreetly, he slipped his phone out and checked Lara's social media profile. Immediately, he saw that she had befriended someone new just days before–*Andres Courtenay*, read his name. He put his phone back in his pocket and bookmarked that for later.

Unsure of what he could add to the conversation, he tried to tune out Lara's stories of this supposedly wonderful man–British, half something as well, smart, worked at the same consulting firm as Mike once had…

The snippets were small and insignificant, but Owen felt intimidated at the thought anyway. It had been exactly a year since the debacle with Lara. One year of maintaining their boundaries. One year of living together, but also being more apart than they ever had been before.

Suddenly, Owen was filled with a sadness that made him feel oppressively lonely even as he was surrounded by friends.

He stood abruptly and made for the bathroom, mumbling something he knew was incoherent as he went.

"What's with him?" He overheard Mateo ask.

"Jealous, obviously," came Monique's answer–in a tone and at a decibel she clearly was not even trying to disguise.

Owen stepped into the bathroom and looked at his phone again. There, he saw the face of a smiling, charming young man–coiffed dark hair, warm, lightly tanned skin. On the few public images on his profile he saw a young man with varied interests: There he was playing the drums, rowing for his college at Oxford, partying with friends in a club. Buried amongst some of these photographs, he found a recent one–tagged just from the week before. It was a large group picture from a party in a swanky apartment, and there was Andres Courtenay, standing next to Lara and a tall Japanese man. In the further corner of the picture was Adora, Lara's sister. Everyone was smiling with drinks in hand.

46
Manila, 2011

For Owen's birthday, all he wanted to do was stay in and do a movie marathon with Lara. Still ever obliging, a trait that Adora insisted Lara should reconsider, Lara found herself cuddled up on the couch with Owen that night, close, but not *so close.* Intimate, but not over any lines.

Owen draped his arm around Lara. "I like this. I feel like we haven't been able to do a lot of this kind of thing in a while."

"We're always on this couch, working side by side, or watching movies," Lara protested.

"But just us, you know. And like, close, like old times."

Lara didn't like where this was headed. She hadn't quite gotten over all the conflict and confusion with Owen, and she wasn't convinced Old Times were times to return to, really.

"I guess," she said after a moment.

"What?" Owen asked, he seemed confused as to why she wasn't responding perhaps in the way he had expected her to.

What does he want me to do? Lean into him? Fawn over him? We'd kill each other, that's what he said. Well. Pretty sure the Old Times are dead now indeed.

Lara nursed these uncharitable thoughts, trying to reconcile them with how life with Owen continued to be this comfortable, predictable, easy thing.

"Nothing," she said, "Just...this isn't really like Old Times is it? The old times are long gone."

Owen was quiet for a moment. Then he said, "I don't get it. You seem so moody and distant half the time. Am I missing something? We're honoring our boundaries. We're being good friends. I don't know what else you want from me, Lara." Owen looked genuinely confused.

"Nothing, Owen. I'm not asking you for anything," Lara insisted. Then suddenly she realized that this was true. She didn't want anything at all from Owen anymore. A sudden lightness came over her. It was good, and red-hot, and confusing. There was anger, and disappointment, and relief. Just over a year since they had set those boundaries, she finally felt like she was looking ahead. Truly.

She took a deep breath then and leaned into Owen, "Nothing at all. This is fine exactly as it is. Happy Birthday, brosky."

***

"These are magical," Monique said, standing in the middle of Lara's room, turning around and around as she looked from painting to painting, each mounted on wood board and propped up against furniture and walls and surfaces in a circle.

These were the fruits of Lara's labor. She had begun several in the latter half of the year before and completed them in an inspired fit after the New Year. Her latest collection: pinprick scenes in a mix of gouache and acrylic of the Philippines covering an area no bigger than her thumb. Owen had seen a few, but even from him she kept much of the work quiet. Part of her wanted something just for herself—free from even Owen's gaze.

Lara watched Monique observing. Her eyes went from one to the next. She used square sheets of varying sizes, washing them in a gradient of color, then in the center composing her intricate scapes.

The sunset on Manila Bay, with all its color and wonder.

The Fort Santiago gate, with all its texture and shadow. Owen.

The summit of Mt. Pulag, with its sea of clouds and sunrise.

The ocean, a meeting of sky and water.

Chinatown, with its red arches.

A pedicab.

An old man selling taho.

An underground river.

And, still, Owen. Most of her reference photos included him, and she struggled to paint him out. So he remained—as vague blots indicating a form, a person, a soul.

"Oh my god, Lara, thanks so much for finally showing me these," Monique said, her face a picture of awe and pride.

"So…like I'd mentioned a few months ago…I am indeed thinking of applying to a few programs. The deadlines are all next week." Lara sat on her bed and concentrated her gaze on her favorite of the lot—the one of Mt. Pulag. It reminded her of a time of hope. Nostalgic and a little sad, but also sweet and promising.

"What, that's awesome!" Monique enthused, plopping down next to her. "Where?"

"New York, Boston, Chicago, and Paris." Lara had researched over the past few months and this seemed the best natural exit from her job. She had done her time in corporate, and after this Masters, she could work anywhere—or in a museum, or could double down on her art and make a living off her paintings. The possibilities now felt endless. It was time.

"Fancy." Monique nudged Lara and threw one arm around her shoulder. "I think you'll do great."

Lara smiled. "Thanks. I wanted to show you because I needed fresh eyes. Is it good enough, you think?"

"They're good, and you know it."

Lara nodded, grinning ear to ear. "Okay. Thank you."

"What does Owen think?"

"I haven't mentioned it," Lara answered, standing up.

"Wait, what?" Monique stood up after her. "You kept something from Owen?"

Lara felt a kernel of irritation. "He's not my keeper. I don't have to tell him everything."

Monique gasped then reached over and held Lara by the shoulders. "You've finally walked off the boat. Like, completely. I had an inkling already, I mean…with the way you were at dinner a couple of weeks ago, I definitely thought…" she trailed off, seemingly out of words.

Lara had to laugh then. "Yeah. Boat's long gone now, I

think.”

***

Two months later, Lara got the news that she had been accepted into the art programs in Paris and New York. To her surprise and delight, however, the New York one came with a special scholarship. A full ride.

The programs were well-known but because the New York one in particular would be free, she began to feel like the choice was a no-brainer. Armed with the last few years of work experience, free admission to a stellar program, and a growing portfolio, Lara felt ready for the conversation that would come up with her parents soon. She just had to tell Owen, too.

***

A couple of evenings after the news came in, Lara and Owen sat in their dining room working separately, quietly. She had not mentioned anything. It felt awkward to bring it up. There was something almost space-bound about their relationship. She wondered what would happen if she moved away. Owen and Lara were a storm, and the eye was wherever they were together. Physically apart, would the storm cease? Did she want it to?

“You’ve been quiet the last few days,” Owen teased.

“Yeah. A lot is going on.” Lara looked at Owen and tried to picture what his life would be like without her. Would he be lonely? Would he miss her? Her heart, as usual, softened at the thought. They had many memories—so many of them good that they almost consumed the bad. Although she had been purposely taking more time for herself–away from him, he was still her best friend. Perhaps he always would be.

“I gave my notice, Owen,” she said.

Owen’s face grew white. “Wait. What?”

“Yeah, yesterday. I’m moving to New York.”

He coughed. “That’s huge. Why didn’t you tell me about this?”

“I wanted to make a choice for myself, without hearing what you’d have to say about it. ”

216

"What's that supposed to mean?"

"Oh, you know, Owen. You always have so much to say. Judgments. Feedback. Opinions. It's fine, but I wanted to see a process through, end to end, on my own. It was important. To me."

Owen shook his head, took a sip of water then eventually said, "Well. Congratulations! What's in New York?"

"I got a scholarship for a good Fine Arts program."

"That's huge! With the new paintings you've been hermiting up in your room for?"

Lara nodded.

Owen took a seat across from her and held his hand out across the table. Lara slid one of her own hands into his, and they held onto one another for a moment.

"This is huge," Owen said again. "I'm happy for you. I'm really proud of you." He turned her hand around in his, his eyes now trained on her fingers.

"Wow, I feel like you've never actually said that aloud," Lara smiled teasingly.

"What, that I'm proud of you? Really? Never?"

Lara shook her head.

"Well, I am. I've always been proud of you."

"Thank you. Sorry, I didn't tell you about the process. I just needed to remind myself that I'm good at what I do, and that I'm an artist in my own right. It's easy to forget. I needed to do it myself."

"I get it. I was the same with my parents and my music. But it's funny you say that. I've always seen it in you."

"Seen what?" Lara asked, her brow furrowing, thrown off.

"Everything."

Lara rolled her eyes.

"Okay, not really. But it was always visible to me."

"What?"

"That you're an artist. And that you're brilliant."

Lara was silent.

"And now you're off. You're off to fly!"

"Yeah… Are you going to be okay without me?" she said jokingly, but she meant it.

Owen seemed to falter. "Maybe." He squeezed her hand. Then he cleared his throat and added, almost too quickly, "No, of course, I'll be fine."

There was a sadness there between them, but in her burned a unique and vibrant hope.

"Anyway," she said, standing up, "Monique promised me a girls' night celebration so I'm going to get ready."

47
Manila, 2011

Owen looked around the living room and thought of Lara. He thought about their life in that apartment. On the bookcase were hundreds of her books and wedged between them, his copy of *The Catcher in the Rye*. On the fridge were recipe cards with both their handwriting scrawled across, her dishes annotated with his notes and vice versa. On one side of the couch, her knitted throw—a shock of orange and yellow—and on the other, his in plain forest green. He thought of these things, and felt that deep sense of loving and knowing. As he internalized her news, he imagined each thing being erased in front of his eyes. A new era for Lara and Owen.

He had the sudden urge to memorize her, as though this version might disappear forever. He called up the image of her sitting before him minutes before. Flowy dark hair, long lashes, freckles, the Foo Fighters T-shirt he'd given her that she'd cut into a crop top and paired with vintage gym shorts, her bare feet.

Later, from where he lay, on his bed, he heard Lara leave, and there, in his throat, were the words he wanted to say, right alongside the feelings he struggled to accept.

I (frustration), love (fear), you (worry), madly (confusion).

And he sighed, rolled over, and tried to sleep.

48
Singapore, 2011

After her last day at work, Lara scheduled a trip back to Singapore. Her plan was to spend a month at home, and then she would swing back through Manila to pick up her stuff and make the big move.

It was great to be back.

Aurora and Lewis were happy to have their daughter home. One afternoon, as mother and daughter sat in the living room, reading quietly and drinking tea, Aurora spoke up: "I'm so proud of you, Lara."

Lara looked up from her book and smiled. "Thanks, Mom."

"No, really. You've done so well. Your art is beautiful, and you've put in the corporate tenure to ensure that you are still marketable after pursuing your art. I'm sure you'll meet incredible opportunities while in New York."

Lara beamed. She was relieved to hear her mother not just supporting her, but also openly accepting her decisions. Both women went back to their books, but Aurora didn't seem quite finished as she kept fidgeting in her chair and clearing her throat.

"What is it, Mom?" Lara asked finally, sliding her bookmark back in and eyeing her mom curiously.

Aurora closed her own book and leaned forward, curiosity bubbling out of her. "Oh nothing," she said in a way that was so overtly casual that Lara knew it was totally contrived. "I was just curious about how Mike and Owen are doing? Feels like I haven't seen either of them in a while."

"Oh, Mike will come over for merienda later."

“That’s nice.”

“And Owen is fine. He’s looking for a new flat in Manila, and I think he’ll probably stay and continue with his work and stuff.”

“Interesting,” Aurora said slowly, her lips drawn into a thin line. Then she added, “Well. Whatever happened there? If I may ask?”

“Where?” Lara looked at her mother.

“With you and Owen.”

Lara sighed. “Nothing. We were just friends.”

Aurora looked at Lara and shook her head. “Oh, my dear, no, you weren’t.” Her eyes betrayed a deep sort of wisdom and almost sadness right then. As though there was a sort of pride mingled with pity that she was trying to convey, but Lara couldn’t quite get to the bottom of it. Before Lara could respond, Aurora leaned back and shrugged, saying, “But if that’s what you are now…okay, then.”

Lara thought for just a moment then responded, “Yes. That’s all we are now, Mom. Yes.” Inside she thought, *Ah, mothers do know all.*

“Good,” Aurora responded then, her tone firm, an almost smile in her voice.

That surprised Lara. She had thought her mother and Owen had gotten on well.

As though reading her mind, Aurora hastened to add, “Don’t get me wrong, I liked Owen. And I did think that you pushed each other so much that your karma would be ending up together forever. But I think you can both do better.”

“Oh, thanks, Mom,” Lara said, with a hint of sarcasm.

“You know what I mean, Lara. I just think there’s a better match out there somewhere.”

***

Message from Andres Courtenay
Hi Lara, I hope you have been doing well. I know it’s been a while but as promised, I am messaging because I am passing through Singapore this week and wondered if you might be in town as well? If you are, it would be wonderful

Lara stared at the message on her phone. It had arrived halfway through breakfast on her penultimate day visiting her family in Singapore.

"What is it?" Adora asked, wandering over and snooping over Lara's shoulder. "Andres…" she read aloud, then she gasped, "CUTE GUY from Tokyo?"

Lara nodded.

"Eee! You guys are still in touch?"

"Not really, I mean occasional comments on social media and a hi or hello here and there, but not *really*."

"Well, he's here now. What are the actual odds?" Adora squealed.

Lara wanted to say that, actually, the odds had been rather high given he had told her he would be in Singapore a few times in the year, and that her trip had been a month long…but it did feel a little bit like kismet.

She read the message again.

"Well, aren't you going to reply?" Adora said impatiently, tapping her fingers on the table.

Lara rolled her eyes. "Fine," she said and she began to type out a response.

Andres! What are the odds! It's great to hear from you.

Just as Lara had said to Adora, they weren't exactly in direct contact. And while they had occasionally interacted very lightly online, she hadn't truly considered the idea of another meet up. Faced with the possibility, she was rather anxious-excited. She continued her message:

*I am indeed in town! Have been for a few weeks, and am
on my last couple of days. I do have time this afternoon
for a quick coffee catch up if you'd like that?*

His reply came about an hour later.

So that afternoon, Lara found herself at Artichoke Cafe in the Bugis area–right by Sculpture Square. She had chosen it because she liked its mix of Greek and Middle Eastern cuisine, but also its coffee, and most of all its proximity to the Singapore Art Museum.

When she arrived, Andres was already there. It would have been impossible to miss him. He sat by a window, a golden ray of light streaming across his face, highlighting his thick, wavy hair. As she approached, she noticed the sun accentuating the caramel tinge in his eyes, a warm rosiness adorned his cheeks–perhaps from the heat outside.

He waved when he saw her and stood up to greet her.

They gave each other polite kisses on the cheek and sat opposite one another.

"So crazy to catch you!" Lara enthused.

"I know, what luck!" Andres said, just as he had in his text.

"How have you been? Have you begun any of your processes towards a change of scenery?" Lara asked.

"Yes, slowly," Andres said, nodding, "Everyday it seems a less remote possibility. Though nothing is set in stone, my intentions have now been made known, so I will likely be traveling to New York after the summer more often–to start networking and seeing about new clients and transitions. From there, it should go rather smoothly, I should think."

At this piece of news, Lara felt that deliciously sweet cautious optimism filling her heart again. Like she was in a Linklater film. Like these were her *Before* and *After Sunsets*. "Well that will be our nth coincidence in a row because, as luck would have it, I will be moving to New York at the end of the summer!" She didn't know why she was volunteering that information right off the bat, but it felt almost weird not to say it given the context was already there.

Andres' eyes grew wide at this, "You can't be serious?"

Lara laughed. "Yes, I'm serious. I applied to a few Fine Arts programs, and the one in New York comes with a full ride…

so it became the top choice."

"Oh, that's right! You had mentioned something to the effect of wanting a change of scenery too…and New York being shortlisted…" Andres said. It impressed Lara that he remembered. He took a sip of his coffee then went on to ask, "What were the other choices?"

"Boston, Paris, Chicago…" Lara rattled off the other cities she had looked at with schools she'd sent applications to.

"And New York gave you the full ride and so here we are, or, rather, there you'll be," Andres said with a smile, "and perhaps there I'll be as well!"

Lara nodded and couldn't help but smile in return. Indeed. Perhaps so. And she wondered for a moment if she could allow herself to be cautiously optimistic.

***

Later that evening as Lara tucked into bed, her phone chimed. She rolled over to check it and saw a message from Andres once more.

Message from Andres Courtenay
Hello, Lara! Thank you for the lovely coffee catch-up earlier today. I wish you continued success on your journey to New York. I hope it's alright with you if I reach out should anything come of my own possible move.

She smiled to herself and wrote back immediately.

Message from Lara Halford
Hey, Andres! I'd like that.

49
Manila, 2011

As the Philippine summer drew to a close, and the last of May gave way to June, Owen welcomed Lara back to their apartment for the last time. She had returned to Manila to pack up her life.

Standing in the doorway of Lara's increasingly empty room, most things relegated to boxes, Owen felt all kinds of mixed up things. There was joy there too–a certain pride and happiness at seeing someone you care about succeed. But there was grief just as well.

"It's all happening." Owen said. He walked in and helped her lift one of the boxes to stack on another.

"It is, indeed. I need to tie this. Help me?" She grabbed some string and threw it in his direction. He caught it mid-air, and they set to work on two boxes Lara had labeled 'Coming with' and 'Fragile.'

He lifted the boxes as they roped the string around to create a makeshift handle. The pair worked in silence.

"I was thinking we should do a going away party?" he proposed when they were finished.

"Yeah, a despedida is a good idea."

"Here works. Same crew?"

"Sure."

***

That night, Owen asked Lara if she wanted to watch a movie. She agreed and suggested they do so in his room. They picked a light one—*The Pink Panther* with Steve Martin. It was a good laugh, and for a moment, it was like old times. With bowls of popcorn, sitting shoulder to shoulder on the bed, they laughed until their sides ached, and mimicked Steve Martin's French accent.

When the movie was over, Lara stretched out and stood up.

"Where are you off to?" Owen asked.

"Back to my room." Lara shrugged. "It's late. Better sleep."

"But it's all dusty and boxed up in there." He hated how desperate he sounded. He loathed how much he wished she'd just stay in his bed for the night and allow them that last bit of closeness.

Lara laughed. "Yes, but the bed's still standing. I'll survive."

He had so many wishes, and questions, but instead he just rolled his eyes and said, "Your choice."

"Exactly, so good night!" she said with a smile as she left the room.

***

Two nights later, Monique, Mateo, Bianca, David, and Niko, along with Lara and Owen, found themselves in the living room, eating pizza, and reminiscing. This was Lara's send-off.

"Everything's changing," Bianca lamented, a hint of sadness in her voice. "Monique and Mateo are super married..."

The couple rolled their eyes and Monique tossed a crust in Bianca's face, but it was true. The two were in the middle of their wedded bliss, and were trying for a child. Niko had announced he would be leaving for his MBA in France in the fall. Bianca and David were likely at the cusp of engagement themselves. Mike was long gone. Lara was heading out.

"Next thing you know, Owen's off, too," Niko declared.

"After all, what's keeping him here without Lara," Mateo joked, and everyone laughed—even Lara and Owen.

"You exaggerate," Lara protested.

But Owen did not. The whole night, he sat close to Lara, and when the friends left, they stood in the kitchen, shoulder to shoulder, doing the dishes in silence.

"How are we going to stay in touch?" Owen asked. It felt a little like grasping at straws, but what could he do? He was going to miss her. His mind wandered to Andres Courtenay, whose social media profile had stated he was based in Boston–and that wasn't far from New York at all. Plus, somehow the more Owen thought about this Andres character, the more the notion of him multiplied and there were infinite Cute Guys like him, all in Lara's league, just waiting to meet her in New York. And they would take it a step further than Owen ever had. And they would deserve her. And this continued to make Owen ache.

"I don't know. Video calls," was Lara's flippant reply. "It doesn't have to be regimented. We can message each other when we have time."

Owen poked Lara in the side. "I'm sure you'll miss me," he teased with a smirk on his face. He couldn't help himself. He knew it sounded like a test.

Lara put down the plates she had been washing and turned to face him. "Of course, I'll miss you," she said plainly, and then turned back to the dishes.

Lara had indeed stuck to her word. She was no longer available to Owen the way she had once been. And while it had been easy enough to brush aside all these changes when they lived together, because, after all, they remained in close proximity and continued to do most everything together, this particular change was a big one. A different one. And Owen knew there would be no ignoring it anymore.

The pair were quiet as they tidied up the rest of the mess. Then Lara said, "I'll miss you, Owen. But it is what it is."

Owen reached over then and pulled her in for a hug. In that embrace, he tried to squeeze in all the things he could not say. How much he admired her, and her drive, and her art, and her kindness. How much he appreciated her compassion, and her patience, and her giving of herself. And how much he would miss her companionship, and her creative energy, and her partnership.

In that hug, he poured out the weight of their years behind them, and the lightness of what could lay before them— together and apart. He felt them both melting into it a little. A soft goodbye.

Chorus

Climax

Is this the part where we become
Just ships
Speaking each other in passing?
A love supreme we can't escape it
We can only change it cause we're
Ships
Just ships
Speaking each other in passing

<h1 style="text-align:center">50
New York, 2011</h1>

New York in November was its own sort of magic. Though the streets still stank of piss, the taxis still ran the reds, and everyone still walked at breakneck speed with no regard for other pedestrians, all this was made more palatable under the golden hue of autumn.

The days were long enough to enjoy an evening stroll, the nights festive enough for a warm cup of cocoa, the mornings crisp enough to pop a window open and catch a breeze, the weather cold enough for a stylish coat. Best of all, the trees were a wonder of red, orange, and yellow, and the pavements were lined with crunchy, golden leaves.

Lara loved New York. She was smitten with its energy, its color, its size. It was like a secret world, tucked away among skyscrapers, hidden in the shadow of brownstones—a land of artists, entrepreneurs, makers. Everyone breathing life into the city.

She stood on the steps of the Met, and sighed for perhaps the hundredth time, in near disbelief that this was her life now. Fond memories from her childhood overlapped with her new reality and she was filled with gratitude. She had, to her own surprise, landed a coveted graduate internship there and had just gotten used to the euphoria she felt every time she said, *"Yes. I work at the Met."*

The internship was ten weeks long, and she was on her last week. It was sad to say goodbye. Lara had been placed on the Educational team. This sat within an interesting space that dealt in both curatorial aspects of museum work, but also events and program management. Lara had not been too enthusiastic at the start, but was pleased to learn she enjoyed working with kids.

In her first two weeks, she had designed an Alphabet

Challenge. Schools participating in a partnership with the museum brought middle school age kids, and each child was given a disposable camera. Then Lara and another museum employee would teach them about what Lara dubbed 'Noticing.'

They would ask the children to take twenty-seven pictures while they were in the museum—first a shot of themselves or their name tag, and then twenty-six pictures depicting each letter of the alphabet.

The catch was that they could not photograph any real letters. Each photo was meant to be of something that suggested the shape of the letter, ideally from paintings, sculptures or artifacts, but also from shadows, or frames. The goal was to get the kids close enough to each piece. In the process, they were talked through the art or artifact, and were able to see more detail than they might have had they not been prompted with such a challenge.

Lara loved all the unique work the challenge inspired. Her personal favorite set had come from a child named Noam Abelman. This bespeckled child with dark hair, and a broad, braced smile had an eye. His 'C' had been the shadow in the curve of the nose of Pablo Picasso's Gertrude Stein portrait. His 'H' the banister on Monet's *Bridge Over A Pond of Water Lilies*. His 'U' the curve in the back of the dress on one of the dancers in Degas' *The Dance Class*.

Feedback was so positive for the activity that the museum was considering bringing it on for future partnerships and field trips. Lara was thrilled. She left on her very last day with a bouquet, glowing references, and a deeper appreciation for where art, education, and inspiration coalesced.

***

"That is gorgeous," Lara approached her friend Zuri from behind during one of their weekly studio sessions.

Zuri's colorful abstract expressionism was the envy of the cohort. Each stroke had an absolute purpose. A single purple line might look out of place one moment, and then she would layer a different color over it and suddenly, it was such an essential part of a meditation on war emblazoned across an eight-foot canvas.

Zuri smiled. "Thanks! What are you working on today?"

Lara pulled out her canvas and placed it onto her easel.

"I'm starting a series." She opened her wooden carry case for all her paints and bits and bobs. "It's reflections on Singapore."

She produced a folder of reference photographs from her backpack. In it were pictures she had taken on her last trip home. She had captured the sometimes blurry, wild-looking mirror images of shop houses in a puddle, cell towers in water reservoirs, skyscrapers in canals. Lara wanted to juxtapose the clean, clinical Singapore with its reality as a tropical island that if left to the elements would overgrow, given to the whims of its wild inhabitants—the crocs, the birds, the otters, but also the people, who lived in their quiet constraints. Lara was working hard toward a more hyper-realistic style applied to surreal concepts. She wasn't there yet, but she knew it was around the corner—if her skills could only improve at the same pace her ideas flowed.

Zuri gave an approving nod and went back to her piece—a dense apartment block, whose windows were the forms of people in the middle of crimes of passion. Edgy, fascinating work.

Lara felt a pang of imposter syndrome and forced herself to push it away. The best thing about doing something new and challenging was knowing there was room to grow. *I must expand into the space around me and grow*, she thought, and so she did.

Three hours of heavy, focused work later, Zuri said, "When we're done, do you want to grab dinner?"

"How soon would that be?"

"Like…now?" Zuri laughed.

"PLEASE," Lara said, packing her things away and making mental notes about what she wanted to change.

The girls threw their coats on and stepped into the chilly evening. Nearby, the neon sign of a pizza parlor glowed. Just as they began to make their way over, Lara's phone chimed. She slipped it out to check.

Message from Andres Courtenay
Hello, Lara! This is Andres. I hope you are well! Guess what? Just as I'd mentioned last we saw each other, here begins my Manhattan journey! I will be coming by New York next week for work and to scope for clients and network with partners. Would love to see you if you're around. How has school been? Has the program started?

The pair found seats and just as Lara took hers she exclaimed, "Cute Guy!"

Zuri nearly jumped in shock.

"Sorry, I didn't mean to say that aloud." Lara said sheepishly.

Zuri laughed along. "No worries."

"I just got a text from someone I nicknamed Cute Guy in my head," Lara explained.

"I see." Zuri smirked. "What did Cute Guy say?"

"His name is Andres. He just said he'd be in town next week and was wanting to hang out."

"Ooooh, a date? Are you going to say yes?"

"Oh, I don't think he means a date, I think he just means a meetup. Last we met–months ago, actually, he was just beginning to make progress on a future move to New York. I think he's still based out of Boston."

"Ah, well…that's not too far away? A four hour train or something. No harm in hanging out, I'm sure."

"True. I'll plan something next week and invite him along. Maybe something for our whole group, and he can drop in."

Message from Lara Halford
Hey, you! Good to hear from you. Nice that you'll be in town, and I am sending as many good vibes your way as you prepare to charm those Partners into giving you that lateral move. Hanging out sounds good. I'm thinking of having a few people over to my apartment next Friday. Would you like to join us? Nothing fancy. Just beer and pizza.

Message from Andres Courtenay
Marvelous! Shall I bring anything?

Message from Lara Halford
Drinks?

Message from Andres Courtenay
Good as done! I'll be at a hotel by Times Square. Can you send me your address? See you next Friday! Cheers

51
Manila and Los Angeles, 2011

Owen in Manila was aimless. It was the middle of October, and two months since he'd last seen Lara. He stopped working out and was thin and pale. Monique, Mateo, Bianca, and David kept inviting him around, but he only showed up half the time.

He insisted, to anyone who commented on the state of him, that it was because he had lost the grounding effect of music, the driving force of a deeply-held dream. But really, it was the loss of Lara—his anchor, his home—that he felt in his bones. And he knew it. Perhaps everyone knew it. Owen had begun to look forward to just two things in the week: Saturdays, when he would call Lara; and Sundays, when he'd call Lola Beth, and his father thereafter.

"So, son," Oskar said on one such call. "How are you doing without Lara?"

Owen feigned surprise at the question. "What do you mean? How should I be doing? I'm totally fine."

Oskar was not convinced. "Really? Because you look awful."

Owen laughed. "Jesus. Thanks, Dad."

"No, really, we're worried," Oskar insisted. "You look miserable. Beth, your mother, and I... We think this isn't healthy."

"Nice to know you guys gossip about me behind my back."

"Please, Owen. We're your family. We care about you."

Owen was silent.

"Look, son. I don't want you to make the same mistakes I did. I'm sure you recall at least a little that your mother and I had a passionate but difficult relationship. I put music before her all the time. In fact, I put music before you, too. And I was convinced love had to be a hard, wild thing. But that's not it. Love is a stable, soft thing. A kind thing. One that shows up every day and considers you. Love, son, is what you and Lara had. You can't just let that go."

Owen felt a strange thing happen inside him then. Nobody, not even he or Lara, had ever described aloud in such clear terms what they shared. He had always been afraid to admit it, scared of what might happen if the words left his body and became real.

But that day, as Oskar spoke, the facts rolled off his tongue into the world and they just sounded right. True. They weren't scary. They were as good as reading out a grocery list or singing the ABCs. They were real. His heart began to thud in his chest at the thought. *He loved Lara.* And the scariest thing about that was refusing to admit it.

Then the reality of the situation came back to him. What they had. *Had.* In the past tense. *Had*, because she was gone now. *Had*, because the chance was there and he didn't take it.

"What are you proposing, Dad?" Considering many of his traumas were thanks to his parents, he didn't feel that they should dole out life advice. And yet, there he was, listening to his father's advice.

"Come back to the US. Do your music or engineering stuff. Come here, get her back. Nothing is keeping you there anymore."

"But I wouldn't even know where to begin?" He would be lying if he said the thought had not crossed his mind. But he felt so lost. No music, no Lara; just work and a nagging feeling of shame and regret.

"Sustainability is coming up now. You'll have no shortage of clients. You could even find something in New York."

"I can't," he said, rather sorrowfully. "We already talked about this, and I gave her my decision. It's over."

"It ain't over 'til the fat lady sings, son."

***

It was wild. And yet, four weeks later, after serving his notice period, Owen found himself packing his life into four suitcases, selling off the little furniture he had, and moving back to the United States.

To try to get the girl back. Maybe.

On his last night, Mateo and Monique took him to dinner. Bianca, Niko, and David dropped by for drinks and goodbyes. The group hugged and teased Owen that they had seen this coming. Then they all parted ways until it was just Mateo and Owen standing in front of the restaurant as Monique went to get the car.

"Are you following Lara, Owen? Be honest," Mateo asked.

Owen thought about the question but couldn't yet bring himself to admit the answer aloud.

When he hadn't responded for some time, Mateo shook his head. "'Cause…I hope you aren't. You had every chance here, and that poor girl… She was just waiting. You should let her find her space without you." Mateo looked out at the pattering rain and then drew in a deep breath, "But if you are… I hope you do it right this time."

Monique pulled up in their car and Mateo gave Owen a final hug, got in, and the pair waved as they drove off.

Owen knew Mateo was right.

He turned and walked back into the restaurant. He ordered a bottle of San Miguel and a bowl of arroz caldo. Steam rose over the rice porridge, smelling of ginger, garlic, and chicken stock. A chicken leg poked out and a drizzle of soy and fish sauce finished off the dish, lending it a punch of umami. It reminded him of sick days as a child when he would lie with one such bowl, watching cartoons, on the road to healing as Lola Beth doted on him.

He enjoyed that simple moment—Filipino comfort food and Rivermaya's '90s classic "214" on the speakers competing with the now torrential rain outside.

Owen had never chased a girl anywhere. Had never followed love any place. Usually, he tried to run the opposite way. But maybe just this once, he could finally say, *"I love you madly."*

***

The first thing Owen wanted to do when he touched down was call Lara, but he knew it was first things first. He had to have at least something lined up; he couldn't just run into her open-armed without a plan. He discussed this extensively with his father—he would find a job for stability, and then he would call Mike, and then they would visit Lara for New Year's, and with that nostalgic atmosphere, he would do it. He would finally make the jump. He would tell her everything. He would do right by them.

He got to work applying for jobs everywhere from New Jersey to Manhattan, and from San Francisco to Los Angeles.

It was mid-November when he received an offer from a start-up seeking someone to lead the waste management and recycling practice. The paycheck was small, but commissions were big. The founder, a young man named Peter Chance with big glasses and a shock of red hair, was fresh out of his Masters at USC. He would spearhead the firm's energy–wind, solar, water practice.

At their first real meeting, Peter pulled up a spreadsheet of prospective clients. "Let's prioritize, shall we?" he said.

On the list Owen spotted an opportunity. The owner of a hotel chain needed his particular expertise. The sheet listed offices in Connecticut, New Jersey, North Carolina, San Francisco, and Oregon. It was almost too perfect. Connecticut and New Jersey were close enough to New York to make it make sense.

"That," Owen pointed.

"That?" Peter said, cocking his head to one side and reading through the columns. "It's not one of the most lucrative deals."

Owen thought quickly. "But it's evergreen. It would rake in repeat revenue. So it's a sustainable first play and simple enough to give us case studies for future, larger hoteliers."

Peter nodded thoughtfully. "Okay, let's go for it. Most of this is on the East Coast, though."

"I can hop over to New York or Jersey for the New Year and work from there. Let's just talk about the budget and targets."

52
New York, 2011

On Friday, Lara found herself drenched in her own sweat in her little studio apartment, busy tidying away all her art materials in preparation for the dinner she was hosting.

Four friends from her MFA program, including Zuri, had agreed to come, along with Andres. People began to stream in, bearing cupcakes, chips, and soda. Zuri helped Lara set the table and move the furniture to make a circle for people to sit and chat as a group. Then the bell rang once more.

Lara opened it and standing there in her doorway was Cute Guy.

Andres was just as attractive as he had been the last time she saw him, although he seemed to have lost his tan somewhat, and his skin shone flushed at the cheeks and nose from the brisk fall wind.

"Andres!" Lara smiled. "Welcome. Come in!" She held the door open and he walked in. He wore a dark gray woolen coat, slacks, and a crisp blue button down shirt. He took his coat off and hung it from a hook near Lara's door. With him, he had brought a box of pizza and a bottle of Martinelli's apple juice.

Lara took both and set them on the table. "Thanks so much. You didn't have to bring all this! We were going to order."

"Ah, I thought if I was going to impose myself on one of your gatherings, it's the least I could do."

"It's hardly an imposition." Lara waved him off, "Everyone, this is Andres. Andres, this is everyone. Zuri, Lorelei, Rashad, and Carly." She gestured with an open palm to each person in the group and then went to order more pizza.

By the time she was off the phone and back in the living room, the group was already seated and chatting. Lara found a spot next to Zuri.

The group was diverse, and the common threads among them were their adventurous spirits and love of travel. Everyone traded stories, and eventually games were taken out, and rounds of *Settlers of Catan* and *Munchkin* were played.

Later that night the last ones standing were Andres, Lara, and Zuri. The three stayed back, cleaning up in the kitchen.

"You know, I saw a trailer for that new George Clooney movie yesterday," Andres mentioned casually as he wiped off a dish and returned it to the rack.

"Oh, the one set in Hawaii? Me too! I'd be interested to see it if anybody else is," Lara said as she walked Andres to the door.

He smiled. "I think that would be lovely."

Lara smiled back. "Cool!"

He shrugged on his coat. "Brilliant. If you're free tomorrow, we can make a day of it. I'll give you a ring to coordinate? Maybe grab lunch, and then see a matinee showing?"

"Sounds good," Lara replied. "Thanks for coming."

"My pleasure. I had a grand time. Thank you for having me," Andres said, and they gave each other a hug before he walked off.

When Lara closed the door behind him, she realized she was still smiling.

"Ooh, he *is* cute, Lara," Zuri gushed.

Lara pulled out her phone to check the time. 11 p.m. There was also a message.

Message from Owen (Music Dude) Weber
Hey, got time for a call?

Zuri pulled her own coat on and gave Lara a kiss on the cheek, "Enjoy your date tomorrow," she teased.

Lara rolled her eyes. "Just friends, just friends."

Zuri stuck her tongue out. "Bye, girl."

After her friend left, Lara headed to her desk and opened up her laptop to call Owen but he must have seen her online because he rang her almost immediately. "I have news!" he said.

"Hello to you, too," Lara replied wryly, but she was smiling in spite of herself.

"Hello, I have news," he repeated.

"Where are you?" Lara asked. It looked like night wherever he was, and she was quite sure it was not night in the Philippines.

"That's the news! I'm back in LA!"

"Oh, what?"

"Yeah, I moved back. A couple of weeks ago."

"Wait, what?"

"I MOVED BACK," he enunciated with extra drama. "Can you hear me? Is the connection bad?"

"No, no. I mean, yes I hear you fine. I was just surprised."

"Oh, well yeah. I moved back!"

"But...why?"

"I didn't have much keeping me in Manila anymore."

This felt like a loaded statement, and Lara wanted to walk right past it. "I see." She grasped for something to say. "Well, so what's on your plate now then? Taking a break? Music?"

"Actually, I bagged a semi co-founder role in a start-up leading their waste management and recycling practice. The actual founder, Peter, is great, Lar. You'd love him. Geeky, funny, smart."

"Oh. Congratulations!" she said, genuinely happy for him, but also a little bit annoyed, though she wasn't sure why.

"But that's only half the news. The other is... I spoke to Mike and he wants to spend New Year here. So I was thinking, wouldn't it be fun to do a reunion? Us three, together again?"

"Sure," Lara said, "Yeah that'd be fun." And she meant it. The idea of bringing back the old group was nice. She liked that Mike would be there, too, and it wouldn't have to be just her and Owen. She had begun to notice that the more distance she had from him, the more she enjoyed that space. She knew she'd love Owen forever, but already she could feel that love changing.

"So, we can come stay with you in New York then?"

"Oh, you mean a reunion here, in New York.... In my flat?"

"Yeah?"

"I need to think about that."

"Yeah, think about it and let us know! It's expensive to book a hotel but if it's too much, I'm sure we can find something."

The way he said it suggested that he was not sure they would find something and he, in fact, felt that it would be better if she hosted them. "Okay. Just give me time."

"Okay. But think fast. We need to know ahead before rates go up. Plus, I can't wait to see you." These days every time they spoke, Owen always sounded uncharacteristically enthusiastic. And again, Lara found this irksome.

"Sorry, just excited!" Owen apologized as though he'd clocked Lara's ire over his bubbly energy. This was also irritating, so Lara decided to close the call early.

"I gotta go, Owen. I'm tired. Just hosted a little house party, and now I need to sleep. I'll get back to you tomorrow, okay?"

"Okay. Sleep well!"

"Good night. Send my love to your dad and the dogs."

***

The next morning, Lara pulled on her work out clothes and set out for a run. The best thing about fall weekends were the morning runs. As the trees changed around her, blowing in the wind and shedding the beautiful old for a beautiful new, she felt a parallel in her own life. She breathed deeply, closing her eyes and savoring every few steps.

When she returned from her run, she had a missed call from Andres so she called him back.

"Hello," came his voice on the other end. "Thanks for calling me back, Lara." She could almost detect the sound of a smile on his lips. "Just checking to see if we're still on?"

"Yes! Sorry I missed your call. I was out on a run."

"Terrific! I'd have loved to join for that. Running in this weather is heaven."

"It is! Maybe next time."

"Shall we meet at a place near you?"

"Sure, and I'll book movie tickets for the afternoon."

"Perfect."

The two settled on a Filipino restaurant in Lara's

neighborhood called Gutom Gang. Andres had not tried Filipino food before and was eager to do so.

As Lara was about to dress for the day, her laptop chimed. Peering over at the screen, she saw that Owen was calling again. Throwing on a sweater, Lara tapped to receive the call and leaned over in front of her computer. "Yo," she said. "What is it?"

"Have you given my question some thought?" Owen asked. He was sitting shirtless with his guitar.

"Isn't it cold there?"

"No. Mild. LA, remember. Hey, where are you going? You have makeup on. And you didn't answer my question."

"It's Saturday, Owen. I'm going out."

"What are you doing today?"

"Well, *if you must know* I'm going to lunch then a movie."

"Ooh with WHOM? Pray tell."

"Andres." Lara was beginning to feel impatient.

"I feel like I haven't heard that name before."

"I mentioned him maybe once. Met him on a plane?"

"Ah yes, the British Chap based in Boston." Owen put on a fake accent.

"Right." Back in the day, Lara might have found this charming, now it was just a little sad.

"What are you going to wear?"

"I'm about to change, Owen. So I'm going to drop the call."

"Show me what you're going to wear! You want to make a good impression, right? I'm your best friend, and I'm a dude."

Lara rolled her eyes but produced the outfit for him anyway—a blue tartan wool skirt, tights, a white buttoned down boyfriend shirt tucked in, and a sage green knitted vest. She planned to wear them with her classic Burberry trench and chunky ankle boots.

"I like it. It says 'I'm artsy and fun.' Quirky and preppy."

"When did you become a fashion editor?"

"Just now."

Lara managed a half-hearted snort of laughter. "Okay, now I really am going, Owen. Thanks for the unsolicited feedback as always."

"Wait! So did you figure it out for New Year's? We want to

book before it gets more expensive."

"Fine, fine." Lara knew she wasn't going to say no. She didn't have the heart to, really. She just hadn't felt like fulfilling Owen's wish immediately. She kind of wanted to make him sweat.

"So we can stay?"

"Yes."

"YES. You still love us. See you. Have fun on your DATE."

Lara hung up.

53
New York, 2011

At lunch, Lara made all the orders at Andres' request. The food came quickly. The scent of garlic, soy, and vinegar filled the air. Before them lay an assortment of platters. On one, there were chunks of meat in a brown sauce. In another, a plate of white rice garnished with fried garlic and onion. In a bowl, a cloudy soup with vegetables and, unmistakably, a fish head, steamed away, warming their faces. The dessert dish appeared to be four chunky spring rolls, drizzled with sesame seeds and a sticky syrup.

"Adobo," Lara said, pointing at the first dish. "Braised pork and chicken in soy and vinegar, with garlic, peppercorns and bay leaves. A Filipino staple."

"Adobo like adobar?" Andres asked.

"Maybe! Do you guys have this in Argentina, too?"

"Not really, but in Spanish, 'adobar' is to marinate. I just found it interesting that the word overlaps."

"I think we'll find many other commonalities soon enough."

"What might this be?" Andres pointed at the rice cheekily.

"This is the fabled Filipino arroz. Grown in the mountain ranges of the Cordilleras. Harvested under the blood moon…" Lara attempted her best David Attenborough impression.

The two laughed.

"Okay, hold up, we need to get through this lunch if we want to make the movie! Now this," Lara said, pushing the bowl closer to Andres, "is sinigang. A sour soup made from fish sauce and tamarind broth. One of my favorites."

Andres licked his lips and began to serve the soup into smaller bowls. He handed one to Lara, then he held his own up to his face and inhaled. "Should we dig in?"

"What do you say in Argentina before you eat? My Filipino grandma always calls us to the table in Spanish. She says, 'vamos a comer.' Let's eat!"

Andres smiled at her then—a bright, open look. She felt warm and giddy as their eyes met. "In Argentina, your host usually must say 'buen provecho,' before anyone can begin eating. Is there a Filipino equivalent?"

"Ooh." Lara stopped to think, and also to admire the subtle change in Andres' accent when he spoke in Spanish. "No, actually. It was always 'just, vamos a comer.' Or in my maternal family's local dialect, 'kaon na ta.' Which also just means 'let's eat.'"

"Ah, well, then, kaon na ta!" Andres tried the words out.

"Buen provecho!" Lara said gamely in return.

Andres grinned back. "You're a good host." He then took a spoonful of the soup and his eyes grew wide. "This is incredible!"

Lara took a sip of broth. It had been some time since she had last had a bowl herself, and something about having it in this cold, crisp setting made the features of the dish all the more pronounced. The sinigang had the full-bodied flavors of the fish head, but was light and tangy thanks to the tamarind.

When she looked at Andres, he was savoring each bite—just like she was, a small smile at the edges of his lips, his eyes wide. It felt, just then, like they were on exactly the same wavelength.

"This. Is. A. Revelation," he said. "I've never had anything like it."

Lara laughed. "Don't get ahead of yourself. Still more to try!"

Andres took Lara's lead and went through each dish, taking the time to sample his way through the flavors and sensations.

"I love the zing of the peppercorns in the adobo. And all that garlic in the rice," he gushed between servings.

Next came dessert. The spring roll was crunchy and sweet. Inside was a banana and slivers of the fragrant, chewy langka.

Andres chewed thoughtfully then said, "Banana and… What's the other fruit in there?"

"Jackfruit." Lara smiled. "We call it 'langka' in the Philippines."

"Fascinating!" Andres polished off his plate and leaned back patting his belly. "Are you sure there's room for ice cream?"

"We'll make some room. Because this place makes their own sorbetes." Lara rubbed her hands together excitedly and stood up, grabbing Andres by the arm and pulling him toward a little traditional Filipino ice cream cart by the register. It was painted colorfully, with tin holders for the assortment of flavors.

The server nearby, whose name tag read 'Joy,' came to help. "Hello! In the mood for sorbetes even in this cold weather?"

"He's a first timer so it's a must."

"Welcome to the world of Filipino food and dirty ice cream!"

"Brilliant! Why do they call it that?" Andres asked, laughing.

"'Cause it's sold on the streets, I think."

"Today we have ube, queso, and mangga," Joy said.

"What now?" Andres startled.

"Can we have two cones with a scoop of each please?"

"Coming right up." Joy scooped three of each flavor onto two cones and handed them back.

"I haven't tried any of these flavors before."

The queso was the first, and both took a lick at it. Lara felt immediately nostalgic. It was creamy, salty, and sweet at once.

She watched Andres as he nodded approvingly.

"Oh, that's rather nice," he said. He then took a bite of the ube, whose bright purple tone was a sight to behold.

Lara also ate her scoop. It was earthy like a sweet potato, but also sweet and rich like chocolate.

Mango was last, and the Filipino sorbetes version was milky and not like sherbet.

"I like them all, but I like ube best," Andres declared after. On their way out, he tipped all the servers extra and pointed at the sorbetes cart, "I'll be back for more of that."

***

247

"So what do you like best about living in New York? Now that you've been here a few months," Andres asked as they walked the ten minutes to the cinema.

Lara shrugged. "Honestly, I think I just like the change."

"The change?"

"Yeah. It's so different from the Philippines and Singapore. I love to be back where the seasons are shifting, the nights grow longer, and the days start shrinking." Lara took a deep breath of the crisp air. "I liked living in the tropics, but sometimes I feel like constant warmth and heat dull one's senses and resolve. The heat muddles the days. Everything is always the same. The sun rises and sets at the same time all year. Nothing changes. Here, it feels like everything is changing all the time."

Leaves were falling from the trees above them and she tried to reach and catch one mid-air. She missed. Andres smiled, just listening, then he did the same and caught one. A perfect maple leaf—red on the inside radiating out in a gradient til it turned a sunny yellow on the edges. A sunburst.

Andres handed it to her. She bowed in thanks and from the little cross-body bag she had strapped to her, produced a favorite she had been rereading as of late (her battered copy of Aldous Huxley's *Brave New World*). She slipped the leaf in to use as a bookmark, and together they entered the movie theater.

***

Lara and Andres had such a pleasant time that they immediately made plans to hang out with Lara's friends that Sunday.

Everyone met up at a blues bar on the Lower East Side. It was a dimly-lit, plush place with hues of black, blue, brown, and purple accented only by the soft lights on the stage.

They found a little leather booth, curved around a circular table, and they all squeezed in next to one another. Behind the bar there was a blackboard with the words "Conversation Starters," where the staff wrote a question people could ask friends new and old. The query for the day was: "What is one wild thing you've always wanted to do?"

The friends in Lara's booth posed the question to one

another. Lara's answer was skydiving. "Jumping out of a plane is high on my list, pun intended," she said.

"Oh, mine too!" Andres said, nudging Lara. They were squeezed so closely to one another, knees touching. "I've always wanted to go skydiving."

"I have this ridiculous fantasy that I go skydiving right into the ocean and then scuba," Lara said.

"Brilliant! Count me in."

They high-fived and drank more gin, and Lara noted the familiar feeling of liquid courage creeping from the pit of her stomach up through her torso, and down to her fingertips. As she looked at Andres, she could see all the little details in his face. Thick eyebrows over soft, warm eyes, shaded by curly, long lashes. Dark hair that was naturally coiffed, with voluminous waves and a little Clark Kent curl over his forehead. A tall nose and on the left side of the bridge, two little scars from a battle with chicken pox or adolescent acne. A five o'clock shadow accentuating a strong jaw. The curl in his hair moved a little and Lara had the sudden, inexplicable urge to touch him.

Without thinking, she reached over and ran a hand through his hair. The table had moved on to other merriment and conversation, and nobody even noticed, but Lara sat, appalled, as though in an out-of-body experience.

"Oh, I'm so sorry. I don't know why I did that," she said, eyes wide and tone sheepish. Her cheeks were flushed, embarrassed.

Andres laughed. "It's okay," he said. "I don't mind. Do you want to see if there are seats closer to the band?"

Lara nodded, still mortified but also a little electrified.

Andres led her through the crowd and found two little bar stools flanking a cocktail table by the stage. He pulled her seat out for her and she climbed onto it a little clumsily. Then he inched his own chair closer to hers and sat down

"Do you like this kind of music?" he asked.

"I do. I like jazz better, but this is still beautiful."

Andres remembered sharing jazz songs on the plane when they first met and he smiled. "Yes, jazz is…more hopeful."

"True. Blues can be a bit…" Lara paused. "Blue." She giggled.

Andres laughed. "I don't recall you mentioning before... Do you play any instruments?"

"A little. Uke. Guitar. I sing as well." She thought about the record deal that never was. "You?" She had seen a picture on Andres' social media profile that showed him at a drum set but she couldn't recall if they'd ever spoken about it. And it could just as well have been simply a picture of him at a set, without it being something he actually did...

But Andres answered then, "Yes, the drums, actually. I loved it. But it's been a long time since I last got to sit down and really play. My favorite genre to play was jazz, though."

Lara's thoughts went back to that one picture again. He had been younger then. She transposed this version of him with the stronger jaw, the longer hair, the stubble into that frame in her mind. She pictured his hair a little tousled, his sport coat off, his shirt a few buttons loose. She decided it would be dangerous to imagine more.

"The drums are sexy," she blurted out.

Andres chuckled. "The guitar is sexy. Singing is sexy."

No teasing, no bickering. Lara realized she had been steeling herself, but as Andres sat next to her, relaxed and himself, it dawned on her she didn't have to do that around him.

The pair were silent for a moment, just watching and listening. Lara did not want to keep flirting with Andres. In the back of her mind, she thought, *God, he is so cute.* But also, *Damn, four hours is still a ways away.* She didn't want to start anything with anyone if the odds were stacked against her or them. *Maybe if he officially moves here, then we'll really have a shot.*

When Lara turned and caught Andres' eye, she realized he had been looking at her. Her stomach did a little flip. She remembered what her sister had said, *I think he likes you.* Could she have been right? They both smiled, and Lara realized that the answer was probably yes.

Lara reached over and this time, with full knowledge, emboldened by the alcohol in her veins, ran her hand through his hair again. She started from the front, following the curve of his curls down to the base of his neck, where she stopped and let her fingers rest against his nape. Despite her reservations, she felt she couldn't help herself.

Andres kept his eyes locked on hers. He reached over and drew their chairs closer still to one another. She let her hand drop back down, and turned back to the music.

That night, Andres walked Lara home. As the sparks of her inebriation began to wane, Lara felt a familiar anxiety descending upon her—a wondering, an uncertainty. But at her stoop, with no warning, no airs, and not a hint of second guessing, Andres leaned over and gave Lara a peck on the lips. It seemed to surprise even him, but when she looked up into his face, she saw that he was smiling. Her anxiety fell away and she giggled in spite of herself.

"Sorry, I hope that was okay," he said.

Lara smiled. "It's fine."

"I had a marvelous weekend. I'd love to see you again after work on Tuesday. If you have the time."

Lara was glad to hear he'd still be around. "Sure, I'd like that."

***

"I have some news," Andres said on Thursday. He was a week into his trip in New York, and on the third meal he and Lara were sharing alone in such a short time.

"Ooh, do tell?" Lara said, half expecting him to drop a bomb. She was almost afraid that he was too good to be real.

"The networking is going well," he said, "I'm not sure if they're going to give me the promotion and move me here yet, but it looks like they've agreed to staff me on a client here. So it seems, for now, I'm a New Yorker. So…not an official move, but… certainly a step in that direction."

Lara stared at him for a moment. "How long is a case usually?" she asked slowly.

"Three to six months," he answered.

"So you're saying you could be here for another six months?"

"Something like that. With occasional travel. But also, after that initial time, perhaps I'm here for good."

Lara grinned in spite of herself. She had nothing to say that she was willing to do so aloud, so she just took a sip of her drink and looked at this ridiculously attractive man in front of her.

"I'm going to assume from your face that you aren't terribly disappointed by this news."

"Oh no, you have it all wrong," Lara joked. "I'm terribly disappointed."

Andres laughed and reached over instinctively to tuck a loose strand of Lara's hair behind her ear.

Lara was, just then, filled with a cautious optimism—a glimmer of hope blossoming in the base of her stomach, warming her all the way through.

November 22, 2011
Email from Owen to Lara

Subject: Thanksgiving!

Hello, my friend. What are your Thanksgiving plans?
We are arriving on December 28th. Hope you're ready for us!

[Attachment: Flight itineraries of both Mike and Owen]

***

November 24, 2011
Email from Lara to Owen

Subject: Re: Thanksgiving!

Happy Thanksgiving! Thanks for sending me your itineraries. Looking forward to seeing you both. Today I am having dinner with some friends. And Andres. He is making a turkey in my oven for the first time. Hope we survive. Will let you know if we don't by haunting you in your sleep.

***

November 24, 2011
Email from Owen to Lara

Subject: Re: Re: Thanksgiving!

Happy Thanksgiving to you too! Also can't wait to see you. Dad sends his love. Believe it or not, Mom is coming to town to do turkey dinner with us. And wow, Andres. Things must be going well then? I looked him up on social media. He's very attractive. How are you batting so high above your average? Practice safe sex. And please don't haunt me in my sleep. You're scary enough when I'm awake.

***

November 24, 2011
Email from Lara to Owen

Subject: Re: Re: Re: Thanksgiving!

Still alive! Hi to your parents and the dogs. Good night

[Attachment: Picture of Andres, Lara, and the turkey]

***

November 24, 2011
Email from Owen to Mike

Subject: Happy Thanksgiving!

I know you don't celebrate, but Happy Thanksgiving! Also, I think
Lara has a new boyfriend.

***

November 25, 2011
Email from Mike to Owen

Subject: Re: Happy Thanksgiving!

Did you have a good Thanksgiving? Thanks for the info? Is that a
good thing? Are you ok? We're still on right?

***

November 26, 2011
Email from Owen to Mike

Subject: Re: Re: Happy Thanksgiving!

Yeah, it was good. Yummy food. Yes, we're still on. Why wouldn't
I be ok?

***

**November 28, 2011
Email from Andres to Lara**

Subject: How is your day going? Here is a cat

I am under a bloody excruciating pile of work. But probably not
as big a pile as you. Since you are likely literally under a mountain
of canvases right now. Are you? This cat is to give you a little
extra strength.

Also, you're doing great!

[link to a gif of a cat flying in outer space]

***

**November 28, 2011
Email from Lara to Andres**

Subject: Re: How is your day going? Here is a cat

Day's going great! I was indeed under a big pile of canvases.
And now I am in front of them, and feel very daunted. Why did I
choose to do this again? Anyway, I take your cat, and raise you
a honey badger.

P.S. I also believe in you. And you are probably doing the greatest

[link to a viral video about honey badgers]

***

**November 30, 2011
Email from Lara to Adora**

Subject: Cute Guy Alert

I have so many updates about Andres. We have been having the best of times. It's been two weeks since he got here, and he has made it known that he will be here for 3-6 more months! AND POSSIBLY FOREVER? We've been doing lots of sports together, seeing movies, and trying new restaurants... I think you might have been right... We are well-suited for each other! Honestly, I feel so safe? Like mentally and physically? Is this normal? I mean, I can't tell what we are yet. But I'm not even anxious about that? I'm just optimistic. Like, cautiously optimistic. He's just so different! Anyway, I dunno. I can't help it. Like I said, cautiously optimistic.

54
New York, 2011

One of the things Lara and Andres had taken up together in earnest was rock climbing. They got memberships at a local gym, and met up there after school and work at least three times a week. Lara's favorite thing to do was boulder. She had been climbing leisurely in the past, but in New York she really hit her stride.

In mid-December, around Andres' sixth week in the city, the two found themselves once again at the wall.

"Do you think you're going to clear that V4 today?" Andres pointed at a problem that Lara had been working on for the past two sessions. It had a tricky forty-five degree overhang and required a dynamic reach from one crimp hold to another. Lara hated crimp holds, but she loved the rush of endorphins and adrenaline after sending a wall proportionately more, so she didn't let that stop her.

"Do you think you'll clear the slopey V4?" Lara pointed at the problem he was tackling on the opposite boulder.

"I think we're both going to try our darndest." Andres winked and offered her a high-five. When their hands clapped together a cloud of chalk erupted between them, showering Lara's hair and clothes with dust. "Oops!"

"HEY!" Lara exclaimed, realizing what he had done. She took a fist full of chalk and smudged it clean across his black dri-fit shirt.

Andres had been approaching this process of getting to know her as slowly and considerately as possible, and Lara appreciated that, but their playful flirtation was only making it more difficult to maintain neutrality and cautious optimism. In fact, she had begun to wonder if she and Andres were forever going to be relegated to centuries-old flirtation with soft Jane Austen-esque touches and meaningful gazes.

Right then, Lara wanted to just grab him and kiss Andres. Full-on. No holds barred.

It seemed his own mind and body were in the same place because he reached over and placed one chalky hand on her lower back and the other on her hip, drawing her close.

"This is a new shirt!" he said, his face close to hers now. He rubbed his chest against hers playfully, getting chalk all over her, too.

Lara laughed. With his face so close she could see the little cupid's bow of his upper lip, a bead of sweat on his brow, the knot on the bridge of his nose giving his face that much more character, the stubble on his chin, and the little gold flecks in his eyes.

She looked up at him and smiled cheekily. "Is this the part where you finally kiss me?" Her heart was thudding in her chest. "Like, REALLY kiss me?"

Andres leaned closer and closer, but he moved so infuriatingly slowly, teasing her. So Lara leaned up and sealed their fate herself.

The kiss was tender and sweet, but deep and hopeful. Instead of her heart thudding harder, she felt it slowing down until her breath matched his. Calm, confident.

They pulled apart and Lara smiled again. She could not remember the last time she was kissed, and it did not matter because she felt that perhaps she had never been kissed in that way before anyway.

Andres smiled back. Then suddenly he stepped aside and bowed at her, gesturing toward the wall, "Now, allez!"

***

That Sunday, Andres took Lara to champagne brunch.

"Wow, what's the occasion?" she said, sliding into her chair.

"I have to head back to Boston for about ten days,"

Andres said, kicking off their first serious conversation. He poked at his Eggs Benedict and looked at Lara meaningfully.

"Oh," Lara said disappointedly. She had been thinking they were on a fancy date to talk about something else.

"But I'll be back before December 23rd. I leave early next week. And that's why I wanted to talk to you."

"Oh," Lara said again, an ember of hope forming in her chest.

"And HR has just given me the news that I will be, in fact, moving to Manhattan—in effect from the day I get back from this trip," Andres said this in a very formal way, with both hands on the table, and his eyes gazing directly into Lara's. "And I am thrilled about this news, not just because I like Manhattan, or the team, and not just because this is what I had been planning for, but because, as I am sure you know by now, I really fancy you. And it just feels so right that our paths keep crossing and have since led us to this moment."

Fancy, Lara blushed. Never had a boy been so forward with her before.

"I've really enjoyed getting to know you. You are beautiful, and smart. Funny, adventurous, intriguing, authentic. I like the things I know so far, and am keen to explore and learn more." Andres reached over and squeezed Lara's hand, then he added with a deep, contented exhale, "Honestly, I'm so glad we met on that plane."

Lara's cheeks burned and she could not hide her smile.

Andres had not broken eye contact. "Do you feel the same?"

Lara nodded, clearing her throat, hoping to find her words. Then from somewhere within her, she heard herself say: "Yes. I get what you're saying. I feel the same."

Emboldened by his honesty, Lara chose to tell him her truth, too. "I've really enjoyed getting to know you as well," she said. "You might be the kindest, funniest, most respectful guy I have ever dated. I just love that there are no airs, no doubts with you. You're honest. And you're real."

"So you fancy me as well?"

Lara scrunched her nose at him. "Yes, I fancy you, too. And I'd like you a lot better if after this you kiss me again."

Andres leaned closer to her and this time gave her a soft, hopeful kiss. "So are you open to building something together? And seeing where this goes?"

"Yes. I am open to building this together. And I like that you say building, because I don't want this to be a passive thing. I don't want to waste my time," Lara replied.

"Yes, absolutely." Andres' smile reached all the way up to his eyes.

They kissed again. And for the days after that until he left, it seemed they did not stop kissing. The night before his trip to Boston, they lay wrapped up in his sheets and in each other, and Lara felt no longer just a cautious optimism. She felt absolutely golden.

And she was.

December 14, 2011
Email from Lara to Owen and Mike

Subject: NY NY TRIP!

Hey guys! So I was thinking we could do a festive sort of pub crawl at some point while you guys are here. And we definitely need to treat ourselves to a good meal. Can you guys look up what you want to try the most and we'll get reservations asap? The guy I'm seeing, Andres, will be tagging along for a lot of the stuff - hope you don't mind. It would be great if you guys could get to know him and vice versa! I really like this one. Anyway, here's a link to some of the top reviewed restaurants - let me know what you think!

***

December 15, 2011
Email from Owen to Mike

Subject: Fwd: NY NY TRIP!

Looping Lara out for a minute. Told you. The guy she's seeing. Boyfriend.

55
Los Angeles and New York, 2011-2012

Owen stared at Lara's email. *I am fucked.*

He felt his frustration and anxiety bubbling to the surface. So in the end this Andres did prove to be a thing. This news really threw a spanner in the works. Owen had wanted to let Mike in on his plans, where he had hoped to pull some kind of small gesture as Lara would have liked—maybe at an art gallery or a gig. He had planned to say it. To tell her. The truth.

"What do I do?" he said to Oskar, who sat across from him at their dining table.

Oskar looked nonplussed.

"Dad…" Owen pressed, desperation building in his eyes and his tone. It was so typical. *Obviously, this would happen to me,* he thought morosely. *The one time I decide I'm finally going to do it, and I'm late. And I'm shitting myself in the bed I made.*

"You'll have to just wait and see, son. If she's seeing someone now, you'll have to gauge how serious it is, or if it's something you might be able to stand in front of and say, *'Choose me instead.'*"

"I am so fucked." Owen sat with his head in his hands trying to regroup, trying to figure out his Plan B, his thoughts.

Oskar reached over and gave Owen's shoulder a squeeze. "It's going to be okay, son. You can't give up just yet. It isn't like they're married."

"The one time I decided to take a chance on love. The one fucking time." Owen threw his arms up in exasperation.

"It ain't over 'til it's over," Oskar said again firmly.

Owen sighed. *I hope you're right,* he wanted to say, but

he just shook his head and left to pack.

***

On December 28th, Owen and Mike rolled up to Lara's flat.

When Lara opened the front door, she looked every bit the same—and yet so different. Her long, wavy hair cascaded around her shoulders in a half ponytail, and she appeared to wear a bit of tint in her lips and cheeks. She wore a wool lounge set—joggers and a loose, crop top, and she had a pair of fleece-lined clogs on.

Owen felt a surge of nerves and affection at the sight of her, his breath caught in his throat.

When the pair walked in, Lara, Owen, and Mike all exchanged an enthusiastic "HEY!"

Then from the corner of Owen's eye, he saw a tall young man come out of the kitchen to join them. Standing respectfully behind Lara, a couple of paces away, he waved at the new arrivals.

"You must be the new boyfriend!" Mike said to Andres.

Lara smiled. "Guys, this is Andres. Andres, these are my good friends, Owen, and Mike. We had many misadventures together during our time in Manila."

"I heard you're a cog in the good old machine?" Mike said as Lara and Andres helped them with their bags, and everyone found a spot in the living room around the couch.

Andres laughed. "Yes! I heard you left for greener pastures?"

"I did! I'm with my dad's business now. Is it still the same?"

"Long hours, delicious food, batty clients?"

"Yeah?"

"Absolutely!"

Listening to the back and forth made Owen feel antsy and before the two could speak more, he heard himself say loudly, almost unwittingly even, "That's super interesting and all, but maybe we can get a tour?"

"Well, there isn't much to see, but sure." Lara led the boys around to the bathroom, kitchen, and her room. When she opened the door slightly, Owen stepped forward and burst in.

"Ah, there was a time when I was the only boy who spent any time in Lara's bedroom," he said before he could stop himself. *Ah, shit,* he kicked himself inwardly. It had just been a thought, he hadn't meant to say it aloud.

Lara gave him a look that said, very clearly, *What the fuck?*

Mike sighed. "Don't mind Owen. He's like a male dog marking anything he can touch."

Owen tried not to take offense. At this point, he was in no real position to argue anyway.

Lara laughed and rolled her eyes then shoved Owen out of her room and closed the door. "My room is thankfully off-limits to pissy dogs."

She gestured at the spot on the floor in front of the couch. "This is where you guys will be sleeping. Andres and I got some blow-up mattresses. So we can set them up every night and collapse them during the day."

"Oh, does Andres live here too now?" Owen asked, finding a seat and kicking off his shoes. He hated how curt he sounded.

Lara looked at him through narrowed eyes, and Owen looked away, feeling ashamed of his own behavior but unable to control how defensive he was feeling.

"No," Lara said simply, a tinge of annoyance in her voice.

***

In bed that first night in New York, Owen lay some feet away from Mike on the blow-up mattress, staring at the ceiling. In the next room, Lara and Andres had long turned in.

"*An-dres Cour-te-nay,*" Owen said, pronouncing each syllable. "What do you think? Is he a good fit for our Lara?"

Mike groaned. "You want to talk about this now? They could walk out and overhear us at any time."

"I'm just saying. Doesn't he seem too perfect? Nobody's that perfect. And he plays the drums, too?"

"Are people not allowed to play the drums now?"

"I'm just saying, maybe there's more than meets the eye."

"The firm does background checks. I'm sure Lara's safe."

"I mean, don't you think he's too pretty?"

"Dude, I hesitate to even say this but…*are you jealous?*"

"NO."

"Okay, because that's what you sound like. Go to sleep. Andres is a nice guy, and they seem happy together. Lara is letting us stay over, and we are going to have a fun reunion. You and your brain won't ruin it."

Mike turned away and closed the conversation, but Owen lay there with his mind whirring. It's too late. Mike knew nothing of Owen's real intentions, and he felt trapped with nobody to vent to,except perhaps Oskar, who was undoubtedly asleep.

The rising panic in his chest trumped everything. The regret, frustration, shame. And he was even more embarrassed now. He had packed up his whole life. And for what? For her to move on and shack up with someone new. But it was his fault, really, and he knew it. He had taken his sweet time. He had taken so many things for granted when he had them. *What a prick you are, Owen. This is why you can't have nice things,* he thought, and he closed his eyes and tried to quiet his mind.

***

For New Year's Eve, the group decided to do something different. A cheesy ensemble film literally entitled *New Year's Eve* had recently come out. None of them had seen it, and they decided to make a joke of it, going together with Zuri and another friend from Lara's program named Lorelei.

They started the evening with a potluck dinner in Lorelei's flat. After, they transitioned to drinks in a nearby bar before stumbling their way to the cinemas to watch Zac Efron and Michelle Pfeiffer zip around New York City on a scooter.

Andres sat next to Lara and in the darkness of the theater Owen saw him reach for her hand. Their fingers locked. Lara turned and smiled at him, and he at her. The entire night they had been so sweet—stealing glances, touching each other on shoulders or backs, fingers through hair, lips brushing cheeks. Andres watched Lara with clear admiration when she walked from one place to another.

Owen could tell because he knew that feeling—what it

was to take Lara in. He saw Andres do so with a smile, and when they sat next to one another, it was clear that Andres never shied away from her touch.

He sat next to Lara on her other side most of the night, noting each little signal in her body. It was the first time that Owen was in a room with Lara and she was organically, with ease and comfort and joy, turned toward something else other than him. It was the first time in so long that they were sitting together, and their knees were not touching.

Somewhere, again, in his throat, the knot throbbed uncomfortably. Feelings. He took a large handful of popcorn, and stuffed it into his mouth as he tried not to think.

***

Mike left New York on January 2. Owen, who had not booked a return flight because of work and all his original intentions, begged Lara for a couple more weeks to stay over and figure himself out.

"Client work," he explained.

With obvious sympathy but some hesitation, judging by the lack of enthusiasm in her voice, Lara agreed to let him stay.

But what was he going to do now? Owen was beginning to flounder. There was nobody to blame but himself, and yet he found himself blaming everyone. How could Lara get over it all so quickly? Had it been just his imagination? Was the love that they'd shared so long expired? Couldn't they have had a way forward? Why had Oskar encouraged him at all? It was so ill-conceived. He shouldn't have been allowed to give love advice anyway. He was terrible at it.

Owen could feel himself taking his frustrations out on the world, and every day he always came back to the only real comfort he knew. Lara. *Call Lara. Vent to Lara. Reach for Lara.* Somehow, this was worse than he could've imagined. Because he had flown all this way to be closer to Lara, but she felt further from him than ever.

On one rare morning when Lara was home and not with Andres, she came out of her room in a bright orange coat, chunky black sneakers, jeans, and a white shirt.

"Wow," Owen said from his perch on the couch. He couldn't help himself. Lara had always had her style, and he had found it charming and artsy. But now in this setting, it grated on him. How cute she always was. And was she wearing makeup? He was no expert but he could see eyeliner and gloss on her lips.

"What?" she asked, looking down at herself then at him.

"Nothing." He turned back to his breakfast and adjusted his work shirt and slacks.

"What?" she said again.

He shrugged. "Nothing. Just not what I would've chosen."

"Well, good thing you have your own closet and I mine," she bit back.

Okay, he deserved that, he knew. But back in the day he could comment on things and she might have bickered back but she'd often hear him out, too.

"Sure." He shrugged, not sure what to say next, to which she rolled her eyes, and somehow that angered him. He felt a sort of irritation bubbling up inside. *Hey, I came here for you*, he argued. But it didn't come out. Instead he said, "And are you wearing makeup? How come you never did that for me?"

And he wanted to kick himself.

She looked at him then, her eyes narrowed and her cheeks flushed. "Have a good day, Owen," she said and then left.

56
New York, 2012

Two weeks later, Lara was at Andres' new flat. His apartment was a one-bedroom with spectacular views. The pair were cuddling while reading together on the couch when Lara's phone rang.

"Hello? Owen?" It was only the third time he had called her that day. The first two times had been about the bathroom. She wondered what it was now. "I don't understand why—but—"

On the other end, Owen was launching into a tirade over the radiators, which had apparently been giving him grief. But Lara didn't want to hear it. In that moment, she was entirely over Owen's voice and presence, and all else.

"Owen, listen—look," she interrupted, "just call the Super if the heating isn't working. I'm not home, and I can't do that for you right now. You're a grown man, and you're staying in my flat free of charge. If something's broken while you're the only one home, the least you could do is be an adult and figure it out."

She hung up and huffed, then turned back to her book, brow still furrowed. She and Owen had been bickering again, and she hated it. All of it vexed her–the relentless teasing, and how he kept leaning into all the sides of their previous relationship, their "secret-boyfriend-girlfriend" status, and their inability to speak directly about their feelings.

She was glad Andres finally had a place, then she could escape almost whenever she wanted.

Andres had put his own book down and was watching her with interest. "Owen again?"

"Yeah, he's just needy."

"Can I ask you something, Lar?"

"Mm?" she said without looking up from her book.

"Could you set that down a moment while we talk about this?"

Lara put her book down and looked up at Andres, taking a deep breath. She had known this conversation would come up eventually, but she hadn't rehearsed all the ways she could address it, so she sat there, nervously wondering what he would say.

"What's gone on with you and Owen?" he said this so gently, so openly, that Lara felt her nerves and defenses whittling away.

She sighed. "Well. Owen is my best friend."

"All right," Andres replied, but his tone said, *"Tell me more."*

"But we also had a weird…physical relationship for a short time. And we also had a fraught…emotional relationship."

"I see. And when did that end?"

"Hmm, let me see…" She thought for a moment. "A while back to be honest. Probably two years ago now? Or close to that? I mean, it never really was properly resolved, if I'm being honest. But. We both knew it was the end."

"I see. So it wasn't a clean break, then?"

"Well, no, not quite." Lara shrugged. "But, at the same time, it kind of was. It was a mutual, conscious moving apart. I think I would have been willing to give it a last ditch effort before leaving Manila if he had been up front with me. But he wasn't, and, really, I think Owen knew we would be awful together. He said so himself, in his own way. And he was totally right."

Andres appeared to think for a moment, digesting the information. Then he replied, "Alright. As long as you are happy now and don't have any one-that-got-away regrets or anything like that…"

Lara drew herself closer to Andres then, hooking her legs into his. "Andres Courtenay, I am not only happy with the choice I made almost a year ago. But also with every other choice I've made since. Especially you."

Andres smiled and gave her a kiss in response, which led to another then another, and for the nth time since they had begun their relationship, Lara felt truly satisfied.

***

Later, when the two lay on the couch, wrapped in each other, with Lara's back against Andres' chest, he whispered, "I hate to bring this up once more but…given your history, isn't it rather odd Owen is living with you again?"

Lara was quiet for a moment, thinking, and then she said, "Yes, I suppose that's true. But I can't possibly kick him out…"

"I wouldn't put it that way. He's an adult with a job. He can find his own flat." Andres shrugged. "And to be honest, as your current boyfriend, it's rather strange for me to see your ex living with you. And he's driving you batty while he's at it."

"He says he'll be out of our hair soon."

"I don't want to force you to do anything out of character, Lara. I find it rather uncomfortable, but I can manage. I'm a grown man. If it makes you uncomfortable in your own space as well, though, perhaps you should do something."

Lara thought this over. Did it make her uncomfortable? Certainly, she was annoyed—almost daily. It just felt like Owen was always in her hair. But was she uncomfortable with that? Perhaps she should have been. It was then that Lara realized just how used to Owen she was—how accepting she was of his antics and their toxic codependency. So much so that even if she had a boyfriend, a new life, and new friends, Owen was still there, breathing down her neck, making her uncomfortable, making her boyfriend uncomfortable. Suddenly, Lara felt angry. A weird sort of acidic feeling in her stomach bubbled up to her throat. She remembered all the times she set a boundary, and every time Owen crossed a line.

God, why do you have to be such a prick sometimes, Owen? she thought.

"I'll talk to him," she promised.

"Be gentle," Andres said, his tone almost a warning. Who was this man who considered her first, and who spoke and thought kindly of even her oddest relations? She knew, of course, this man was hers. That knowledge gave her such a deep feeling of contentment, and that night she slept beautifully.

***

"I'm just so frustrated," Lara growled into the phone walking back and forth across the length of her room on a day that Owen was off in Connecticut seeing a client.

She had returned home feeling gentle and calm, ready to face Owen, and was greeted instead with his groceries stacked on the kitchen counters, and his clothes hung against her book shelves. The calm had quickly turned to impatience, and it was all only made worse by the note he had left tagged to a box of half-eaten hazelnut truffles which read, *Got these for you for being such a gracious host but since you're never home they couldn't wait anymore and I helped myself and had some. Oops. They're good though! Made sure to leave you half still. Sorry about the mess, I promise I'll tidy up when I'm back. Away only a day and a half, so be in your hair again before you know it!*

"I know," came Adora's comforting voice.

"I just can't believe that after all this time, even when I'm with someone new, Owen can still get under my skin!"

"But you let him, Lara," Adora said gently. "You let him do this to you. You don't have to."

Lara stopped pacing and sat on her bed. The truth was, ever since Owen had first arrived, she had been growing weary of him. And her recent conversation with Andres only made it that much easier for her to admit to that weariness. She was annoyed that Owen could have such a presence in her life even long after they had set boundaries. She was hurt and frustrated that he still kept infringing on her space.

"You know he's broken, and you feel bad for him." Adora sighed on the phone. "And now you're letting that pity and your friendship and your past cloud your judgment. You know he loved you. Everyone knew that. But you guys broke up," Lara almost protested this but Adora was a step ahead and raised her voice, "Don't even try to say otherwise! It. Was. A. Break. Up. Anyway. What I mean is, he doesn't get to just keep having his cake and eating it, too."

Adora was right, of course. "True," Lara conceded. "I do. I know what I have to do."

57
New York, 2012

Owen sat across from Lara in that diner, feeling anxious and queasy. This was it. This was the moment. When Lara had come in that morning and said, "We need to talk," he could tell, it was going to be a serious one. And he probably wasn't going to like it.

"Is everything okay?" Lara leading with this question only made Owen feel worse. She was being so nice, so calm. She had this air of professionalism, of maturity about her. It made his stomach churn. He sat back in his chair and stared at her, maintaining an apathetic distance. This was his opening, his chance to tell her. But he couldn't. Not anymore. Not without it being an unwelcome intrusion.

"I would like to help if something is the matter. I know you said you're here for work but like...if it were work, wouldn't you have your own place? Or is there maybe something you're not being honest about? Or like, do you need help finding a place? Is your start-up in a scrappy budget crunch phase?"

"Why, Lara? Why do you want to help?"

"Gosh, Owen. You know why. You're my best friend." Then she smiled a little. "Even when you're noseying in on my space at your own convenience."

Owen looked at her and then shook his head. He knew, as he gazed into her eyes, that she didn't realize this was meant to be his big gesture. That he had come for her—not to make her uncomfortable, not to wiggle into her life because it was convenient, and certainly not just for work, but to be with her.

He felt like a fool.

"I don't think there is anything that you can help me with, Lara," he finally said.

"Well, look, Owen. I don't think you can stay at my place anymore. I don't think it's appropriate. I'm with someone now. Whatever it was between us, you and me, that's been over for some time now. You're still my best friend, but I don't think you can be here. It's too weird."

When Owen remained silent, Lara kept talking. "Life is different now, you know? And we have to give each other space. We can't call each other all the time, we can't live together, we can't bicker like an old couple. We can't go back to the way things were. I really like Andres...and I really want our relationship to work..."

"Did Andres put you up to this?" Owen asked in spite of himself. He felt strange listening to his own voice—so tight, defensive, gruff.

Lara's eyes grew wide. "No. I mean, he was honest about how he felt about you staying at my place. And I had to be honest with him about what our relationship once was. But no. This was my idea, and what I want out of it is my choice."

Owen let out a long, tired exhale. "Just making sure."

"Sorry, Owen. But you know we were messed up. You really hurt me. And not just physically. And I acknowledge it takes two to tango. I'm sure I've hurt you. *So we both need time.*"

Owen sat there scratching a stain out of the table in front of him, quiet, processing. The waitress came and set down their plates of cheese burgers and fries. They ate for a few minutes as Owen tried to collect himself. Finally, he felt it was time to speak.

"Thank you," he said softly. "I appreciate that you brought this up. I guess we haven't had a lot of one-on-one time for me to explain. But. Like I said, I've got work to do here. I have a big client on the East Coast, particularly in New Jersey and Connecticut. I wanted to make Manhattan my base because, well, you're here and I thought it'd be nice to be in the same city again. I should have been looking for a flat of my own. I'm sorry for imposing myself on your space and making you and Andres uncomfortable. I think I just fell too easily into our old rhythms." He took a deep, shaky breath, "As you know, you're like family. Home. And I guess I missed that."

They let the silence sit between them, and Owen felt his eyes stinging, tears forming at the edges. *I miss you,* he repeated in his mind. He clenched his fists on the table and bit his lip, thinking, *I'm sorry. Just say it, Owen. Say it.*

But before he could gather the courage to speak, Lara said, "Thank you for explaining. I think it's clearer now. And, hey, it's great that you have all that going on. I am sure you are going to do great things. We're still friends, and always will be, but this is where we are now. "

"Thanks…and…you're right," Owen said. "I especially did not consider all the ways that our relationship affected you. I'm sorry for that. And even now I've been neglecting how my presence might be affecting your new life and relationships." He sighed and rubbed his forehead. He felt defeated. *You are a loser,* he scolded internally. What would he allow himself to say? *Stop being a coward.* "I miss you so much, Lar… I miss you but I know we're busy. Especially you. I know you're building something, and I'm so happy for you because this is a good time in your life, and Andres seems honest and real. I mean, fuck all the shit I've said, okay. He's not out of your league. You are worthy of him and more."

Lara sat, mouth slightly agape, looking surprised. Even he was a little shocked that he'd managed to get those words out. And now that he'd begun, he wanted to say as much as he could.

"You seem so happy and I don't want to get in the way of that, but we have something. We've always had something. And I hope that will always be so. There's so much more I want to say… but…I just… I can't." He licked his lips and shook his head. "I hope one day I can reach joy and clarity, too."

Then Owen noticed Lara was crying.

"Why are you crying?" he asked.

She sniffed and scrunched her nose, and then shook her head as if shaking out the emotions. "It's kind of sad, isn't it? I miss you, too. And I want you to be happy, too."

Owen paid for their meals, and the two stood and walked back up to Lara's apartment where Owen began packing immediately and made some calls to a nearby hotel for the night.

As they stood in her doorway, they hugged goodbye. When they finally let go, Owen said, "I never said this really, or if I did I didn't do it enough: I learned a lot from you. So thank you."

Owen felt like they were breaking up—again and for real. He knew that as the door closed, a window should open into a new version of Lara and Owen as a pair. He hoped eventually for that version to be friendly, peaceful, joyful, and clear. *Two People...on different paths. Two happy people; two whole people.*

58

New York, 2012

"I'm sad you're going."

Lara fiddled with the collar of Andres' shirt as the pair stood in the middle of Penn Station, facing one another, the bustle of commuters ebbing and flowing around them. She felt silly saying so, but she couldn't help herself. She couldn't keep even her cheesiest, silliest impulses from him. That's how much she liked him.

"It's just a two day business trip, darling. Then I'm back."

Lara was full of affection for this man. This man with whom the days were so elegantly simple that Lara's own joy and peace delighted her in the best of ways. "I know, I know," she said.

"Just focus on your latest paintings and then tell me all about them."

"Deal," Lara smiled.

Leaning forward, Andres gave her a kiss and hug, and then the next thing she heard was "I love you."

She giggled a little in spite of herself and tried to pull away to look at Andres' face but couldn't. "What did you say?" she said to his chest instead.

"Nothing," came his swift response.

"What?"

"I mean…nothing."

"What was that?"

Lara finally pulled away and they looked at each other, and they were both blushing fire engine red.

"Well, I'd best be off!" Andres said.

Love was a big word. Did he love Lara? Did he mean it? In that moment, Lara realized she hoped he had. And as much as she wanted to say it back, the words were stuck in her throat. Had it been a fluke?

"Get well soon!" Andres said suddenly, his voice shaking slightly, clearly nervous. He made to walk away but they were still holding hands and Lara wouldn't let him off so easily. He slapped himself on the forehead. "Rather, see you soon. I'll miss you!"

The two laughed and kissed then parted. Lara was filled with a buzzing, nervous energy.

The entire way home, she smiled to herself. Andres loved her. It was real. She turned the idea around in her mind and felt the butterflies in her belly rising up to greet her, filling her mind with hope and joy and promise.

That afternoon she painted a watercolor scene—a thousand tiny birds and butterflies and bees flooding a large page. She felt like she was in the middle of that Ben Folds song. In the verses he sings of mistakes and possibilities, but each wondering leads to an affirmation in the chorus, and Lara knew she was *the luckiest.*

59
New York, 2012

Owen's new flat in New York was a studio. It had everything he needed—a little kitchen with just one burner and a sad excuse for an oven, a snug bathroom, and a view of the wall of another apartment building.

On the plus side, it had enough space for a comfortable king-size bed, and it came furnished with some decent modern, minimalist furniture.

The only thing he really had to do was buy a bit of art and a couple of plants, but he had been traveling across the client's properties in New Jersey and Connecticut, and now North Carolina too, that as a result, Owen was traveling every week for two or three days at a time, and struggling to make actual roots in New York, or even make his flat a home.

Still, he was going to try. So on a Saturday morning, Owen skipped to a local market and picked up the largest leafy green plant he could find and a cheesy watercolor of New York which made him think, *Lara can do better.* Perhaps after a big commission, he might buy one of her pieces.

Back at the flat, he placed the plant by the window, and the painting on the wall behind the dining table, and stared around with both hope and apprehension. Whenever he was alone, he found his thoughts drifting back to Lara. What might she be up to? How odd it was to be in the same city and not together.

It had been weeks since their talk, and he was trying to give her as much space as possible, but he couldn't help reaching out now and then. He tried to keep his messages sporadic—once a week or so. They had not seen each other at all. But looking at his new apartment, he thought, Maybe a house warming is in order. And Lara was still the only person he thought he wanted to invite.

He picked up his phone and texted her a short, casual invite, making sure to include Andres as well.

Ten minutes later, she replied.

From Lara Halford
Sure! We are free tomorrow, if that works? What time should we come? What should we bring?

Owen's heart skipped a beat and he realized he had been waiting with bated breath. The words he had kept repeating to himself were wearing out. 'I love her madly' was becoming 'I miss her badly' instead. Was it nice to see Lara with a good man? Yes. Was it hard? Of course it was. Was it weird to see "we" and know it meant her and someone else? Absolutely.

Tomorrow is good, he wrote back. *Around 6? I'll take care of the food. You guys bring a couple of drinks.*

Perfect! See you! came her swift reply.

60
New York, 2012

That Saturday, Lara and Andres sat on his couch, reading. In the middle of a lull in the novel she was working through, Lara eyed Andres over the top of her book. The curl on his forehead was impossibly cute, and he chewed his lower lip each time he seemed to approach a serious passage. When she squinted to read the title, she realized he was reading Viktor Frankl's *Man's Search for Meaning*, and she felt such an odd, warm rush of affection for him.

She nudged his foot with her toe. "Psst," she said.

Without looking up, he poked her back. "Yes, darling?"

Her skin tingled. She loved when he called her that. "Learning anything new about man's meaning?"

"Maybe."

"Care to share?" Lara inched closer, stroking his thigh.

This time, he looked at her. "Is someone getting frisky here?"

"Can't help it. You looked so hot there."

"Ooh. Reading a book. Sexy."

"Super."

Andres put his book aside and took Lara by her legs, pulling her closer until they were tangled in each other once more. Lara exclaimed in surprise and put her book down, too. She leaned her face up close to his and kissed him. She tried to imagine a time when she felt so safe with a boy that she might do that—go the full mile, make the first move. She couldn't remember. In the past, she'd wait for a signal. She used euphemisms, analogies—a glance, a touch, the naive hope that her truths could be communicated without letting them step out of her heart into the world. But with Andres once they started, she did not want to stop, and she never worried it was too much. She didn't feel the need to restrain herself.

A kiss was so intimate, sometimes even more so than all that often followed, because it was the spark that started the fire. Lara imagined each kiss in almost chromatic, electric terms. All the invisible nerve endings firing, a web of color emanating from two separate points, meeting somewhere in the middle, crossing lines. That afternoon as Andres kissed Lara, she felt completely lit up, like the Christmas tree in Rockefeller Center.

***

On Sunday, Lara and Andres walked hand in hand up to Owen's new apartment.

"Thanks for doing this," Lara said to him. "I know he's not your favorite person."

"I have nothing against Owen. As long as the boundaries are respected, and you're happy, then I am too."

Lara felt so lucky just then. "You're too nice."

"No, darling, you're too nice. I'm just confident. And I trust you." Andres winked. "I know he's your best friend, and you're his. It wouldn't be fair to make you walk away. People grow and change. We should leave room for that."

61
New York, 2012

Upstairs, Owen had prepared tacos and a cheesecake. Andres and Lara were glad they had brought beers as this made the perfect combination.

The three sat around Owen's table and the couple took turns complimenting his new space.

"I like your furniture. Modern," Andres said graciously.

Lara nodded. "Yeah, and I love that plant," she added, referring to the fiddle leaf fig by the window.

Owen thanked them and then put on some music as they proceeded to share pleasantries and updates about their lives. And as he watched the two, the little knot in his chest tightened and loosened in turns. The way Andres looked at Lara, the way he touched her hand, stroked her hair out of her face. Owen thought about the times he had done the same, and he thought about the times he actively avoided such things.

He observed Andres' attention—how he always refilled Lara's glass. How he looked at people when they spoke. And how he never interrupted Lara to give her grief. If he were to tease her, he did so almost tenderly, as though sharing an inside joke. Whereas Owen and Lara leaned into each other in sarcasm and irony, Andres' tools were authenticity and affection.

When Lara patted her belly and declared she was too full for more, Andres saw her watching him make one last taco out of the corner of his eye, and he smiled and teased her. "Too full for your own plate but not too full to take bites off of mine?"

She flushed but laughed. "Just little bites!"

Andres made no snarky retorts. He didn't point out Lara's

body, or call her a symbiotic parasite–a comeback Owen thought was fitting and funny in his own way. No, Andres gave her the extra bite, the sip of beer, without comment.

"Remember when we went to La Union and you insisted you only needed the small coconut? Then you ate some meat out of mine!" Owen said.

"You gave me so much grief, but they were worth like a quarter, and you bought another for yourself right after!" Lara protested.

Andres laughed, at ease. "Good tip. When we finally make it to Southeast Asia, you get your own coconuts, Lara."

He did not seem threatened by Owen. Owen wasn't sure if that made him even sadder. That he wasn't even a consideration in that sense. That it was so clear as day that the best man had won. Even though they were never fighting to begin with.

He thought about the Joni Mitchell song, "Both Sides Now," whose chorus changed slightly each time but always ended with a confession. In one, she would sing about not knowing love, and then thereafter not knowing life. Owen felt that.

***

Right around Thanksgiving, Owen sat in a cafe, puzzling over the various things on his plate. Peter was struggling balancing the growing West Coast portfolio alone, and the travel for their hotelier client was unsustainable for Owen's social life.

Being closer to Virginia, though, meant he could spend more time with Lola Beth and his mother, which he did every month. The dinners with Andres and Lara had also become regular, monthly occasions. They had started off formulaic—they would talk about the same things, like business, news, films, and music. But over time, they expanded. They began to play Settlers of Catan together as almost a tradition.

At one such dinner, they were at Andres', and Lara had won another round.

"I'm going to grab more beers," Andres declared, getting up, and walking to the kitchen.

Owen watched him go and turned to Lara saying, "I feel like you've always been good at strategy, even if you don't actually

283

know it. You're very thoughtful in the way you do things. It helps in these kinds of games. I lose these games because I have no patience. And I'm a little blind to nuance…"

"You've been really nice lately," Lara teased in response.

"What do you mean?"

"I mean, I can't remember the last time we bickered."

"Well, we're past that now, aren't we?"

"I suppose. You don't miss making me squirm?" By her tone, Owen could tell she was joking.

"Nah." Owen laughed a little, then it occurred to him it wouldn't hurt to give her an honest answer. "I'm sorry I ever wanted to make you squirm. I kept pressing your buttons. It was childish."

Lara sat back. Her eyebrows shot up in surprise. "I appreciate that. But it wasn't all bad."

Owen sat with that. As he looked at her, he felt proud and enchanted by the woman she had become. He wondered what she thought when she looked at him. Had he also evolved?

62
New York, 2013

"By now, you should all be knee deep in planning for whatever series you're putting together for the big year-end show."

Lara's mentor, Professor da Silva, addressed the small room of painters, all of whom were under her charge, benefiting from both her guidance and critique. There were three of them in total, and they all sat in front of their easels, their backs to their work, and their faces turned toward the small, bespeckled woman in the center of the room with skin the color of burnt caramel, and a black and gold kaftan draped over her little frame.

"This work should reflect not only what you have learned in these rooms, these halls, but also everything else that has brought you to this point. As of today, you will have only twenty weeks to complete these works. In the past, I've had students who began even before the designated kick off." Professor da Silva cast a pointed look at each of her charges. "Though nobody in this room has, as far as I know." She cleared her throat and adjusted her glasses. "So you better get started."

Lara's heart thudded a little. She had worked through many series across her time in the program, but none she wanted to include in the final showcase. And she had not quite thought through her thesis. She had indeed done a lot of research, asked former students about the process, and even spoken with Professor da Silva about what to expect. From making the pieces to introducing and defending them in a final oral presentation, she felt mentally prepared for the challenge.

The only thing missing was the series itself.

Professor da Silva walked around the room thereafter,

speaking directly with each artist. In hushed tones, Lara overheard small snippets of her peers' plans. A whisper about charcoal here, a murmur over mixed media there. Something about self-portraiture.

Lara stared at the blank canvas in front of her. In her time in the program, her portfolio had grown and her skill along with it. She had dozens of paintings now, from portraits to self-portraits to still life. From landscapes to seascapes.

But where she was really finding her stride was in surreal pieces of art, painted hyperrealistically. Her most recent work had received gushing, positive critique from her professors for its technical strengths. It had been a large, ultra close-up of a dog's face in whose eyes were reflected an even closer up image of a different dog, in whose eyes in turn an even tighter image of a different dog had been depicted, and so on and so forth. However, it didn't mean very much beyond something silly she'd dreamt up. And she knew that she wanted this final project to mean something.

"Lara," Professor da Silva spoke softly, suddenly right next to her. "Any thoughts for your final project?"

Lara looked from her mentor to her canvas then back again. "I'm not sure," she replied. "I want it to mean something."

"I was on the panel when you applied, you know." Professor da Silva pulled a chair over and sat down.

"I remember," Lara agreed.

"I think you've grown a lot since you've been here"

Lara nodded. "For sure."

"The paintings of the Philippines you submitted for acceptance into the program—they were lovely, creative, and full of heart. But I also saw that they were full of yearning." Professor da Silva crossed her legs and squinted up toward the ceiling as though thinking far back in time. "I saw that you were somehow removed from your own work. These teeny tiny scapes that you had created in the center of large canvases, covered in white space that you filled in shades and color and gradient and ombré…"

Lara was flattered that Professor da Silva remembered her work at all, let alone in such detail. But then again, she was her mentor, and it was part of her job to know.

"Anyway, since then I have seen you fill canvas after canvas with many stories," Professor da Silva continued. "Your work has grown in size and scale, as well as technique and skill. Do you know where that came from? That growth? Because artists come to school to network and be guided, but the journey they are on is already underway well before school, and has much more to do with what is happening in their individual lives than it does with what happens in the studio."

Lara thought about what her professor was saying. She knew her growth in just the last few years had been exponential. Why? How?

As she traced her steps backwards, she found herself seeing those crossroads—the moments that had served as turning points, leading her out of university, into the Philippines, toward music, through heartache, back into the arms of her paints and her brushes, and then into a whole new world.

The pieces began to fall into place before her eyes. Like a puzzle. And in her head, as always, came the familiar tunes of jazz and blues, and folk and rock, the soundtracks in her creative heart.

Lara smiled. "I think I have an idea."

"Wonderful," Professor da Silva smiled back. "Best get started on that then. And don't forget to type up a thesis statement and a draft abstract for me. I expect it on my desk in the next three days." Then, she got up and walked away.

Lara's mind whirred. She had just the thing.

63
New York, 2013

One weekend in February, both Lola Beth and Vicky decided they would like to visit Owen for a change. Vicky drove and booked a hotel where she and Lola Beth could stay.

"I usually have dinner with Andres and Lara on the third Saturday of every month," Owen told his mother and grandmother as he got them settled. "But I can clear my schedule."

"Why don't we all go together?" Lola Beth suggested, "Perhaps at a restaurant. We wouldn't want to change all your plans."

Owen considered this. Vicky and Lola Beth had never met Lara. It might be nice. "Okay, I'll suggest something."

That evening, they met Lara and Andres in a small yet well-regarded steakhouse. The pair had arrived before them, and Owen could see them through the window in the warm glow of the restaurant. Lara smiled widely at something Andres said and Owen felt his heart skip a beat.

How stupid that I still respond to her this way after all this time.

At the table, Owen introduced everyone. "Mom, this is Lara, and her boyfriend, Andres. Guys, this is my mom, Vicky. And my grandmother, Beth."

"It's a pleasure to meet you both! I really appreciate your music," Andres enthused, shaking Vicky's hand. He helped Lola Beth with her chair and regarded her warmly.

Lara smiled and took Vicky's hand in hers. "I am so happy to meet you. Owen has told me so much. Can't believe it's taken us this long to get together!" She then also took Lola Beth's hand and placed her forehead on top of it in a mano gesture, a Filipino custom of greeting elders.

But Lola Beth pulled Lara in for a hug. There were no words exchanged yet, but Owen watched this with his heart in his throat.

"So glad to meet you, hija," Lola Beth told Lara. "Thank you for taking care of our Owen."

Everyone sat down and placed their orders.

"I listened to the music you made together," Lola Beth said as she cut her steak. "It was so special. You're talented."

"Thanks," Lara said, a small, embarrassed smile on her face.

"Would you go back to making music?" Vicky asked.

"No, I think it was never really for me. But I'm grateful for the experience!" Lara said, looking at Owen when she said so.

Andres smiled at them both encouragingly. "Your work did generate some lovely songs." Then he turned to Vicky. "Would you?"

Vicky shook her head. "I'm too busy with other things now. My voice probably wouldn't be able to do what it once could. And Ma and I are having fun in our retirement. Right, Ma?"

Lola Beth laughed. "Too much."

Owen, who had been mostly quiet, observing, smiled as well then. "It's nice that you're together. And one of the only positives to New York is being able to bus over and see you guys every month."

"Are there no other nice things about New York?" Andres teased. "What about your awesome friends?"

Owen laughed. "Yes, that and my friends. But one of them never gives anyone a chance at Catan. I'm sure they are cheating." He winked. "Or otherwise the luckiest person in the world."

Owen noticed Andres squeeze Lara's hand as he responded, "Maybe I am exactly that."

As Owen walked his grandmother and mother back to their hotel after, Lola Beth spoke in a soft, patient voice. "Hijo, you're going to kill yourself sticking around Lara. If you are hoping to outlast this new relationship, you will be disappointed."

Owen stood, taken aback. Was that what Owen was

doing? Was that what it looked like? And was this really it for Lara?

He looked at his feet. "Is that what it looks like?"

"Who cares what it looks like." Vicky shrugged. "What matters is what it is. I doubt they think that's what you're doing, but we're your family. As much as you might think I don't know anything about you, I'm still your mother, and I still have my instincts."

"Owen, anak," Lola Beth stopped walking, which made the other two stop too. She turned to face Owen, she took his hands in hers and looked up at him, squinting and searching his face. "I know you have loved Lara for years. I knew it even before. Maybe I should have said something, because you let that pass you by. You had every opportunity. But it is time to let her go now and move on. She is a beautiful, wonderful person. I can see why you love her. But I'm afraid this is it for you both, anak. You have to take what you learned from this loss and move forward."

64
New York, 2013

"Good choice for a change," Lara said as a server came to set platters stacked with burgers and fries in front of Owen, Andres, and herself.

"Yeah, this looks delicious," Andres agreed.

They sat in a shiny red booth with fake leather couches, white linoleum tile beneath their feet. Neon lights adorned the walls and servers came and went on roller skates.

"It's cool, isn't it?" Owen enthused. He was glad they liked it. For their monthly dinner, he thought they could try out the new diner near his place, and thus far they were not disappointed.

"It is, and this milkshake is divine." Lara raised her glass—a tower of thick, creamy peanut butter chocolate.

Owen returned the favor, raising his classic strawberry milkshake, and Andres his vanilla. They all clinked glasses.

Wiping her hands on her jeans and smiling widely, Lara stood. "Hold up, quick bathroom break," she declared, walking off.

Andres watched her go and when she was clearly out of earshot, he turned to Owen and said, "So, I have some news…" He took a deep breath. "I'm going to propose to Lara."

Owen stared at him. What was this feeling? Shock? Envy? Of course, Lola Beth was right. He would never outlast this relationship.

"Wow, man," he managed to say. "Congratulations! Have you talked to her parents?"

"Not yet. But I sort of hinted at it when we met over Christmas. Not sure if they got it but they're arriving next week to celebrate Lara's graduation, so I'll formally ask for permission then."

The look in Andres' eyes told Owen everything he needed to know. This man was serious. This man was sincere. This man was worthy.

"In the summer, we'll be going to Argentina. If all goes well, I'm hoping to propose while we're there," Andres added.

"That's amazing!" Owen reached over and punched him in the arm. But inside his heart sank at the finality of it all, even though he knew it was good, and right, and that he should be thrilled.

At home, alone, that night Owen found himself reassessing his life choices. It had become such that each day spent with Lara became more salt in the wound. And it was only his own doing. He checked the clock on his wall and saw it was too late to call Lola Beth, so instead he phoned his father.

Oskar picked up on the third ring. "Hey, Dad, got a second?"

"Sure, son. What's up?"

"Lara is getting engaged, probably. Andres plans to propose."

"I see..." Then Oskar went quiet for a moment.

Owen cleared his throat, "And I was thinking..." But he couldn't find the words so he stopped.

"You were thinking it's time to come back to California?"

"Yes, something like that."

There was another short pause, and then Oskar said: "That sounds wise. And I'm sorry, son. I'm sorry it ended this way. I know I encouraged you to go over there, and I worry now I caused you only more hurt."

"No, this was an essential experience, I think." Owen sighed. "I guess I'll speak with Peter about my next priorities."

"Yes, I'm sure your firm has plenty of West Coast clients for you to service."

"That's true."

"You'll be fine in all the other areas soon enough too, son. Your room is ready here whenever you are."

"Thanks, Dad."

65
New York, 2013

Two weeks later, on graduation day, Lara walked that storeyed stage and picked up her diploma. In the crowd, Andres and her parents cheered. Afterwards, they all went to the university gallery where the annual student show, THE NEW NOW, was in full and final swing.

The graduates had their own section, and Lara's final masterworks stood vibrantly out against white matte walls under soft bars of light. There were three pieces in the set, each an oil painting of a place reflected in an instrument. The treatment was both hyper realistic and surreal. She had been inspired to illustrate her journey through creation—the seasons and steps through which she had found herself and her art and her place and her person.

In the sunburst face of an acoustic guitar, she had painted the reflection of the first bar she and Owen had played in together, where their original music had first touched someone's ears.

Against the seductive slope of a saxophone was a warped self-portrait of Lara painting alone in a fictitious studio that was more a depiction of her inner world than her outer reality—walls covered in work tangentially similar to Dali's long-legged elephants or Keith Haring's chunky figures.

On the shiny black keys of a piano was a hazy portrait of herself and Andres walking towards one another, separated by the white keys, where soft and slender hands meant to be her own darted across the keyboard, blurred and in motion.

Each piece was massive—nearly six feet by four—and Lara had only ever shown those in the studio what she had been working on. That day, however, they stood for all to see. Aurora, Lewis, Adora, Andres, and Owen gathered around Lara in her corner.

"They are wonderful, dear," Lewis enthused, hugging Lara.

Aurora nodded. "Are the pieces for sale?" she asked. "Where can I get mine?"

"They are, but I'll do you one better, Mom. I'll make you a commission, free of charge. For your decades of support."

Aurora blushed then gave her daughter a kiss on the cheek. "I'm so proud of you," she whispered in Lara's ear, and Lara was filled with love.

***

A few weeks after her graduation, Lara found herself sitting in a pizza restaurant. It was stuffy and warm, and filled with the smell of charred cheese, basil, and oregano. Against one brick wall, tables had been drawn together to accommodate a party of ten and Owen sat at the head of the group. On one side sat his few friends— Lara, Andres, and a couple that Owen had introduced as his neighbors; on the other, were work contacts.

From his perch, Owen cleared his throat. The table quieted down and turned their attention to him.

"Thanks for being here, guys," Owen said, smiling. "Most of my work buddies know this already, but I thought I'd bring everyone together for a fun evening and a proper farewell, because I'm going back to California."

Everyone raised their beers to Owen and erupted into conversation, back-patting, and questions.

Lara watched Owen for a moment, trying to read past his smile, but she didn't get much, and he wasn't meeting her gaze. She knew outright it would be a lie to say she wasn't a little surprised at this news. He hadn't really mentioned anything overtly to her. Sure, here and there, he had mentioned that work was moving more and more back to the West Coast. But he had never said that he would be leaving. She had grown rather comfortable with the new way in which their friendship worked, and she knew she would miss him when he was gone. It would be good to chat a little one on one about this. *Maybe later*, she thought, as she turned back to her meal and the small talk around her.

Later, when everyone was shuffling out onto the sidewalk, Lara hung back to leave a tip as Owen settled the bill.

"You didn't tell me you were leaving," she said, leaning on one elbow against the counter as Owen shrugged on his coat.

"Ah, you knew it was coming eventually." He waved a hand dismissively. "It'll be better for me. And for everyone."

Lara paused to give this statement some thought. It seemed there was more to it than just a move because of work, and just then it occurred to her that perhaps Owen was finally feeling ready to go out there and find his own space too. Just like she had meant when she'd spoken with him in the diner that day and laid out the boundaries. With all his work travel, Owen had never become fully settled in New York, and if he wanted to really find his footing it would need to be somewhere he wasn't traveling so much for work, and not spending so much time with Lara.

"I guess," Lara agreed, "Anyway, you'll probably find your stride in California. Maybe really bloom there."

Owen nodded. "Maybe. I'm taking a few weeks off. Heading to Virginia first."

"Great idea. I'm sure your mom and Lola Beth are happy."

"Very." Owen slipped his wallet into his coat and turned to face Lara. She looked up at him, smiled, and then opened her arms to offer a hug. He obliged, and they held each other for a moment.

When they pulled apart, Owen was smiling too but his eyes were a little glazed over. On one hand, Lara felt a little worried and apprehensive, but on the other she was proud and excited. She had a good feeling about this. Something told her Owen would be fine.

66
Fairfax, Virginia, 2013

The primary purpose of taking a much needed break in Virginia for two weeks was not just to spend time with his mother and Lola. Owen was in need of a retreat.

Armed with his guitar, he sat in his room and wrote. For two whole weeks, he wrote nonstop. Song. After song. After song.

When he was finished, he put his guitar down, packed his bag, took Vicky and Lola to dinner, and left the next morning for California with nothing but a backpack and his briefcase. The music was now behind him—a demo, cut onto a disc that would never be heard. An homage, a secret.

But also, still inside him. In his mind, the tunes kept playing.

> *I can't wait this one out—I shouldn't*
> *I once thought I was brave—But I couldn't.*
>
> *If there's one thing left to say—Just one thing*
> *I will take it to my grave—This one thing*
> *Cause there's nothing left to save*
> *But that one thing*
> *Just the one thing.*
> *Still wanting.*

Subject: Demo

I cut a demo the last couple of weeks and I wanted you to listen to it. I've zipped a file to this email. Let me know what you think? I don't really have any intentions for this music. Just an outlet. Something.

Before Lara, music was my salve and savior. But after us, it's become an echo of my grief. It all reminds me of her and all my failures. It sounds melodramatic to say, but you grieve for the people you lose–no matter which way you lose them. And you grieve for the battles you cannot win. Even the ones you didn't fight to begin with. Who knows if I will make music again after this. Who knows if I have that tenacity. That gift of endurance. Lara found her artistic voice. Her story is just now beginning. Beginning again. Her song is moving into the bridge. It's my turn to find my own tune. Whatever that may be.

67
San Carlos De Bariloche, 2013

Every summer season, when New York was oppressively hot and humid, and the Philippines was rainy and muggy, Argentina was in the middle of a beautiful, white, sunny ski season.

To propose, Andres decided to take Lara on an adventurous wintry holiday at Bariloche. San Carlos de Bariloche was a resort town known for its chocolate, skiing, and iconic lake.

On the first evening, from their chalet with a view of the lake, as they sipped hot chocolate and sat cuddled up on the couch, Andres cleared his throat and turned to Lara. "I've been thinking about what's next for us. Do you think about that too?"

"Sure, all the time."

"I've been thinking that… Well, I can't imagine being with anybody else but you. And you know that we had discussed at the very beginning we'd only do this if we were building together toward something. I've been wondering if maybe that time is now."

"Now?" The topic had come up before, and she had of course thought about this. But were they ready?

"Yes. So I was wondering… Should we get married?"

If anyone was ever looking for a flaw in Andres, it was this. He was not very romantic. And yet, something about that endeared him even further to Lara. He was so authentic, so himself.

"Are you asking me to marry you?" Lara asked, smiling.

"Are you saying you would?"

"Yes." Lara reached over and held Andres' face in her

hands. "A million times." She kissed him, then released him, just looking at him. Taking him in. "So are we engaged now?"

Andres smiled. "I'd like to think so. Because I don't think they have a good return policy where I got this."

From his back pocket he pulled out a little box and flipped it open. There, nestled in its little velvet pillow, was a beautiful, sparkling diamond ring.

Lara had never been the sort of girl who imagined her wedding. When she was younger, her friends had long lists—what sort of flowers they wanted, what cut of diamond, how many carats. She scarcely even pictured an ideal man. These sort of dreams simply never occurred to her as a young girl, and yet there she sat, staring at her future, imagining it, knowing it, seizing it. Andres slipped the ring onto her finger, and they embraced.

July 1, 2013
Email from Owen to Lara

Subject: San Francisco in the summer is amazing

Where are you in the world these days? Dad says hi. Peter and I are moving the LA office to San Francisco. Better everything. Including the weather. Way better than New York and LA even. You should come visit.
Send my love to Andres. Are you engaged yet?

[Attached: picture of Owen with the Golden Gate Bridge behind him]
[Attached: picture of Owen and Peter with two employees in a new office]

***

July 2, 2013
Email from Lara to Owen

Subject: Re: San Francisco in the summer is amazing

My friend! HELLO! Congratulations on the new office! Will pop a bottle in your honor. And, we are, indeed! We're on our last couple of days in Argentina. Say hi to Oskar.

[Attached: picture of Lara and Andres together on the slopes]
[Attached: picture of Lara's hand with the ring on it]

***

July 2, 2013
Email from Owen to Lara

Subject: Re: Re: San Francisco in the summer is amazing

CONGRATULATIONS! You guys look beautiful together - you three, including the mountain. Who else knows?

***

July 8, 2013
Email from Lara to Owen

Subject: Re: Re: Re: San Francisco in the summer is amazing

Sorry it took a while to get back to you! We are in New York again and will start wedding planning in a couple of weeks. I think I've told everyone who matters at this point. Feel free to gossip about us behind our backs. Haha. Jk. You wouldn't do that – would you? You'd just say it to my face.

***

July 9, 2013
Email from Owen to Lara

Subject: Re: Re: Re: Re: San Francisco in the summer is amazing

I love Northern California. Maybe I can find my people here. Keep me posted on wedding plans. Mike and I were talking about you the other day. Totally gossiping. Imagining your dress and your hair and your ring, and you being bridezilla. Ooooooo. Just kidding. I mean, we were talking about you. But we don't really care about that shit. Can't imagine you as a bridezilla anyway. Maybe your mom bridemomzilla. HAHA. Don't tell her I said that. I still value my life.

68
San Francisco, 2013

By the end of the summer of 2013, Owen had moved to San Francisco. He and Peter were fielding inquiries left and right.

Owen's latest client, Nicholas, was trying to build a new zero-waste cafe. The two men were seated in Owen's new office, a shaft of light streaming in and illuminating the natural wooden table between them and creating a warm cast on both their faces. Nicholas was young and fashionable, with a blue linen button down shirt and khakis. His hair was curly and coiffed, and he wore thick dark-rimmed glasses. He looked more like the third member of Kings of Convenience than a seasoned restaurateur and cafe owner.

"Thank you for your time. I'm looking forward to this." He patted Owen on the shoulder after a productive meeting.

"For sure, I am super excited as well."

"You mentioned you're new to the area, right?"

"Yes, I am! Relatively. I'm more of an East Coast guy. Though I've lived in LA too. Kind of."

"Well, San Francisco is the best in the West." Nicholas grinned. "Even though it's not as charming as it used to be. Maybe you would like to come out with some friends and I later? There's a new bar that hosts standup comedy and live music. Not sure if you like art and such, but it's definitely in that scene."

"That sounds great. Thanks. I'd love to come."

The idea of going out with Nicholas was appealing first and foremost because it gave Owen a little bit of hope in the face of one of the challenges he struggled with: finding his footing socially. As it always was with him, every time he met someone, he felt familiar judgments creeping in. Perhaps they were melodramatic, or lacked substance, or only ate gluten free products even if they didn't have celiac disease. Little things continued to serve as excuses to hold others at arm's length.

He knew it was wrong. Still, all the new dating apps were not the place, it seemed, to correct this. They only encouraged him to swipe based on limited information and face value. If anything, he was at risk of regression if he got used to them. So a night out with a cool guy like Nicholas could be promising.

Owen waved Nicholas off as he drove away and turned back to his desk with a small smile on his face. *Nice*, he thought.

***

The address Nicholas gave Owen led him to a vibrant part of town full of bars and galleries and restaurants. Owen followed the directions to a spot just a few streets off the bustle, where he found himself in an old converted firehouse. It was all exposed brick, plants hanging from the ceilings, and vines crawling over walls. There was a stage up front, and a bar made of recycled glass bottles in many colors, through which LED lights shone and created a church-like stained glass effect.

On stage there was a stand-up comedian. She was tall and slim, with thick dark hair to her waist, a shimmery purple top over ripped jeans, Doc Martens, and a mischievous glint in her eye. She caught Owen's attention immediately.

When he found Nicholas in the crowd, he was surrounded by friends and they were all tuned in to the performance.

"That's a friend of ours," Nicholas pointed out, jutting his chin in the direction of the stage after he'd made brief introductions.

Owen nodded. "Oh, cool."

The woman on stage was funny. Her set was primarily about her Indian heritage. Her impressions of her mother were hilarious and relatable to anyone with some Asian background, but she also focused a lot of her comedy on self-deprecation and her own "complexes" as she had put it. Owen found himself laughing along.

When she was done, she walked right over to them and

threw her arms around Nicholas. "You came!"

"Wouldn't have missed it!"

"Oh, and you brought a friend." She regarded Owen, looking him up and down. She smiled and extended her hand. "Ganavi," she said as a self-introduction.

"Owen." He shook her hand and smiled back.

"Comedian by night, corporate lawyer by day."

"Environmental engineer by day," Owen replied. "Nothing yet by night. Though once upon a time, I was a musician."

"What happened, lose your voice?" Ganavi joked.

Owen laughed softly. "Something like that."

"Well, you'll find it or something else soon enough."

The group ordered food—sweet potato fries, quorn tacos, and naked bean burritos. They found a long table to sit at that still had a good view of the stage.

Owen sat between Ganavi and Nicholas. The conversation revolved primarily around food and startup culture, but Owen found himself getting small tidbits of other things. Everyone had their own hobbies—some were brewing their own alcohol, others cultivating sourdough starters and making bread, a few were into music, and almost all of them did some form of exercise and meditation.

Owen felt transported to a foreign land, dropped into a version of San Francisco he'd only read or joked about, but he felt comfortable. An odd sense of fitting in.

His phone chimed. When he pulled it out he saw an email from Lara. *Subject: Save the Date.* He slipped it back into his pocket without opening it and tried to ignore the feeling in his chest. All the live music was bringing Owen back to the days with her—creating, performing, building a life.

On stage, a new band began a set. They were in the middle of a Mumford and Sons cover. The chorus, an homage to the way love is a means to be free, not to be caged, not to be limited, but to be allowed to fly, to be allowed to become.

The lyrics rang so true for Owen. It felt honest, and raw. He found himself lost in thought, a black hole of memories that swallowed him up and took him back to Lara.

Next to him, Ganavi was speaking and pulled him out of his reverie. "Have you ever done yoga, Owen?"

"Not really."

"Come join us on Saturday. I run a class nearby."

"You?"

"Yeah, I forgot to mention that. Lawyer by day, comedian by night, yoga instructor on the weekends." She winked.

"Your average Asian overachiever," Nicholas interjected.

Owen smiled. "Sure," he said. "Can I get your number? We can keep in touch on the details."

***

"Place your thumb on your right nostril, and breathe in…"

It was a Saturday morning, and Owen was seated in a room of twelve other people, attending his very first yoga class ever. At the front of the room sat Ganavi, her hair curled up into a large bun at the top of her head, a color-coordinated pink and gold yoga outfit accentuating her every curve and muscle. From her perch on a thick ocean blue yoga mat, she called out words of guidance and encouragement. She used a different voice when she led a yoga class. It sounded like it came from deep in her diaphragm.

She spoke so softly, like a whisper, and yet she could be heard all across the room, a comforting, low sound that Owen could feel in the pit of his stomach.

"Now take your middle finger and cover your left nostril, release your right, and breathe out…"

Owen followed. He tried to push away any feelings of self-judgment. *Don't think about it*, he reprimanded himself each time the notion that he looked ridiculous popped into his mind. *Shut up and breathe*, he thought whenever it felt like this was going too slowly. He wanted to get something out of it. He knew it would be possible to. He was willing. *What else did he have to lose?*

"Release whatever thoughts are getting in the way of your practice this morning. Focus on your intention. What is the intention you want to bring to today? Honestly, mine is to be less judgmental. I want to be kind. Not only to others, but to myself."

More breathing.

"What are the toxic things the world has told you? Have you been told that you are not worthy? That love cannot find you? Has the world taught you to fear and be feared?"

Ganavi continued to lead the breathing patterns with patience and what Owen could only describe as perseverance, because even if they were not moving, this required a mental and emotional stamina that he did not yet have.

"I invite you to find a place of trauma inside your body today. We all have one of those. Breathe into that place. What is the part that hurts the most when you are stuck in toxic patterns? For me, it's my shoulders. My shoulders are tight and sore from carrying a burden I did not choose—the burden of being the Good Indian Daughter. Now, I inhale into my shoulders, I create space for healing, and I exhale out the burden."

Owen thought about his feelings, where they sat in his throat, chest, and stomach. His fears of commitment, abandonment, connection. His worry and confusion over loving and being left behind. He inhaled into these spaces and felt himself expand.

He had once heard that deep breathing practice can create an experience of euphoria from the sudden increase of oxygen in the body, and the endorphins releasing into your bloodstream. He was not sure if that was what he was feeling, but he suddenly felt light as a feather. As he exhaled, he felt wide awake. Even with his eyes closed, he could see new possibilities ahead. He couldn't yet make out what they might be, they were but silhouettes, suggestions. But he knew they were there. And that was enough.

In this space he found something new, a certain compassion. An understanding: *Hurt and grief can last a long time, can keep us from our full selves. But if we allow them to be what they are, they can become a part of us. And we can be whole and healed.*

The Mumford & Sons song played in his mind again. Reminding him of love and how love did not turn away, how it transformed, how it set free, how it bettered. For the first time in a very long time, he felt that the man he was meant to be was more than just a remote possibility.

The group were directed to go into savasana. Owen lay

on his back, palms up, eyes closed, and he smiled.

***

Two weeks later, in Owen's therapist's office, he sat with his head in his hands at the end of a heavy session. Taking deep, shaky breaths, he fought to compose himself. His eyes were damp, but no tears would come, and he felt clammy, queasy, and tired.

His therapist, Dr. Harvey, a slight, unassuming man with round specs and a crooked, closed-lipped smile, reached over and patted him on the shoulder.

"I have studied about trauma for the better part of my career. Perhaps you think you have had a rather typical life, but all lives carry trauma. Not just from our present, or our past, but also from those before us. Generational trauma is real. You told me a lot today about your childhood. Being left behind is difficult, but that is only the tip of the iceberg. Your mother was left behind. You were raised by your grandmother, who was also left behind. These patterns of abandonment can create fear. Can make us build walls around us. Can make us hesitate to allow ourselves to be whole, safe, loved."

Dr. Harvey paused and took a sip of water.

"I know you have lost some love in your life this way as well. Missed out," he then continued, "I'm here to help you not only process that, but also move forward. The thing we need to remember is that there is always hope. Now, we've done a lot of unloading today. It's given me a good understanding of your baseline. In the coming sessions, we'll work through some of these things that have come to the surface."

Owen nodded.

"Now to help you decompress a little, I always like to ask my patients to do something that is regulating. Is there something in your life that you have used in the past as an outlet for the pain you've felt? You mentioned music at one point earlier?"

"Yes, music. Though I kind of thought I was taking a break from that."

"Well. Humor me for today. What kind of music?"

"Guitar and vocals."

"That's perfect, because I have just what might help." Dr.

Harvey stood up and walked over to the wall behind his desk where Owen, for the first time, noticed a little soprano guitar hanging on a hook. "Would you perhaps play me something? Anything?"

Owen smiled and took the instrument. He felt a little nervous. He hadn't picked up a guitar since he had recorded that demo months before in Virginia. The file sat in a disc on his desk in Fairfax, and also in a draft on his email account that he had no plans to ever send.

But with Dr. Harvey there looking at him, he felt an odd sense of security. A safety in picking up that guitar, and obliging him.

"Sure. Yes." Owen began to tinker with the strings a little, and already felt his heart growing lighter, his stomach settling, his mind quieting. The relief that came over him when he realized music was still there—still his salve, his friend, his companion, his comfort.

That day the song that came out of him was one he had not heard for a very long time. It went: "No, not ever enough is the falling grace of feeling, failing appetite…"

At the chorus: "Life, oh life, oh life…"

When he finished, his eyes were closed and he was breathing evenly, calmly again.

"That was a lovely song. I've never heard it before. Did you write that yourself?"

"No," Owen answered. He smiled. "Someone I care very much about did. It felt good to get it out."

"Great. How about every week we do some sort of music bit at the end, if it helps. What do you think?"

"I think that would be great."

Subject: Happy Thanksgiving!

Happy, happy thanksgiving, Lara. It has been a crazy time here in SF. I have been doing a lot of inner work. I started yoga. There is so much to share and feel and be. I wish I could write it all down, but I'm not quite ready. I feel like we haven't spoken in ages. And I think we haven't?? This must be the longest time I've gone without hearing your voice, or seeing your face. I guess that's why I'm sitting here thinking about you. There's a song that reminds me of you, and I wanted to send it to you today. I hope you don't mind. *[Link to video of "In The Long Run" by The Staves]*

Thank you for everything you were, are, and will be for me, but also in general, as a human being.

Sending you and Andres much love. I already expressed my availability on the RSVP form for the wedding – not sure if you saw. Looking forward to seeing you both in the new year – if not sooner, then at least for the wedding festivities.

***

69
Singapore, 2014

In the lush, green courtyard of the Raffles Hotel, there stood over a hundred white Tiffany chairs on either side of a grass aisle leading to a small altar covered in wild flowers and adorned with two candles. Against the backdrop of the hotel's beautiful, white colonial style architecture, the flowers provided a welcome whimsy, still elegant, but just that little bit of playfulness, too.

Owen idled at the edge of the scene as guests began to walk in. Behind them the morning sun shone just above the black and white architecture of the historic hotel. The blue sky above promised good weather for the rest of the day. It was so like Lara to have a daytime wedding. In his cream linen suit and white dress shirt, Owen hoped he was channeling calm, tropical, happy. Inside, his stomach churned.

Suddenly, a hand slapped him on the shoulder and he blinked and turned. It was Mike. "Long time no see, my friend!"

Mike wore a black suit and sharp deep blue leather shoes that were definitely designer.

"Pretty nice setup." He gestured at the garden. "And I heard there is going to be some whole roasted pig!"

He jerked his chin back toward the dining area behind them, which was set up with ten large round tables, a small stage, silver tiffany chairs, wildflowers, and scrap cedar table centerpieces. Everything had Lara written all over it.

"Lechon. Yeah, I wouldn't be surprised. At Lara's family Christmas party, there were several of those," Owen said. "And whole roasted calves, too."

Mike whistled softly, clearly impressed.

"You're not the only fancy one here," Owen teased.

Mike laughed and then jerked his chin in the direction of the group who had walked in. It was the groom's party. Everyone wore charcoal gray three-piece suits with sage waistcoats and matching ties. Each of them gave off the same air of sophistication. Andres had friends from every corner of the globe. The groom's entourage resembled a United Colors of Benetton ad out of the '90s. They were made up of a British Royal Marine, a Ugandan Private Equity executive, a Chinese-Indonesian heir to a conglomerate, and an Indian technology consultant. And amidst them all stood the groom himself, Andres Courtenay.

Owen was happy. Not that his opinion greatly mattered. but Lara had made a good choice. *No, not just a good choice. She had made the right choice.*

Andres waved when he saw Owen and Mike, and immediately made his way toward them. Owen had not seen him in a year, and he had not considered how much of a shock it would be. He felt an almost visceral reaction—his heartbeat ran ahead of him, his palms grew sweaty. It was as though he were meeting an old adversary. But Andres was not that. Andres was a friend.

"So nice to see you," Andres said as he approached, opening his arms for a hug.

Mike was the first to reciprocate. "Congratulations, man!"

Andres then turned to Owen, who leaned in his direction. They shook hands and pulled one another in to bump chests and shake each other's shoulders.

"Nervous?" Owen asked, eyebrows raised.

Andres rubbed his hands together and smiled. "Just excited. I can't wait."

Just then, the best man came over and patted Andres on the shoulder. "Time to get ready to march." He nodded in the direction of Owen and Mike.

"Oh, Arch, meet Lara's best friends from Manila. Owen and Mike," Andres said.

Archie grinned and offered his hand to shake. "Nice to meet you." Then he turned to the groom. "But we really gotta go. You can catch up with your guests later. Let's just get you to that altar!"

Andres waved at Owen and Mike apologetically, and was whisked away. Owen watched him go, and Mike watched Owen.

"You alright, man?" Mike asked.

Owen nodded. "Yeah." He smiled. "Everything is alright."

He had indeed been undergoing, as he had told Lara, plenty of inner work in San Francisco with his new friends, and his yoga, and his therapist. He felt, for all intents and purposes, "on the mend." But that did not seem to make this weekend any easier.

He tugged on his suit and smoothed it over. He took a deep breath. *Like a Band-Aid*, he thought, and he walked into the developing crowd of guests to mingle along, awaiting, just like everyone else, the arrival of the bride.

70
Singapore, 2014

Lara stood in her suite. She had been awake since three in the morning. They had poked her, prodded her, pulled at her, and now as she looked at herself in the mirror, she took it all in. Her gown was a vintage-inspired number with a full lace top, three-quarter sleeves with scalloped edging, an elegant high neckline, and a cinched waist leading to a sweeping A-line skirt and a modest train. Her hair was pulled up into a bun meticulously styled to look messy, with tendrils alongside her face and a matching lace headband.

A photographer snapped away, and her family buzzed around her, fussing over her veil, her hair, her lips. Adora was her maid of honor, of course, and stood guard as she directed the people around Lara to give her space, be quiet, and get her water. Aurora and Lewis stood to the side, constantly wiping away happy tears.

It was absolute madness all around, but Lara felt nothing but peace. She was marrying Andres. It had been a bumpy road, full of questions Lara had never thought would have kept her up at night, seating plans and guest lists and menus and the satisfaction of in-laws and parents and everyone in between.

Still, nothing could ruin this day. This day was about celebrating their life together with those who loved them, not just as individuals, but also as a unit. And she didn't care about anyone's judgments or feelings on this matter. This impulse, so confident and pragmatic, made Lara feel proud of herself.

She remembered a time when approval would have counted for more to her, and when she would have felt compelled to rise to her own defense. But the years had taught her that there was power in subtlety, silence, patience, and grit. That perseverance was less about fighting against the storm, and more about weathering it.

And, now with Andres, it was good to have someone to weather together–forever.

When it was time for her to go downstairs, Adora helped her with her train and bouquet, and the entourage headed, giddy, and smiling, to the courtyard.

Tucked away in a separate room as the march began, Lara allowed her mind to meditate on the moment. All the movies she had seen to date had shown her that wedding days were stressful, that one might get cold feet, that brides and grooms were bundles of nerves, but all she felt was peace. Her heart beating slow and steady in her chest, she smiled. Then it was finally her turn. She stood behind the double doors leading out. She could hear the music. A string quartet rendition of "Hoppipolla" by Sigur Ros. Such a bold, and hopeful sound.

The doors opened, and Lara stepped into the sun.

Bridge

Relief

We were the five o'clock bulletin
Bad News Bears
Bonnie and Clyde
And we said we didn't care
What it looked like
But we lied
And now we're ships, just ships
And that's all right.

May 15, 2015
Email from Owen to Lara

Subject: Happy Birthday!

Happy Birthday, Lara! Can't believe we haven't seen each other since your wedding. Hope you're doing well. Miss you. Send my love to Andres, too!

***

May 16, 2015
Email from Lara to Owen

Subject: Re: Happy Birthday!

Thank you, my friend! I suppose now is a good time to tell you that WE'RE PREGNANT! Just 8 weeks on. Haven't told many others besides family. How are you doing? Tell me more about your daily work and the inner work too. I'm sorry we haven't seen each other in so long!

***

May 16, 2015
Email from Owen to Lara

Subject: Re: Re: Happy Birthday!

WHAT? That's huge news! Congratulations!
At the moment, we have taken on an investor to expand the company and we have a big national client coming up. Really exciting.

My inner work is going well. My therapist and I have worked through a lot. It's an ongoing thing, but it has been really good to peel away the layers that made my walls so hard to breach. Also, I think I'm in love!

***

June 10, 2015
Email from Lara to Owen

Subject: Re: Re: Re: Happy Birthday!

I am SO SORRY for the late reply especially on such amazing news! I was super morning sick for a while and I'm only now feeling more like myself again. I'm so happy to hear that the therapy is going well. BUT MOST IMPORTANTLY: LOVE! WHAT A JOY! WHO IS SHE? Tell me EVERYTHING!

***

June 12, 2015
Email from Owen to Lara

Subject: Re: Re: Re: Re: Happy Birthday!

Her name is Ganavi (I call her Navi), which means "singer" or "song." Can you believe that? She's not a singer, though. Haha. She is a comedian! And a corporate lawyer. And a yoga teacher. But at the moment, she really wants to quit law and go into yoga full-time. She is so bright, and I think you would get along great. One of the smartest people I know. We met in 2013, but it's been a slow burn to get to this point. Btw, did you get the invite to Bianca and David's wedding? Are you going? It's about time they tied the knot! Took long enough. Hope the morning sickness is on its way out. Sending you good vibes.

***

June 14, 2015
Email from Lara to Owen

Subject: Re: Re: Re: Re: Re: Happy Birthday!

So happy for you!!! Love is a big word, and it's good you are now putting it out there. Sending you AND Ganavi hugs and love. And unfortunately, no! I'll be too pregnant to make the trip by then. If you go, send my love!

***

December 7, 2015
Email from Lara
cc Owen, Monique, Mateo, Bianca, Niko, David, and Mike

Subject: Welcome Sebastián Halford Courtenay!

[Attached: Photo of Baby Sebastián]

Sebastián Halford Courtenay was born on the 1st of December, 2015 in Manhattan to two beaming, terrified, exhausted, joyful parents.

We hope you guys are doing well! Sending love.

71
San Francisco, 2016

Message From Lara Halford–C.
Hey Owen, hope you're doing well. On our end, things
are mostly good. In fact, we're in San Francisco now.
Unfortunately, my grandfather passed away. So we've
all had to make the trip over. On the one hand, it's nice
to all be together again. On the other hand, it's sad, of
course. Anyway, just wanted to mention we were in town
in case you are too and want to meet up. We're here until
tomorrow night. If you'd like to grab coffee, let me know.

Owen was lounging in Navi's flat that afternoon with
a cup of tea and a book on conflict resolution when his phone
chimed and he saw a message from Lara.

"So, Lara's in town," he said, slipping his phone towards
Navi to let her see the message.

Navi, who had been sitting on the other side of the couch
from him watching something on her phone, glanced at his screen.
"Lara, your ex-girlfriend?"

"No." Owen said, but Navi gave him a stern look and he
smiled sheepishly. "Yes?"

"Nice." Navi smiled.

They were trying something out—a real relationship.
Navi had not been in one in a long time, and neither had Owen.
By his assessment, they were both a little out of practice, but
Owen knew that developing, terrifying, warm, soft feeling in his
soul well. Love. And this time he refused to let it pass him by.

"Are you sure that's a good idea, though?" The way Navi
was looking at him was so open, so neutral, simply curious, just

concerned. "I know that might be a trigger point or pressure point for you. Do you think it's conducive to your healing?"

Owen thought about it. "I think it would be good to go. Right, even. You could come with me? She'd love to meet you, I'm sure. You'd get on really well."

"Don't say because we're alike."

"Actually you're not very alike. But you'd get on really well anyway because you're similar at the very least in how sharp, smart, and bright you are. In your own, very unique ways. Also, she's very artsy."

"No, it's okay, Owen. I think if you do see Lara, especially for the first time in a long time, it should be just you."

"Are you sure you don't mind if I go?"

"Owen, it's not at all my business to mind you catching up with a loved one. Even if she's your ex." Navi smiled, and Owen felt so lucky then. He leaned into that feeling and shimmied over to her side of the couch, giving her a deep, grateful kiss.

"Okay, I'll go see her."

Message From Owen Weber
My condolences to the whole family. I remember him from the Christmas party in Bacolod all those years ago. He was a bright spark of a man. I would love to meet for coffee tomorrow. Where is best?

***

Owen and Lara had scheduled to see each other at her hotel. When he arrived, it was Andres who greeted him downstairs.

After exchanging hugs and pleasantries, Andres explained, "Lara is breastfeeding and Basti is falling asleep as we speak, so unfortunately, the lobby cafe won't work."

"Oh, I can come back later."

"Nonsense. Just come up to the room. I've been instructed to usher you up." Andres played up his British accent and bowed with one hand on his belly as though he were a butler.

Owen smiled and patted his back. "Let's do it. Thanks, man."

Upstairs, in their room with a view of the bay, Lara was sitting on a couch by a large window, a cape over her shoulders, covering her front, and a baby's foot poking out from underneath.

When Owen walked in, Lara smiled, nodded, and then adjusted herself. Moments later, she pulled the cape off and put it aside. On one arm was a napping baby boy—chubby cheeks, chunky thighs, long and curly lashes. Even in his sleep, Owen could see he had inherited Lara's huge eyes. Lara quietly walked to the other side of the room where she put baby Sebastián down in a travel cot. She came back and wordlessly headed straight to Owen and hugged him.

They had not seen each other since her wedding day, and Owen knew that he looked different. He had lost some weight, gotten fitter, and felt brighter himself. And yet, in her arms, he felt that strange familiarity of home in someone else once more. Of being one with another person in some way, shape, form. As Rumi once wrote, *This is a subtle truth: whatever you love, you are.* Owen felt that. For in this world, no matter the time, place, no matter the years, or space between them, Lara would always be one of his greatest loves, and he would always feel connected to her in one way or another.

He returned the hug, squeezing her tightly. She smelled exactly the same as always. She looked the same and yet different. On the one hand, she had lost any puppy fat in her cheeks, and suddenly looked a lot less like a girl and entirely a woman. On the other hand, those wide, warm eyes were just as they had been years before. It somehow overwhelmed Owen with emotion—to see Lara this way, with a baby, in a totally new place, and to be himself somewhat different, a newer person. And yet...

"I can't explain it but." Owen shook his head and stepped back, still looking right at her. "It feels like everything and nothing has changed at all."

Lara smiled. "Ditto." She took him by the elbow and led him to the couch. "We have to leave for the airport in two hours, but come sit, have some tea, and tell me everything I've missed."

"I don't even know where to begin," Owen replied in earnest.

"Well, try. Because as you can see, I have my own little show and tell here." She gestured to herself, Andres, and Sebastián, and Andres laughed. "But you. I must know everything. How's life? Therapy? Inner work? Ganavi? Everything?"

Owen was touched by Lara's interest and earnestness. He struggled at first to find the words but he did try and once he started, it was hard to stop. They sat on that couch for the entire two hours. Owen told Lara about his therapist, his business, his yoga practice, and Navi.

Lara told Owen about married life, Andres' bid for Partner, their plan to retire young and move to Oxford, her paintings, which had been picked up by a gallery in the Lower East Side, and early motherhood. Occasionally, Andres joined them to chat, but mostly spent his time packing and tending to Sebastián, allowing these old friends precious moments of reconnection.

At one point, Andres took Sebastián downstairs for a short walk in the sun. When he had gone, Owen felt the need to take advantage of getting Lara alone. He turned to her and spoke, "Thank you for inviting me to hang out today, Lara. I had mixed feelings about meeting up with you. I mean, we haven't seen each other in a while, and sometimes I even hoped maybe you'd forget me. Just end our song. I had so much shame...and guilt...But now that we're here, I'm glad we're reconnecting after all."

Lara looked at Owen, taken aback. "Shame and guilt? Still?" she said, "I would never have wanted to forget you. I think we should count ourselves as so incredibly lucky in this life if we have had the privilege to love and be loved. I can't speak for you, but for me, I'd like to always remember every great love. Each is a teacher. I learned so much from what we shared. And all of that led me to the wonderful life I have now with my little family, and my art. You're right to draw an analogy with a song. 'Cause that's what life is. A grand song. With highs and lows. But each note matters. Each note makes the song what it is."

Owen stared at Lara. "There is honestly still so much I want to say to you but can't. Just know, I also treasure the time we shared," he replied. "To say I was learning is not really enough to encapsulate all the places we were able to go and the things I managed to find in myself. Thank you for being a part of all that."

The two friends sat in silence for a moment. Then Owen sighed and smiled.

"You know, you were right to say that every note matters," he said, "I love this life I have thanks to the verses, the rests, the rhythms that got me here. Perhaps you can imagine my gratitude, and the words I can't give you aloud. Maybe like old times you can hear them in the silence…"

Lara seemed to search Owen's eyes for a moment, and he wondered if she could still see past all his walls. He had worked hard to dismantle them, so maybe now it might be clearer. He tried to channel the same energy he had had that day after he had hit her. That moment when he had said, "You're like home."

Lara nodded slowly. *She gets it,* he thought, a little awed, a touch relieved.

"I think I know," she assured him. "And everything else—it's all water under the bridge. I mean, there's a whole lot of it and all that, but it's just water." She winked.

"You are too forgiving, you know," Owen said—slightly playfully now. He felt like he was coming out of the shadows, and into the light.

"Holding a grudge does the most damage to the holder," Lara said, "I hope you forgive yourself. And I hope you forgive me, too. I wouldn't change a thing."

Owen smiled. "We are where we were meant to be."

Lara reached over and squeezed Owen's hand. "Absolutely."

When Lara saw Owen out, they hugged one another one last time. Owen closed his eyes and took a deep breath—remembering the smell of the shampoo in her hair, the detergent in her sweater. Trying to hold on to the details. The curl of her lashes, the pulse of her skin, the little wisps of baby hair around her forehead and temple.

Contained in that two-hour span of time, Owen saw the past near-decade of his and Lara's lives flash before his eyes.

Lara at that club—sweet, soft, full of self-doubt; him—defensive, wounded, hopeful.

Lara when she took a leap of faith, and him when he had forfeited his chance.

Lara in New York—confident, motivated, careening toward the future, him stuck in the past.

Lara on her wedding day—radiant, whole, happy; and him learning to take the bitter with the sweet.

And finally, Lara that morning—wise, still sweet, strong, full of grace. And him–learning, open, healing, again full of hope.

Much had changed, and yet they remained.

Outro

Closure

I'm glad we've floated on
To where we do belong
A sea of love between us
And the parts of our song
Because we're ships
Just ships now
Speaking each other in passing

November 3, 2019
Email from Owen to Vicky

Subject: HAPPY BIRTHDAY and a gift

Hi Mom, HAPPY BIRTHDAY! What are you guys up to today? Navi and I wanted to come visit for Thanksgiving. Let's coordinate? Anyway, I know your birthday is coming up, and I wanted to give you something. In my desk in my room there, maybe in a drawer, there should be a demo. Something I've never shared with anyone before. Those songs, when I'd written them, were for Lara. And maybe they kind of still are. But I realize now, looking back, that they're also for you and Dad. They are for all of us. So...please, have them. Thank you for giving me the gift of music.

With love,
Your son, always,
Owen

Acknowledgments

This book would not exist without the people, places, experiences, events, and - yes - even music, that shaped the basis for its story. While this is a work of fiction, instances in my own life, and the emotions and memories that they created for me, have heavily inspired the journeys of the main characters (Lara and Owen).

It is with that in mind, that I must first thank my husband, Jay, my real life Andres, whom I did meet on a plane, and with whom it all took off from there. Thank you for your constant, steadfast support. You are the kindest, truest person, and I am so glad that we get to be partners and teammates in life. As I always say: I am the luckiest.

I am also grateful to my mother, Tina, and my father, Victor, who have believed in me and every single one of my hopes, dreams, and hyperfixations. From the moment I was born to this very day as I type this, they have been my champions. To my mom especially, thank you for reading every single thing I write and providing honest, open feedback. Recently, I was asked the question "how do we build up our daughters' confidence and make sure that as teenagers they have a good foundation of self-esteem and positivity?" I simply thought of my mom then, and how it is our closeness, and her honesty and openness, that have created the right scaffolding around me so that I can build myself up, safely and securely. *Thank you.*

Thanks as well to my sister and girl friends - Andrea, Bernice, Sabrina, Katrina, Karen, and Amanda - whose personalities informed the characters of Monique and Adora, and who have always provided me with their honest opinions, unwavering support, and many shared laughs and sass.

I have had the great honor of being surrounded by many other friends and family who have supported me on this journey - playing parts both big, and small. Especially to my friend Nigel, whose creative support and friendship was a vital component to the creation and completion of this manuscript. And to my brother - Gab, all my cousins, titas and titos, and of course my grandparents - they have always obliged and nurtured me. To them, I am most thankful.

This book also would have been next to unreadable without my incredible editor - KB, who provided nuanced, professional, and supportive insight at every turn. Through my experience with her, I learned that a good editor is kind of like a good therapist - mirroring your work back to you and making you think once, twice, three times about what you really want to say.

And speaking of therapists, I will also forever appreciate my own therapist, Cecilia, who helped me through one of the most difficult moments in my life, and gave me the tools to find the light again even when it felt like I was lost in the dark.

Finally, to my kids - Lucas and Leia. Those two little humans inspire me everyday to tell stories I would want them to hear, and impart lessons that I would want them to internalize.

Writing a novel at the end of a global pandemic, whilst managing a cross-continental move, caring for two young kids and two dogs, moving between two houses, and doing all kinds of other work and projects was not easy. It is only with the support of all of the above, and many others I have probably failed to mention, that any of this was possible.

Thank you, thank you, thank you.

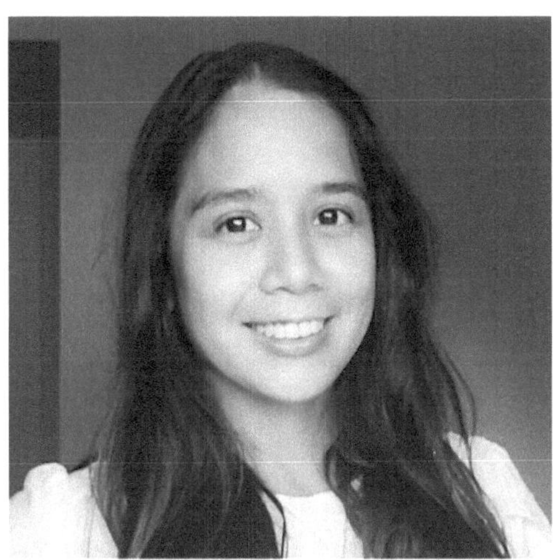

Alexandra Del Rosario Romualdez (also known as Alexandra Romualdez Broekman) is a writer, artist, and entrepreneur. She spent most of her career in marketing at Google, but left some years ago to focus on her family and pursue her dreams. Now she is the founder of Kado Publishing, an indie publisher that champions work by Filipino artists and writers. She has written and illustrated many children's books, such as the *Fabulous Fiestas of the Philippines* and the *Myths and Legends of the Philippines*. You can learn more about her work and advocacies through *kadopublishing.com* or on Instagram at @kadopublishing, @kado.novels, or @arbroekman.

Alex lives in the Netherlands with her husband, their two children, and their dogs. She loves the outdoors, nature, travel, sports, and storytelling. "Parts of a Song" is her first novel.